D0280099

Falling f...

They're working side by side, nine to five…

But, no matter how hard these couples try to keep their relationships strictly professional, romance is undeniably on the agenda!

Will a date in the office diary lead to an appointment at the altar?

Find out in this exciting series!

THE TYCOON'S RELUCTANT CINDERELLA

BY
THERESE BEHARRIE

First Published in Great Britain 2017
By Mills & Boon, an imprint of HarperCollins*Publishers*
1 London Bridge Street, London, SE1 9GF

© 2016 Therese Beharrie

ISBN: 978-0-263-92266-0

23-0117

Our policy is to use papers that are natural, renewable and recyclable products and made from wood grown in sustainable forests. The logging and manufacturing processes conform to the legal environmental regulations of the country of origin.

Printed and bound in Spain
by CPI, Barcelona

Therese Beharrie has always been thrilled by romance. Her love of reading established this, and then spilled over into her writing and her way of life. Fortunately she married a man who constantly exceeds her romantic expectations and is an infinite source of inspiration for her romantic heroes. She lives in Cape Town, South Africa, with her husband and their two Husky furbabies, and is absolutely amazed that her dream of being a romance author is now a reality.

This is Therese's first book for Mills & Boon Cherish!

This book is dedicated to my husband,
my best friend and my biggest supporter,

Grant, thank you for working so hard so that I could
follow my dream. Thank you for believing that I would
be a published author when writing was only a vague
possibility for my future. And, most of all, thank you
for loving me so well that there is no doubt in my mind
that good men and happily-ever-afters exist. I love you.

To my family and friends,

Thank you all for supporting me.
For listening to me as I went on about my dream of
writing and the plans I had to get published. To those
who allowed me to talk about plot lines and characters
even though it might have bored you, thank you.
You have all contributed to this, and I am so grateful.

To my editor,

Flo, you invested time and effort in me even though
there was no guarantee I would be worth it. Over
and above that, I have experienced so much growth
as a writer in the months we've worked together.
I can't wait to continue this journey with you.
Thank you for everything.

CHAPTER ONE

'PLEASE HOLD THE ELEVATOR!'

Callie McKenzie almost shouted the words as she ran to the closing doors. She was horribly late, despite her rushed efforts to get dressed after her shift at the hotel had ended. She wouldn't be making a very good impression on the big boss if she arrived after he did, so she was taking a chance on the elevator, ignoring her usual reservations about the small box.

Relief shot through her when she saw a hand hold the elevator doors and she hurried in, almost colliding with the person who had helped her. She had meant to say thank you immediately, but as she looked at him her mouth dried, taking her words away.

Callie thought he might be the most beautiful man she had ever seen. Dark hair sat tousled on his head, as though it had travelled through whirlwinds to get there, and set off the sea-blue-green of his eyes. He was a full head taller than her, so that she had to look up to appreciate the striking features of his face. Each angle was shaped perfectly—as though it had been sculpted, she thought, with the intention of causing every woman who looked at it to be caught in involuntary—or voluntary—attraction.

Her eyes fell to his lips as they curved into a smile and she felt her heart flutter. It was the kind of smile that transformed his entire face, giving it a sexy, casual expression that stood out against the sophistication of his perfectly tailored suit. It took her a while to realise that she was amusing him by staring, and she forced herself to snap out of it.

'Thank you,' she said, aware of the husky undertone her evaluation of him had brought to her voice.

His smile broadened. 'No problem. Which floor would you like?'

Callie almost slapped her hand against her forehead at the deep baritone of his voice. Was there *anything* about the man that wasn't sexy?

She cleared her throat. 'Ground floor, please.'

'Then it's already been selected,' he said, and pressed the button to close the elevator doors. 'So you're also going to the event downstairs, then?'

She frowned. 'Yes. How did you know?'

'Well, I'd like to think that this hotel doesn't require its guests to dress up in such formal wear to have supper.' . He gestured to her clothing, and Callie once again resisted the urge to slap herself on the head. She was wearing one of her mother's formal gowns—one of the few Callie *didn't* think was absolutely ridiculous—and nodded.

'Of course. Sorry, it's been a long day.' Callie wished she believed that was the reason for her lame responses, but she knew better. She wasn't sure why, but he threw her off balance.

'I can relate. This isn't the most ideal way to spend the evening.'

Callie was about to agree when the elevator came to an abrupt stop. The lights went out barely a second later and Callie lost her balance, knocking her head into the back wall. The world spun for a bit, and then she felt strong arms hold her and lower her to the ground.

'Are you okay?' he asked, and Callie had to take a moment to catch her breath before she answered.

She wasn't sure if she was dizzy because she was in his arms or because of the blow to her head. Or, she thought as the situation finally caught up to her, if it was her very real fear of being trapped in enclosed spaces that had affected her breathing.

'I'm fine.' Her breath hitched, but she forced it out slowly. 'I'm sure it's just a bump on the head.' *Inhale, exhale*, she reminded herself.

'Are you sure? You're breathing quite heavily.'

Her eyes had now acclimatised to the darkness, and she could see the concern etched on his face. 'I'm a little… claustrophobic.'

'Ah.' He nodded his head and stood. 'The electricity must have gone off, but I'm sure it won't take long before someone realises we're here.'

He removed his phone from his pocket and tapped against the screen. A light shone dimly between them but Callie could only see his face, disproportionately large in the poor light. She felt a strange mixture of disappointment and satisfaction that she couldn't make out his features as clearly as she had before, but she did manage to make out the scowl on his face.

'I don't have any reception, so I can't call anyone to help.'

'You could press that button over there,' she said helpfully, pointing to the red emergency button on the control panel.

Her breathing was coming a little easier—as long as she didn't think about the fact that she was trapped. She wanted to stand up, but didn't trust herself to be steady. And the last thing she wanted was to fall into the arms of her companion for a second time within a few minutes.

'Of course I can.'

He pressed the emergency button and quickly conversed with the static voice that came through the intercom. He'd been right. There had been a power outage in the entire grid, and the hotel's generator had for some reason gone off as well. They were assured that it was being sorted out, but that it might take up to thirty minutes before they would be rescued.

He sighed and sank down next to her, and Callie squeezed her eyes shut. She thought it might make his proximity—and her fear—less overwhelming. Instead, the smell of him filled her senses—a musky male scent that almost made her sigh in satisfaction. She swore she could hear her heart throbbing in her chest, but she told herself it was just because of the confines of the elevator. She opened her eyes and looked at him, and before she could become mesmerised by his looks—even in the dim light he was handsome—forced herself to speak.

'I wonder what's going on downstairs. There must be mass panic.' She couldn't quite keep the scorn from colouring her voice.

'I take it that you're not a fan of tonight's celebrations,' he said wryly.

'I wouldn't say that. I'm just…' she searched for the word '…sceptical.'

'About the event, or the reason for it?'

The innocent question brought a flurry of emotions that she wasn't ready to face. Her brother, Connor, had warned her that the hotel they both worked at hadn't been doing well for years now. Despite his efforts as regional manager, Connor was still struggling to bring the Elegance Hotel back from the mess the last manager had created. The arrival today of the CEO—their boss—held a mass of implications that she didn't want to think about.

So, instead of answering his question, she asked, 'Are you here to meet the CEO?'

'Not really, no.'

'A very cryptic answer.'

She could sense his smile.

'I like the idea of being a little mysterious.'

She laughed. 'You realise I don't know who you are, right? Everything about you is mysterious to me.'

As she said the words she turned towards him and found herself face to face with him. Her heart pounded, her breath slowed, and for the briefest moment she wanted to lean forward and kiss him.

The thought was as effective as ice down her back, and she shifted away, blaming claustrophobia for her physical reaction to a man she barely knew.

She shook her head, and was brought back to the reality of the situation. Soon she didn't have to pretend to blame her shortness of breath on her fear. She felt a hand grip her own and looked at him. She could see the concern in his eyes, and gratitude filled her when she realised that reassurance, not attraction, was the reason for his gesture.

'Your date must be worried about you,' he said, and nodded, encouraging her to concentrate on his words.

'He might be,' she agreed, 'if I had brought one.'

He laughed, and the sound was as manly as the rest of him. What *was* it about the man that enthralled all her senses?

'And yours?' Callie asked, and wondered at herself. This wasn't like her. She was flirting with him. And even though she knew that she shouldn't, she wanted to know the answer.

Their eyes locked, and once again something sizzled between them.

'I don't have a date here.'

'Your girlfriend couldn't make it tonight?'

She turned away from him as she asked the question, and leaned her head back against the elevator wall. She didn't want to succumb to the magnetism that surrounded him, but she had already failed miserably. She shouldn't be asking him about his personal life. But every time she looked at him her heart kicked in her chest and she wanted to know more. If she looked away, the walls began to close in on her.

So she chose the lesser of the two evils and turned back to him. His eyes were patient, steady, and she gave in to the temptation. 'Couldn't she?'

'There's no girlfriend.'

Was she imagining the slight tension in his voice?

'And you don't have a boyfriend, I assume?'

'You assume correctly—although I probably shouldn't be telling you that.'

'Why not?'

'Well, you're a strange man and we're stuck in an elevator together. What's going to deter you from putting the moves on me now that you know I don't have a boyfriend?'

Callie said the words before she could think about what they might provoke. But he just said, 'You don't have to worry about that. I don't "put the moves" on anyone.'

'So women just drop at your feet, then?' She couldn't take her eyes off him as she dug deeper.

'Sometimes.'

He smiled, but even in the dim light she could see something in his eyes that she couldn't decipher.

'Ah, modesty. Charming.' She said it in jest, but her heart sank. This man—this very attractive man who made her heart beat faster just by looking at her—wasn't interested in *one* woman. *Women* fell at his feet—and she wouldn't be one of them.

He laughed, and then sobered. 'Mostly I stay away from them.'

Callie felt herself soften just a little at the heartbreak she could hear ever so slightly in his voice. And just like that her judgement of him faded away. He didn't want women, or even just one woman—he wanted to be alone. Callie couldn't figure out which fact bothered her the most.

'I'm sorry. She must have been a real piece of work.'

He didn't answer her, but his face told her everything that she needed to know. She placed a hand over his and squeezed it, hoping to provide him with some comfort. But when he laid his hand over hers in return, comfort was the last thing on her mind. His hand brought heat to hers, and lit her heart so that it beat to a rhythm she couldn't fathom. He leaned his head towards hers, and suddenly heat spread through her bloodstream.

This couldn't be right, she thought desperately as she pulled her hand away. They barely knew each other. She wouldn't let herself fall into a web of attraction with a man who was as charming as a fairy-tale prince.

Before she could worry about it the elevator lurched and the lights came back on. He stood and offered a hand to her, a slight smile on his gorgeous face. Did he know the effect he had on her? Or was he simply aware that he'd helped distract her from one of her worst fears?

As Callie took his hand she had to admit that he *had* kept her thoughts off being stuck in an elevator. And she blamed that—and his good looks—on her uncharacteristic reaction.

'Thank you,' she said as the elevator doors opened. 'I hope you enjoy the rest of your evening.'

The breath of relief that was released from her lungs as she walked away was because she was out of the enclosed space, Callie assured herself, and ignored the voice in her head that scoffed at the lie.

* * *

Blake Owen stopped at the doors of the banquet hall and resisted the urge to walk away. He had never been a fan of opulence, but rarely did he have a choice in the matter. Which was fine, he supposed. In his business, events of an extravagant nature were integral to success, and the welcome for him tonight was an excellent example of that. He would be introduced to the Elegance Hotel in Cape Town in a style that would keep the hotel's name at the forefront of the media's attention while he sorted out the troublesome operation.

So he accepted his lot and walked into the room, snagging a flute of champagne from the nearest waiter's tray before taking the whole scene in.

Glamour spread from the roof to the floor and fairy lights and sparkling chandeliers twinkled like stars against the midnight-blue draping. Black-and-white-clad waiters wove through the crowd while men and women in tuxedos and evening gowns air-kissed and wafted around on clouds of self-importance.

Blake almost rolled his eyes—until he remembered the guests were there in *his* honour. The thought made him empty the entire champagne glass and exchange it for a full one from the next waiter. He noted that the power outage hadn't seemed to dampen the evening's festivities. But when he looked at the scene with the eye of a manager he could see some slightly frazzled members of staff weaving through the crowd doing damage control.

He managed to get the attention of one of them, and took the frightened young man to a less populated corner of the hall.

'What happened when the electricity went out?'

As Blake spoke the man's eyes widened and Blake thought that 'boy' might be a more appropriate description.

'It was only a few moments, sir. As you can see, everything is running smoothly again. Enjoy your evening.'

The boy made to move away, but at Blake's look he paused.

'Was there anything else, sir?'

'Yes, actually. I was wondering if you brush off the concerns of *all* your guests, or if you reserve that for just a handful of people.'

If the boy had looked nervous before, he was terrified now. 'No…no, sir. I'm sorry you feel that I did. We're just a bit busy, and I have to make sure that everything is okay before Mr Owen gets here.'

'That would be me.'

The words were said in a low voice, softly, but for their effect they might have been earth-shatteringly loud.

'Mr… Mr Owen?' the boy stammered. 'Sir, I am *so* sorry—'

'It's fine,' Blake said when he saw the boy might have a heart attack from the shock. 'You can answer my original question.' At his blank look, Blake elaborated. 'The power outage…?'

'Oh, yes. Well, it wasn't such a train smash here. The candles gave sufficient light that there wasn't much panic, and Connor—Mr McKenzie, I mean—managed to calm whatever concerns there were.'

Blake was surprised the boy had been able to string enough words together to give him such a thorough explanation.

'And that was it?'

'Yes, sir. The generator was back on in under thirty minutes, so it wasn't too long. Although I *did* hear there were people trapped in the elevator.'

Blake thought it best not to tell the boy *he* had been one

of those who had been trapped. He wasn't sure if he would be able to handle another shock.

'When was the last time the generator was checked?'

'I... I don't know, sir.'

Blake nodded and left it at that, making a mental note to check that out when he officially started on Monday. The list of what he would have to do at the hotel seemed to grow the more time he spent there, and he wasn't having it. Not any more. Somehow the Elegance in Cape Town had flown under his radar for the past few years, while he had focused on his other hotels in South Africa.

And while he focused on rebuilding his self-respect after letting himself be fooled into a relationship that should never have been.

When he had eventually started reviewing the financials he'd realised that although Connor McKenzie *had* pulled the hotel out of the mess that Landon Meyer, the previous regional manager, had made, it wasn't enough. The hotel hadn't made a profit for three years, and he couldn't let that continue.

But that wasn't tonight's problem, Blake thought as he scanned the crowd. He knew it would only take a few minutes before he would be recognised, and then he would have to start doing the rounds as guest of honour. He paused when he saw the woman he had been stuck in the elevator with a few moments ago. She was standing near a table full of champagne, and before Blake knew it he was walking towards her.

As he came closer he saw that his recollection of their time spent in the elevator didn't do justice to what he saw now. He had noticed that she was attractive when she'd walked in, but he had taken care not to stare. And with the darkness that had descended only a few moments later, he hadn't been able to look at her as he was now.

The red dress she wore clung only to her chest and then flowed regally down from her waist to the floor. Her black hair stood out strikingly against the dress, her golden skin amplifying the effect, and for reasons he couldn't quite place his finger on it disconcerted him. Her round face held an innocence he hadn't been privy to in a long time, and her green eyes persuaded him to consider pursuing her.

The thought shocked him, as there was nothing in her expression to prompt it. There was also nothing in his past that encouraged him to trust a woman again. Yet now he felt an intense desire to get to know *this* woman. One he had only just met an hour ago.

'I think that after being stuck in an elevator the least we could do is have a drink together.'

Callie heard the deep voice as she reached for a glass of champagne. Her hand stilled, and then she continued, hoping that her pause wouldn't be noticed.

'I don't know if I'm inclined to agree,' she said and took a sip of her drink. 'I never have drinks with anyone I don't know.'

'Really? But you have nothing against flirting with strangers?' He gave her an amused look, his smile widening when she blushed.

'Must have been a temporary lapse in judgement.'

'How do you date if you don't flirt?'

'I don't.' She sipped her drink.

'Which would explain the lack of a boyfriend.'

Callie aimed a level look at him. 'Yes. And it would also explain why I don't have to deal with conversations like this very often.'

'Touché.' He smiled and lifted his glass to her in a toast.

Her lips almost curved in response, but then she stopped herself. What was she *doing*? A memory flashed into her mind, of him sitting with her in the elevator, patiently talking to her to distract her from her fears. And then she remembered. She was flirting with him because there was something about him that had kept her calm when she should have had a panic attack.

Heaven help her.

'And you've told me everything I need to know about why *you're* single, then?' she asked, and immediately regretted it when his expression dimmed. 'I'm sorry, I didn't mean to upset you.'

'No,' he responded, 'it's fine.' But he changed the topic. 'Since you seem to want to know so much about me, how about you offer me the same courtesy? You can start with your name.'

She smiled. 'Callie.'

She held out her hand, proud that her voice revealed none of the strange feelings he evoked in her. He took it and shook it slowly, making the ordinary task feel like an intimate act, and she shifted as a thrill worked its way up her spine.

'Blake? I'm so glad I've found you. I was about to send out a search party.'

Callie stared dumbly at her brother as he strode towards them, his tuxedo perfectly fitted to his build and perfectly suited to his handsome features.

'Hey, Cals, I'm happy you made it without missing too much.' Connor gave her a kiss on the cheek, and angled his face so that Blake wouldn't see his questioning look. 'I see you've met the reason we're all here.'

It took a full minute before Callie could process his words. '*This* is Blake Owen?'

'Yes.' Blake intercepted Connor's reply. 'Although, to be fair, I was about to introduce myself. Connor just got here before I could.'

Blake shook Connor's hand in greeting, and Callie couldn't help but notice how much more efficient the action was now than when he had done it with her.

'How do you two know each other?'

'Connor is my brother,' Callie said, before her brother could say anything. All the feelings inside her had frozen, and she resisted the urge to shiver.

'So you're here to support him? That's great.' Blake smiled at her.

Connor laughed. 'No! Callie's a good sister, but I'm not sure she would attend an event so far out of her comfort zone for *me*.' At Blake's questioning look, Connor elaborated. 'Callie works at the hotel.'

Connor's simple words shattered the opportunity for any explanation Callie might have wanted to give. Blake's eyes iced, and this time she couldn't resist the shiver that went through her body.

'Well, we should probably get going,' Connor said when the silence extended a second too long.

'Yes,' Blake agreed, his gaze never leaving Callie's. 'You should probably start introducing me to the other *employees*—' he said the word with a contempt that Callie hadn't expected '—before I make a mistake I can't rectify.'

Callie watched helplessly as they walked away, wondering how she had already managed to alienate her CEO.

CHAPTER TWO

BLAKE WATCHED AS the crowd in the banquet hall began to thin. There must have been about three hundred people there, he thought. And, the way he felt, he was sure he had spoken to every single one of them. No, he corrected himself almost immediately. Not *everyone*. There was one person he had avoided ever since learning who she was—an employee of the hotel.

Julia, his ex, had been an employee. She had been a part of the Human Resources team in the Port Elizabeth hotel, where he spent most of his time.

He had been enamoured of her. She was beautiful, intelligent, and just a little arrogant. And she had a son who had crept into his heart the moment Blake had met him. It had been a fascinating combination—the gorgeous, sassy woman and the sweet, shy child. One that had lured him in and blinded him to the truth of what she'd wanted from him. The truth that had made him distrust his judgement and conclude that staying away from his employees would be the safest option to avoid getting hurt.

He narrowed his eyes when he saw Callie walking towards him, and cursed himself for the attraction that flashed through his body. But he refused to give in to it. He would ignore the way some strands of her hair had escaped from her hairstyle and floated down to frame her face. He wouldn't notice that she walked as if someone had rolled out a red carpet for her. He hardened himself against the effect she had on him—and then she was in front of him and her smell nearly did him in.

The floral scent was edged with seduction—a description that came from nowhere as she stood innocently in front of him, those emerald eyes clear of any sign of wrongdoing.

'What do you want?' he snapped, and surprised himself. Regardless of the way his body reacted to her, he could control it. He *would* control it.

Her eyes widened, but then set with determination. 'I wanted to set the record straight. I know you must be confused after finding out I work here.'

'That isn't the word I'd use.'

'Well, however you would describe it, I still want to tell you what happened.'

She took a breath, and Blake wondered if she realised how shakily she'd done it.

'I had no idea who you were when we were stuck in that elevator. If I had, I wouldn't have—'

'Flirted with me?'

Something in her eyes fired, and reminded him that he had flirted with her, too. But her voice was calm when she spoke.

'Yes, I suppose. It was an honest mistake. I didn't seek you out to try and soften you up, or anything crazy like that. So…' She paused, and then pushed on. 'Please don't take this out on Connor.'

Blake frowned. She was explaining to him that she'd made a mistake—and the honesty already baffled him— but she didn't seem to be doing it for herself. She was doing it for her brother, and that was…selfless.

Almost everything Julia had done had been self-serving.

But then he hadn't known that in the beginning. He'd thought that she was being unselfish, that she was being honest. And those qualities had attracted him. But it had all been pretence. So what if there didn't *seem* to be a deceitful motive behind what Callie was saying? He knew better than anyone else that she might be faking it.

But when he looked at her, into those alluring and devastatingly honest eyes, that thought just didn't sit right.

'So,' he said, sliding his hands into his pockets, 'I can take it out on *you*?'

Was he still flirting with her? No, he thought. He wanted to know what she thought he should do about the situation. Yes, that was it—just a test. How would she respond now that she knew he was her boss?

She cleared her throat. 'If need be, yes. I understand if you feel you need to take disciplinary action, although I don't believe it's necessary.'

'You don't?'

'No, sir.'

The word sounded different coming from her, and he wasn't sure that he liked the way she was defining their relationship.

'I apologise for my unprofessional behaviour, but I assure you it won't happen again.' She looked at him, and this time her eyes pleaded for herself. 'I didn't know who you were. Please give me a chance to make this right.'

Blake was big enough a man to realise when he had made a mistake, and the sincerity the woman in front of him exuded told him he had done just that, in spite of his doubts. He straightened, and saw that there was almost no one left in the room for him to meet. Relief poured through him, and finally he gave himself permission to leave.

But before he did, he said, 'Okay, Miss McKenzie. I believe you. I'll see you at work on Monday.'

* * *

By eleven o'clock on Monday morning Blake had had enough. He had got in to the office at six and had been poring over the financials since then. *Again*. But no matter how he looked at it—just as he'd feared the first time he'd reviewed them—there was no denying the fact that this hotel was in serious trouble.

How had he let it get this far? he thought, and walked to the coffee machine in the office he would be sharing with Connor. The man had set up a makeshift space for Blake, which made the place snug, but not unworkable. Right now, he was tempted to have a drink of the stronger stuff Connor kept under lock and key for special occasions—or so he claimed. But even in Blake's current state of mind he could acknowledge that drinking was not the way to approach this.

With his coffee in his hand, he walked to the window and looked out at the bustle of Cape Town on a Monday morning. The hotel overlooked parts of the business district, and he could feel the busyness of people trying to get somewhere rife in the air as he watched the relays of public transport. But he could also glimpse Table Mountain in the background, and he appreciated the simplicity of its magnitude. It somehow made him feel steadier as he thought about the state the hotel was in.

How had he let this happen?

The thought wouldn't leave his head. He had picked up that the hotel had been struggling years ago—which was why he had fired Landon and promoted Connor—but still this shouldn't have got past him. But he knew why it had. And he needed to be honest with himself before he blamed his employees when *he* was probably just as responsible for this mess.

He had been too focused on dealing with Julia to notice that the business was suffering.

His legs were restless now, as he got to the core of the problem, and he began to pace, coffee in hand, contemplating the situation. About five years ago the Elegance Hotel in Port Elizabeth had started losing staff at a high rate. When he'd noticed how low their retention numbers were, he'd arranged a meeting with HR to discuss it.

It had been at that meeting that he'd first met Julia.

She hadn't seemed to care that he was her boss, and had pushed the boundaries of what he had considered appropriate professional behaviour. But the reasons she had given him for losing staff had been right, and he'd had to acknowledge that she was an asset to their team. And as soon as he had she'd given him the smile that had drawn him in. Bright, bold, beautiful.

To this day, whenever he thought about that smile he felt a knock to his heart. Especially since those thoughts were so closely intertwined with the way it had softened when she'd looked at her son. The boy who had reminded him eerily of himself, and made him think about how Julia was giving him something Blake never had—a mother.

Until one day it had all shattered into the pieces that still haunted him.

He knew that Julia had taken his attention away from the hotels. And now this hotel was paying the price of a mistake he'd made before he'd known better. The thought conjured up Callie's face in his mind, but he forced it away, hoping to forget the way her eyes lit up her face when she smiled. He had just remembered the reason he didn't want to be attracted to her. He didn't want to be distracted either, and she had the word *distraction* written all over her beautiful face. *And*, he reminded himself again, he knew better now.

He grunted at the thought, walked back to the desk, and began to make some calls.

And ignored the face of the woman he had only met a few days ago as it drifted around in his head.

'Yes, darling, include that in my trip. I would *love* to see the mountain everyone keeps harping on about. And please include some cultural museums on my tour.' The woman sniffed, and placed a dignified hand on the very expensive pearls she wore around her neck. 'I can't only be doing *touristy* things, you know.'

'Of course, Mrs Applecombe.' Callie resisted the urge to tell the woman that visiting museums was very much a 'touristy' thing. 'I'll draw up a package for you and have it sent to your room by the end of the day. If you agree, we can arrange for the tour to be done the day after tomorrow.'

'Delightful.' Mrs Applecombe clasped her hands together. 'I just *know* Henry will love what we've discussed. Just remember, dear, that it's—'

'Supposed to be a surprise. I know.' Callie smiled, and stood. 'I'll make sure that it's everything you could hope for and more.'

After a few more lengthy reminders about the surprise anniversary gift for her husband Mrs Applecombe finally left, and Callie sighed in relief. She loved the woman's spirit, but after forty minutes of going back and forth about a tour Callie knew she could have designed in her sleep, she needed a break.

Luckily it was one o'clock, which meant she could take lunch. But instead of sneaking into the kitchen, as she did most days, she locked the door to her office and flopped down on the two-seater couch she'd crammed into the small space so that if her guests wanted to they could be slightly more comfortable.

It had been a long morning. She'd done a quick tour first thing when she'd got in, followed by meetings with three guests wanting to plan trips. Usually she would be ecstatic about it. She loved her job. And she had Connor to thank for that.

She sighed, and sank even lower on the couch. Officially she was the 'Specialised Concierge'—a title she had initially thought pretentious, but one that seemed to thrill many of the more elite guests she worked with at the hotel. Unofficially she was a glorified tour guide, whose brother had persuaded her to work at the hotel to drag her from the very dark place she had been in after their parents' deaths.

She didn't have to think back that far to acknowledge that the job had saved her from that dark place. Once she had seen her parents' coffins descend into the ground— once she had watched people say their farewells and return to their lives as usual— she had found herself slipping. And even though her brother had been close to broken himself, he had stepped up and had helped her turn her life into something she knew had been out of her grasp after the car crash that had destroyed the life she had known and the people she loved.

The thought made her miss him terribly, and she grabbed her handbag and headed to Connor's office. Maybe he felt like having lunch together, and he could calm the ache that had suddenly started in her heart.

As she walked the short distance to his office she greeted some of the guests she recognised and nodded politely at those she didn't. She smiled in sympathy when she saw her friend Kate, dealing with a clearly testy guest at the front desk, and laughed when Kate mimicked placing a gun to her head as the guest leaned down to sign something.

Connor's door was slightly ajar when she got there, and she paused before knocking when she heard voices.

'If we keep doing what we're doing, in a couple of years—three, max—the hotel will be turning a profit again, Blake.' Connor's voice sounded panicked. 'I'm just not sure *this* plan is the best option. Surely there's something else we can do? Especially after we've stepped up in the last few years.'

'Connor, no one is denying the work you've done at the hotel. You've increased turnover by fifty per cent since you took over—which is saying something when you consider the state Landon left it in. But three years is too long to have a business running in the red.' There was a pause, and then Blake continued. 'Would you rather we move on to the other option? I've told you that it would come with a lot more complications...'

'Of course I would prefer *any* other option. But you know what's best for the hotel.'

Callie felt a trickle of unease run through her when she heard her brother's voice. It wasn't panicked this time, but resigned, as though he had given up hope on something.

'All right, then.' There was a beat of silence. 'I suppose we should start preparing to lay off staff.'

The words were fatalistic, and yet it took Callie a while to process what she had heard. Once she did, her legs moved without her consent and she burst through the office door.

'No!' she said, and her voice sounded as though it came from faraway. 'I can't let you do that.'

CHAPTER THREE

'EXCUSE ME?' BLAKE LIFTED his eyebrows, and suddenly Callie wished her tongue had given her the chance to think before she spoke.

'I'm so sorry, Mr Owen… Connor…' She saw the look in her brother's eyes and hoped her own apologised for interrupting. 'I just heard—'

'A *private* business conversation between members of management. Do you make a habit of eavesdropping?'

His eyes were steel, and she could hear the implication that he thought she had more poor habits than just eavesdropping.

'No, of course not. I was on my way to ask Connor if he'd like to do lunch, and then I heard you because the door was open.' She gestured behind her, although the action was useless now, since it stood wide open after her desperate entrance. 'I didn't mean to listen, but I did, and I'm telling you that you *can't* lay off staff. Please.'

Blake's handsome face softened slightly, and she cursed herself for noticing how his dark blue suit made him look like a model from the pages of a fashion magazine. It was probably the worst time to think of that, she thought, and instead focused on making some kind of case to make him reconsider.

'There are people here who need their jobs. Who *love*

their jobs.' She could hear the plea in her voice. 'Employees here who have families who depend on them.'

'I'm aware of that, Miss McKenzie.' Blake frowned. 'I've thought every option through. This one is the best for the hotel. If we downsize now we can focus on operations and then expand again once we turn enough profit. It would actually be fairly simple.'

'For you, maybe. And for the hotel, sure. But I can assure you it would be anything but simple for the people you lay off—' She broke off, her heart pounding at the prospect. 'This is a business decision without any consideration for your employees.'

His eyes narrowed. 'I *have* considered my employees, and I resent your implication otherwise. You have no idea what any other option would require from us. This is the most efficient way to help Elegance, Cape Town, get back on its feet.'

'Are you listening to yourself?' she asked desperately. 'You've been tossing around words like "downsizing" and "efficiency" as though those are *good* things. They aren't!'

'Callie—'

Connor stepped forward and she immediately felt ashamed of her behaviour when she saw the warning in his eyes. She knew she was embarrassing him in front of their boss. She even knew that she was embarrassing *herself* in front of her boss. So, even though more words tumbled through her mind, and even though the shame she felt was more for Connor than for herself, she stopped talking.

'It's okay, Connor.' Blake eased his way into one of the chairs in front of Connor's desk. 'I understand your sister's anger. However unprofessional.'

Callie's heart hammered in her chest and she wished that she hadn't said anything. But then she thought of Kate, and Connor, and of the fact that her job meant the world to her, and she straightened her shoulders. She wouldn't feel bad for standing up for their jobs. Not when it meant that she'd at least tried to save them.

'There is another option, Callie.'

Blake spoke quietly, and she wondered if he knew the power his voice held even so.

'I've looked into other investors.'

'Why did you dismiss the idea?'

Something shifted in his eyes, as though he hadn't expected her to ask him about his reasons.

'The Elegance hotels are the product of my father's hard work, and mine, and I don't want an outside investor to undermine that. Not at this stage of the game.'

He looked at her, and what she saw in his eyes gave her hope.

'Of course I *have* considered it. Especially an international investor, since that might give Elegance the boost it needs to go international. But it would be a very complicated process, and it would require a lot of negotiation.' He turned now, and looked at Connor. 'Like I told you before, I would have to think through the terms of this thoroughly before I make any decision.'

'But you'll reconsider it?' There was no disguising the hope Callie felt.

Blake looked at her, and those blue-green eyes were stormier than she had thought possible.

'I don't want another investor. This hotel group has been in my family for decades, Miss McKenzie. It's a legacy I want to pass on to my children.' He paused. 'But if we can secure an international investor, that legacy might be even more than I thought possible. We'll talk about it.'

He gestured to Connor, and then moved to sit behind the desk Connor had had put in his office for Blake.

Callie waited, but the look on her brother's face told

her she had been dismissed. She nearly skipped out of the room, because despite his non-committal response Blake Owen *was* considering an option other than laying off staff. If Blake chose an investor it would mean that everything her brother had worked so hard for wouldn't have been for nothing.

He had toiled night and day to try and get the hotel running smoothly again, and the news of Blake's arrival had been a difficult pill to swallow—it had been a clear sign that everything Connor had done hadn't been enough. Callie knew he loved the hotel, and the last thing that he wanted was for his employees to lose their jobs. And, she thought, the last thing *she* wanted was for him to lose his job—and for her to lose hers.

So before she left she wanted to say one more thing to Blake.

'Mr Owen... Blake?'

He looked up, and she smiled.

'Thank you for reconsidering.'

Blake couldn't sleep. He had been working with Connor until just past midnight, trying to draft an investment contract that he was happy with. A contract that would require all his negotiation skills to convince an investor to accept—although he knew it was possible. He had put out feelers even before he had spoken to Connor, when he had initially thought of finding an investor, and the response had been positive. But he still wasn't convinced that this was something he wanted or if it was something he was being persuaded into by a pretty face.

He threw off his bedcovers and walked downstairs to the kitchen of his Cape Town house. He had bought the place without much thought other than that he would need somewhere to stay when he visited his father, who had retired here. Now he was incredibly grateful he had, since he didn't know how long he would be in town.

The house was a few kilometres from the hotel, and had an amazing view. He could even see the lights of the city illuminating Table Mountain at night through the glass doors that led out onto a deck on the second floor. But he wasn't thinking about that as he poured himself a glass of water and drank as though he had come out of a desert.

Since the house was temperature-controlled, he knew he wasn't feeling the heat of the January weather. No, he thought. It was because he was considering something that would complicate his life when all he'd wanted was a simple solution.

Blake had been raised in the family business. His father had opened the first Elegance Hotel four decades ago, and had invested heavily in guest relations. He had made sure that every employee knew that the Elegance Hotel's guests came first, and seen that vision manifested into action. Eventually, after two decades, his investment had paid off and he had been able to expand into other hotels.

Blake had been groomed to take over since he was old enough to understand that his father was not only building a business, but a legacy. And he hadn't been given control of the hotel until his father had been sure that he could do it.

That was why he wanted to lay off staff instead of considering an outside investor. He would be able to solve the problem that had arisen while he'd been trying to fix his relationship with Julia easily, and make the reminder of his failure disappear. It would mean that his feelings of losing control and being helpless would be gone.

A memory of himself standing at the front door, watching his mother leave, flashed through his mind, but he shook it away, not knowing where it had come from, and forced his thoughts back to the matter at hand. Laying off staff might have been the simple option, but it was also a selfish one. Especially when he thought of the hope he had seen written on Callie and Connor's faces.

He sighed as he made his decision. He would do this— but not for Callie. The slight heat that flushed through him every time he thought about her, the intensity of it every time he saw her, was a sure sign that he should stay away from her. He *wouldn't* make this big a decision based on his attraction to her or her need for him to do so. He wouldn't make that mistake again.

'Mr Owen, do you have a moment?'

Callie stood awkwardly at the door, wishing with all her might that she didn't feel quite so small in his presence. But she straightened when he looked up and gestured for her to come in.

She knew Connor had to attend one of the conferences at the hotel today, and she was using the opportunity to speak to her boss without her brother's disapproving look. And without the disapproving lecture she would no doubt receive—like the one she'd received just after midnight— which, she had been told, was when Connor and Blake had finally finished their meeting.

She knew she'd been out of line when she had spoken up, and she hadn't needed Connor to tell her that. So once again she was preparing to apologise to Blake.

She walked in and swallowed when he looked up, the striking features of his face knitted into a stern expression.

'What can I do for you, Miss McKenzie?'

'It's Callie, please.'

He nodded. 'Okay, then. What can I do for you, Callie?'

Her stomach jilted just a little at the way he said her name. She cleared her throat. 'I wanted to say sorry.'

He almost smiled. 'It's becoming a habit, then.'

She let out a laugh. 'Seems like it. I've made quite the mess since meeting you.' She stepped forward, resisted pulling at her clothes. 'But I *am* sorry. The first time I apologised it was because I'd made a mistake. This time it's because I shouldn't have barged in here and spoken out of turn.'

'I'm not upset with you because you spoke out of turn.'

Blake stood, walked around the desk and leaned against it. He was wearing a blue shirt, and the top button was loosened. She swallowed, and wondered if the temperature in the room had increased.

'I'm not your school principal.'

'Aren't you, though? In some ways?'

This time he did smile, and it did something strange to her heart.

'I won't take the bait on that one.'

He paused, and then crossed his arms. She could see the muscle ripple under his shirt, and the heat went up another notch.

'You say you're sorry for barging in here. But not that you eavesdropped?'

'No, I'm not sorry about that. If I hadn't you wouldn't have considered investors. Which you *have* been doing, right?' she asked, and knew that subtlety was not her forte.

'I have. I made a few calls this morning, and I have a few people interested.'

He walked towards her, and though the distance between them wasn't small her heart thudded.

'So the answer to your real question is yes, I am going to do this.'

'You *are*?' Relief washed over her. 'Oh, wow!' She pressed a hand to her stomach. 'That's amazing.'

'But I need your help.'

Relief turned into confusion. 'What do you mean?'

'Like I said yesterday, we need a very specific kind of investor. An international one who will be willing to invest in the hotel, but also in this city. Especially if I want him to agree to my strict terms regarding the expansion of Elegance Hotels.'

His hands were in his pockets now, and he moved until he was just close enough that she could smell his cologne. It reminded her of when they were in the elevator together—a time when she hadn't had to think of him as her boss.

She shook off the feelings the memory evoked, but when she spoke, her voice was a little husky. 'And how can I help with that?'

'You can help me sell the city. You are the "Specialised Concierge", right?'

He smiled slyly, and she realised he knew about her made-up title.

'Or, in more common terms, a tour guide,' she said.

'Exactly. So I'll need you to help me sell Cape Town to potential investors. Your knowledge of the city will be an asset to any proposal I make. I'll take care of the business side of it, of course, and once that's done we can take them on the tour you will custom-design to fit my proposal.'

'How do you know I can do it?' She felt her heart beat in a rhythm that couldn't possibly be healthy.

'Because your job depends on it.'

He smiled now, and she couldn't read the emotion that lined it.

'Callie, are you prepared to work with the boss?'

She stared helplessly at him, and despite everything inside her that nudged her to say otherwise she answered, 'Yes, I am.'

CHAPTER FOUR

'YOU'RE HERE BECAUSE you want to keep your job. You're here because you want to save Connor's job. You're here because you're saving your colleagues' jobs.'

Callie repeated the words to herself as she walked into what had previously been known as Conference Room A. Blake had turned it into an office. Not one he would share with Connor. No, that had ended the minute she had agreed to work with him. This conference-room-turned-office was hers and Blake's to share. It was one of their medium-sized conference rooms, and Callie had only been in it a few times when she'd had tours with groups of more than six. But, despite its reasonable size, Callie felt closed in. And this time she wasn't fooling herself by attributing the feeling to claustrophobia.

Her heart hammered as she saw him sitting at one end of the rectangular table, a large whiteboard behind him already half filled with illegible writing.

'Are you sure you weren't meant to be a doctor?' she asked, hoping to break the tension she felt within herself.

Blake looked up at her, his eyes sharp despite how hard she knew he had been working. The hotel had been rife with the news that Blake had been holed up in the conference room for the entire week it had taken for Callie to sort out her schedule. She'd done her tours for that week, but had cancelled everything beyond that. Blake had made it very clear that Callie's full attention would be needed for the investors, and that was what she was doing.

She tilted her head when he grabbed a cup of what Callie assumed had once been coffee from in front of him. By the look on his face, it was something significantly less desirable now.

'I'll get you some more,' she said, and placed her files and handbag a few seats away from his.

This was their first official day of working together, and Callie wasn't sure what it would be like to work with the boss. She was already distracted by being alone with him in the same room, she thought as she poured coffee into two cups that sat on the counter along one side of the conference room. The hotel staff had made sure that everything their boss could possibly need was in that room.

She'd heard them whispering amongst themselves, and had taken it upon herself to defuse their curiosity.

'We're going to try and save the hotel,' she'd told Kate, knowing her friend couldn't keep a secret for the life of her, 'and if we do things will stay the same for the foreseeable future.'

Since she'd let that little titbit go, her colleagues had done everything in their power to make sure they had the fuel to save the hotel. And maybe the world, she thought, and wrinkled her nose at the extensive display of pastries that lined the rest of the counter.

'How many people are eating this?' she wondered out loud, and set the coffee in front of Blake.

'Two today.' He sighed as he sipped from the coffee. 'It's been like that ever since I started working in here. I think they think I'm a competitive eater in my spare time.'

She laughed. 'Or a man who needs as much energy as possible so that he can work to save their jobs.' He frowned, and she elaborated. 'People were getting restless about what you being here means. I told a friend, and she told everyone else. Trust me—it's better this way. Otherwise they might have been planning to starve you instead of feed you.'

She grinned, and felt herself relax. This wasn't so bad. They were having a normal conversation. Just as she would with any of her colleagues. But then Blake smiled in return, and her heart thumped with that incredibly fast rhythm she was beginning to think was personalised for him. Like a ringtone.

She cleared her throat. 'How's everything going here?'

'Good.' He took another sip of the coffee, and settled back in his chair. 'I've created interest amongst my contacts by highlighting how beneficial it would be for them to be a part of my business, so we're looking at a few potential prospects.'

She stared at him. 'You're good.'

He grinned at her. 'Thanks. It's going to be a lot easier for both of us now that you've realised that.'

She felt her lips twitch. 'It's a good thing I have, then. Now, what do you need from *me*, Mr Owen?'

'Blake,' he said, and shrugged when she frowned. 'I feel like my father every time you call me that.'

'Fine,' she said, and forced herself to say his name without feeling anything. 'Blake, what do you need from me?'

There was a pause as the question settled between them, and it made her feel as though she'd said something inappropriate. And the way he looked at her made her feel like she wanted to give him whatever he thought he needed from her—even if it wasn't something that was strictly professional. She exhaled slowly, and hoped that the tension inside her would seep out with her breath. It did—but only because he finally responded.

'Well, we need to start working on a proposal. But, since

I'm still at the stage of securing possible investors, please start drawing up a list of places you think we can include in the tour portion of the proposal. Include your motivations for why you think we should visit them. We can take it from there.'

'Okay,' she said, and then frowned when he grabbed his coffee and hung the tie that had been carelessly thrown across his chair over his shoulder. 'Where are you going?'

'To work in Connor's office for a while. Just so we don't disturb each other while I'm busy with my calls.'

He nodded at her, and then left her wondering why he had asked her to work with him in the conference room when he wouldn't even be there.

'Welcome back,' Callie said later, as Blake entered the room.

'Thanks.' He nodded, and opted for a glass of water instead of the coffee he knew he should take a break from. Especially since his throat was nearly raw from all the talking he had been doing for the last few hours.

He had been successful—had spoken to many of the parties who had contacted him—and he could no longer justify staying away from the conference room. Not when he had insisted Callie work with him and that they should do things together.

'What do you have so far?'

Callie gave him a measured look, and immediately he felt chastised that he hadn't made small talk first. But he didn't trust himself to do that just yet. Not while he was still trying to convince himself that working with her had been a *business* decision, and had nothing to do with the way she made him feel. Especially after he had told himself that he would stay away from her.

Even now, as she sat poised behind the table, her white

shirt snug enough for him to see curves he didn't want to notice, he could feel a pull between them that had nothing to do with business.

And it scared him.

'Well, I've done exactly as you asked. I've drawn up a list of must-see locations that I think we should consider for your proposal.'

She stood and handed him the list, and he saw that her black trousers were still as neat as they had been that morning, when she'd first walked in. She looked pristine—even though, based on the papers in his hands, she had been working extensively on her planning.

'You can have a look at them and let me know what you think, but I don't think there will be a problem with any of them. I've also tentatively set up some tour ideas.'

Blake struggled to get over the way her proximity threatened to take over his senses, but he forced it to the back of his mind and listened to her explain some of the ideas she'd had. As she did, his own began to form. A business proposal that would complement what she had in mind. But he didn't know if it would work without seeing it first.

'Okay—great.' He put down his glass of water and gestured towards the chair where her jacket lay. 'Grab your things and we can go immediately.'

'What?' Her eyes widened.

'I want you to show me these must-see locations. I mean, what you have is great—theoretically—but I need you to show them to me so that I know they work in practice.'

'And you want to go right now?'

'Yes.' He walked to the door and opened it for her. 'The longer we wait, the longer we delay finalising plans. And that's not the way I work.'

Callie stood staring at him, as though at any minute he was going to say, *Just joking!* When she realised that it wasn't going to happen, she grabbed her jacket and hand-bag and walked past him through the open door.

Her scent was still as enticing as it had been that first night, and for a brief moment—not for the first time—Blake wondered if he was making a mistake. He had asked her to work with him on impulse, although he had known it was a logical, even smart way of approaching the inter-national investor angle once he'd had a chance to think about it. So why was it that he'd avoided working with her for the entire morning if he was so convinced that it was all business between them?

It didn't matter, he thought, and shook away any linger-ing doubts. He had a job to do. And that job would come first.

Callie waited as John, the parking valet, pulled up in Blake's silver sedan. This evidence of his wealth jostled her, though she knew she shouldn't be surprised. Of *course* her boss had money, she thought, and watched Blake thank John and wave him away when the valet moved to open the door for her. Instead, Blake did it himself, and she got in, her skin prickling when she brushed against him by accident.

She ignored it, instead focusing on the car. It was just as luxurious on the inside as it was on the outside—as she'd expected—with gadgets that she didn't quite think were necessary. But, then again, she drove an old second-hand car that made her arms ache every time she had to turn the wheel. Perhaps if she had thought about gadgets, she wouldn't have to worry that her car might stall every time she drove it.

Nevertheless, she was proud of the little thing. It was the first car she'd ever bought, and she'd worked incredibly hard since leaving high school and saved every last rand to buy it. Granted, she'd worked for her parents, and she knew they had been liberal in their payment.

She smiled at the memory, and caught her breath when he asked, 'What's that for?'

She hadn't realised he was paying attention to her. She should have known better. *Always be on guard*, she reminded herself.

'I was just admiring your car. And comparing it with mine. It doesn't,' she said with a smile when he gave her a questioning look.

'I bought it when I knew I was coming to Cape Town. I had no idea how long I was going to be here, and I didn't want to impose on my father and use one of his indefinitely. I'll probably sell it as soon as I know where I'm going next.'

Though her heart stuck on the information that he would be leaving, she asked, 'You didn't own a car before?'

'I did. But I sold it a while ago—when I realised I would be travelling a lot more.'

'But don't you need one for when you're at home?'

He took a right turn and glanced over to her. 'I don't have a home.'

For some reason Callie found that incredibly sad. 'I'm sorry.'

'Don't be. It's a choice.'

She wanted to ask him why, but the silence that stretched between them made it clear that he didn't want to reveal the reasons for that choice. She respected that. There were things she wouldn't want to reveal to him either.

'Blake, shouldn't *I* be driving?'

He frowned. 'Why? Can't you direct me to where we're going?'

'I can, but that won't give you the experience we'd be giving potential investors. And that's what you want, isn't it? That's why we're here?'

'I suppose so.' He signalled and pulled off to the side of the road.

They switched seats, and for a moment Callie just enjoyed the sleekness of the car. A car *she* would be driving for the day. She resisted the urge to giggle—and then the urge disappeared when she became aware of the other things sitting on the driver's side meant. The heat of his body was almost embedded into the seat. She could smell him. She traced her hands over the steering wheel, thinking how his had been there only a few moments ago.

She cleared her throat, willing the heat she felt through her body to go away. After putting on her safety belt, she pulled back into the road and aligned her thoughts. But they stuck when she realised he was looking at her.

'What?' she asked nervously. 'Am I doing something wrong?'

'No.' He smiled, and it somewhat eased the tension between them. 'I just didn't think this was how the day would turn out. You driving me around in my car.'

'Are you disappointed?' Callie turned left, a plan forming in her mind for their day. It was more of an outline, but she was sure it would suffice for something so last-minute.

'No. You're doing quite a remarkable job—especially considering I'm not a fan of being a passenger.'

'Really?' She glanced over in surprise. 'I thought you would be used to being chauffeured.'

'When the need arises, yes. But I try to keep those occasions to the minimum.'

'Because you like to be the one in control?'

He frowned, and for a minute Callie thought she had gone too far.

'Maybe, though I think it has more to do with my father. He loves his cars, and couldn't wait to share that love with me. So I like to drive him when I can so we can talk about something other than the hotel.'

Callie felt her heart ache at the revelation she didn't think Blake knew he had let slip. And, though a part of her urged her to accept the information about his relationship with his father without comment, she couldn't help but say, 'It must have made him proud that you took over his legacy. The hotels,' she elaborated when she felt his questioning glance. 'I read the article *Corporate Times* did on the two of you when he retired.'

She didn't mention that she'd read it—and many others— just a few weeks ago, when she'd heard Blake would be coming to Cape Town. When he didn't respond, she looked over and saw a puzzled expression on his face. Nerves kicked in and she felt the babbling that would come from her mouth before it even started.

'I just meant that he must be proud of you since he loved the hotel business so much. And since you're also, in some ways, his legacy, it's like his legacy running his legacy…' She shook her head at how silly that sounded. 'Anyway, that's why I said he must be proud.'

Blake didn't respond, and she wondered if she'd upset him. She should probably just have left it alone, she thought as she drove up the inclined road that led to Table Mountain. But it wasn't as if she was prying. Okay, maybe it was. But she'd only said something she thought was true. Surely he couldn't fault her for that?

'I think you might be right.'

He spoke so softly that she was grateful the radio was off or she might have missed it.

'He doesn't talk about it much, but I think maybe he is.'

Callie nodded, and was amazed at how those few words confirmed what she'd suspected earlier about his relationship with his father. She considered pressing for more information, but he asked her a question before she could.

'Where are you taking me first?'

She bit her lip to prevent her questions about his family from tumbling out. 'Table Mountain. Our number one tourist attraction, and also an incredible experience if you live here. This would be the first place I'd want to see if I hadn't been to Cape Town before.' She frowned. 'But, since you *have* been to Cape Town before, I'm sure this trip is redundant for you.'

'No. I haven't been up the mountain.'

He shrugged when she shot him an incredulous look.

'I've only been here for business or to visit my family. I don't do touristy things.'

'But…' She found herself at a loss for words. 'Don't you and your family go out together? I mean, this is the best outing for a family.'

'For certain kinds of families, yes, I suppose it is. But our family isn't one of those.'

Again, Callie felt an incredible grief at his words. They'd been driving for less than twenty minutes and already she knew that Blake didn't know if his father was proud of him or not, that their conversations mostly revolved around business, and that his family didn't do outings together.

She didn't know what was worse, she realised as she parked. Having a family—parents—and not having a great relationship with them, or having no parents but wonderful memories of them. She had always known that her parents were proud of her. And suddenly, for the first time since they'd died, she was grateful for those memories she had of her parents, no longer pushing them away.

CHAPTER FIVE

'IT'S BEAUTIFUL, ISN'T IT?'

Callie's voice was soft next to him, and he turned slightly to her, not wanting to move his eyes from the view.

'I don't think I've ever seen anything like it,' he said, knowing that the words couldn't be more true.

They stood at the top of Table Mountain, looking over the city and the harbour. If he walked to the other side, he knew he'd see the beaches and the ocean in a way he'd never experienced before. They weren't the only ones up there, but for the peace Blake felt he thought that they might as well be. He didn't think about failure or disappointment here. He felt so small, so insignificant, that thinking about his own problems seemed selfish.

Though he'd just done it, he walked back to the other side of the mountain and looked down at the ocean. There were houses scattered across the peaks of the hills above it, and he felt a tug of jealousy that the residents there were privy to such a spectacular view every day of their lives.

'I wonder if those people know how lucky they are to live there,' he said, aware that Callie was standing right next to him.

From the moment they'd stepped into the cable car to get up the mountain she'd left him to his thoughts. Thoughts that were tangled around her and her questions about his family. He hadn't wanted to talk about it, and he thought she'd realised as much when she'd remained quiet after her last question about going out as a family. But even though she was silent he had never been more aware of her presence. That peaceful, steady presence that he hadn't expected.

'Well, most of them are rich tycoons who purchase those houses and rent them out. Some are wealthy Cape Townians who invest or buy just because they can.' She paused, seemed almost hesitant to continue. 'And others are very aware of how lucky they are.'

'You know some of the others?'

'You could say so.' A ghost of a smile shadowed her lips. 'I live there.'

He struggled not to gape at her, but he couldn't resist the words. 'You *live* there?'

'Yes.'

The smile was full-blown now, and it warmed something inside him that he had thought was frozen.

'Right over there.'

She pointed, and he wondered which of the spectacular houses was hers.

'Connor said he lives in one of the main parts of town.'

'*He* does, yes. But we don't live together. He moved out of the house when he went to university. My parents were devastated, but they had me, and I had no plans for moving out. I commuted to university for my first year and then…' She trailed off and cleared her throat. 'And now I still live there.'

Her words made him want to ask so many questions. He wanted to break through whatever barrier she'd put up and find out why she hadn't continued with her story. Instead he settled for one of his many questions.

'Alone?'

She looked at him, and the pain in her eyes nearly stole his breath.

'Alone.'

Silence stretched between them while Blake tried to find words to comfort a hurt he didn't know anything about. But words failed him, and all he could do was wait helplessly.

'Come on—there's a lot more to show you,' she said, after what felt like for ever, and he followed her back to the cable car.

Somewhere in the back of his mind he was reminded that they were there for business, and as soon as the thought registered he took his phone from his pocket. He opened a memo and recorded Table Mountain as an approved place for the investors to see.

'This must be a really popular place for your tours,' he said as the cable car began its descent.

'It is.'

Was that relief he heard in her voice?

'I usually begin here or end here. Ending here usually works when the tour starts in the afternoon and we can make it up the mountain for sunset.'

'I'd love to see that.'

She smiled. 'It's definitely something to see. Maybe some day I'll take you.'

They were simple words, but Blake felt them shift something inside him. An emotion he hadn't experienced until he'd met her jolted him. *Hope.* He hadn't hoped for anything in a long time. Nor had he thought he would want to watch the sunset on top of a mountain with a woman who made him feel things he didn't want to feel.

'Where to next?' he asked when they reached the car.

'That, Mr Owen, would take all the fun out of today.'

She grinned, and he felt himself smiling back, despite what he was fighting inside.

* * *

'If Table Mountain is included in a morning tour I usually schedule it for about ten. We'd usually end there at about twelve, and then either have lunch at the top of the mountain or take a drive down to Camps Bay to have lunch.'

She nearly purred at the way the car was handling the curves of the road.

'I usually prefer driving down, because then our guests get to experience this amazing drive. And once there they can have lunch at one of the many upper-class but affordable restaurants.'

'I can't fault you on that,' Blake said, and she glanced over to see he was looking out of the window. 'This view is amazing.'

'I know.'

She smiled, and thought that her tour wasn't going badly. She hadn't shown him much yet, but she wanted to take him to the places she knew would provide opportunities to market the hotel to his investors. And she hadn't been able to resist showing him the best attraction—Table Mountain—first.

'If they like it, I tell them they can stay at the beach for the afternoon and we'll send a shuttle to fetch them when they're ready.'

'Sounds like a tourist's dream.'

'It is,' she agreed. 'Although, to be fair, it's a resident's dream as well.'

'The grateful ones.'

He looked at her and smiled, and she had to force her eyes back to the road.

'If you live here, you must drive this road every day?'

'Mostly, yes,' she said, and thanked her heart for returning to its usual pace. 'But I live further up, so I wouldn't take this part of the road. It leads to the beach,' she continued, when she realised he was probably just as much of a tourist in Cape Town as her guests were.

'Do you often go to the beach?'

She slowed down as they turned onto the road along the beachfront. 'Probably once a week. Never to swim or tan.' She smiled and drove into an underground car park. 'I usually go in the evenings for a run or a walk. It helps clear my head.'

They got out, and she suddenly realised that she hadn't told him she thought they should have lunch. Self-doubt kicked in, and she said nervously, 'Um…there isn't really much to do here unless you have your swimming trunks hidden under your suit.'

She flushed when she realised what she had said. Even more so when she thought about him in swimming gear.

'But I *can* introduce you to the management at some of the restaurants the hotel guests usually frequent during the tours. And we can grab lunch on our way to the next stop.'

She didn't wait for his response but instead led the way to the beachfront, where the line of restaurants was. The idea of sitting down and having lunch with him was still slightly terrifying to her, so she was taking the easy way out.

As she introduced Blake to the different restaurateurs she watched him slip into a professional mode that oozed charm and sophistication. He asked the right questions, said the right things, and ensured that everyone respected him. Which meant that many of them—whom Callie knew quite well—were now even more interested in the Elegance Hotel, having met its CEO. And they genuinely seemed to like him.

She grudgingly admitted that it made *her* like him a little more, too, but told herself that she was talking about her boss—not the man she'd met in the elevator.

Desperately trying to distract herself, she asked if he'd like to eat and then took him to one of stores that did take-away wraps and salads. They ordered, and stood in silence. Callie waited for him to say something—anything—about all the people they'd spoken to, but instead he sat down at one of the tables and stared out at the ocean.

She joined him, and yet the silence continued. When she couldn't take it any more she asked, 'So, do you like the beach?'

Callie knew it wasn't her best shot, but the silence had made her observant, and the more she observed, the more she responded to Blake. She felt the movement of her heart, the heat in her body, but she refused to succumb to them. She just wanted to talk, to take her mind off what being in his presence did to her.

'Who doesn't?'

His eyes didn't move from the ocean, but she could see a slight smile on his lips.

'I didn't go nearly as much as I would have liked to when I was younger. And when I took over the hotels there just wasn't time. I don't know when I was last at a beach like this.'

'You should make the time.' She offered a tentative smile when he glanced back at her. 'At both our stops so far you've seemed... I don't know...at peace with the world.' She blushed when he turned his body so that he was fac-ing her. 'I just think that if something makes you feel at peace, makes you happy, you should make the time for it.'

He didn't respond for a while, and Callie bit her lip in fear that she might have said the wrong thing. His eyes lowered to her lips then, and the heat she'd felt earlier was nothing compared to what flowed through her body at his gaze. If he had been anyone else she would have leaned forward and kissed him. But he wasn't anyone else, and she couldn't look away when he looked back into her eyes.

'What do *you* make time for, Callie McKenzie? What makes you happy or makes you feel peaceful?'

The question would have been innocent if he hadn't still been looking at her as if she was the only woman on earth.

She cleared her throat. 'Gardening. I garden.'

Blake tilted his head with a frown, and then grinned. 'I would never have guessed that.'

She smiled back at him, grateful that the tension between them had abated. 'I don't blame you. I'm terrible at it. I buy things and plant them, but mostly I pay someone to look after them.'

He laughed, and Callie couldn't believe how attracted she was to him when he looked so carefree. 'So you plant things but don't look after them? And that makes you happy?'

She nodded, remembering the first time she had done it.

'Yes, it does. It reminds me of my mother. We used to do it together—though I was just as bad then as I am now.' She stared out to the ocean, memories making her forget where she was. Who she was with. 'But my mom would just let me plant, and then she'd fix what I did wrong. When I was old enough to realise, I asked her why she let me do it.' She looked down, barely noticing how her hands played with the end of her top. 'She told me that it was because it made me happy, and that if something makes you happy you should do it.'

She looked up at him and saw compassion in his eyes, before she realised that tears had filled her own. She lifted her head, embarrassed and raw from what she'd told him, the way she'd reacted, and only looked back at him when she was sure she had her emotions under control.

He took a hand from her lap and squeezed it, but before

he could say what he clearly wanted to their order number was called.

They grabbed their lunch and without saying anything ate as they walked back to the car.

She wasn't sure what had prompted her to tell him that. Maybe it had been the moment...the setting. But the more likely answer—the one she didn't want to consider—was that maybe it was *him*. He made her feel things—things she would fight as long as she could. Feeling safe enough, secure enough to open up to someone would take a lot more than just a few hours with him.

And it wouldn't be with her boss. No, she thought as she threw away her half-eaten wrap. She couldn't open up to her boss.

Blake had wanted to say something to her from the moment she had told him about her mother. He wanted to comfort her, tell her that it was okay that she'd told him, that the fear and surprise he'd seen in her eyes when she'd realised what she'd said wasn't necessary. But instead, like the coward he was, he stayed silent and went along with the rest of the tour as though she *hadn't* just let him see such an intimate part of herself.

On their way back from the beach she drove him up to the Bo-Kaap, where colourful houses lined the streets. She told him about the rich cultural heritage of the area—how it had come to be a place of refuge for the Islamic slaves who had been freed in 1834. She pointed out the museum that had been established over a century later, and had been designed according to the typical Muslim home in the nineteenth century.

'The design is in the process of changing at the moment, but the museum will tell you quite a lot about one of the most thriving cultural communities in Cape Town.' She turned the car around and drove back down the hill. 'You should make an effort to visit it some time.'

After that she took him to the V&A Waterfront—another cultural hub of the city. It was both a mall and a dock, he discovered as they walked past a mass of shoppers to get to the actual waterfront. The large boats there were either docked for repair or in to pick up cargo, and the smaller ones either belonged to private citizens or were available for hire.

They also transported people to Robben Island, he discovered as he climbed into a boat and sat next to Callie.

Since it was the last trip of the day the boat was quite full, and he was forced to sit closer to her than he would have liked. Her perfume made him feel a need he had never felt before. Even mixed with the salty smell of the sea, its effect on him was potent. He wanted her to turn to him so that he could kiss her, just so that he could make his need for her subside.

He couldn't shake it off even when they arrived at the island where Nelson Mandela had famously spent twenty-seven years of his life. His thoughts were filled with her as the tour guide walked them through a typical day in the prison, as he told them about the ex-President of South Africa and showed them his cell.

By the time they had got back to the waterfront, it was late enough for their day to end. But he didn't want that. No, he didn't want the day to end. Because then he would have to go back to the hotel...back to being her boss.

'We should go for dinner,' he said, without fully realising it. 'It's been a long day and we've barely eaten. I think the least I can do for you after today is take you out.'

Her mouth opened and closed a few times, and his heart pounded at the prospect of her saying no. But then she answered him.

'Yeah…okay. Where do you want to go?'

'Somewhere you love.' He cleared his throat. 'I want to see more of Cape Town, but not just the side that your guests see.'

'Um…' She looked lost for a second, and then she nodded. 'Okay, I'll take you to one of my favourite places. But you can drive this time.'

He nodded and climbed into the driver's seat, following her directions until she'd finished typing the location into his GPS.

'You weren't lying when you said you haven't seen much of Cape Town, were you?'

The question was so random that he didn't take the time to think his answer through. 'No. My father and stepmother moved here when he retired, which was about eight years ago. I've probably been here twice a year since then to see them, and a few more times for the hotel. But that's the extent of my travels to Cape Town.'

'Where did you live before?'

'Port Elizabeth, for the most part. But, like I mentioned, I travelled a lot between hotels.'

'Do you miss it? Port Elizabeth?'

He thought about telling her the truth—that he didn't miss being there because it reminded him of his relationship with Julia, and how he had failed at that and let his business down. But that would only open himself up to more questions, and force him to face things he didn't want to remember.

Luckily the GPS declared that they had arrived, and he used the opportunity to deflect the question.

'What *is* this place?'

She tilted her head, as though she knew what he was doing, but answered him.

'It's called Sakari—which means "sweet" in Inuit. They

specialise in dessert and have the most delicious milk-shakes—though the food is pretty incredible, too.'

They walked inside, and Blake took a moment to process the look of the restaurant. It wasn't big, but it comfortably fitted its customers without seeming stuffy. There were even a few couches in front of a fireplace. Since it was still summer, the fire wasn't lit, but the couches were filled with people ranging through all ages. The doors were open and a slight breeze filled the room, causing the candles that had been lit for atmosphere to flutter every now and then.

It was a perfect summer's evening, he thought, in a perfect—and intimate—restaurant. He shrugged off what the thought conjured inside him and returned his attention to the hostess, who was greeting Callie with a warmth that he'd never witnessed before.

'Hi, Bianca, how are you?'

Callie spoke to the hostess as though she were her best friend.

The woman had a full head of black and blue curls that complemented her gorgeous olive skin.

'Great, thanks. Ben and I just found out we're having a girl!'

Blake only then realised the woman was pregnant as he looked at the slight bump under her apron. He figured she was probably around four months, and waited as Callie congratulated Bianca and asked if she could squeeze them in.

'Of course. Give me a second.'

Callie turned to him and her eyes were bright. 'Bianca is my father's business partner's daughter. She opened this little restaurant about eight years ago. My dad was so proud of her—almost like she was his own.'

'Was…?'

'Yes.'

Her eyes dimmed, and suddenly he put together all

the bits and pieces that she'd told him throughout the day. Her house, the almost-tears when she'd spoken about her mother, and now the past tense with her father. And just as quickly he realised he'd pressed her when he shouldn't have.

'Callie, I'm so sorry.'

CHAPTER SIX

'Don't worry about it.'

Callie cleared her throat and smiled when Bianca led them to a table in the corner. She knew the woman had probably squeezed it in herself, and she thanked her and rolled her eyes at the wink Bianca sent her after looking at Blake.

Callie busied herself with looking at the menu, and though she could feel him staring at her eventually Blake did the same. She sighed in relief, knowing that she didn't want to talk about her parents' deaths with him. She just wanted to have dinner and go home, where she would be safe from the feelings that stirred through her when she was with him.

'Their burgers are really good. And of course you should have one with a milkshake.'

She spoke because she didn't want to revert to their previous topic of conversation.

'Sounds good,' he said, and placed his menu down. And then he asked exactly what she'd tried to prevent. 'When did you lose your parents?'

She didn't want to talk about this, she thought, and shut her eyes. But when she opened them again his own were filled with compassion and sincerity. So she gave him a brief answer. 'Almost a decade ago now.'

He nodded, and was silent for a bit. 'My mom left when I was eleven. It's not the same thing, of course, but I think I may understand a little of what you feel.'

She stared at him—not because his mom had left, but because he'd shared the fact with her. It made her feel—*comforted*. That was terrible, she thought, but then he smiled at her, and she realised that comforting her had been his intention. She found herself smiling back before she averted her eyes.

How did he *do* that? And in this place that was so personal to her? She'd brought him here out of instinct, because she'd honestly had no idea what else to do. He'd put her on the spot and the only place she'd been able to think of was the one her friend owned—the one she had so often come to with her father in the year before his death.

She tried to pop in as often as possible, even just to grab one of the chocolate croissants that Sakari was known for. Maybe it was because she didn't want to lose the connection she'd had with her father. But it had taken a long time after his death for her to realise that.

'I know this isn't what you're used to.' She changed the subject to a safer topic. 'I mean, it isn't a five-star restaurant or anything, but it is highly rated.'

He laughed. 'It isn't what I'm used to—but not because I'm a snob, which you seem to be implying.'

She blushed, because maybe he was right.

'I just don't have time to find places like this. I usually eat at the hotel, or go out to dinner for business.'

'Do you enjoy it?'

'My job?'

She smiled, and wondered if he knew how cute he looked when he was confused. 'No—being so busy.'

He didn't respond immediately, and when the waiter came to take their order he still hadn't said anything. She didn't press, because somehow she knew he was formulating his answer.

'It works for me.' He shrugged. 'Keeping busy means I don't have to think about the problems in my personal life.'

She hadn't expected such a candid answer, but she took the opportunity to say, 'Your family?'

He nodded, though he didn't look at her. 'Partly, yes. And some other things.'

Callie suddenly remembered what he'd said about dating, and how he had told her without words that a woman had made him cynical about it. As much as she wanted to know, she didn't ask. She didn't want to tell him about how her parents had died, or how she'd fallen apart when they had. And clearly there were things that *he* didn't want to speak to her about either. And that was fair. Though a part of her hoped that it would change.

'Well, I hope that one day, when this mess is all over, you'll take a day to relax.'

'Relax?'

'Yes, it's this thing us normal people do—usually in the evenings or over weekends—when we try to put aside thoughts of business and enjoy the moment.'

He leaned back in his seat and grinned. 'Never heard of it.'

She laughed. 'I could show you some time. It's pretty easy.'

'I'd like that.'

He spoke softly, and suddenly the noise in the restaurant faded to the background as she held his gaze. Thoughts of the two of them spending evenings together, weekends, made her heart pound. And yearn.

He lifted a hand and laid it over hers, and suddenly the sweetness of her thoughts turned to fire. She wanted to lean over, kiss him. She wanted to know what it would be like to feel his lips on hers, his hands on her body. His hand tightened on hers and she wondered if he knew her thoughts. The way his eyes heated as he looked at her made her think he did, and she leaned forward—just a bit. If this was going to happen, then she didn't want him only to be a spectator.

And then the waiter brought their milkshakes, told them their burgers were about ten minutes away, and the spell was broken. Immediately Callie pulled her hand from under his and placed it in her lap, where it couldn't do anything ridiculous like brush his shampoo ad hair out of his face. She drank from her chocolate milkshake, and wished she'd ordered something that would actually help quench her suddenly parched throat.

'Do you ever bring Connor here?'

She looked up, saw the apology in his eyes—or was it regret?—and nodded in gratitude.

'Sure. If we do supper we either do it here, or somewhere close to the hotel. It depends on whether we're working or just meeting up.'

They continued their conversation, steering clear of any topics that might reveal anything personal about each other. And, though she longed to know more, she didn't ask about his family, or the mysterious woman in his past. She didn't think he spoke of it very much, regardless, and she didn't want to be the one he did it with. She ignored her thoughts that screamed the contrary, and instead focused on eating her food.

At the end of their meal, he offered to take her home.

'No, thanks. I'll just get a taxi.'

'That's silly. It isn't that far, and it's unnecessary for you to pay—' He stopped when he saw the look on her face. 'What?'

'I don't want you to take me home,' she said, because

the alternative, *I'd want to invite you in if you did*, wasn't appropriate.

'Of course.' He frowned, and stuffed cash inside the bill. 'Can I at least call you that taxi?'

She smiled her gratitude at his acceptance. 'Sure.'

He waited with her for the taxi. Since Sakari was only a few kilometres from the sea she could smell it, and feel the chilly breeze it brought even in summer.

She shivered, and he glanced down at her. Without a word he took off his jacket and laid it over her shoulders. The action brought him face-to-face with her, and gently he pulled at the jacket, drawing her in so that she was pressed to his chest. She felt her breathing accelerate at the feel of his body against hers, at the look in his eyes when they rested on her face.

'What is it about you that makes me forget who I am?' he asked, his voice low and husky, and her skin turned to gooseflesh.

'I could ask you the same thing,' she responded, before she even knew what she was saying.

But their words only encouraged whatever was happening between them, she thought. Especially as they stood together, frozen in time, looking at each other. Neither of them moved—not away from each other, nor any closer— and Callie could feel the hesitation, the uncertainty that hung between them. She could also feel the want, the need, that kept them there despite the ambiguity of their feelings.

The longer she stood there, the more pressing her desire to kiss him became, and she moved forward, just a touch, so that their lips were a breath away from each other's. His eyes heated and he leaned down. Callie closed her eyes, lost in anticipation of the kiss…

The sound of a car's horn pierced the air and they jerked apart. She lost her balance, and was sure she would soon be landing on her butt, but a strong arm snaked around her waist and pulled her upright. Again she found herself in Blake's arms, almost exactly as she had been a few moments before, but the magic had passed.

She cleared her throat. 'Thanks for...um...saving me.'

'Of course.' His words were stilted. 'I assume that's your taxi?'

She turned and looked around and saw that the hoot had indeed come from a taxi. She closed her eyes in frustration and then turned back to him.

'Yeah, it is. Thanks again.' She gestured towards the restaurant and felt like an idiot. 'And...um... I hope you feel more confident about the tour for the proposal now, having seen some of the stops.'

He stuffed his hands in his pockets. 'I do. I enjoyed today. I'll see you tomorrow.'

She nodded and smiled, and then awkwardly walked to the taxi, knowing he was still watching her. She lifted her hand as the taxi pulled away, and resisted the urge to look back at him.

'Blake?' Callie pushed open the conference room door and saw him sitting at the head of the table, where she'd found him the first time.

Was that only yesterday? she wondered, and nodded a greeting when he looked up.

'Morning,' Blake said, his tone brisk, and immediately Callie's back went up. 'Grab a seat and we can start talking about the proposal.'

Callie stood for a moment and wondered if this was a joke. There was no familiarity in his tone, no semblance of the man she'd spent the day with.

The man she had nearly kissed.

When he looked up at her expectantly she walked to a seat at the table and felt her temper ignite.

'So, I've gone over your list of places—including the ones we saw yesterday.'

Oh, she thought, so he *did* remember it. 'Yes…?'

'I have some ideas on how to complement the business side of the proposal with the tour. Have a look at these and let me know what you think.'

Callie took the papers he offered her and began to look through them. But somehow she kept reading the same line over and over again.

What was wrong with him? He was treating her as he had after that welcoming event. Cold, brisk, professional. The aloof and unattainable boss. She knew she shouldn't expect more from him—or *anything* from him, for that matter—but she'd hoped that their day yesterday, the things they'd learned about one another, the attraction they'd *both* felt, would have eased things between them. She didn't want her spine to feel like steel from the tension in the room. And yet that was exactly what was happening.

She cleared her throat as she built up the nerve to address it. 'Blake, did I upset you last night?'

He barely acknowledged that she was speaking, but she pushed on.

'When I told you I didn't want you to take me home? Or when we nearly—'

'Callie, I don't need you to explain anything. I just need you to read through the document and tell me your thoughts on it.'

He continued working on his laptop and didn't see her jaw drop. Just as quickly as it had dropped, she closed it again. This wasn't the man she'd spent the day with yesterday, she realised. Now she was dealing with her boss.

The one who had made her feel as if she was dishonest and nosy when she'd first met him.

Suddenly all the regrets she'd had about not letting him take her home, about not kissing him, about not telling him more about herself faded away. All the questions she'd wanted to ask him about his mother, his father, the woman he wouldn't talk about, no longer mattered.

She should be thanking him, she thought. He was saving her, really. She didn't have to worry about developing feelings for him. She didn't have to think about opening up to him. She didn't have to open up to her boss. She could be just as brisk and aloof as he was.

'Of course,' she replied, and read through the document, making notes and ignoring the disappointment that filled her.

Blake threw his pen against the door five minutes after Callie had left for the day. It had been a week since their tour together. Seven days of complete torture, five of which she'd spent sitting across from him, answering all his questions politely, only speaking when it had to do with work.

And *he'd* done that. He'd pushed her away with his professionalism. The stupid professionalism that he'd prided himself on before Julia. No, he thought. He'd never been this bad before Julia. She'd made him into this cold person. This person who didn't open up even when he wanted to.

He closed his eyes and leaned back in his chair. That wasn't completely fair. Julia may have brought it out in him, but he'd made the decision to be cold. Just like now, when he'd decided that after the day they'd spent together—after he'd almost told her too much…after he'd almost kissed her—that Callie was too dangerous to his resolve to stay away from relationships.

So he'd ignored the fact that their day had meant something to him and dealt with her just as he dealt with any other employee. And each time he did, he could sense the animosity growing inside her.

She didn't deserve this, he thought, and loosened the tie which seemed to be strangling him. She didn't deserve to feel as if she had been the only one to want something more than professionalism.

But it had to be this way. Or else, if they started something, he might begin to need her—to want her and want things he'd forgotten about a long time ago. Julia had done a number on him, he knew, but he'd deserved it after the way he'd reacted to her. He'd been attracted to her like no one else before, and she'd had a sweet kid who'd needed a father.

He rubbed his hands over his face and thought about the first time he'd met Brent. He and Julia hadn't been dating very long—perhaps a month—when she'd brought the boy to work with her because her babysitter for the school holidays was sick that day. Brent had been sitting with Julia at the table when Blake had got to the restaurant where they'd planned to have lunch. Blake had known Julia had a son, but hadn't thought too much about it until he'd met the boy.

'I'm glad you two finally get to meet,' she'd said, her arm around her son's chair. 'Brent, this is the man that I've been telling you about.'

The boy had looked up with solemn eyes, and examined him for a long time. Then he'd asked Blake, 'Are you going to be my new daddy?'

It had shocked him, and he'd resisted the urge to laugh nervously. But then he'd looked up into Julia's eyes, seen what he'd wanted to see, and replied, 'Maybe.'

He shook his head and stood now, his body tight from sitting at the table for the entire day. And from the direction of his thoughts. Being around Callie brought up all sorts of emotions inside him, and awakened memories he'd thought he'd put to rest.

Such as the fact that he had wanted to give that boy a family like the one he'd never had.

His mother had done a number on his father as well, and since then he and his father had always focused on their joint interests instead of on family. He'd never had a normal family situation. Just as he had told Callie.

Which was exactly why being professional with her was so important. He couldn't afford to fall for her. She was everything he had tried to stay away from, and he'd already revealed things to her that he didn't even think he'd known about himself.

It was the best decision to distance himself, Blake decided. And he didn't question why it felt so wrong.

CHAPTER SEVEN

'CALLIE, BLAKE NEEDS TO see you in Conference Room A.'

Kate popped her head into Callie's office and then disappeared almost immediately. But not before Callie saw the expression on her face. She recognised that expression. It was the sympathetic one Kate usually wore when Callie told her about a horrible tour she'd been on.

Was Blake annoyed with her? She'd left him a note in the conference room to tell him that she wanted to prepare alone before their first potential investor arrived at ten. As she made her way to the conference room she faced the fact that it was certainly a possibility. He might have wanted to talk to her about the proposal and run through it one last time.

But she hadn't wanted to deal with him that morning, when her nerves had already been tightly coiled. Just being in his presence made her feel so tense that sometimes she felt sick. So this morning, before the most important tour of her life, she'd just wanted a bit of peace.

When she arrived at the room she saw Blake standing with his back facing the door.

'Blake? Kate said you wanted to see me?'

He turned to her, his face calm, though she thought she saw an eyebrow twitch. She took a step towards him and then stopped when she realised she'd mistaken calm for professional. It was the same look he'd had on his face when she'd walked in on him and Connor talking the day all this had started.

'What do you need me for?'

'Both Mr Vercelli and Mr Jung arrived this morning. Apparently Mr Jung had an urgent matter to resolve in South Africa, and so took an earlier flight to Cape Town. Instead of individual proposals, customised for two different potential investors, we're going to have to do them both today.'

Callie felt her stomach churn, and sat down on one of the conference room chairs so her legs didn't give out on her. She closed her eyes and let her mind go through the possibilities. Could they still do two different proposals? No, that wouldn't work. And nor could they make one of the men wait, do it in two shifts, since both proposals included dinner.

'Callie?'

Blake was crouched in front of her when she opened her eyes.

'Are you okay? You're pale.'

He brushed a piece of hair out of her face and her mind, which had been so busy before, blanked. And then she remembered that they had a job to do and nodded.

'I'm fine.' She stood, and he rose with her, and for a moment they were so close she could feel his body heat. 'What does this mean, though?'

'It means we need to work on a new plan that merges the two proposals.' He said it confidently, his voice back to its usual formality, as though this had always been his plan and he hadn't just shown his concern for her.

'And you aren't in the least worried that this might turn out poorly?' she asked, her own fears motivating words that she wouldn't have spoken if it didn't irk her that he had recovered from their contact much faster than she had.

'No, Callie, I'm not. This is what I do.'

He shrugged and walked around her, and she thanked the heavens when her mind started working normally again.

'And, today, this is what *we* do.'

His emphasis stiffened her spine and she realised he wanted her to step up. So she took a moment, searching through the possibilities, looking for some way to maintain the two proposals they'd worked on. She knew both tours like the back of her hand, and before she could consciously think about it she started pulling threads of commonality from each of them.

'Okay…so Mr Vercelli wants to experience the Italian side of Cape Town—family was our angle on that one.' She spoke almost without realising it, needing to hear her ideas out loud to figure out whether they made sense. 'And Mr Jung wants to experience Cape Town culture, which we know is so different from his own Chinese culture.'

She frowned, and then looked up at Blake.

'But isn't family in a place fondly called the Mother City an important part of our culture?'

Blake smiled at her, and she felt the knot in her stomach loosen.

'I'd say so, yes. I think you're on to something.'

She returned his smile. 'So we focus on the common aspect of the two proposals—family. We use tour stops and business details focused on that.'

'Yes, that should work.'

She waited for him to grab his tablet from the table to note things down. But instead he just stood leaning against the table slightly, with a satisfied look on his face.

'You'd already thought about that, hadn't you?' she asked.

'I had. But you needed to get there yourself.'

She shook her head and sat down, not sure if she was relieved that her idea was one he approved of or annoyed that he'd already thought of it and had let her panic for nothing.

'So what's the plan?' she asked in resignation, and listened as he outlined his thoughts, only objecting when she thought she had something valuable to add.

And even though she knew he was good at his job—even though his calm and commanding presence gave her some stability—she still found herself saying the words that mingled with her every thought.

'This *is* going to work, right?'

He looked at her, and something on her face prompted him to sit in the chair opposite her. He placed his hands on her arms and the heat seeped through her jacket right down to her blood.

'This is going to work. And I would know, since I've already seen you in action when you haven't had the time to plan anything.' He squeezed her arms. 'You're good at what you do spontaneously, and you still have some time to prepare now, while Connor is with them. Think about how awesome you're going to be with weeks of preparation and fifteen minutes of practice.' He smiled, and her lips curved in response. 'This is going to work.'

'Thanks,' she said as he stood, and something made her want to offer him the same comfort, even though she knew he didn't need it. 'Blake? I've seen you work. And your passion, your dedication, doesn't come close to anything I've ever seen before. I know you didn't *have* to get new investors, or do as much as you have to save our jobs when the hotel would have probably been more successful if you had downsized.' She shrugged and then continued softly, 'I'm still not sure why you agreed to this, but I'm thankful that you did. We all are.'

He nodded, with a mixture of emotions on his face that were complicated enough that she didn't try to read them. Instead, she simply said, 'Shall we do this?'

'As you can see, this is the best place to see Cape Town from and look around. Families—tourists and residents alike—all come here to experience the best of the Mother City. This is such an integral part of the family culture of Cape Town—the culture our tourists specifically come for—and now you get to experience it for yourself.'

Blake smiled, though he was sure their two potential investors barely saw it. Not when they'd hung on to Callie's every word from the moment she'd introduced herself in the conference room that morning. She had done so confidently, as if they had always expected Mr Vercelli—who had insisted they call him by his first name, Marco—and Mr Jung to arrive at the same time.

He looked over at the two men who were admiring the view of Cape Town from its signature attraction. Mr Jung caught his eye and nodded, as though silently agreeing that this might be one of the most beautiful places in the world, his grey hair blowing in the wind. He wasn't a man of many words, but he wielded a lot of power.

Blake had his finger in pies that didn't have anything to do with the hotels, and in his previous dealings with Mr Jung he had been fair and open to suggestions. And that meant fertile ground for his expansion plans, he thought, and knew he had to do everything in his power to make sure this proposal was the best it could possibly be.

'At sunset, this experience is even more beautiful.'

Callie smiled at him, acknowledging that these were words she'd said to him once before. Except then it had just been the two of them, and Blake had felt something inside him longing, which was decidedly not the case now.

'I think that would be a…er…wonderful thing, Callie.' Marco's Italian accent was thick, and his words were punctuated by pauses every now and then, but otherwise his English was flawless. 'I would love that.'

'And I would love to bring you up here.'

She smiled again, and Blake knew that part of the reason she was handling these businessmen so seamlessly was because of their appreciation of that smile.

'If you invest, our hotel's connections with the staff here would mean we wouldn't even have to wait in line.'

She smiled again, and Marco burst out laughing. She even coaxed a smile out of Mr Jung.

'You have a firecracker here, Blake,' Marco said. 'I might even steal her for one of my hotels in Italy!'

'You would have to get through me first,' Blake said, and saw Callie's eyes widen. It reminded him of her expression just before they'd almost kissed that night so long ago, when he had pulled her in closer to him…

She bit her lip and he realised that he'd been staring. And that Marco was looking at him with amusement.

He turned his attention back to the Italian man and smiled. 'Unless you invest, Marco, in which case we can negotiate!'

The boisterous laughter that erupted from Marco made him think that perhaps he hadn't lost face. But he'd nearly lost his composure, he thought, and forced himself to focus.

Clearly the businessmen weren't the only ones captivated by Callie's smile. Her proximity made him say things, do things that he wouldn't otherwise. Even as she stood now, prim and proper in a black dress and red heels, a matching jacket lying over her arms, he wanted her with a need that surpassed even that which he had felt for Julia.

He cleared his throat. 'Now that you've had a chance to see it for yourself, gentlemen, you can understand how the

Elegance's proximity to Table Mountain is an asset for the hotel. We arrange for free shuttles on request, to drop and fetch our guests at the location, with the added benefit of guided tours if the guest desires it. We've also negotiated special rates for families with the Table Mountain tourism management, so all our guests will be able to enjoy this experience together.'

He assumed that the nods from both the men meant they were on board thus far. Now, he thought, to keep going for the next seven hours…

'I think we actually pulled that off,' Callie said as she watched the two businessmen being escorted back to the Elegance from their final stop at the V&A Waterfront, where they'd had dinner.

As soon as they'd been driven away she turned and grinned at Blake.

'We did,' he agreed, and shocked her by picking her up and spinning in a circle.

She laughed, but when he put her down and they stood in each other's arms she felt herself wanting him. She wanted to slide her hands around his waist and pull him close. To celebrate the success of the day. The stars gleaming down on them seemed to encourage her, seemed to tell her that it was the perfect moment to lean forward and kiss him.

But a couple of people nearby whistled at them, and broke her from her trance. She stepped back from him and smiled at their spectators. And when she turned back to Blake he was smiling at her.

'What?' she asked, wondering what the strange look on her face was.

'Nothing,' he responded, and tucked her hair behind her ear.

His hand lingered there, and again Callie found herself

wishing that he would just kiss her. Then he took his hand away and stuffed it in his pocket, as though it was being punished.

'We should go and have a celebratory drink.'

'What?' Shock seeped right through to her bones. Based on the last five minutes they'd spent together, the last thing they should be doing was spending time alone with each other.

'I think we should grab a drink to celebrate.'

He took her hand and led her through the throngs of people who were out and about, despite it being a weekday evening.

'And you can actually eat something instead of answering questions while we're at it.'

Before Callie could fully process what was happening they were walking towards the dock. She frowned, knowing that there were very few bars or restaurants on this side of the waterfront. And then she stopped dead when he led her to a boat with two men standing on either side of the steps that led to its entrance.

'What is happening, Blake?'

'We've having drinks. Come on.'

He walked towards the steps, but she didn't budge.

'Callie?'

'I don't think you understand.' Now she did take a step forward. 'This is a boat. They don't just serve drinks on private boats for people who decide that they should celebrate.'

'No, they don't,' he agreed. 'But they *do* serve drinks on boats for people who own them and decide to celebrate.'

She stared at him. 'You *own* this boat?'

'As of two weeks ago—yes. Now, will you come with me?'

Callie followed him purely on instinct. Her mind was too busy thinking about the fact that she was having drinks on a boat with her boss. And that the boat belonged to him. Two weeks ago? That had been after they'd spent the day together...

She still hadn't come to terms with it all when he pulled a seat out for her at a table in the centre of the deck. The edges of the boat were lined with tiny lanterns, which lit the boat with a softer light than the full moon offered from the sky. Champagne chilled in a bucket next to the table, and one of the men who had waited for them to get on the boat now filled their glasses with it. The other still waited at the entrance to the boat, she saw, though he didn't make any move to cast off.

'How did you do this?' She finally looked at Blake, who was wearing a very self-assured grin.

'I called a few people.'

'But when?' she whispered, afraid she would embarrass him. 'We've barely had fifteen minutes since Marco and Mr Jung left.'

'Oh, that.' He was still smiling as if he had just pulled off the world's biggest heist. 'During dinner. I knew today had been successful, and I wanted to do something on a par with what we pulled off. So I made a few calls and here we are.'

'Firstly, I'm pretty sure this *surpasses* what we pulled off. And, secondly, dinner was only about an hour ago.'

'Are you complaining?'

'No, but I feel sorry for these men. How often do they have to do this?'

'I'm not sure about their previous employers, but since they've only worked for me for two weeks this is the first time I've asked them anything. Don't worry—I've made it worth their while. Besides, this is minimal effort since we aren't going anywhere. Now...' he lifted his champagne glass '...shall we toast to what we did today?'

Callie lifted her glass and toasted, but she still couldn't

believe she was on a boat. Okay, they weren't sailing any-where, but privacy after the day they'd had was exactly what she needed. Although she wasn't sure if privacy with Blake was the smartest kind.

'Did you buy this boat after our tour together?'

'I did.'

He didn't offer anything else, and Callie thought per-haps she should be more specific.

'Did you buy this boat *because* of our tour together?'

'Not really—although our time on the boat did give me some fond memories.' He grinned and ran a hand through his hair. 'You're thinking too much about this, Callie. I wanted a boat so that I can have some peace when I need it. That's what you told me, right? To do things that make me happy.' He shrugged when she frowned at him. 'Let's just focus on tonight, okay? I wanted to do something nice for you to say thank you. And well done.'

'Well, you didn't have to. Especially not this.' She ges-tured around her, though she could see that maybe he was trying to reassure himself more than he was her. Especially after telling her that he'd bought the boat to make himself happy. 'I was just doing my job. And I wouldn't have been able to, I don't think, if it wasn't for you.'

'If you're talking about the fact that these proposals might help to save your job, and all those at the hotel—'

'Actually, no. I'm talking about what you said to me be-fore we left this morning.'

He frowned. 'That you could do it?'

'Yeah.' She laughed a little, feeling silly for telling him this. 'It made me feel like I really *could* do it. And…you know…gave me a boost of confidence.'

He didn't say anything, and she had a sudden burst of doubt. 'I'm sorry, I know that sounds corny—'

'No, it doesn't.'

She felt herself flush when he smiled at her. There was something different about this smile, she thought. It wasn't the cordial you-smiled-at-me-and-I'm-returning-the-gesture type she usually got from him. No, it was a genuine smile that made her remember the completely different Blake she'd first met in the elevator.

The memory awakened other things inside her. Like how much she enjoyed looking at him. The planes of his face, the way his hair fell across his forehead, made butterflies stumble through her stomach.

It's just the atmosphere. Which woman wouldn't have butterflies if a man took her on a boat in the moonlight?

Yeah, she thought, *keep telling yourself that.*

But before she could ponder it further the man who had poured their drinks—she realised now he might very well be a waiter—placed two platters on the table. One held a variety of cheeses and the other a variety of breads and crackers. And, she thought to herself as the waiter described them, she hadn't heard of most of them.

'So you arranged this at dinner? While we were eating?'

He grinned. 'Yes, because even from the starters I could see that you weren't eating very much.'

'Very perceptive,' she said as she spread Camembert on one of the crackers. 'Marco was incredibly interested in some of the sites we took him to. So whenever you were discussing something with Mr Jung he would lean over and ask me about them.' She chewed slowly, contemplating what he had asked her. 'I'm actually not sure if he was asking out of interest or if he was testing me.'

'Well, he definitely seemed impressed. Especially when he told me how much he'd enjoyed the novelty of today's proposal. I don't think he's ever been pitched to for business along with a tour.'

'No wonder you're doing all this. Maybe now would be a good time to ask for a raise.'

He laughed. 'I'll take that under advisement.'

'I'll have Connor put in a good word for me!'

When Blake's face sobered, Callie realised how that might have sounded.

'I was joking, Blake. Connor would never do that.'

'That's not exactly what he told me.'

She frowned, and then remembered the time when he'd told her she would have to pitch to their investors with him. He already seemed to know that her title wasn't a normal one.

'What do you mean?'

Blake drank the rest of his champagne and then asked the waiter to bring him a glass of whisky. She shook her head when he raised his eyebrows and the waiter nodded, presumably concluding that he would only need to bring one glass.

'Connor told me he gave you a job after your parents died.'

'Well,' she said, grasping for something that would make the situation sound better, 'I didn't get paid at first, so it was more of an internship than anything else.'

'He also said that you had been studying towards a degree in anthropology. A degree which, if your human resources file is accurate, you didn't complete.'

Callie opened her mouth and then closed it again. How was she supposed to respond to that? That it had been an internship was true, but she knew it didn't make sense since she hadn't studied tourism or anything related to what she was now doing. The fact that she hadn't finished her degree made an even stronger case for nepotism, she thought, and cringed when she realised that she was going to have to tell him part of what had really happened.

'Yes, that's true. But Connor was just trying to help me.' She had long since stopped eating, but the food felt like lead in her stomach. 'I… I didn't cope very well with my parents' deaths. So, yes, maybe Connor wasn't being completely professional when he got me the internship. But I've worked incredibly hard for the hotel. And I've built up a good reputation with our tours. I can show you—'

'Callie.'

Blake was looking at her strangely, and she felt her heart stuck in her throat.

'I'm not asking you to defend your job.'

'I know that,' she said, and resisted the urge to shake out her shoulders. 'I just…just thought you should know that Connor has never done anything like that again. It was a one-time thing.'

Blake didn't say anything for a while. The waiter brought his whisky and Blake thanked him. After what seemed like an eternity he drank, put his glass down and settled back into his chair.

'I was there when we hired Connor. Did you know that?'

She shook her head, wondering where he was going with this.

'My dad was still in charge then, and Connor started out as the operations manager of the Cape Town branch. During his interview I remember thinking that he was going to be a good fit for the hotel. He understood our values and seemed just as dedicated to our guests as we were. And then he worked his way up and I had the honour of seeing how much of himself he invested into the job. And the pride he took in the work he did. When I promoted him to regional manager he told me that he would make sure we got out of the mess Landon had made.'

He paused, and bit into a piece of cheese.

'Of course neither of us really knew the extent of the

damage Landon had caused. But that's beside the point. What I'm trying to tell you, Callie, is that I was always fairly sure of your brother's character. Only one thing has gone against the opinion I had of him—*your* appointment.'

Callie wished she could stand up and give her restless legs something to do. But she didn't think that would be wise, considering that she was on a boat with men who would probably think she was crazy if she did. Instead she pushed a hand through her hair, resisting the urge to pull at it.

'You know, Blake, sometimes we do things for our family that go against what we believe in.' She cautioned herself against the fury she felt behind her words, but it didn't work. 'I know *your* family wasn't like that, but in mine we did things for one another. Helped each other. Supported each other.'

She rubbed her hands over her face and almost immediately her anger fizzled out.

'I'm sorry. That was uncalled for.'

Blake's face had blanched at her words, but he nodded. 'It was.'

Callie bit her lip, and hated herself for lashing out. 'It's just that Connor saved my life with this job. No, he really did.' Tears pricked at the backs of her eyes but she forced them back. 'My parents' deaths nearly destroyed me.'

There—she'd said it. The words she'd never really said aloud to anyone else. She was afraid to look up, to see the pity she knew would be in his eyes. She didn't want that. It would remind her of how almost everyone had treated her after her parents had died. As if she was something to be pitied.

She looked up at him when she felt his hand gentle

on hers, and there was no pity in his eyes. Just compassion. And she felt the coldness that had started to chill her bones thaw.

CHAPTER EIGHT

BLAKE KNEW HE shouldn't have pushed, but he'd wanted to know. He'd needed to. Callie awakened desires in him that had been dormant since…well, since Julia. And even then, he hadn't needed to know her this badly.

Ever since Callie had told him about her parents' deaths Blake had wanted to ask her about it. He wanted to know how she'd handled it, who had been there to support her. The information he had gathered from Connor after she'd mentioned it and the little he had shared with Callie a few moments ago had only made him more curious. Especially since he knew that her specialist job wasn't something that existed in any of the other hotels.

But now, seeing her anguish right in front of him, he felt like an absolute jerk.

'I'm sorry you had go through that,' he said, wishing there was something more he could say.

She slid her hand from beneath his and laid it on her lap. 'I am, too.' She attempted to smile, but her sadness undermined its effect.

'Well, you don't need to talk about it.' He gestured to Rob, the man who had been serving them all night. 'Could you bring some tea for Miss McKenzie, please?' Rob nodded, and Blake turned his attention back to Callie. 'I figure you could use something a little more soothing than champagne.'

'Thanks.' She smiled again, and this time it wasn't quite as sad. And then she took a deep breath and said, 'Blake, I… I want to tell you what happened when my parents died, okay? But only because I need you to understand why Connor did what he did. And then can we pretend this conversation never happened?'

She looked at him with such innocent hope that he nodded, even though he knew that pretending it had never happened would probably—well, never happen.

She angled her head, and didn't meet his eyes as she spoke.

'My parents were on their way home from a weekend away. It was their anniversary, and every year they celebrated by staying at the hotel where they'd had their wedding. They'd been married twenty years.' She cleared her throat. 'A drunk driver overtook when he wasn't supposed to and crashed into them. They died instantly.'

She looked up at him.

'I was nineteen. Old enough to survive.'

But still young enough to need them, he thought, but didn't say it in case it interrupted her.

'My parents meant the world to me. We were incredibly close, and losing them…it felt like I'd lost a piece of myself.'

He reached for her hand again when he saw she was fighting back tears.

'I was incredibly depressed. I couldn't go back to university. I shut my friends out. I shut Connor out. I just felt like I was in this dark room and I was flailing around, trying to find a light.'

She paused when Rob, the waiter, returned with a pot of tea, but barely waited until he'd left before she continued.

'My friends couldn't deal with the morbid person I had

become. One by one, each of them disappeared. Until even my best friend—well, I thought she was—couldn't do it any more.'

She lifted her eyes to his, and gave him a sad smile.

'Death is one of those things that you can only truly understand when it affects you. Sure, people are there for you at the funeral, and sometimes a few weeks after. But when you realise that this is your life now—that you have to live without the family who were so integral to your existence— even those people fade away. Because how can they understand that the life you knew no longer exists when theirs is going on as normal? Connor struggled too, but he had his job. Something that gave him purpose. I think that's probably around the time he started climbing the ladder at the Elegance. But when I didn't go back to university I think an alarm went off for him and he realised how lost I was. So he pitched up at my house one morning and forced me to go to work with him.'

She smiled at the memory.

'I hated him for it, but he just told me to start shadowing the concierges. He did that every day for two months. And then one day I realised that I wasn't walking around in a coma any more. I found myself asking questions and engaging with the guests. And that's how the tours came about.'

Blake had known that it would be something like that. He hadn't been lying when he'd told Callie he knew Connor pretty well, and the man he knew would have never given his sister a job just because he could. But the truth was he didn't really care why Connor had done it. He was more interested in Callie, and in the events that had had her starting at the hotel. That now had her desperate to save it. All of a sudden, it made sense to him.

'I wondered why you wanted to save the hotel so badly.' He looked at her and wished he could do something about that wounded expression on her face. 'I knew it was because of Connor. And, of course, your job. But now I understand that the reason behind it is because they saved you. Connor and your job helped you cope with your parents' deaths.'

'Yes,' she said, surprise coating her features, 'that's exactly it.'

He drank the last of his whisky and put the glass down with a little bit of a bang. 'I'm definitely glad I listened to you, then.'

She laughed—a husky sound because of the emotion she had told her story with. 'I'm glad you listened, too. Or I might be out on the streets and not out on a boat.'

Blake grinned, and slowly began to realise that he believed what he'd said. He *was* glad he'd listened to Callie. If he hadn't he would have had to let staff go and face another example of his own poor judgement. He would have had to tell his father what had happened and face his reaction. And all the hard work he had put into building his own legacy—not merely being a part of his father's—would have been for nothing.

As he asked Rob to bring him coffee he realised that Callie's ghosts weren't the only ones that had been stirred that night.

'What's wrong?' Callie asked, holding her breath at the expression on Blake's face.

Emotions she couldn't identify flashed through his eyes, but then he shook his head and smiled at her.

'Nothing. Just thinking that it's been a tiring day.'

And it had been, she thought. Except that *wasn't* what he was thinking. Maybe he was thinking of a way to fire her. Or to fire Connor. She had just admitted that Connor had given her a job—or rather an internship—to help her through her parents' deaths. And even though Connor's intentions might have been good, that didn't matter in the real world. Professionalism mattered. Ethics.

She shouldn't have told him any of it, she thought. She had just been trying to get him to see that she had earned her job. Why did the way it had started out matter? But at the same time she had told him about the worst part of her past. She had opened up to him. Her heart accelerated at the thought. She had done exactly what Connor had encouraged her to do so often. Except she'd done it with her boss. The man who had the power to kick her out of his hotel and make sure she never worked in the hospitality industry again.

She bit her lip and searched Blake's face, hoping she would find the truth of what he was thinking somewhere. What she saw worried her even more.

'Blake...look, I'm sorry if I overstepped. I probably shouldn't have told you any of this.'

'What?' He looked up at her distractedly and whatever he saw must have alerted him to her paranoia. 'Callie, no—I am so glad you told me. I understand.'

His face softened and something made her think that perhaps he wanted to say *I understand you so much better now*.

He laid a hand over hers. 'Thank you for telling me. I know it wasn't easy for you.'

'It wasn't.' The heat from his hand slid through her entire body. 'And if you're not upset with me, that means you're thinking about something that isn't easy for *you*.'

He frowned up at her.

'Come on, Blake. We've spent almost all our time together for the last two weeks. You don't think I know when something's bothering you?'

'Look, it's honestly nothing. I was just thinking that getting investors is probably the best solution for the hotel.'

'And that upsets you?'

'No.' Rob placed coffee in front of him, and Blake waited until he was gone before continuing. 'I was just so set on saving the legacy of the hotel that I would rather have retrenched staff whose livelihood was on the line—as you so nicely reminded me—than think about my father being disappointed in me—'

He stopped abruptly, and Callie realised he hadn't meant to say that. But because he had, things began to fall into place for her. Snippets of their conversation on the day of their tour filled her mind. His relationship with his father. His mother leaving. The legacy. As she put them together she thought she knew what was bothering him.

'There's nothing wrong with wanting to make your father proud,' she said gently.

He shook his head. 'I don't know where that came from.'

She smiled, wondering if he realised how much of a man he was being. 'You were being honest with yourself.'

He angled his head, didn't meet her eyes, and she realised he didn't enjoy being honest with himself. Which, if she knew him well enough to guess, meant that he had halted any thoughts that would continue along those lines.

'Blake, was your dad upset when your mom left?'

He looked up at her in surprise. 'Of course he was. But I don't see what that has to do with anything.'

Of course you don't.

'So they'd had a good relationship?'

'I don't know.' He shrugged. 'My dad always used to say they were partners—so, yeah, I guess so.'

'Do you know *why* she left?' Callie didn't want to ask, but she knew that the answer would help her put the final piece into place. And help Blake to do the same.

'Callie—'

'Blake, please…' she said, seeing the resistance in his eyes. 'I want to understand.'

Especially because I still feel raw from telling you about my parents.

'My father said she didn't want us any more.'

He clenched his teeth, and Callie resisted the urge to loosen the fist his hand had curled into.

'That she'd left us for someone else.'

She felt her heart break for the little boy who had heard those words. For the man who still suffered from them.

'She disappointed him?'

He drew a ragged breath. 'And me.'

'And now you don't want to disappoint him, or yourself, like she did?'

He didn't answer at first, and then he looked at her. She saw his eyes clear slightly, and resisted the urge to smile at his expression.

'I guess so.'

Now she did smile. 'Should I ask the waiter to warm up your coffee?'

'What?' He was still staring at her in bemusement.

'Your coffee.' She gestured towards it. 'It's probably cold. Actually, so is my tea.' She signalled to the man and asked him to bring them fresh beverages.

'Callie, did you just psychoanalyse me?'

'No,' she said, putting on her most innocent expression. 'I was merely pointing out why it's important to you to make your father proud.'

He stared at her for a moment, and then shook his head with a smile. 'I think you missed your calling in life. You would have had a field day with me when I got married.'

Callie felt her insides freeze. The smile she had on her lips faded and she thought time slowed.

'What did you say?'

Blake was still smiling when he answered her. 'I said you've missed your calling in life.' And then he saw her face, and his eyes widened. 'Callie—'

'You're *married*?'

'No, I'm not. I got divorced a long time ago.'

'Oh…okay,' she said shakily, and wondered why she hadn't thought about it.

He was, after all, an attractive, successful man in his thirties. It shouldn't surprise her that he had been married. Though the divorce was a surprise, she thought, and thanked the waiter—why didn't she know his name yet?—as he placed her tea in front of her.

She went through the motions of making a cup, and remembered the first time they'd met, when Blake had told her that he tried to stay away from women. She'd attributed it to a bad relationship. She'd known there was a mysterious woman. So why hadn't she considered an ex-wife until just now?

'So she was the piece of work we spoke about in that elevator?'

'I don't think we've ever spoken about that.'

'Yeah, we have.' She didn't look up at him, just kept on staring intently at the milky colour of her tea. She hadn't let it stand for long enough, she thought. 'When you said that you don't put moves on women, that you stay away from them, I told you that whoever had made you feel that way must have been a real piece of work.' She lifted her eyes to his and asked, '*Was* she?'

His face hardened. 'Callie, this isn't any of your business.'

'It isn't.' Suddenly the surprise that she'd experienced only a few moments ago morphed into anger. 'But neither was my parents' deaths yours.'

'That isn't the same thing. You told me about that because you wanted to explain why Connor hired you. And since he hired you into *my* company I had the right to know.'

She quickly realised that the reason she'd told him about her parents' deaths, about how she'd coped and how Connor had saved her—the reason he had just provided—was a lie.

'You and I both know that I wasn't telling you because I work for you,' she said in a measured voice. 'But, since we're talking about it, was what you told me about *your* parents any of my business?'

'No, it wasn't.' His tone mirrored hers, but it was lined with the coldness she was beginning to recognise he used when he spoke to her as her boss.

'And all of this—' she gestured around her '—is what you do for someone you don't want in your business?'

'I was just saying thank you to an employee for a job well done.'

She stared at him, wondering if he really believed the nonsense that was coming out of his mouth. She gave him a moment to come to his senses, to salvage the progress they'd made, but he said nothing.

'Well, in that case remind me to compare notes with Connor about employee rewards.'

She gathered her things and walked towards the man who had stood silently at the entrance of the boat since they arrived.

'Would you please help me off this boat?' she asked him, and realised that she didn't know *his* name either.

He smiled kindly at her. 'Of course, ma'am.'

Before she climbed the steep stairs up to the dock, she turned back to Blake. 'She must have done something really awful to you, Blake, for you to push away something that could have…' She faltered, but then said it anyway. 'That could have *been* something. But don't worry. The next time I see you we can pretend nothing that happened this evening actually happened. Just to ensure that we stay out of one another's business.'

He didn't move in his seat—in fact he hadn't even turned while she'd been talking to him. She shut down all the hurt flooding through her and nodded at the man who was waiting to help her.

She murmured a thank you when she reached the top, and then she was walking as fast and as far from the boat— from Blake—as she could.

CHAPTER NINE

CALLIE SIGHED AS she stared at the clock on her desk. It was almost eleven. She had been back at the hotel for almost an hour now, after taking a taxi, and she'd spent that hour clearing her office of the mess she'd made after hastily preparing for their unexpected double proposal.

She was waiting for Blake to arrive and return to his house, so that she didn't bump into him when she popped into her brother's office to give him an update. Connor had said that he'd wait for her to return, and though she knew it wasn't nice of her to make him wait even longer she didn't want to deal with Blake until she'd had a good night's rest.

Or at least that was what she was telling herself.

She sighed and paged through the file she kept on the proposals. So many things had happened that day—that evening. And the evening's events made her want to throw the file in her hand at the door. When Blake had swooped her up into his arms after they'd finished the proposal and taken her to celebrate on his boat—a *boat*—she'd almost laughed at how unbelievable it was. Now she thought that it wasn't as unbelievable as Blake's claim that he was just 'rewarding an employee' by taking her there.

After the things they had shared with one another, after the romance of the evening—and, yes, she acknowledged, to her the whole boat event *had* been heartbreakingly romantic—the fact that he could claim she was just an employee to him hurt. After she had bared her soul to him—and she gritted her teeth at that—how could he callously say such a thing? All because he didn't want to talk about his stupid marriage.

It hurt her more than she wanted to admit that he wouldn't talk to her. Sure, he had told her about his parents' split, and he had been open—however reluctantly—to her conclusion about his subsequent relationship with his father. But then he'd completely shut down when she'd asked him about his ex-wife, going right back to being the stubborn boss she knew and intensely disliked. The one she would never have considered telling about her parents' deaths and how it had broken her.

This was the reason she didn't open up to people, she thought as she began to gather her things. People let you down. One day you had them around you, and you thought that you wouldn't ever feel alone, and the next day they were gone. It didn't matter *why* they left—those reasons always changed—the leaving was the one thing that was always consistent.

So she should be glad that this had happened. Blake was saving her so much heartache by pushing her away. And she would listen to *herself* in the future, not to Connor or any of her colleagues, who insisted that she should open up to people. That she should date.

It was just a waste of time, she thought, and locked her door. Especially if the person she opened up to wasn't ready to do so themselves.

As she made her way to the exit of the hotel she saw that her brother's office door was slightly ajar. Guilt crept in as she remembered that she was supposed to give him an update, and she sighed and detoured to his office. Subconsciously she was hoping that he had already gone home, and she could send him a message when she got home with a quick summary. But he never left his door open after he'd left for the day, so she resigned herself to having to tell him how the day had gone.

It was dark when she peered into the office, with only the city's lights shining through an open window illuminating the room. When her eyes adjusted she saw the outline of a figure in Connor's chair. Her heart thudded and she rushed to his side.

'Connor, are you okay?'

Only when she knelt beside him did she realise that it was Blake, not Connor, sitting at her brother's desk.

'Oh, I'm sorry—I thought you were Connor.' She rose awkwardly to her feet and wished she hadn't let the guilt of responsibility lead her into the lion's den.

'I got that,' he said dryly, and his voice was lined with something she couldn't place her finger on. But she knew it was dangerous.

'I just wanted to fill him in on today.' She eyed the door she had shut when she'd thought something was wrong with her brother, desperately wishing she had left it open.

'I did that. He left a few minutes ago.'

'Oh, okay...' Why was her voice so shaky? 'I'll go, then.'

'No.'

She exhaled sharply. 'What do you want, Blake?'

'I want to apologise.'

'For what?'

'For being a jerk earlier.'

A part of her wanted to brush it off, to tell him that it didn't matter. But she couldn't because...*it did*. It mattered. Everything she had told herself earlier about it being for the best faded somewhere into the background of her mind as she realised this. But she didn't respond to him.

With her eyes fully adjusted, she could see that he no

longer had his tie on, and the first few buttons of his shirt were undone. She swallowed, all thought leaving her mind as she noticed that his neck was bare, ready to be kissed. She shook her head and shifted her eyes to his face. It was as gorgeous as it had been the first time she'd admired it, but the danger she had sensed from him earlier was clearly outlined there.

Somewhere at the back of her mind a voice was shouting that she should leave before she had the chance to find out what that danger meant for her. But she didn't move, not until Blake stood, and then she took a step back, bumping into Connor's bookcase. It shuddered, barely moving, but it knocked some of the breath from her.

'I... I can't do this with you, Blake.'

'Do what?'

He was a few feet away from her now. She could smell him, and the sexy scent nearly sent her to her knees. She was suddenly incredibly grateful for the bookcase behind her that held her steady.

'Whatever you have in—'

Her words were cut off as he walked slowly towards her. Her heart rate—which was never really normal around him—kicked up even higher.

'What are you doing?' she asked breathily when there was barely any space between them.

'I'm apologising,' he said, and placed his hands on either side of her.

'It's okay. It's fine.'

She didn't care that she hadn't been ready to accept his apology a few minutes ago.

'Good. But now I'm saying sorry in advance...for doing this.'

And he kissed her.

His lips were soft on hers, and she could barely breathe

from the electricity that the contact sparked. She was aware of every part of him—of his hands that were no longer braced beside her but had moved to her waist. Heat seeped through her clothing where he touched her, but it was nothing compared to the inferno of their kiss. He had deepened it, and as though she was outside of her body she heard herself moan.

Her hands slid through his hair and she loved the feel of it through her fingers. Before she knew it he'd pressed her against the bookcase, so that her body was aligned with his. She shuddered at the feel of him against her, and moaned again when he trailed kisses down her neck. She pulled at his shirt and then, with frustration, when she couldn't find his skin fumbled with his buttons. Just as she'd thought, muscles rippled across his chest when the shirt was finally opened and she greedily took them in.

And then froze when his hand slid up her thigh and settled at the base of her underwear.

'Blake…' she rasped, her breath still caught by their passion, 'Blake, we can't.'

His lips stilled at her collarbone, and she could hear that he was just as affected by what was happening between them. He lifted his head and looked at her, and something on her face had him nodding and moving back. She stayed where she was, afraid that her legs wouldn't work if she tried to move.

In the shadowed light from the window he looked amazing, his shirt undone and his abs ripped, just as she'd felt them a few moments before. She wished she could do this, she thought as she took him in. She wished that she hadn't stopped and that they could let their desires control them. But that would only get her more of the hurt she already felt when she was with him.

'I forgive you. For this,' she said breathlessly. 'But I can't do this with you.'

She straightened her dress, picked up the handbag and jacket that she had thrown across the room in her haste to get to her brother. And then she took the minute she needed to organise her thoughts.

'You may have convinced yourself that taking me out on your father's boat was an employee benefit for a job well done, but you can't claim that *this*—' she gestured between them '—is how employees and their employers behave with one another.'

'You're right, it isn't.'

She hadn't noticed that he'd fastened his buttons again. A faint wave a disappointment threaded through her.

'Callie, I meant it when I said I was sorry about earlier.' He braced himself against Connor's desk. 'You didn't deserve that.'

'No, I *did*,' she said, and ignored the surprise on his face. 'I deserved it for believing that letting someone in would do me any good.'

He looked up at her, and something had him moving towards her.

'No—stop.' She held up a hand. 'We've already let this go too far.' She sighed, wishing she could pull her hair out. Anything that would make her feel better about what she was going to say. 'Blake, your ex-wife clearly hurt you. And you'll never really let me in because of that. So, for both of our sakes, I think we should just pretend this never happened.'

'The kiss?' he asked, stuffing his hands into his pockets.

'Everything. Every single thing that's happened between us that shouldn't have happened between a boss and an employee.'

He didn't say anything, and she took that as agreement.
But as she left the office her heart ached at the thought
of forgetting what they'd shared.

CHAPTER TEN

'I THINK WE should just pretend this never happened.'

Blake welcomed the cold water on his heated and fatigued body. He knew that at some point hot water would be needed to soothe his screaming muscles, but for now the cold took away the pain his two-hour gym session had yielded.

'I think we should just pretend this never happened.'

What it failed to do was wash away the memories of the previous evening. The memories of him acting completely out of character.

Completely out of control.

He'd tossed and turned the entire night, so despite the incredibly long day he'd had, and despite how tired he'd been, he hadn't been able to get a wink of sleep. Which was why he had instead, at four in the morning, made use of his home gym.

He adjusted the water when he felt the cold down to his bones, and closed his eyes as heat pounded against his body. He had probably pushed himself too far, he thought. And he knew he would pay for it the entire day. Hell, probably for the entire week. But it had kept his thoughts off the mess he had made. For a few hours, at least, he thought, when his mind yet again looped back to the single thing he couldn't stop thinking about.

'I think we should just pretend this never happened.'

He wished he could. He wished he could pretend he hadn't spent the day watching her work. He wished he hadn't noticed how well she had done—how she had taken an unimaginable scenario and turned it into what he was almost certain would be a victory for Elegance. More than anything, he wished he hadn't given in to the impulse of taking her onto his boat.

Yet that wasn't the reason why her words had haunted him from the moment she'd said them. Because, as much as he wished he could pretend everything that had happened between them *hadn't* happened, he couldn't—for one simple reason:

He didn't want to.

He turned the water off and towelled himself dry. He knew the moment Callie had started asking him about his mother that her line of questioning wouldn't be easy for him. He didn't talk about his mother to anyone—he hadn't even mentioned her to Julia—and yet he'd told Callie about her the day they'd had supper after their tour. When he had barely known her.

He had convinced himself that it had just been to comfort Callie, after he'd figured out that her parents had died—especially since she hadn't offered the information freely. But it hadn't taken him long to realise that it had also been because he'd felt comfortable with her. And, if he was honest with himself, that was part of the reason he had insisted on maintaining a professional relationship with her.

If he was comfortable enough to share his most hidden memory with her, it wouldn't take long before she lodged herself in his heart. And then she would be able to hurt him. And if his instincts weren't wrong—as they'd been before—and she'd fallen for him, he'd be able to hurt her, too.

As he began dressing for work he thought about his mother for the first time in years. She *had* disappointed him.

He had watched her pack her bags into the car, and then she'd knelt in front of him and said, 'I'm sorry, Blake. I hope one day you can understand that I couldn't do this. This life was never for me.'

She'd kissed him on the forehead and driven away, and he had watched the car fade into the distance.

He couldn't remember feeling more helpless—or more heartbroken—than at that moment when he was eleven and his mother had left. He didn't know if it mattered to him now that it had been the last time he had seen her or the last time he had known some semblance of a normal family life. But what he *did* know was that he had vowed he would never feel that way again. He didn't ever want to feel as if he didn't have control or to feel heartbroken again. Most of all, he had assured himself that if he were ever a father he would never let his child feel the way he had. He would make sure that *his* child had the family he'd never had.

Something clicked in his head and he realised that Julia had made him feel all those things—had forced him to break all those promises he had made to himself such a long time ago. And the worst thing was that now he was terrified Brent would be feeling the same way he had—helpless and disappointed.

The mess of his mother, Julia and Callie swirled through his head, and he began to think about his relationship with Julia in a way he'd never considered before. To think of why he'd reacted the way he'd reacted to her, why their relationship had broken down so completely. And though there were many layers to it—most of which seemed hazy to him at the moment—one layer suddenly became incredibly clear.

Blake closed his eyes and resisted knocking his head against the wall. And he thought one thing repeatedly—that he was a fool.

Callie got into work early that morning, not bothering with breakfast at home because she knew she could sneak into the hotel kitchen and grab some of the food that would be warm and ready for the breakfast buffet in half an hour.

After doing just that, she unlocked her office and thanked the office angels who had helped her clear her desk the previous night. Because now she could set her breakfast and her coffee on a desk that she could actually see, instead of on a pile of papers she hoped weren't important.

She sighed as she bit into a warm slice of toast, and moaned when it was accompanied by the coffee boost she so desperately needed. She hadn't slept very well, her mind muddled with thoughts, and at about three in the morning she'd forced herself to stop thinking about the events that had caused the ache in her heart and instead focused on business. She knew the proposal the previous day had gone well, but she wanted to kick it up a notch. At five a.m. she'd had a fully drafted email about what she thought would do just that. Now she just had to find the courage to hit 'send'.

She took her time eating her breakfast, and then read through the email a couple more times. When she couldn't procrastinate any longer she sent the email to Blake, and copied Connor in just in case. She hadn't spoken to him about the proposal, but he'd sent her a message congratulating her. Which she'd only read after midnight, since she had been too busy kissing her boss and dealing with the resulting anguish to switch on her phone before then.

It was barely ten minutes later when she received a response, and she held her breath as she opened it.

Come and see me.

That was it? Nothing about the perfectly outlined event she had just sent him the plan for?

She bit back her disappointment and pulled out her compact mirror to make sure she didn't have breakfast crumbs on her face. She gave herself a pep talk on her way to the conference room and told herself she was as prepared as she would ever be before seeing her boss, with whom she had so hungrily made out the night before. An image of him with an open shirt standing in the moonlight flashed through her mind, but she forced it away.

She was a professional. She could do this.

But her resolve nearly faltered when she saw him. He looked nothing like the dishevelled man she'd left in her brother's office the night before. His hair was slicked back and his suit was pressed. Worst of all, his face was expressionless when he looked up at her.

'Morning, Callie. I just got your email.'

'Yes, I know.' She forced herself to match his demeanour. She was the one who had wanted him to be like this. Except now it didn't seem to be what she wanted at all.

'So…what do you think?'

He ran a hand through his hair and just like that the neat style collapsed as a piece fell over his forehead. He didn't seem to notice, but she did, and she wanted to walk over and fix it for him. And then she could sit on his lap…and then they could continue where they'd left off last night…

She shook her head. Where had *that* come from? She had been so sure that she had made herself immune to him. She'd forced herself to replay every moment of the previous evening and repeated all those words that had hurt her so that she could strengthen her resolve. And then she had forced herself to forget the way his hands had felt on her body, the way he'd kissed like Cupid himself.

She had even dressed the part—loose white linen pants and a cream waterfall jersey that hid the curves of her body effectively. And then she had resolved never to think about him and what he did to her body, to her heart, again. She had focused on her work and come up with a pretty decent idea, even if she said so herself. Now she was just waiting for him to acknowledge it.

'It's a good idea. A really good one.' He tilted his head. 'A gala event for all our potential investors would do wonders for their interest in the hotel. Especially if they're introduced to the competition. I just don't know how you'll be able to pull it off in seven days. Maybe we should push it back?'

'Timing is important.' The words were so formal that she resisted the urge to roll her eyes at herself. 'We should hold the event when the proposals are still fresh in the investors' minds and before the negotiations start, so it can help influence their decisions. That means next Friday is our best bet.'

She sighed when he didn't respond.

'It's just an idea,' she said. 'But I think that if we do this we'll have an opportunity to show the investors the possibility of much larger events in the hotel. So far we've only done corporate events, but if we started adding birthdays, anniversaries, weddings, I think it would be a source of revenue for the hotel that will increase profits immensely.'

'Yes, I saw all that in your email. But how?' Blake stood now, and leaned against the table as he had so many times in the weeks they'd worked together. 'How are we going to pull off the best event the hotel has ever given in a week?'

She faltered. 'We *could* do it. We've racked up favours from all kinds of vendors and services, and I know a lot of them would be grateful for the opportunity to—'

'How long did it take you to organise my welcome event?'

'I didn't organise that. Connor did, mostly.'

'How long did it take Connor to organise the event?'

She bit her lip, and didn't answer him immediately.

'Callie, how long did it take for Connor to organise the event?'

'Fourteen weeks.'

He raised his eyebrows. '*Fourteen?* And you want to throw an event bigger than that in one week? In addition to working on the proposals we'll be doing for four of those seven days?'

She locked her jaw and looked at him. 'Yes.'

'I don't think—'

'Forget it—it's fine.' She turned away.

'Callie, wait,' he said, before she could leave. 'I was going to say I don't think you can do it alone. We'll have to get everyone involved. We need to call in all our favours, with every vendor and every service provider, and make this happen. Because we *can* do it. Together.'

Suddenly Callie was transported back to the previous day, when similar words had made her feel more valued than she ever had before. And she cursed him for still having the ability to make her feel that way.

'Okay, great.'

He smiled at her, though there was something behind it that she hadn't seen before. 'So let's get to it. There's a lot of work to be done.'

Her heart stopped. '*You're* going to help with this?'

He nodded. 'That's generally what's meant by "together".'

'I just thought you meant all the staff.'

'Oh, everyone will help. But you and I will be running it.' He sat down and started typing on his laptop. 'We seem to work well together.'

She stared at him, wondering who had kidnapped the surly boss she'd worked with before and replaced him with this cordial man in front of her.

'Yeah, apparently we do.'

CHAPTER ELEVEN

'ARE YOU READY to go?'

Blake stood in the doorway of her office and she nodded, scribbling a note to remind herself to check when the lights for the gala event would arrive for set-up.

'Let's do this.' She grabbed her handbag and locked up, following him to the front of the hotel. 'I think I might actually be looking forward to this.'

He laughed and nodded his thanks when John pulled the car in front of them. 'It's food—what's not to look forward to?'

How about the fact that we have to do this together?

But she smiled in response, clinging to the truce that had settled between them over the last few days. The proposals were going well, and now, since the German investor they had seen today had had to attend another meeting in the afternoon, they had some more time to work on the gala event.

Blake had arranged that they do a tasting to ensure the catering for the event was good, and she had resigned herself to the fact that she had to go. Eating together—even professionally—seemed dangerously close to a date, but Callie had agreed because she didn't want to rock the boat between her and Blake. She almost rolled her eyes at the description—why did it need to be a *boat*?—but then remembered that Blake always seemed to be watching her recently. And she didn't want to invite any questions she wasn't willing to answer.

'We never really spoke about how you chose this restaurant,' she said once they were in the car, hoping to stop her annoying train of thought.

'This is one of the rare restaurants I've actually been to in Cape Town.'

She looked at him in surprise. 'Really?'

'Yes.' He glanced over at her, but his expression was closed. 'My father has been friends with the owner since before I was born. When we did go out together, it was generally there.'

She frowned. 'Then why are we doing a tasting, if you already know how the food tastes?'

'For several reasons. One being that they've recently hired a new chef. He came with new menus, and I haven't had a chance to taste anything on them yet. Another is that I need you to make sure I've made a decent choice and not just gone with something I know because I trust that the catering will be reliable.'

It made sense, she thought, though she wished he might have said, *Oh, I see your point—we can just skip this.*

'There's a lot to be said for reliability,' she said. 'The last thing we want on Friday is to worry that the food won't be good or won't arrive when it should.'

'Which is why I hope you'll give this place the stamp of approval.'

Callie didn't answer, instead looking out of the window at the hills they passed. She didn't come to this side of Cape Town very often, she thought, as the hills become vineyards. It was a popular venue for large events— weddings, especially—and many of the vineyards offered wine-tastings. Though she had recommended it as a weekend activity for her guests, she had never considered including it on her tours since she knew they would always be battling traffic to get back to the hotel in the afternoons. And, more importantly, she didn't want to deal with tipsy guests and the potential problems they brought.

As Blake turned on to a gravel road that slowly inclined Callie looked up to the top and saw a building made mostly of glass. It was beautifully designed, with curves that spoke of specialised techniques and artistry even to an amateur eye like hers.

'Is that it?' she breathed, but didn't need an answer when Blake pulled into the car park. 'It's *amazing*.'

'It is,' he agreed. 'And the inside is even better.'

He guided her into the restaurant, where they were greeted politely, and while Blake spoke to the maître d' Callie looked around and was forced to agree with Blake about the interior design. Wooden tiles swept across the floor and chandeliers hung from the roof. The glass exterior meant that the restaurant's patrons were treated to a spectacular view of the winelands and, from their position at the top of the hill, some of the city as well.

They were led up spiralling stairs, from where Callie could appreciate the decor of the restaurant even more. It was definitely an upper-class restaurant, but the subtle touches of warmth—like the soft yellow and white table settings—made her think that the owners wanted to avoid the alienating effect more expensive restaurants often had.

When they finally stopped climbing she was out of breath, and she looked around, realising that they had climbed to the top of the building while she had been distracted by aesthetics. And then the maître d' led them through a door and she lost her breath altogether.

'Blake…' she said, but couldn't even continue as she took in the beauty of their location.

She was standing on the rooftop of the restaurant, over-looking the view she had thought so spectacular only a few moments ago. Except now she felt that description had been overzealous, since what she was looking at from here was better than the view through the glass walls.

Blake smiled at her reaction and led her to a table at the edge of the rooftop, from where she could see everything merely by turning her head to the left.

'How did you arrange this?' she asked, when they were seated and the maître d' had been replaced by a perky waitress.

'Connections,' he said, and shrugged as though sitting on the roof of a restaurant was normal. 'I take it you like it?'

'I really do.'

'So do I,' he said, and looked out to the view. There was a slight breeze that helped lessen the effect of the summer sun and rustled through Blake's hair like leaves during the autumn. 'I don't think I will ever get tired of this.'

She had been wrong, she realised. Even though getting them to the rooftop might have been easy for her boss, the experience wasn't lost on him. That loosened something inside her—something that had stuck the night she had told him to forget everything that had happened between them. The fact that something so simple, something so small, could make her heart ache for him again told her she was in trouble.

So she pulled back, forced herself to act professionally. She made the right sounds when the food was served, agreeing on some dishes, asking for variations on others. She made polite conversation with Blake about the weather, about work, about the event preparations that were coming along nicely. She had almost congratulated herself on sur-viving when the waitress brought out dessert.

'We've prepared a variety of dishes for you to taste,'

said the pretty blonde, who had been incredibly helpful throughout the tasting.

Callie wondered if she had been warned about who she would be dealing with.

'Chocolate mousse, strawberry cheesecake with berry coulis, pecan pie, and a cream cheese and carrot cake trifle.' She pointed at the individual dishes, which were lined up on a long plate. 'You can choose three of these desserts to be served at your event. Please do let me know if you have any questions.'

She smiled brightly at them and then moved to join her colleagues.

Callie frowned as she looked at the plate in front of them, and her stomach dropped when she realised that the waitress wouldn't be bringing out a second. And then she saw the spoons on the table—two of them—and mentally kicked herself for thinking that the restaurant must be encouraging romantic dessert-sharing.

'I suppose we start at each end and move in?' she said, hoping to sound logical about it.

His lips twitched. 'Yes, let's do that.'

She frowned slightly, but chose to ignore him, and instead took a bite from the chocolate mousse. She closed her eyes as it melted in her mouth. She had never tasted anything like it, she thought, and greedily dipped her spoon into the small dish for another bite.

But as she lifted it to her mouth she realised Blake was watching her, and she felt heat flush through her body when she saw the desire in his eyes.

She put the spoon down slowly and said huskily, 'I'm sorry, I suppose I'm being selfish by taking another bite.'

She cringed at her words, knowing full well it wasn't selfishness that had caused her to pause.

He didn't respond, but reached over and took the spoon

from her plate instead. 'I don't mind you being selfish,' he said, and lifted the spoon to her mouth.

She opened it on a reflex, though her eyes never left his, and felt a thrill work its way through her body. The mousse melted in her mouth, just as it had the first time, but she didn't taste it now. No, she was remembering the way *he* had tasted when they'd kissed, the way his eyes had heated just as they did now, the electricity that had sparked between them.

The sun was setting behind him, and it cast a glow over them that made everything seem a little surreal—as if they were in a romantic film and about to shoot the perfect ending. She wished it were that which made Blake look like a movie star, but she knew that Blake's looks were not an illusion. Her handsome, gorgeous boss was all too real, and with each moment she spent with him she wanted him to become a part of her reality. She wanted that heat, that electricity, his taste to be hers.

And, even though it couldn't be, for once she didn't fight showing how much she wanted it.

His eyes darkened at what he saw in hers and he placed the spoon down on her plate again and leaned over to kiss her. She felt it right down to her toes…the slow simmer of passion although his lips were only lightly pressed against hers. The taste she had longed for only a few moments earlier was sweeter than the dessert she had just eaten, and it wiped away the memory of it.

She wanted to deepen the kiss, to take more, but the sane, rational part of her brain—the part that was half frozen by his kiss—reminded her that they were in a public place and she pulled back, feeling embarrassed and needy from what she knew had only been a brief kiss.

She reached for her glass of water at almost exactly the

same time he did and she drank, grateful that the glass hid the smile that crept onto her face for one silly moment.

He cleared his throat. 'I can tell why you wanted another taste of that.'

She looked up at him in surprise, and bit her lip to stop the bubble of laughter that sat in her throat. But nothing was funny about this, she realised, and the thought banished her lingering amusement.

So she just smiled at him politely, and said, 'We should probably finish the tasting and get back to the hotel. There are a couple more things I need to do before tomorrow.'

And just like that the mood between them shifted.

'Are you done for the day?'

It was like déjà vu, Callie thought as she looked up to see Blake at her office door. It was only a few hours since she'd last seen him there, before they'd gone for the tasting. *Before they'd tasted each other.* She shook her head at the thought, resenting her mind for reminding her of the part of their afternoon that she really wished she could forget.

'Yeah, just about. Why?' She looked down at the papers in front of her, taking care not to look him in the eye.

'Great. Connor's asked me to take you home. He said something about your car breaking down yesterday?'

She was going to kill Connor. 'Yeah, it did. But he said *he* would drop me at home.'

'Something came up.'

Blake didn't seem nearly as concerned as she did about spending time alone together in a car. Even after the tension that had mounted between them on their way back to the hotel. And the awkward parting they'd shared when they'd arrived.

'It's fine. I'll call a taxi.'

Blake placed a hand on her own, which was reaching for her phone. 'Callie, I'll take you. I don't mind.'

'It's really okay, Blake. I don't want to put you out.'

'This is the second time you've said no to my offer of taking you home.'

She looked at him in surprise when his words were spoken in a terse voice.

'*Why* won't you accept my help?'

'Because you're my boss,' she said, grasping at the one thing that she could cling to. The very external thing that she held on to instead of admitting the real reasons she was pushing him away. 'It isn't appropriate.'

'Can we both stop pretending that's still a factor here?'

'Excuse me?'

'It's the card you pull out every time you want to put distance between us, Callie. We both do.'

She stared at him as he walked into her office and closed the door.

'I know I messed things up between us that night on the boat. I used our professional relationship as an excuse because I was scared. We were getting too close...and my judgement has failed me before.'

He didn't look up at her, but for some reason she could tell his expression would be tortured.

'My ex-wife was an employee. And marrying her was probably the worst decision I've made in my life.'

He lifted his eyes, and she could see that she'd been right. The look on his face tore her heart into two.

'I just don't know if I can trust my judgement any more.'

She could see that the admission had taken a lot from him. And she wished that she could take away the pain that had come with it.

Instead, she bit her lip and said softly, 'I *do* use our professional relationship as an excuse.' She played with a stray thread at the bottom of her jersey. 'To distance myself from you—yes. And because…' She sighed, and gave up on the resistance every part of her screamed out when it came to him. 'Because I don't want to have feelings for you. I don't want to open up to you and have you shut me out again.'

Or, worse, have you leave.

But she couldn't bring herself to say it.

'Do you…? Have feelings for me?'

She shouldn't have said anything, she thought immediately, and then saw the sincerity in his eyes. *Trust me*, they seemed to say, and she spoke as honestly as she could.

'I don't know, Blake. I haven't given myself the chance to entertain even the possibility.'

He nodded. 'And if I promise to…to be open with you, too. Would you entertain the possibility then?'

Her heart accelerated. 'Maybe.'

'Okay.' He held a hand out to her. 'Can I take you home?'

She laughed, and nodded. 'I guess so. I just need to put my shoes on.'

She slipped her left shoe on her foot, and was about to do the same for her right when Blake knelt in front of her.

'Let me.'

He took the shoe from her hand and fitted it onto her right foot. For one ridiculous moment Callie felt as if she was in a fairy tale. Her Prince Charming was kneeling in front of her, fitting onto her foot the shoe that would make her his princess.

But then he looked at her, and all fairy-tale notions fled from her head. There was a heat in his gaze that made her burn from the place where his hand still lay on her foot right up to the hair follicles on her head. For a moment she wondered what would happen if she pinned him against the wall and continued where they had left off a few nights ago…

She shook her head and he smiled at her. But his smile

was a wicked one, as though he knew exactly what her mind had jumped to as he'd slipped her shoe on.

He straightened and held out a hand to her. 'Shall we?'

She exhaled shakily and took his hand. 'Yes.'

CHAPTER TWELVE

BLAKE OPENED THE car door for Callie and felt his body tighten when she brushed past him to get in. He supposed he hadn't recovered from their interactions earlier today. That kiss at the restaurant… Whatever it was that had happened in her office…

He didn't know what had possessed him to put her shoe on for her, but he was glad that he had. If he hadn't he wouldn't have seen the way her eyes had sparked with a desire that matched his. She might not know if she had feelings for him, but she definitely wanted him. And that meant they were on the same page.

He watched as she typed her address into the GPS on his dashboard, and when the voice gave him his first direction he followed it. He glanced over at her, and frowned when he saw that her arms were crossed.

'Are you okay?'

'I think so.' She didn't look at him.

'What's on your mind?'

'Nothing,' she said, almost immediately, and then she sighed. 'Everything. I'm just not used to this.'

'To…us?'

She ran a hand through her hair. 'To any of it. This is all new territory for me. Worrying about work. About whatever's going on between the two of us. I don't know—I guess I just feel...*raw*.'

Blake forced himself to keep focusing on the road, even though he wanted to pull over and hold her in his arms. He wanted to comfort her, to tell her that everything was going to be okay. Instead he settled for saying the one thing he thought she might need to hear right now.

'You're not alone, Callie.'

He took a right and didn't look at her, even though he knew her eyes were on him.

'I worry about what's going on between us, too. But you don't have to worry about work, okay? Everything is going to be fine.'

He wanted to ask her if he'd made her feel worse—about her worries over them, about the things she had just told him—but he forced himself to wait. She was opening up to him again and he wanted to earn it. So he just said it again.

'You're not alone.'

The rest of their trip was quiet. Blake didn't know what she was thinking about, but her hands now lay on her lap, and he took it as a sign that maybe she didn't feel so vulnerable any more. He wanted to kick himself for making her feel that way in the first place, but there was nothing he could do about the past. When he'd realised he'd made a mistake about Callie—when he'd realised that the failure of his relationship with Julia had had very little to do with them working together—he had wanted to call her immediately and tell her that he was sorry, that he wanted to make it up to her.

But his words wouldn't have meant anything at that point, he had reasoned, and so instead he'd tried to show her through his actions. He'd made an effort not to keep up the act of being the boss she expected—the hard, cold act he had clung to in order to keep his professionalism with her. Instead he'd acted as he did with every other employee. Well, perhaps not *exactly* the same way, but he figured she'd earned some preferential treatment since her standard of work was higher than most he'd encountered.

He'd also enjoyed the way her eyes widened every time he engaged with her without the cold formality that had coloured his interactions with her before.

When his GPS announced that their destination was on the left, Blake pulled up in front of a light-coloured house with a rush of flowers planted in flower beds along the pathway.

'I'm not sure who to compliment on your garden. You for choosing the flowers, or your gardener for planting them.'

She laughed and unlocked the door. 'Both, I suppose. Thank you. I'll pass the message on to Ernesto.'

He frowned. 'Your gardener's name is *Ernesto*?'

'Yes. He's from Italy. What are the chances of finding a young, attractive male from another country to do your garden for you?'

He couldn't quite keep his face neutral when he thought about it, and she took one look at him before bursting out into laughter.

'I'm just kidding, Blake. My gardener is a lovely man in his fifties called George.'

Her eyes twinkled, and he felt himself relax. And then she gestured to the door.

'Do you want to come inside?'

He barely took a second before saying, 'Sure.'

Her house was spacious, filled with light and bright flowers from her garden. The open plan meant that the lounge, dining room and kitchen led from one room to the other, and all the furniture complemented the warm and rustic theme of her house.

'Did you do the interior of the house?' he asked, walking past a shelf that held pictures of the McKenzie family.

His eyes were drawn to a picture of Callie and Connor, standing next to a woman and a man who looked so much like them he thought that if he'd met them on the street he would have recognised them as Connor and Callie's parents. They looked so happy, he thought, and his heart broke for reasons he couldn't describe. Somehow it made him think of his own family, and the fact that Callie wouldn't ever see a picture like this anywhere in his place.

'Some of it.'

He turned when she answered him, and the compassion in her eyes tugged at his heart. How did she continue to see through him?

'But mostly I've kept it as it was when my parents were alive,' she pressed on, and took off her jersey, throwing it over one arm. 'My mom had great taste.'

'Yeah, she did.'

He was still thinking about her family when she said, 'I'm going to change. It shouldn't take too long, but feel free to make yourself comfortable.'

She walked through a doorway in the kitchen and he heard her footsteps on the floor and a door closing. He turned back to the shelf with the pictures and tried to keep his mind off the thought of her changing in the next room. But his thoughts kept shifting back to how she would be slipping off those heels that made her legs look as if they never ended. And she was probably taking off that dress that had done nothing to hide the curves that had been in his thoughts ever since he'd touched them.

He swallowed, and walked to the kitchen to pour himself a glass of water.

There was an empty glass in the sink, and he rinsed it and filled it with water from the tap. As he drank he looked up through the window that was just above the L-shaped kitchen counter. It overlooked a tidy little yard which was completely free of flowers, but had a large palm tree that shadowed a swing seat just beneath it. But the real view was of the mountain just above it.

'That's Lion's Head.'

He turned back to see Callie looking past him through the window. She had changed into a long floral skirt and a mint-green T-shirt, and had loosened her hair so that it fell in waves down her back. She looked so effortlessly beautiful that his heart stopped for a few minutes just looking at her. She walked towards him until she was next to him and then pointed to the right of the mountain he'd seen.

'Table Mountain is over there.'

But he couldn't keep his eyes off her, and her proximity overwhelmed his senses. When she looked back to him her eyes widened in that way they did whenever something she hadn't expected happened.

He put his hands on her waist, cautiously, asking permission without saying a word, and she took a step towards him so that there was barely any space between them. His arms slipped around her and his body heated at finally being able to feel hers again, and then he leaned down to her until his mouth was next to her ear.

'I'm going to kiss you now,' he whispered, and felt her shudder. He moved his head back so he could see her face, flushed and beautiful, and asked, 'Is that okay?'

'Yes.'

She had barely said the word before his lips were on hers. She had expected hunger, passion—everything that had burned with their first kiss. But there was none of that. Instead it felt as though he was trying to make up for that, to show her there was more to whatever was going on between them than just pure lust.

She thought vaguely that this might be the way their kiss on the rooftop would have felt if they'd let it continue for a while longer. And as the sweetness of their kiss swept through her she felt her heart open and be filled with it. He pulled her closer, and her heart beat at double its speed as she let her hands explore his body.

As soon as she did, the sweetness turned into need and she deepened their kiss, wanting more.

'Callie.'

Blake had ended the kiss, but he didn't let her go. She opened her eyes to see his own were closed, and he leaned his forehead against her.

'Do you want to give me a heart attack?'

She laughed breathlessly. 'I'm sorry. I didn't realise I had that in me.'

He lifted his head and smiled, and for the first time she noticed the crinkles around his eyes. She'd never really seen them before, she thought, and brushed a thumb across one of them.

'I think you have a lot in you that you don't realise,' he responded, and then took a deliberate step away from her.

As he did so she suddenly realised where she was, who she was with. Where had all this come from? Why was he was saying all the right things? About how she wasn't alone, how she shouldn't worry about the hotel, how they would deal with whatever was happening between them together. She had let her guard down enough to invite him in, and now he'd kissed her—in her own kitchen.

She turned her back to him and braced her hands on the sink as the uncertainty of the situation overwhelmed her.

'Hey,' Blake said, and moved to next to her. 'What's going on?'

'Nothing.' She turned to him and forced a smile to her face. 'Can I get you something to drink?'

'Callie, come on. I thought we agreed we were going to be open with one another.'

'Yeah, we did. So tell me where all this is coming from. How are you so calm and determined to be open with me when the last time you did this you pushed me away?'

The words had rushed from her mouth and she sighed, wishing she had some semblance of control over it. Especially when she saw the pain on his face.

'I'm sorry, Blake. I told you I was feeling a bit raw. And kissing doesn't help.' She resisted the urge to touch her lips.

He nodded. 'You're right. We should probably straighten things out before we do that again.'

Her heart accelerated even at the thought of it.

'Is that drink still up for offer?'

'Sure. Would you like some wine? I have a really good red.'

'Yeah, that's great.'

She poured the wine and joined him on the couch. It overlooked the garden when the curtains were open, and the amount of light it offered the house meant she kept them that way most of the time.

She handed him his glass and took a sip of her own wine as she snuggled into the corner of the couch. There was enough space between them that she felt safe from doing something she would likely regret if she were any closer.

'The last time I messed things up between us it was because of my ex-wife.'

He spoke suddenly, and Callie didn't know what to make of the way her stomach clenched at his mention of the woman. So she just nodded, and waited for him to continue.

'She was one of my employees at the Port Elizabeth Elegance Hotel. I met her a few years after my father retired, when I realised that the hotel in PE was losing staff at an incredibly high rate. I arranged a meeting with HR and they sent Julia.'

Callie watched as the tension on Blake's face tightened. She wanted to reach out to him, but she resisted. He needed to tell her about this without any help. But he had stopped talking.

She waited, then finally she asked, 'What was it that made you fall for her?'

He looked at her, and she saw a mixture of emotions in his eyes. Emotions that almost mirrored her own. She didn't really want to hear about what it was that had attracted Blake to this woman. But she needed to if they were going to make any progress together.

Then he exhaled sharply. 'I don't exactly know, to be honest with you. I guess it was because she had all the ingredients of the perfect woman. She was smart and beautiful, and I was attracted to her. But I didn't want to date her because—well...' he smiled wryly '...I was her boss.'

He continued now without any help, and she thought it was almost a compulsion for him to tell her.

'But professionalism didn't really mean as much to me back then, so after about six months of resisting I asked her out. And it felt good. But what drew me in was Brent—her son.'

Blake didn't look at Callie but he paused, as though letting her process what he was telling her. She already had so many questions, but she refused to speak. Especially when she didn't think she would have the voice to do so.

After a few more moments he continued. 'She had always been honest with me about him. She'd told me that his father hadn't been in the picture from the beginning and that she'd been raising him by herself. And the way she told me that...'

He leaned forward now, bracing his elbows on his knees, and Callie realised he had long ago placed his wine, untouched, on the coffee table in front of them,

'That was, I think, what made me fall in love with her. She had this softness about her when she spoke about Brent that seemed so out of place in this woman who was all sass all the time.'

Callie didn't realise she was holding her breath until he looked at her, and the torment she saw in his eyes made her untangle her legs from under her and move closer to him. They sat there for a while in silence, and Callie thought about what he'd said. She remembered the way his eyes had dimmed when she'd spoken to him of his mother on the boat, what felt like a lifetime ago. It was quite simple for her to come to a conclusion then.

'She was a good mother. So different to what you'd had.' She hadn't realised she'd spoken out loud until he took a shaky breath.

'Yeah, I think that was it. And when I met Brent I fell in love with him, too. He reminded me a lot of myself.' He frowned, as though unsure of where that had come from. 'In hindsight, I suppose I fell for Brent more than I did for Julia, but they were intertwined. And then one day I found her crying in my office. She told me that she didn't think she was a good enough mother to Brent, that she wasn't giving him stability because he didn't have a father. And just like that she had me.'

He pushed off from the couch so fast that Callie felt her heart stop.

'I thought she was being honest with me. That she was being unselfish, thinking of her son first. Maybe she was. But the way she did it...' He shook his head.

She'd shown her son all the things Blake hadn't had

growing up, Callie thought, and wished she could have been there for him then.

'I fell for it. I comforted her, told her she was an amazing mother, and started making plans to propose. I'd only known her for a year then, had been dating her for six months, and I *married* her.'

He looked at her, and she thought she saw embarrassment in his eyes.

'I married a woman I barely knew because she pulled at my heartstrings. My father insisted that we sign a prenuptial agreement, and we did—though she made some noise about that. The right noise, too. About how we didn't need a prenup when we were going to last. We were a family, and we were going to make it work. And for a year we did.'

He joined her on the couch again, and Callie took his hand, wanting to provide as much comfort as she could.

'Callie, I didn't think I would *ever* be as happy as I was being a husband and a father. We were a family. *I* had a family.' He rubbed a hand across his face. 'But I was in a bubble, and I only noticed the way Julia had changed when it began to affect Brent. She had become snarky and mean. Only to me, luckily, but she was doing it in front of Brent, and I could tell that he hated it. When I challenged her on it she told me it was none of my business because Brent wasn't even my son.'

He looked at her, and then lowered his eyes.

'I tried to save the relationship—I really did. I even went so far as to look into adopting Brent. I hired an investigator to find Brent's father so that I could ask him to relinquish his parental rights to me. I was going to surprise Julia with it. But then one night she told me it wasn't working, and that what was happening between us was hurting Brent. That was the last thing I wanted, so I agreed to a divorce. I had just wanted to give Brent a home, a family.'

'I'm so sorry, Blake.' Callie spoke because she had to. She couldn't take the pain in his voice any longer.

He looked at her now, smiled sadly. 'Thanks, but I was in that relationship for the wrong reasons. For my own reasons. Julia had her reasons, too, so we were both wrong— though I do think she thought she was doing the right thing for Brent. She wanted to make sure that he never lacked for money.'

'Wait—what?'

Blake shot her a confused look. And then he nodded. 'Oh, yeah, I didn't mention that. When we spoke about the divorce she told me she had only married me so that she could live the life she knew she and her son deserved. And then she realised that she was hurting him instead, and she didn't want that.' He shook his head. 'That was pretty much the end of it.'

'Did she get anything in the divorce?' Callie didn't want to ask, but it was one of the pieces of the puzzle she needed to understand him better.

'No, the prenup prevented that. And Brent didn't either, since the contract stated he needed to be legally mine before I was required to pay anything.'

'Do you still see him?'

'No, I don't. Julia resigned shortly after we divorced and moved to back to Namibia, where she's from.'

'Blake…' Callie shifted over and put an arm around him. 'I'm sorry.'

He lifted his own arm, put it around her, and sat back so that she could lay her head on his chest. They sat like that for a while, and Callie wished she had words to say that would take the pain away. Suddenly everything made sense to her. His resistance to dating an employee. His pushing her away when she got too close. He was broken inside, and he didn't want anyone to know.

'I've created a trust fund for him.' Blake spoke softly. 'When he's twenty-five—old enough to decide what to do with his own money—he'll get something from me. It may not mean much to him—'

'But you needed to do it.' She leaned back and watched him nod, before putting her head on his chest again. 'You're a good man, Blake Owen.'

CHAPTER THIRTEEN

CALLIE LOOKED AT HERSELF in the mirror and tried to be critical. She was wearing a blue floral dress with a white jersey and matching heels, and her hair was tied into a loose bun. She had to lead a meeting about the gala event that day, and she wanted to look her best. She placed a hand on her nervous stomach and forced herself to admit that she wanted to look her best for Blake, too.

He hadn't stayed for very long after they'd spoken last night. Callie knew that telling her about his past had made him feel uncomfortable, so she hadn't pushed him. Instead she'd brushed a kiss on his cheek and waved him away, all the while worrying about what it meant for *them*. She could no longer deny that there was something between them, but even the thought of it terrified her. Especially as they hadn't defined it yet, and she didn't even know how long Blake would be staying in Cape Town.

Or if he would be staying at all.

She shook her head and told herself that there was no point in worrying about it now, when everything was still so new and fresh. She would just have to wait and see how it played out. She sighed, and wished that was enough for her.

She grabbed her handbag when she heard a car hoot outside and locked up quickly, not wanting Connor to wait. Her car would probably be ready after the weekend, her mechanic had told her, and he had also cautioned her that it didn't have much life left in it. This she knew—though part of her wanted to keep it, even if she left it in the garage, just because it reminded her of the days when she had been part of a family.

'Hey, Cals. How are you?' Connor asked as she climbed into the car and kissed him on the cheek.

'Fine—no thanks to you. What were you thinking, throwing me to the wolves yesterday?' Callie wasn't sure why she'd said that, but somehow she felt it was what he would expect her to say if she hadn't shared anything personal with their boss.

'Sorry about that.'

He grimaced and she thought her gut instinct had been right.

'Urgent matter at home.'

She looked at him in alarm. 'Is everything all right?'

'Not really.' Connor focused hard on the road ahead of him and didn't even look her way.

'Connor,' she said, in the stern voice she only used with him, 'what's going on?'

After a few more moments of silence he said tersely, 'Elizabeth is pregnant.'

Her jaw dropped before she consciously realised. 'Oh, Connor…'

'She only found out a few days ago. Told me yesterday.' He shrugged, though the movement was heavy with tension. 'I guess I'm going to be a dad.'

Callie wished she had the right words for him, but she didn't. Connor had been dating Elizabeth for less than six months. And, while she was a perfectly lovely girl, she knew Connor didn't want to start a family this way. Family was a responsibility that deserved attention, and she and Connor had lived by that because that was the way *they* had been raised.

Her heart cracked for him, but she knew that all she could do was offer her support. 'How do you feel about this?'

'I'm not sure. I think I'm still a little numb from the shock. It wasn't planned.'

She laughed a little. 'Yeah, I got *that* part.'

He gave her a wry smile, and then sobered. 'But… I *want* it, Cals. I want to keep the baby. And so does she. You know how much family means to me. And after Mom and Dad died I thought I'd lost that. Do you know what I mean?'

'Yes, I do.'

'Now I get to have my own…and I don't think that's a *bad* thing.'

'Of course it isn't!' She felt excitement bubble inside her at the prospect of seeing her brother as a father. And ignored the voice in her head that threatened to temper it. 'I think you're going to be an amazing father. I mean, an amazing brother, not so much—but definitely an amazing father!'

He laughed, and she could tell some of the tension had gone from him. Feeling an urge to make even more of it go away, she placed a hand over his and said, 'I think Mom and Dad would be so proud of you. There's no doubt in my mind that you're going to give your child what they gave us—a good, solid, wonderful family.'

He smiled at her, and they drove the rest of the way to the hotel in silence.

She'd meant every word she had said to him. She could picture Connor running around with a little boy or girl in the backyard, could see herself spending holidays with him and his family. So why did she feel so strange? Perhaps it was because she wished her parents could have been there to see their grandchildren? Yes, she knew there was some truth in that. But something niggled inside her, and she knew that wasn't quite all of it.

No, she thought suddenly, it was because now she wondered where *she* would fit into Connor's new life.

Something inside her broke, though she couldn't explain why. But before she could examine it they'd arrived at the hotel.

'Thank you.'

'Of course. Cals?' Connor looked over at her. 'Are you okay?'

She forced her doubts and her fears away, and smiled over at him. 'Yeah.' She got out of the car and hugged him when he joined her. 'It's going to be okay, Connor. I promise.'

She repeated the words to herself as she walked to her office, and then tried to force the situation out of her mind altogether so that she could focus on preparing for the meeting in less than an hour.

But her mind kept wandering, until finally she sighed and went to get herself a cup of coffee. Before she got to the kitchen she saw a flurry of activity around it, like bees weaving in and out of a beehive, and did a neat three-sixty turn and instead headed for the conference room.

Her heart beat a little faster as she knocked at the door, and it accelerated one hundredfold when she heard the muffled, 'Come in.'

'Hey,' she said as she walked in.

'Hi.' Blake smiled at her, and stood up at the end of the table. 'What are you doing here? I thought you were going to prepare for the meeting in your own office.'

'I was, but then I couldn't really focus and I needed coffee. And, since nowadays coffee in the kitchen comes with the dozens of questions my colleagues seem to have every time they see me, I thought I might persuade you to share.'

'No persuasion needed.' He grinned and walked to the counter to grab a mug. 'Can I pour you some?'

She nodded, and wordlessly took in how attractive he looked. She would never tire of it, she thought. Admiring him in a suit was definitely on the list of things that she most enjoyed doing.

'Black, one sugar, right?'

She shook herself, and blushed when she saw the amused look on his face. 'Yes, please.'

She walked to one of the conference room chairs and sat heavily, needing a moment to process everything. She was all over the place, she thought, and forced herself to be *present*. To be in the moment. She had so many important things to do. Her job depended on the tours she still had to do this week, and so did her brother's. And while she *was* struggling with processing her brother's announcement, she still wanted to support him. One of the biggest ways she could do that was to fight for the hotel he loved…and the job that he needed if he was going to be a father.

Then there was Blake, and all her feelings for him that were knotted in a ball at the base of her stomach. She took a deep breath in, and exhaled slowly.

'Hey, is everything okay?'

Blake handed her the coffee and sat on the chair next to hers.

'Thanks,' she said, and then answered him. 'Everything is fine. Just the usual concerns.' She smiled, but she could feel that it was off.

'About the event?'

She nodded, because she didn't know what else to do.

'Look, I know this isn't your thing. I remember the night we met Connor mentioned it was out of your comfort zone,' he elaborated when she looked up in surprise. 'Which makes me respect your suggestion for doing it all the more. But you don't have to worry. After the meeting today we'll know exactly where we stand with the planning, and we can take it from there.'

She stared blankly at the cup of coffee in her hands, and blew at the steam in an attempt to cool it down. She had heard him, but her thoughts had almost immediately drifted away to Connor's situation. What would it mean for *their* relationship? She knew his child would come first, of course, but would that mean that she would lose him, too?

'Callie?'

'Mmm?' She looked up at Blake and realised he was waiting for a response when she saw the questioning look on his face.

'Yes, I know it's going to be fine.' She laid a hand on his cheek, finding the warmth there comforting, and then stood. 'I need to prepare. Thanks for the coffee.'

'Are you sure you're okay?'

'I'm fine.' She brushed a kiss on his lips. 'I'll see you at the meeting.'

She walked out the door, her mind already wandering back to Connor.

Blake leaned against his car and resisted the urge to pace.

Callie had been so unlike herself today that he had wanted to corner her as soon as he could to demand that she give him something other than her generic 'I'm fine.' He hated to think that it was about him, but after what he had shared with her the previous evening, the thought kept strolling through his head, making him restless.

He knew he hadn't stayed very long after he'd told her about Julia, but he'd thought it was best for them to spend some time apart to process what had just happened. Because something had shifted between them, and he'd wanted to give her space—and, yes, give himself space too—to come to terms with it.

He hadn't worried that he'd done the wrong thing until he'd seen her in the conference room. She'd been pale, and her usual vibrant demeanour had seemed almost brittle. She had looked...*fragile*.

Again he despised the thought that it might have been because of him. But the more he'd seen of her that day, the more he'd thought that it might be. She had still been professional—she had handled the meeting with a grace and leadership that had had him thinking about her future at Elegance—but underneath it he'd been able to see that something was wrong.

So he had gone rogue and told Connor that Callie would be working late that night, that he shouldn't worry about getting her home because Blake would drop her. Connor had dubiously accepted, but had thankfully been distracted enough not to verify it with Callie. He knew the man had been under a lot of strain lately, and there were rings under his eyes that looked like thunderclouds. But it would be over soon enough, and none of his employees would have to worry about their future any more.

He looked at his watch and wondered if Callie had got his message that *he* would be taking her home. He was just about to call when he heard the click of heels coming towards him. He looked up and was blown away by her beauty all over again. He had been right that first night they'd met, he thought, about her walking as though on a red carpet. She was so graceful, so elegant, that it made him square his shoulders and take his hands out his pockets.

She looked up at him and smiled—an utterly exhausted smile, but a smile nevertheless—and tightened her grip on the handbag under her arm.

'Are you making up for lost time with these lifts?' she asked easily, and something in Blake's heart released.

'Maybe. Or maybe I just like seeing if I can trick your brother into forgetting how protective he is of you.'

Her smile dimmed, and then she said, 'We should probably get going.'

Blake frowned, wondering what he had said wrong, but he opened the car door and waited as she got in. Then he decided to drive to his house instead.

She didn't say a word to him—not even when he drove in completely the opposite direction to her house. She only looked up when the gates to his house opened.

'Where are we?'

'My place. I figured I could make you some dinner.'

She looked at him in surprise. 'You *cook*?'

'Yes, I do. And I'll try not to be offended by the incredulity in your eyes.' He smiled at her. 'Do you have anything against steak?'

CHAPTER FOURTEEN

CALLIE TRIED TO KEEP a neutral expression on her face as she looked up at the place where Blake lived.

The house was a combination of brick and glass, with brown frames outlining the doors and windows. A deck on the upper level of the house overlooked a vast estate, including a small pond that Callie could see from where she was standing outside his car. She walked forward, caught a glimpse of the city lights, and imagined that standing on his deck would be quite an experience.

When Blake had unlocked the large oak door he stepped aside for her to walk past and her neutral expression gave way to a jaw-drop.

Brick walls, wooden furniture and sparks of green were scattered across the living room in a design that screamed warmth. A fireplace was the focal point of the room—and rightly so, she thought as she took in its impressive design, and then walked through the room to a passage that opened onto the kitchen and dining room.

The kitchen space was huge, and had the same homely yet modern design as the living room. Granite counters were highlighted by pops of colour and a window looked out onto a garden that made her salivate. The dining room was more elegant—wooden floors and a black dining room set that was decked out with cutlery and crockery that looked incredibly expensive.

'This is not what I expected from you.'

'Did you think I lived in a cold black and white room?' He smirked as he said it, but his eyes grew serious when she nodded.

'Something like that. This is a lot more…*inviting* than I expected.'

He looked around, as though seeing it for the first time. 'It is, isn't it? Though it's wasted on me. I've barely spent any time here, and the decor was pretty much left to the interior designer I hired.'

'Perhaps they decorated according to what they thought the house needed instead of thinking about its owner.'

He narrowed his eyes. 'I'm not sure if you just complimented me or insulted me.'

She laughed, and felt a bit of the tension of the day leave her. 'I was only agreeing with you that this house needs to be somewhere people are invited to.' She ran a hand over the kitchen counter. 'It deserves a family.'

The words felt fatalistic as she said them, and although she knew why it felt that way for her, she wasn't sure what the expression on Blake's face meant.

Then it cleared and he smiled. 'Well, you haven't seen the second floor, where I spend most of my time. It's a lot colder than this.'

He winked and she laughed.

'Now, shall we have some supper?'

She nodded, and settled back on a bar stool at the kitchen counter. Though she wanted to offer her help, there was something about watching him go through the motions of making a meal that helped soothe the turmoil inside her. She also wanted to speak, to tell him of all that was going through her head, but she couldn't bring herself to interrupt what seemed surprisingly easy for him. So she just sat and watched him—watched as he spiced the meat, seared it in a pan, and popped it into the oven.

He took out two wine glasses, poured a liberal amount of wine into each, and handed a glass to her.

'Now, will you tell me what's happening in that head of yours?'

'What do you mean?' she asked, but she didn't look him in the eye.

'Callie, come on. You and I both know you've been distracted today. We promised each other we would be open.'

She looked up at him when he paused, and felt alarm go through her as he clenched his teeth.

'If this is because of Julia, then—'

'What?' she exclaimed, and then she placed her wine down and walked around the counter until she was in front of him. She brushed the piece of hair he should really have cut out of his face and kept her hand on his cheek for a moment. 'No, Blake. This isn't about Julia—or you.'

He took her hands and squeezed. 'Then what's wrong?'

She bit her lip and then she said, very softly, 'Connor is going to be a father.'

Blake felt his eyebrows lift, and then carefully rearranged his features. 'And that's a *bad* thing?'

'No, I don't think so.'

She walked back around the counter, and Blake thought it might be symbolic, somehow, her placing an obstacle between them.

'I mean, it isn't the *best* thing that could happen to him right now, what with our jobs being on the line and him only knowing his girlfriend for six months…'

This time Blake didn't try to hide his surprise, and Callie grinned at him.

'That's not like the man you thought you knew so well, is it?'

'No, it isn't.' He looked up at her, and saw something in her eyes that prompted him to ask, 'Or is it?'

'I'm beginning to think it is.'

She lifted her wine glass slowly, not meeting his eye. And when she did, he saw a flash of pain that quickly settled into something he couldn't quite identify.

'I mean, not the getting-a-girl-pregnant thing. But the baby…' She trailed off. 'I think it helped Connor cope with my parents' deaths when he had to help *me*.'

'What do you mean?'

She looked at him, then sighed. 'Should we be making a salad, or something else to go with the steak?'

He didn't respond, recognising her ploy, but walked to the fridge and started removing vegetables. He was glad he had made a visit to the shop the day before—he'd wanted steak and his conscience had guilted him into buying the ingredients for a salad. He'd have to do it more often if Callie visited regularly.

And then he stopped, remembering her earlier words about his house needing family, and something nudged at him. But he forced it away and handed her cherry tomatoes and an avocado to cut. Before he knew it—and, he thought, before she was ready—they were done.

'Nothing left to distract you now,' he said, and laid a hand on her cheek. 'Tell me.'

She sighed again, walked back around the counter and sat down. Then she spoke without looking at him. 'I just mean that family has always *meant* something to Connor. To both of us, really, but to him most of all. And when our parents died they left a void that we both felt.' She paused. 'I thought that we'd filled it for one another. But I think this baby is going to do it for him.'

Blake watched her as she spoke. Her shoulders were tight, and he realised that she was embarrassed by what she was saying. Suddenly it clicked.

'And you're going to be left alone?'

She didn't look up at him, but he thought he saw a tear roll down her cheek.

'Yeah, that's it. Except that admitting it makes me sound selfish.'

Before she had finished speaking Blake pulled her into his arms. He wanted to comfort her—needed to, perhaps—because he was feeling less and less comfortable with what she was saying and he wasn't sure why. So he focused on her, and said what he thought she needed to hear.

'Callie, I know that Connor helped you get through your parents' deaths. And you have every right to be grateful to him for that. But he isn't the reason you got through it.' He leaned back so he could look into her eyes. '*You* are.'

She blinked, and two more tears escaped from her eyes. 'Connor *did* help me get through my parents' deaths.' She said it slowly, deliberately, as though trying to convince him of the fact.

'I know he did. But just because he helped you, it doesn't mean he's the *reason* you made it through.'

He repeated it, stopping only to check how his words were affecting her.

'Callie, when you told me about how you dealt with everything you said that *you* were the one who became interested in your job. *You* chose to start interacting with the guests. *You* were the one who took the initiative to start tours. Connor could never have forced you to do it, even if he'd waited outside your house every single day for a year.'

He stopped, trying to gauge whether she was taking it in.

'I know Connor is important to you, and that the two

of you have been through a lot together, but that doesn't mean you can't do it alone. Besides, you won't be alone.'

She looked up at him now, and the hope in her eyes knocked him in the gut.

'I mean, I don't think Connor won't be there for you any more just because he's having a baby.' He said the words quickly, for reasons he didn't want to examine. Not when they were so entwined with feelings he couldn't explain. The hope in her eyes was quickly dimmed, and although he knew he had spoken in response to that hope its extinguishment disappointed him.

'Yeah, maybe you're right,' she said, and was quiet as she waited for him to dish up.

And even though the meal was one of his favourites to make on the rare occasions he was at home, he didn't taste it. His thoughts were too busy with why he had tried to back out of the support he wanted to offer her.

'I think I forgot that Connor's baby will be my family, too.'

Callie spoke softly, and dragged him from his thoughts. Her expression was pensive, but when she met his eyes there was a sparkle there that had been missing the entire day.

'I've been thinking selfishly all day.'

'Your reaction was completely normal. You weren't being selfish.'

'Maybe normal, but definitely selfish.'

She smiled at him, and his lips curved in response. 'Maybe just a little.'

She laughed lightly, cut another piece from her steak, and then looked at him. 'You're the first person who's ever made me feel like it's okay to be alone. Or that I might have helped *myself* get out of my depression. Thank you.'

Her words were so sincere that they ripped at his heart,

and immediately he felt like a fraud. He didn't deserve her gratitude when he couldn't even tell her that he would be there for her. When her simple comments about family had frozen him up.

'You're welcome.'

They ate the rest of their meal in silence, each lost in thought, and when they were done she ran the water for washing the dishes. He sat back, watching her as she pulled plates into the soapy water, rinsed them, and then placed them on the dish rack. Slowly, almost without realising it, he began to picture her there after a long day at work.

He could almost see the rain outside the window above where she was washing up, could hear the fire roaring in the living room. He even saw himself walking to her and offering a hand, drawing her close to him as he touched her stomach, where she was carrying their child...

'You know, I think before today I hadn't thought about family outside of my parents and brother. But it's nice to think that we could expand.'

He was ripped out of his fantasy, felt his heart racing faster than he'd thought possible. 'Yeah?'

'Yeah.' She turned to him and her expression softened. 'Wasn't your time with Brent good?'

His heart still pounded as he answered her. 'Yes, it was.'

'I thought so.' She nodded, and started washing again. 'Connor's going to be an amazing father. And being an aunt won't be so bad.'

It was almost as though she was thinking out loud.

'I'll get to practise for when I have my own kids one day. *Ha!* I hadn't even thought about having my own family until now.'

'Do you *want* to have a family?' he asked, before he could stop himself. He didn't think he would have been able to stop himself even if he'd had the chance. Not when he still saw that picture of her pregnant in their house—no, *his* house—vividly in his mind.

She turned around and wiped her hands with a dry cloth. 'Yeah—yeah, I think I do.' She tilted her head and said, 'It's our legacy, I guess.' She smiled at him. 'Building on the foundation of family that our parents gave us.'

The words hit him right in the stomach, and finally he realised what it was that was bothering him. *Family.* The word that described his biggest disappointments. And now, he thought in panic, his biggest fear.

'Callie, do you mind if I take you home?' he asked, and ignored the voice in his head that called him a coward. 'It's getting late and I still have a couple of things to do before our next proposal tomorrow.'

'Um…okay—sure,' she said, and his heart clenched when he saw her bewildered expression.

He helped her with the dishes in silence as he tried to work through the thoughts in his head. He wanted it. Family. With Callie. Never before had he felt a need more intense. Never before had he seen something this clearly. But he'd lost things before. Things that hadn't meant nearly as much to him. And those things had nearly broken him.

Like Brent, he thought as they made their way to the car. He'd loved that boy more than he'd thought he could, and his heart was still raw from not being near him. And like his parents, who had both, in their own way, left him. He fought the memories of those heartbreaks every day, still carried the scars of them with him.

More so than he had realised, he thought, remembering his conversation with Callie on the boat when she had pointed it out to him.

If somehow this didn't work out between them—if, for some reason, Callie left him—he knew he wouldn't be able to go on as though nothing had happened. No, he would be a broken man. And she would carry the pieces of him with her, so that he would never be able to put himself together again.

And even if she didn't leave he would risk disappointing her. He knew nothing about family. Nothing about the foundation she spoke of—her *legacy*. He didn't have much to contribute to that. His mother had left him and his father was more business partner than parent.

It didn't matter that he wanted to be a part of her life, he thought sadly, and it didn't matter that he wanted to have a family with her. What mattered was that he would fail her—just as he had Brent. And he knew that it would kill him if he failed her. And more importantly, he realised, it would devastate him to hurt her like that.

'Hey, what's going on?' she said softly, taking one of his hands.

Blake turned to her and realised that he had pulled up in front of her driveway. He wondered when that had happened.

'Nothing,' he answered, feeling his heart hurting from the lie, but knowing it was for the best.

The only way to avoid disappointing, failing or hurting her—*and* himself—was to put some distance between them. And, though it killed him, that meant not talking to her about the way he felt. Not when he still needed to figure out what to do about it.

'Really?' she scoffed. 'So we've been sitting here for ten minutes for you to think about *nothing*?'

He resisted the urge to tell her what was wrong, and forced himself to think about the look on Brent's face the last time Blake had seen him. The memory of the mixture of emotions in the little boy's eyes—especially the heartbreak—helped him steel his heart.

He *never* wanted to see that expression on Callie's face.

'It's just been a long day, that's all.'

She looked at him for a while, and then moved her hands to her lap. 'So, is this "being open" you reminded me of earlier something that only *I* have to follow?'

Though his heart tightened at the emotion in her voice, he ignored it. He was doing the only thing that would protect both of them. 'Look, there really isn't anything going on. I've just had a long day, and I still need to get things done. I was thinking about that.' He tried to smile, but knew he was failing miserably at it.

'Fine. If that's what you're going with.'

She picked up her bag and got out of the car, but the tiny moment of relief Blake felt was shattered when she slammed the door shut.

'Callie.'

He got out quickly, not knowing what he could say—not when he wanted space to think about everything—yet he needed her to be okay with him.

'Please.'

She stopped on the first step of the path up to her house and then turned to him. He knew the hurt in her eyes was a picture that would stay with him through the night.

'Look, if you need time to work through whatever's going on, that's fine. But don't lie to me about it.'

He walked towards her, but stuffed the hands that itched to take hers into his pockets.

'Okay.' He paused, then exhaled slowly. 'I need time.'

She nodded. 'Okay.' She kissed his cheek and walked to her house, shutting the door after a slight wave.

And for a long time afterwards Blake stood outside her house, thinking about the choice he needed to make and why he needed to make it.

CHAPTER FIFTEEN

IT WAS FINALLY FRIDAY, the day was gorgeous, and the final arrangements for the gala event were going well.

It was being held on the Elegance's rooftop—an idea Callie had had after she and Blake had gone for the tasting. It had taken some planning—and a lot of convincing—to change the venue so soon before the event, but as she looked around she was glad she'd managed it.

Pillars stood at each corner of the rooftop, with minilanterns draped between them. A stage had been set up at one end, adorned with light. The band they'd hired were setting up there, and any speeches during the evening would be made from it. Tables had been set around the centre of the roof, with white flower centrepieces and napkins on black tablecloths, leaving space for a dance floor. The food would be plated, there was a bar up and ready, and the bustle of the staff doing the final touches should have given Callie a sense of accomplishment.

Except that as she stood there, looking at everything, she wasn't feeling anything except dread.

All she'd been able to think about for the last few days was the way Blake had decided to take her home after the dinner they'd had at his house. The way he'd lied to her about what was bothering him. And although she told herself to be patient, although she reassured herself that he would tell her when he was ready, every time she saw him the feeling of dread deepened.

Because somehow she knew he was slipping away from her.

She'd tried to brush it off at first as paranoia. He wasn't acting differently around her—at least not on the surface. But her heart knew that there were no more lingering looks, no more affectionate touches. Those had been replaced with smiles that had no depth and words that didn't say what he meant. She'd hidden the hurt, hidden the concern, and waited in vain for him to tell her what was wrong.

And the wait was breaking her.

'It's amazing.'

She turned to see Blake surveying the area. He offered her a smile, and again she was struck by how different it was.

'Yeah, I can't believe we actually pulled it off.' She looked around again, and then returned his smile tentatively. 'I think it's going to be a success.'

He nodded, and she saw something flash across his eyes.

And then he said, 'Shouldn't you be busy with your hair? We only have four more hours until the event. You're cutting it close.'

She tilted her head, trying to figure out his mood. 'No, I have my things downstairs. I'll get ready once I'm sure everything is done up here.'

He stuffed his hands into his pockets. 'I was joking, Callie.'

'Were you?' She shrugged, ignoring the pain in her heart. 'I can't seem to tell with you lately.'

'Look,' he said, and then took a deep breath.

He stood in silence for a moment—his hands still in his pockets, his face tense—and Callie felt her nails cutting into her hands as she clenched her fists, waiting for him.

'Did you say you have your things downstairs?'

'What?'

'You don't have an afternoon of pampering planned after this week?'

'No, Blake, I don't.' She brushed off the irritability that threatened. 'I didn't have time to make the appointments this week nor do I want to spend a ridiculous amount of money on a new dress—'

'You don't have a dress to wear tonight?' he interrupted her.

'Of course I do,' she said defensively. 'It's just not new. It's one of my mom's. But what does that have to do with anything?'

Callie was ashamed of the desperation that coated her tone.

He looked at her for a few moments, and then pulled out his phone, his fingers speeding over the screen. A 'ping' sounded almost immediately, and he nodded and put it back into his pocket. Then he looked at her, and something in his eyes softened her heart.

'Would you come with me?'

His voice was hesitant, as though he wasn't quite sure of what she was going to say. That, combined with the look in his eyes, made her insides crumble, and she took the hand he offered. Even though everything inside her wanted to say no, wanted to ask him why he was allowing this uncertainty to eat at them, she let him lead her down the stairs.

And felt hopeless when the thought that she would follow him anywhere flitted through her mind.

They didn't speak when they reached the parking garage, and she waited for him as he moved to open the car door for her. But his hand stilled on the handle and he stepped back.

'What's wrong?' she asked—and then she saw the look in his eyes and felt herself tremble.

She was standing just behind the front door of the car, and when he took a step towards her instinct had her moving back against it. Her heart thudded as his hands slid around her waist and he pulled her closer, until she was moulded to his body. She looked up at him, breathless, and her knees nearly gave way at the need, the desperation in his eyes.

She closed her own eyes when he moved his head—closed them against the onslaught of emotions that flooded through her at the look on his face—and thought that their kiss would be filled with hunger, with the passion that need brought.

But instead it was so tender that she nearly wept. She slid her hands through his hair and shivers went down her spine when he deepened their kiss, taking more. She felt herself being swept away with it, but her heart cracked, just a little, as she thought that he must be trying to memorise the way she tasted, the way she felt.

Her heart demanded the same, and she slowly opened the buttons of his shirt and slid her hands up and down his chest, over his abs and back up again. She shook when the muscles beneath her hands trembled.

And then he moved back, breathing heavily, with his forehead against hers. She realised that she was breathing heavily too, and she stepped away from him, laying a hand on her racing heart. Finally, time and place caught up with her and she looked around, half expecting to see a colleague looking at them with shock. But the parking garage was empty, and for some strange reason she felt disappointment.

'I'm sorry,' he said, and she saw that he had buttoned his shirt up.

'Why are you apologising?' she asked, and braced herself for his answer.

But he simply said that someone might have seen them,

and she nodded, not trusting herself to speak when she realised *why* she felt disappointed that no one had.

Because now there was no proof that everything that had happened between her and Blake hadn't only been in her head.

He opened the car door for her, and when he'd got in he pulled out of the parking garage and started driving towards the business centre of Cape Town.

'Where are you taking me?' she asked, when she thought she had her thoughts—and her body—back under control.

'To a friend. You'll see when we get there,' he said quietly, and again Callie wondered what was going on with him. With them.

She had never felt this unsure in her life. Even when her parents had died she had had certainty. She'd known they were gone, and the only thing she'd been unsure of then had been herself. Now she was wondering if she'd made up their relationship—could she even call it that?—in her head. The feelings, the sharing... Had that just been wishful thinking? Was she just a fling to him? Someone to pass the time with?

No, she thought. That couldn't be it. Not when they'd shared things that she knew had been new for both of them. Besides, he'd never tried anything besides kissing with her. And, yes, the kissing had been hot and delicious, but he'd had the opportunity to press for more. Like the evening they'd been at his house... But instead he'd just dropped her off at home. That didn't seem like a man who wanted a fling.

But why hadn't he defined what they were? an inner voice asked her. He'd never told her that she was his girlfriend. A mistake, she realised, and suddenly she was immensely tired of the back and forth of her thoughts. She was going to ask him, once and for all. She would demand to know what they were to one another, and why he had pushed her away that night. She would demand the truth from him.

Satisfied with her resolution, she opened her mouth to speak—but the words stuck when he pulled up in front of two large bronze gates. Blake pressed the buzzer and told the crackly voice who he was, and the gates opened.

Callie held her breath as they drove up the path and she saw the large white house in front of them. Blake pulled into one of the designated parking bays and they walked to the front door, barely having enough time to press the button before the door opened and a woman stepped out and pulled Blake into her arms.

Callie might have felt threatened if the woman had done it in a remotely flirtatious way. But her hug was almost maternal, and Callie felt interest prickle when the woman drew back and said, 'Let me take a look at you.' She scanned Blake from his head to his toes and back up again, and then she smiled, and Callie thought it made her look years younger. 'Blake, you're an adult. I can't believe it.'

He laughed. 'Yes, Caroline, I have been now for quite some time.'

'Which I would have known, had you visited me at any point during that time.' She gave him a stern look, and then waved a hand. 'But that's water under the bridge now that you're here.'

She turned and Callie felt her back stiffen as she was sized up.

'And who are *you*, darling?'

'This is Callie. She's…a friend of mine.' He paused, as though thinking about what he had called her, and then continued. 'She needs a new dress for an event at the hotel tonight.'

'Oh, why didn't you just say so? Come on, let's go in.'

She walked past the two of them down the passage, and entered a room right at the end. Callie and Blake followed, and she whispered, 'Who *is* this woman?'

'She's an old family friend. My mother's, actually, though she didn't want us to hold that against her when my mother left. Her name is Caroline Bellinger.'

Callie stopped in her tracks. 'You *know* Caroline Bellinger?'

'Yes. Why?'

'Why?' She looked at him incredulously. 'Caroline Bellinger is Cape Town's top designer. She's designed dresses for local celebrities for almost all of our glamourous events. She isn't just someone's "family friend".'

'Do you plan on joining me, or are you going to stand in the passage whispering about me all day?' Caroline called from the room.

Blake grinned. A genuine one this time, she noted.

'She's astute, isn't she? Come on, let's find you a dress for tonight.'

From that moment Callie felt as though she had been selected for a makeover show. Caroline examined her even more critically than she had when they'd met, and Callie had to resist the cringe that came over her when Caroline announced that she had a body 'like a movie star'. She could tell Blake was enjoying the show, but Caroline shooed him out before she pulled out any dresses.

'You can follow Darren, Blake. He'll take you to the restaurant where we make all the men wait while we do this.'

The man who appeared when his name was called nodded at Blake, and Blake gave Callie a reassuring nod before leaving. She held her breath when she realised that Caroline was now looking at her, and she felt the weight of the woman's stare.

'So, you and Blake are...*friends*?'

Caroline didn't believe it for a second, Callie thought, but answered, 'Yes, I think so.'

'I didn't need an answer, dear. I just wanted to see your face after my question.'

Caroline didn't elaborate on what she'd seen there, and walked past Callie to a rack of dresses on the other side of the room.

'I met another friend of Blake's a while ago. Except it was at their wedding.'

Callie quickly realised what Caroline was implying, and it had her shaking her head. 'No, no. This isn't anything like him and Julia.'

Caroline raised her eyebrows. 'No, it can't be if he's told you about her.'

She returned to Callie with four dresses, each of which looked as though they were fit for royalty.

'He didn't bring her here, you know.'

'Excuse me?'

Caroline handed her a midnight-blue dress that Callie worried might not cover nearly as much of her body as she would have liked before answering.

'I always thought I would be the one to make Blake's bride's wedding dress. Though he didn't even ask me.' She looked at Callie again, and this time the gaze felt distinctly more piercing. 'And yet here you are. For a dress for an event at the hotel.' She paused again, and then simply said, 'You can get changed over there.'

She pointed to a dressing screen and Callie followed, not sure what else she was supposed to do. Or whether she was supposed to speak at all. The woman had given her so many innuendoes that Callie wasn't sure she was able to process them all.

She dressed as quickly as she could, and almost sighed when she felt the silk on her skin. It was luxurious, she thought, grateful for the distraction of something as simple as a dress. Except that this dress was anything *but* simple. She thought she could easily become used to such luxury… until she walked out and Caroline shook her head.

'Oh, *no*, that's dreadful.'

Callie felt her face blanch, but Caroline waved a hand.

'No, darling, it's not you—it's the combination of you and that dress. Try this one instead. I think it'll do wonders for that rich skin tone of yours. And it won't hide your curves either.'

She winked, and Callie took the dress wordlessly.

She knew that artists could be eccentric—but, honestly, she hadn't ever experienced it first-hand before. It was strange that this woman was a part of Blake's life. Her conservative boss—she'd settled on using that term, since she wasn't sure *what* to call him personally—didn't strike her as someone who would be familiar with a person so—well, *unique*. Especially when Caroline seemed to see things Callie didn't think most people would want her to see—especially not someone as private as Blake.

She looked down at the dress, noting how much tighter it was than the previous one, and resisted pulling at the neckline that lay just a touch too low for her liking. When she walked out in the emerald dress Caroline clasped her hands together in what Callie could only imagine was delight.

'This is *it*. This is the *one*.'

Callie doubted the dress required that much enthusiasm, and was still thinking about it when Caroline asked her what size shoe she wore. She responded automatically, even though she wanted to tell the woman that she had some shoes she could wear with the dress. But then Caroline brought out the most gorgeous silver pair Callie had ever seen and she kept her mouth shut.

'Gorgeous—though there's something missing…' She

looked at Callie for a few more moments, and then went to fetch something from a glass cabinet.

Callie didn't realise what it was until Caroline presented her with a diamond necklace.

'Oh, Caroline, I couldn't—'

'You can, and you will.' She fastened the necklace around Callie's neck herself, and then led her to the mirror.

Callie was almost afraid to look, but she caught her reflection before she had a chance to close her eyes and nearly gasped. She looked… *Wow*, she thought. Maybe the dress *had* required that much enthusiasm. She almost didn't recognise herself.

Caroline had been right about the colour, and the gown fitted her perfectly. The necklace sparkled up at her, matching the shoes that she could see beneath the slit that ran up her left leg. She had never seen herself like this before. Not even on the night of Blake's welcome event had she looked this elegant.

She remained silent when Caroline stood behind her and twisted her hair into some kind of chignon.

'You should wear your hair like this. And just a touch of make-up. We don't want to hide any of your natural beauty.'

Callie nodded wordlessly, not trusting herself to speak. What could she possibly say to this woman who had made her look like a princess?

'It's okay, dear. You don't have to thank me. That look on your face is more than enough.' Caroline smiled at her, and for the first time since they'd met Callie could see what it was about the woman that Blake cared about.

She returned Caroline's smile and walked back behind the screen, undressing slowly so that she didn't do any damage to the dress. When she was done, she handed it over to Caroline along with the shoes and the necklace.

'Caroline, I don't think I can take these from you.' She

gestured to the accessories she knew must have cost a fortune.

'You can't have the dress if you don't.'

'What?'

Caroline put the dress in a clothing bag and said again, 'You can't wear this dress if you don't take the accessories.'

'Why…why not?'

'Because you need the whole package for Blake to get that feeling *you* had when you looked in the mirror.' Caroline smiled kindly when Callie lifted her eyebrows. 'You don't think I saw the surprise on your face when you looked at yourself? I think it would give Blake a good kick in the behind to see you like that. And, from what I know about that man, he could use it.'

Again, Callie didn't respond.

'I'm *so* glad he brought you here.'

Suddenly Callie found herself in Caroline's arms.

Hesitantly, she put her arms around the woman, and she felt an odd sense of comfort when she said, 'Be patient with him. He'll get there eventually.'

She drew back, and Caroline smiled again, and for a moment Callie wondered what 'there' meant. She realised too late that she'd asked Caroline out loud, and waited with bated breath for the answer.

'You'll know soon enough, dear,' she said, before calling Blake, and Callie knew her chance to probe was gone.

'Are you sorted?' Blake asked when he walked in.

'Yes, she is.' Caroline patted his cheek. 'No need for thanks. You can just send the things back after the event.'

'Of course. We can sort out payment at a later point.'

Callie immediately wanted to offer payment too—even though heaven only knew how she would be able to afford it—but Caroline had narrowed her eyes.

'Blake, you say something that offensive to me again,

and I swear I will tell the world that you stole this dress from me.'

He laughed, and then sobered. 'I appreciate it, Caroline.'

'Anything for you.' For the first time, Caroline looked completely serious. 'I'm just so happy to see you, Blake. You look good.'

As they drove away Callie didn't say anything. Caroline's cryptic words kept swirling around in her head, rousing the thoughts she had refused to have for such a long time. Rousing feelings she had ignored even when they had demanded attention. Because she couldn't give in to them. Not when she didn't know where she stood with Blake.

One moment she felt as if she didn't know this man she'd spent so much time with, the next he was kissing her as if he was a dying man and she was his last breath. And then he'd arranged this trip to a fairy godmother.

How could she love a man like that? she thought, and then went very still when she realised it.

The very simple truth that made his strange behaviour so difficult to swallow.

She looked away, out of the window, although she didn't see any of the buildings they passed. She just needed to look away from him. She didn't want him to know that she loved him. That she—Callie McKenzie, who hadn't thought she would ever open herself up enough to fall in love—was in love with her boss.

She squeezed her eyes closed, letting herself process the novelty of her thoughts.

Except that they weren't new, she thought. They had been there since—well, she didn't even know. But then Caroline had nudged her and cracked the armour she'd protected the thoughts in. She was in love with an incredible man. A man who cared about his company, about people, about *her*. A man who made her feel she wasn't alone. A man who had helped her work through feelings from the most difficult part of her past.

If she'd had to pick him from a list on paper, Callie would have put money on herself picking Blake, and a part of her took joy from that. But that joy was quickly dimmed by the fact that the man she had fallen in love with wasn't the man who was sitting next to her. And it terrified her—wholly and completely—to consider the reasons why that was the case.

She was so deep in thought that she didn't even notice that they'd stopped until Blake put a hand on her thigh.

'Callie?'

'Yeah?'

'We're here.'

She looked around in surprise. 'This isn't the hotel.'

'No, it isn't. This is the salon my stepmother goes to. I made an appointment for you, and a car will come and get you in a few hours.'

'Blake, this really isn't necessary...'

'A car will come and get you and bring you back in time for the event,' he repeated, and then he continued, 'There will probably be someone inside to help you with all the make-up stuff, too.'

'Blake—'

'No, don't say it. Don't tell me that you don't want this. Because this isn't about you. This is *for* you. You deserve this. After all you've done...' He lifted a hand to her face and she thought that it was as if he *needed* her to believe him. 'You deserve a few hours of relaxation. When people do things for *you*. Let me do this for you, okay?'

She wished she could just accept his words at face value. Her heart was full of him, of his compassion, of his gesture for her. But something told her that he'd said them out of obligation. Out of a need for her to accept this from him. And how could she resist such a plea?

'Okay.'

He leaned over and kissed her cheek. 'I'll see you in a little bit. Go and have fun.'

CHAPTER SIXTEEN

BLAKE WAS SURE he would burn a trail in the carpet if he didn't stop pacing.

But he felt unsettled and couldn't stop. Not when some of his employees passed him, smiling politely to hide their curiosity, or even when guests did, aiming puzzled looks at him as he walked back and forth in front of one of the rooms. He wasn't sure if it was adrenaline for what was to come during the evening that fuelled his legs, or anticipation at seeing Callie when she finally emerged from the room she was using to get ready in.

He hadn't seen her when she'd got back, so he didn't know what she had thought about the limo he had sent to pick her up. It might have been overkill, but he wanted her to feel like a princess tonight. He wanted her to know that the effort she had put into the hotel hadn't been for nothing. He wanted her to know that what they'd shared together *meant* something to him. Especially when he wouldn't be able to tell her himself…

He paused. He didn't want to think about those plans. He didn't want to think about the way he had put distance between them, about Callie's face every time he'd done so. He didn't want to think about leaving her when it was all too painful. When he was doing it because he couldn't bear to lose her, to disappoint her. He just wanted to spend one night with her without worrying about what it would do to them when he left. Or, worse, what it would do to her if he stayed and couldn't give her what she wanted.

But he wasn't running, he assured himself. He was just saving them both from the potential hurt.

But all thoughts froze in his head when she opened the door and hesitantly took two steps towards him.

The neckline of her gown lay lazily over her chest, hugging her curves and accelerating his heart. Especially when he saw a diamond necklace sparkling just above her breasts, as though it wanted to distract him and draw his attention to them at the same time. The rest of the dress was just as flattering, clinging to her curves and revealing legs that Blake now realised he had vastly under-appreciated. She wore silver shoes that wrapped around her legs from just below her knee, and never before had he found a pair of shoes more attractive.

Finally, when his body had settled, he rested his eyes on her face. Her hair was like silk, tied into some kind of intricate knot at the base of her skull. And her face was glowing, slightly red at his appraisal, and absolutely gorgeous.

'Hi…' she said huskily, and Blake had to check himself before he could speak.

'Hi. You look amazing.'

She smiled hesitantly, closed the door behind her, and Blake had the pleasure of seeing how much skin the back of the dress revealed. He wasn't sure which side of it he appreciated more, he thought, and smiled when she turned back to him. Just one night, he promised himself—and his conscience—and offered his arm.

'Thank you,' she said as she straightened the tiny train of the dress behind her.

When they got to the elevator he looked at her in question.

'It would probably be best if we took the elevator today,' she said, without moving.

He squeezed her hand. 'Don't worry, the electricity won't go off tonight. And if it does I've made sure the generator is working, so we won't get stuck.'

'Famous last words…' she breathed, and then straightened her shoulders and walked into the small box.

He smiled at her bravado, and selected the button for the rooftop. He knew she held her breath as they steadily moved up, and when the doors pinged open she let out a huge sigh of relief.

'You ready?' she asked, and turned to him, the tension of a few moments ago only slightly abated.

He refused to think about what the remainder of that tension meant.

'I think so.'

'Then let's do this.'

'Dance with me.'

Callie turned to Blake and had her refusal ready when she saw he had the same look on his face as that afternoon when he'd kissed her.

But he didn't wait for an answer. Instead he took her glass and placed it with his own on the closest waiter's tray. Then he led her to the dance floor and pulled her in close. Every nerve in her body was awakened and prickled with awareness at the feel of him against her. His hand pressed against her naked lower back and sent shivers down her spine, and when she looked up at him her breath caught.

He looked at her with longing, with a sadness she hadn't expected. But she didn't want to think about it. She didn't want to think about all that had plagued them over the last few days. No, tonight she wanted to stand in the middle of the dance floor on the rooftop, under the moonlight, and sway to the music with the man she loved.

'Callie?'

She lifted her head and the illusion of a few moments ago was gone. And it had taken any thoughts she had about love with it.

'What is it?'

He looked at her, his eyes filled with an emotion she knew only too well.

'We need to talk.'

She clenched her jaw as a voice in her head told her that she wasn't being paranoid. She stiffened in his arms and looked at him, trying to read him even though it pained her to do so. And what she saw gave her the answer to all the questions she'd had.

'You're leaving.'

His arms tightened around her, and she had to stop herself from pulling away from him.

'Callie—'

'Don't.' She didn't look at him, and was grateful when the song ended. 'Just *don't*.'

She wanted to hate him for it—for doing this to her after making her feel like a princess. After making her fall in love with him. But she forced all feelings aside and worked the room, pretending everything was normal.

She clapped along with everybody else when Blake walked up onto the stage to thank everyone for coming, and laughed jovially when he told them he looked forward to taking their money the following week. But when the formalities were done she couldn't take it any more. She slipped away to Connor, and asked him if he could wrap things up for her.

'Yeah, sure. Things shouldn't go on too long anyway.' He looked at her, and then frowned. 'Are you okay?'

'I'm fine.' She brushed a kiss over his cheek. 'Thanks. I've spoken to all the investors, so I know they're happy with the event. You just need to facilitate the clean-up afterwards. I'll see you soon, okay?'

She didn't wait for his response, though she could tell that his gaze was on her as she walked away from the event. She didn't look back as she took the stairs in her evening gown, too distressed to take a chance on the elevator. They had pulled it off, she thought, and immediately felt grief at the use of 'they' for her and Blake. There would be no more of that, she knew.

She laid a hand on the railing of the staircase, bracing herself for support, and took a moment—just one—to close her eyes and soothe her aching heart. But she knew that soothing wouldn't be possible—not when her pain could only be compared to what she'd felt after her parents had died. But still she stood, rubbing a hand over her chest, as though doing that would make a difference somehow.

The look on Blake's face flashed through her eyes— the look that had told her all she needed to know about the awkwardness between them over the last few days—and another wave of grief rushed through her.

But instead of giving herself another moment, she hurried back to the room she had got ready in to change and get her things. Before she changed she looked in the mirror for one last time, wondering who the woman who looked back at her was. That woman looked so glamorous she might be royalty—nothing like the broken woman Callie knew really stood there. The one who was using every last bit of her strength to keep standing, not to fall into a heap on the floor and cry until she couldn't think about him any more.

Until she couldn't feel the pain that sliced through her at every memory of him.

She carefully took off the necklace and the shoes, placing them back into their boxes, and peeled the dress from her skin. When she was done she laid the dress bag over her arm and took the boxes in one hand, her own things in the other. She struggled out through the door and smiled her thanks when Tom, one of the bellboys, offered to help her.

She'd just handed over her things and asked him to call her a taxi when she heard Blake's voice.

'Callie—wait. Callie!' he said, more loudly when she didn't stop. 'I've been looking for you all over. We need to talk.'

She gestured for Tom to go ahead, and stiffened her spine when she saw Blake walking towards her even as the pain crushed through her chest.

'I'm on my way home. I was going to put this in your office with a note for Caroline. Actually, I think I'll do that now.'

She walked past him to his office, silently thanking Kate for getting her a room on the ground floor, so that she didn't have to get into an elevator again. She opened the door and laid the things gently over the desk Connor had put up for Blake, and turned when she heard the door slam.

'Let me explain,' he said, tension in every part of his body.

'Explain what?'

'Why I'm leaving.'

'So you *are* leaving.' She nodded as her heart broke, but coated it with anger. 'I thought you were just going to let me assume something was wrong, like you've been doing for the last few days.'

'I'm sorry. But—'

'I don't want to hear it, Blake.'

'Callie, I think the least you can do is let me explain myself.'

His tone was testy now, and she felt anger clutch at her.

'*Why*, Blake? Why should I let you explain yourself? You've been pushing me away for days. You've lied to me. And now you're leaving. So give me one reason why I shouldn't walk out of here right now and forget about whatever we had?'

'Because we care about each other. At least I care about you.' His hands were on his hips; his face was fierce. 'I care enough that I'm leaving because it's what's best for you.'

'What's *best* for me?' she repeated, almost shocked at his audacity. 'You've decided what's best for me based on what?'

'Based on the fact that I know you,' he said angrily. 'You need someone who can be a father to your children. I can't do that.'

Pieces began to fall into place somewhere at the back of her head, but she didn't take the time to see it. 'Of course you can't. Not when you're so stuck in your own world that you don't really care about how I feel.'

'Excuse me?'

Although she heard the warning in his voice, she couldn't stop now. 'I can't actually believe that I thought you might tell me what was going on in your head. I made excuses for you. I went against my gut.'

Tears pricked at her eyes, and for once she didn't care.

'That night you took me home from your house—the night you lied to me—I told myself that you needed time, and that I needed to be patient. But I waited and waited and waited. And all I got was distance, a day of pampering— because you needed to distract me from the fact that you were leaving, right? And from a decision made for my best interests. All because of what?'

She wiped at the tears that came when she realised that he had been saying goodbye to her from the day he'd dropped her at home. Today had just been the finale.

'Because you couldn't have a conversation with me about having a family?'

The shame she saw in his eyes confirmed her words.

'You have no idea what it's like to care about someone and realise that you can't give them what they want,' he said.

'*You* have no idea what it feels like to have someone you love decide they don't want to *give* you what you want,' she snapped back at him, and then stopped when the words fell between them like the blade on a guillotine.

'You *love* me?'

'I'll get over it—don't worry.'

It felt like a weakness, now—a mistake. Loving him. One she would rather have kept to herself. But she hadn't, and now she had to keep herself from falling for that expression on his face. It made her want to beg him to stay, to face his fears, to let himself love her.

To let her love be enough for him—for them.

But then she saw the sadness behind his surprise at her declaration—the sadness that told her he wouldn't let go of whatever was keeping them apart—and she felt devastation rip through her. With tears still threatening, she walked to the door, and then she paused, the fire inside her burning just enough for her to turn back to him.

'You could've missed it, because I made the mistake of saying I love you, so I'm going to say it again. You think that you're leaving because you can't give me what I want. But what I want is exactly what *you* want—a family. So don't use me as an excuse, Blake. The real problem here is *you*.'

'Callie… I'm trying. I mean, I've tried it before, and I failed miserably at being a father.' He said the words through clenched teeth. 'I'd rather walk away than have you witness me failing at it again.'

She choked back the sob that threatened, and felt completely helpless as she said, 'Well, then, luckily for both of us I'm used to the people I love leaving me.'

And with those words she walked out through the door, slamming it shut on him and on their relationship.

And breaking whatever had been left of her heart.

CHAPTER SEVENTEEN

BLAKE STOOD LOOKING OUT of the window of the office he shared with Connor, and felt the weight of his decision heavy on his shoulders. The weight that had settled there the moment Callie had shut the door to the office—to them—what felt like years ago.

He rubbed a hand over his face, tried to get his thoughts in order. The first day of negotiations had gone well—he thought he already knew who would be giving him a call, even though they still had four more days to go. It would take a few days after that to draw up the contracts, and then that would be the end of the personal responsibility he felt after letting the Elegance Hotel, Cape Town, slip through the cracks because of Julia.

He wouldn't be needed in Cape Town after that. He could run operations for the hotels from anywhere in the country. From anywhere in the *world*. Logically, he knew that. Which was why he couldn't figure out why every part of him wanted to stay in Cape Town.

Except that was a lie. He knew exactly why he wanted to stay. The part he couldn't figure out was how he could even consider it. He'd broken things off with Callie—whatever they'd had was now completely and utterly broken. His heart seemed to be, too—so much so that he couldn't remember the reasons he had given her, had convinced himself of, for why they couldn't be together. The reasons that had seemed so clear before.

'You should be at home, celebrating the deal that will be coming in soon.'

Blake turned to see Connor behind him, his hands in his pockets.

He nodded, failing to muster the energy required for a smile. 'I'm not in the mood.'

'I can see that. Seems you and Callie may have taken a drink from the same fountain. She's as miserable as you are.'

Blake hated it that there was a part of him that took comfort in that. 'She is?'

'Yes.' Connor waited a beat, and then said, 'In case you didn't pick it up, the fountain was a metaphor. The reality is that you two have been in a relationship that has now broken up. Correct?'

Blake stared at Connor, wondering why on earth his heart was thumping as though he had been caught making out with a girl by her parents, like some teenager. 'How did you find out?'

Connor let out a bark of laughter and Blake wondered if he had spoken with the guilt he felt.

'Blake, *you* may be able to hide your feelings quite well, but my sister can't.'

He smiled at that. 'Yes, so I've realised. She told you?'

'She didn't have to. I could see it from the way she looked at you.'

Connor studied Blake for some time, and Blake had to resist the urge to shuffle his feet. He was becoming increasingly aware of the fact that he was being sized up by his employee. No, he corrected himself. By the brother of the woman he cared about.

'Blake, do you know how long it took for me to get Callie to consider dating?' Connor shook his head. 'It was like talking to a rock. She would let me speak for however long my words of encouragement for that day required, and then she'd smile and tell me she wasn't interested. So, as much as I'd like to avoid getting involved in my boss's affairs, the fact that Callie opened up to you tells me that she cares about you. What happened?'

Blake felt another blow to his heart at Connor's words, and wondered why the reminder that Callie had been willing to let him in hurt so much.

'It doesn't matter. We can't be together.' He shrugged, as though to show that he had come to terms with it.

'Well, clearly it *does* matter—to both of you—because of exactly that.' He stopped, gave Blake a moment to contradict him, but when it didn't happen, he nodded. 'That's what I thought. Was it you or her?'

'What do you mean?'

'I mean did you end it or did she?'

Blake thought about it. 'I'm not actually sure. I suppose it was me—though she was the one who actually walked out.'

Connor stared at him, and then shook his head. 'Of course she would fall for you. You're *safe*.'

'Excuse me?'

'You're safe,' he repeated. 'You're not here permanently and you're her boss. She wouldn't have to worry about falling for you because you would never feel the same way about her.'

'That's not—'

'In fact she probably never told you how she really felt. She may not be able to hide her feelings, but verbalising them is completely different. So if you weren't looking, and she didn't say anything, you'd never know and she'd be able to tell herself that she tried and then move on.'

'Stop.'

The single word was said so sharply it might have sliced through metal.

'You have no idea what you're talking about. She put *everything* on the line for me.' Blake ran a hand through his hair. 'She told me exactly how she feels, and she was perfect. *I'm* the problem.'

Finally, after repeating the words had Callie told him the last time they'd spoken, something cleared inside his head. He *was* the problem. He had pushed her away because he'd thought that was best for them—for her.

He turned to Connor, saw the look on his face, and realised he'd been baited.

'How did you do it?' he asked Connor, who was watching him with serious eyes. 'How did you get over your parents' deaths? In your relationship?' He saw the surprise on Connor's face and realised there was no point in pretending he didn't know. 'Callie told me you're expecting. Congratulations.'

'Thanks.' Connor paused, as though trying to gather his thoughts, and then he said, 'I'm sure you know that losing our parents broke both of us.' He rubbed at the back of his neck. 'When I found out Elizabeth was pregnant it scared me. I don't know how to be a father, and I was terrified of caring about her, about our baby, and then losing them. And then I realised that going through life being scared wasn't living. I thought about coming home to Elizabeth, to our child, and I realised my parents would have *wanted* that for me. They wanted me to live, to be happy.'

Blake thought about how he'd imagined the same thing, and how it had thrown him into a panic. 'And that was it?'

'Pretty much.' Connor shoved his hand back into his pocket. 'I'm still scared of losing them. I still don't know how I'll be a father. But the thought of not being with them, of *not* being a father, scares me more.'

Something shifted for Blake as he realised he felt the same way. The misery he felt now because he had lost her—the irony of that gave him a headache—was testament to that. But he still couldn't shake off that one thing...

'You had a father to learn from.'

'We all do. Even if they aren't perfect,' Connor continued when Blake opened his mouth to interrupt. 'We learn from them. We learn what to do and, sometimes more importantly, we learn what *not* to do. And we should have a partner to help us through it.' He smiled slightly. 'It's not so scary when you realise you're not alone. Unless, of course, you choose to be.'

He stopped, and then nodded at Blake.

'I think I'll head home now. And by the way...' Blake looked at Connor. 'I don't care if you're my boss. If you hurt her again I'll kick your butt.'

Blake smiled wanly in response, and then sat down heavily at his desk. Connor had a point. With Brent, Blake had tried to be there as much as possible, and he'd thought he had succeeded until the divorce. It was still a sore point for him, the fact that he couldn't be there for Brent now. One he had used when he'd decided he couldn't give Callie the family she needed.

She would be an amazing mother, he thought. She was caring—passionately so. And she would sacrifice her own happiness before letting anything happen to the people she cared about. He could only imagine what she'd do for her child, for her family. She would never leave them—not for one moment...

She would *never* leave, Blake realised. If Callie had any choice in the matter she wouldn't leave the people she loved. But *he* had left. He'd left her, failed her, disappointed her, lost her. All the things he'd wanted to protect her—

and himself—from had happened, because he'd chosen to leave the woman he loved.

The realisation hit him like a bomb, and he leaned forward, bracing his arms on his knees. He loved her. And he had hurt her. So much so that the woman he knew in his heart would never leave the person she loved—*him*—had left. Because he had left her first. He'd done the very thing she'd been afraid of. He'd shown her that opening up to him had been a mistake.

Convincing her to take him back would mean she'd have to trust that he wouldn't leave again. And how could he do so when he'd already left?

The weight on his shoulders nearly crushed him.

Callie's heart broke over and over again each time she thought about it—which felt like every second of every day.

She had taken the week off work, which no one had questioned, despite the fact that she hadn't taken any time off since she'd started—because she couldn't bear to see Blake every day. Not when there was a hole in her chest where her heart was supposed to be.

She knew the pieces lay somewhere, broken in her chest, and would no doubt remind her of their brokenness when she saw him. She would forget, just for a second, about the fact that he had left her and she would run into his arms, feel his warmth, smell the comforting musk of his cologne.

And then she would break when she realised that would never happen again.

She shrugged her shoulders and forced herself to breathe as she walked into the hotel on Friday. Kate had called, telling her that a young honeymooning couple had begged her to arrange a tour for them, and since Kate had no idea what to do she'd called Callie. Her favourite tours were those she organised for honeymooners—they were always so happy to be with one another it was infectious—so she'd reluctantly agreed to come in.

Even though she didn't want to see the man who'd broken her heart. The man who, according to her brother, was a negotiation tsar.

Of course she was happy that the negotiations were going well. But somehow it just didn't seem important any more. So she would just focus on what she'd come to do.

Kate had told her the couple wanted to see Table Mountain at sunset. That would be in an hour, giving her enough time to introduce herself and travel there with her guests. And to remember that the last time she had been up there had been with Blake.

She stopped when he materialised in front of her. And blinked just to make sure she wasn't imagining things. That she wasn't dreaming of him again.

'Callie.'

'Blake.'

She nodded, and hated it that her body heated at the memory of his. Even worse, that her heart still longed for him.

'I've missed you around here.'

'I've...er...' She cleared her throat. 'I've been on leave.'

'I know.' He put his hands in his pockets. 'I was hoping we could talk.'

'Yes, well...let's pretend you've left already, when there won't be any more talking between us,' she said, and then tried to walk past him.

But she stopped—as did her heart—when he placed a hand on her arm.

'Callie, please. I have to tell you something.'

She looked up at him, and though her heart urged her to agree her mind warned her not to. And for once she chose to listen.

'I think it would be best if we didn't speak any more.'

Their eyes locked for a moment, and then he let go of her arm.

'Okay.'

She nodded and walked away with an aching heart and the sinking feeling that this might be the last time she spoke to her boss.

To the man she loved.

CHAPTER EIGHTEEN

'AND IF YOU look over there you'll see Camps Bay Beach and the Atlantic Ocean. Beautiful, isn't it?'

Callie pointed out the area for her guests, and watched the sun cast its orange glow over the city, grateful that Cape Town was showcasing its romance for the couple. She smiled and walked to the other side of the mountain, giving them privacy. And giving herself time to think, to grieve for the man she would have loved to share the experience of sunset on the mountain with.

'I don't think I've ever seen anything quite as beautiful in my life.'

Callie heard the words and for a brief moment wondered if she had conjured him up again. But when she turned around Blake was standing in front of her, looking directly at her.

She squared her shoulders. 'What are you doing here?'

'I came to talk. I thought that you would have no choice on a mountain.' He smiled slightly.

She bit her lip, feeling the heat of tears threaten. Why couldn't he just leave her be?

'How did you know I was here?'

'Kate. Connor. A number of other people who gladly offered me the information when they realised we were together.'

'You told them that?'

He took a step closer. 'I did. I wanted them to know how serious I am about the talk we're going to have.'

Her heart ached with longing, with heartbreak. The combination left her a little breathless.

'I have guests here, Blake' She gestured to the couple. 'I don't think I'll have much time to talk.'

'That's okay. They're with me.'

It took Callie a moment to process that. 'What do you mean, they're with you?' She repeated the words slowly, hoping it would help her make sense of it.

'I mean I asked some friends of mine to request a tour. I knew you wouldn't come if it wasn't for your guests, so I called in a favour.'

His eyes were so serious, so hopeful, that her indignation faltered. And her heart wondered what was so important that he'd had to pull strings to see her. She turned to the couple, who waved gaily at her, and felt the ends of her mouth twitch. And then she noticed that the mountain had cleared in the moments she'd spent with Blake, and that her pretend guests were also moving in the direction of the cable car.

'Blake, I think the last cable car of the day is leaving.' She said the words even as her mind told her that it wasn't supposed to happen for at least another hour.

'No, there's one more. For us.'

She looked at him in surprise. 'How did you…?' But she trailed off when she saw the determination and the slight desperation in his eyes. 'You did all this for a moment alone with me?'

He nodded and took her hand. Tingles went up her arm as he led her to the end of the mountain where it overlooked the ocean. They stood there like that for a while, and then he spoke.

'I've been trying to find the words to tell you how sorry I am since the moment I realised how wrong I was.' His hand tightened on hers, and then he stuffed it in a pocket. 'I did things so poorly. I made decisions for you, for us, without talking to you. I let my fears become more important than my need for you.'

He turned to her and she resisted the urge to comfort him.

'And I *do* need you—more than I've needed anything else in the world.'

Her lips trembled and she took a deep breath, trying to figure out what to say. But he continued before she had a chance to respond.

'I have been so miserable since you walked out through the door of that office. I justified my actions, and cursed them, and I went back and forth doing that for a long time. And then I spoke to Connor, and I knew I was wrong.'

'You *what*?'

Blake gave her a nervous smile. 'He caught me moping in the office and offered me some advice.' Then he grew serious. 'My whole life I've tried to avoid disappointing the people I care about. I thought that by being in control I could do that. And then you came along, and I've never felt less in control in my life.'

He exhaled, looked out to the ocean.

'I was falling for you even when I was trying not to. Then we got to know one another, and I knew the falling would never stop. Not with you.'

He looked back at her and she felt her breath catch.

'It scared me, Callie. I've *never* felt the way I feel about you. And I began to think about how I'd lost my mother, how much it would break me if you left. I thought about Brent, about disappointing him, and how it would hurt if I did that to you. How I had failed in my marriage, with my family, and how I wouldn't survive if I failed *you*. If I failed to give you the family you deserved.'

He reached a hand up and touched her cheek, and without even realising it Callie leaned into it. 'I thought the only way to prevent that was to leave. I couldn't break you, disappoint you or fail you if I left. But by doing that I did *all* those things, and I'm so, *so* sorry.'

His voice broke and Callie took a step forward, wanting to comfort him.

'I know, Blake. I know that you thought you were doing the right thing.' She looked up at him, drew a ragged breath. 'I was scared, too. I realised I was in love with you but I had no commitment from you besides the things we'd shared. I convinced myself that it was enough. I convinced myself that loving you would be okay even if I lost you. *Because* I loved you.'

She couldn't stop the tears now, even if she wanted to.

'And then I *did* lose you, and it hurt more than I could imagine because you *chose* to leave me.'

'I'm sorry.'

He pulled her into his arms, and the pieces of her heart stirred.

'For everything. I can't imagine ever hurting you like that again.' He drew back. 'I'm not going to leave, Callie. I will *never* leave you.'

'Why should I believe you?' She whispered the words that whirled around in her mind, keeping her from accepting what he was saying.

'Because this week has been the worst of my life.' He gently brushed a piece of hair from her face. 'And it's made me realise that I want to give you the family you want. I want to create a legacy with you.' He tipped her chin up so that she could look at him. 'Believe me, because I'm telling you I won't leave you. Trust me.'

'Why?'

'Because I love you, Callie. And if you still love me let me prove to you for the rest of my life that I will stay with you. That I will fight for you. For *us*.'

And with those words—the words she'd dreamed about hearing from him—her broken heart healed and filled.

'I still love you.'

He smiled tenderly at her. 'I hoped you would.'

'So much that it scares me.'

She looked at him, and the agreement in his eyes comforted her.

'I am, too. So let's be scared together.'

He got down on one knee and Callie's heart pounded and melted at the same time. Suddenly she became aware that the sun had set and that their only source of light now came from candles and lanterns, all over the top of the mountain. And then she saw the ring—a large diamond sparkling brightly up at her surrounded by what seemed like a thousand smaller ones—and she realised Blake was offering her the biggest assurance he could that he was staying.

'Will you marry me, Callie McKenzie?'

'You want to *marry* me?'

'I really, really do.'

She laughed, and nodded, and was swept up into his arms before she had a chance to wipe the tears from her cheeks. Her hand shook as he slid the ring on her finger, and then he kissed her, and any remnants of fear she'd had disappeared. The kiss was filled with all the longing they'd felt for one another since they'd been apart, with the joy of their future together, with the heat of their passion. And when they finally drew apart they were both breathing heavily.

'We're engaged,' she said when she'd recovered, and she looked at the ring on her finger.

'We are.' He smiled and drew her back against him. 'I'm

thinking we should get married at the hotel. A rooftop sunset wedding could be pretty amazing.'

'I think that would be perfect.' And then she realised she hadn't even asked him about the deal. 'Did we get an investor?'

'We did. Marco signed the papers a few hours ago. He's going to be a silent investor. Although he *did* say he will still actively try to poach you.' He waited as she laughed, and then said, 'I have so many plans for the hotels. I can't wait to do it all with you.'

'So I'm going to help with the Owen legacy, huh?' She smiled and drew his hands tighter around her waist as they looked down at Cape Town at night.

'Yeah. Which means it's probably only fair that I help you with *your* legacy.' He looked down at her with a glint of amusement in his eyes. 'Family, right? I think the best way for me to show my commitment to you is if we start on that as soon as possible.'

Her laughter rang out on the top of Table Mountain, and for the first time since her parents had died Callie finally felt whole.

EPILOGUE

'ARE YOU READY for that?'

Blake gestured towards the chubby toddler who was steadily making his way over the grass in their backyard to his father, knocking down every toy they'd put out for him. He gave a happy gurgle when Connor picked him up and spun him around, and Callie smiled when she saw the absolute love in her brother's eyes as he did so.

'I keep thinking about a little girl with your eyes, or a boy with your hair. And every time I do I fall in love with the little person in my imagination.' Callie snuggled closer to her husband—she would never tire of the thrill that went through her when she thought that Blake was her *husband*—and kicked at the ground so that the swing seat they were sitting on would move.

She couldn't quite believe they were already celebrating her nephew's first birthday. Tyler was such a little ball of happiness, with his father's steady presence and his mother's zest for life, that it made her excited to see what combination her own child would be.

She resisted the urge to rub her stomach and imagined how happy her parents would have been if they'd been there. They would have loved enjoying their grandson in their home—the home that she and Blake now shared and had gladly offered to host Tyler's birthday at—and feeling the comfort of family. Connor and Elizabeth hadn't wanted a big party for their son when he wouldn't remember it, so instead they'd just organised a day when the McKenzies and the Owens—she *and* her brother had married within a few months of each other—could spend time together.

Callie couldn't think of a more perfect way to celebrate. Or to share her very exciting news.

'What if they have *your* eyes or hair?' Blake said, distracting her from her thoughts.

He pulled her in and she felt the warmth right down to her toes, before it quickly turned into a sizzle the moment he began to run his fingers up and down her bare arm.

'I suppose we'll have to accept them as they are. It won't be *their* fault after all.' She gave a dramatic sigh, and smiled when Blake laughed.

She loved seeing him like this—relaxed, happy, content. He had become a part of their family so smoothly she sometimes felt that he had always been a part of it. And she wondered where the man who had feared family so much had disappeared to.

'Look how beautiful it is,' Blake said, and gestured to the mountain and the ocean they could see from the swing seat. She smiled when she saw the peace settle over him, the way it always did when he looked out onto that view.

'Are *you* ready for it?' she asked quietly, not wanting to be overheard by her brother and sister-in-law.

'What?' He followed her eyes with his as she looked at her nephew, and then settled them back on her. 'I was ready the moment I met you. And then again when you told me you'd marry me. I believe I was willing to start right at that moment.'

She laughed. 'You were. But there were a few things we needed to sort out first.'

He rolled his eyes—a clear indication of a man who had

heard the words before. 'Yes, I know. We had to set up our operations for the hotels from Cape Town, and then we had to support Connor and Elizabeth during their wedding and Tyler's birth, and then we had our own wedding.'

'Exactly. Points to you for remembering.' She grinned at the amusement in his eyes, and then felt it soften to a smile. 'But all that's done now.'

'Yes—thankfully. So I don't have to be reminded about it all the time.'

She felt her lips twitch. 'No, Blake, all that's done now.'

'I heard you the first time.' Blake frowned at her, and then sat up a little straighter. 'You mean we can start trying for a family?'

'I mean that it's happened without us really trying.' She whispered the words, unsure, even though she knew that this was what they both wanted. 'I think my body knew about our timeline, too.'

He took a moment to process her words, and then whispered back, 'Do you think you're pregnant?'

'I *know* I am. The doctor called yesterday.'

She had barely finished saying the words before Blake pulled her into his arms, needing the contact with her more than he'd thought possible. His heart was exploding, and it was a long time before he let Callie go.

'Hey, none of that in front of my kid.'

Blake heard Connor's amusement and smiled, unable even to pretend that he was upset. 'Well, I think expressions of love are important. Maybe we should start making notes of all the things we've learnt from Connor about what to do and what not to do before *our* baby gets here, honey.'

Connor's eyes widened. 'You're *pregnant*?'

Blake laughed, and thought he had never felt this good in his life. 'No, not me personally—but Callie is.'

The announcement was met with laughter and congratulations, and even though he accepted the hugs of his family, even though he toasted his unborn child, he couldn't take his eyes off Callie. She was radiant, he thought, and saw her blushing every time she caught him looking at her.

It made him love her even more.

When Connor and Elizabeth had left, Callie and Blake moved back to the swing seat in the backyard. It would be a special place to him for ever, he thought. This house where he had finally found a home, where he had finally found himself be a part of a family. This yard where he had celebrated his godson's first birthday. And now this swing seat, where he had found out he was going to be a father.

'How have you made every dream of mine come true?' he asked, his heart filled with the love that overwhelmed him every time he looked at her.

She gave him that soft smile of hers and moved closer to him. 'We've made each other's dreams come true.' She laid a hand on his cheek. 'You're going to make the best father, Blake Owen.'

'Our child will have the best parents in the world.'

And then he kissed her, and knew without a doubt that he had finally found his home.

* * * * *

"If you know Juliette so well, why did you break in?"

"She was supposed to leave me a key, but I couldn't find it."

He squinted at her. "Where was she supposed to leave it?"

"Under a planter. She wasn't specific, and, as I said, I couldn't find it. That's when I saw the open window—"

Ethan held up his hand, silencing her.

"Just give me your cell phone."

"I don't have it on my person."

His mouth twisted in a dubious expression and he grunted. "On your *person*? I've been giving you the benefit of the doubt. If you don't want to cooperate, I can call Joyce back and we can sort out what's what down at the station."

He held out his hand again, this time moving his fingers in a "give it to me" gesture.

"It's in the car." Now he was starting to irritate her. "I'm certainly not hiding it." She ran her hands down the silhouette of her body to emphasize that she was wearing a T-shirt and a rather snug skirt that didn't leave room for secret pockets.

When she realized that Ethan Campbell's gaze was meandering the same path her own hands had traced she regretted issuing the invitation.

* * *

Celebration, TX:
Love is just a celebration away…

THE COWBOY'S
RUNAWAY BRIDE

BY
NANCY ROBARDS THOMPSON

First Published in Great Britain 2017
By Mills & Boon, an imprint of HarperCollins*Publishers*
1 London Bridge Street, London, SE1 9GF

© 2016 Nancy Robards Thompson

ISBN: 978-0-263-92266-0

23-0117

Our policy is to use papers that are natural, renewable and recyclable products and made from wood grown in sustainable forests. The logging and manufacturing processes conform to the legal environmental regulations of the country of origin.

Printed and bound in Spain
by CPI, Barcelona

National bestselling author **Nancy Robards Thompson** holds a degree in journalism. She worked as a newspaper reporter until she realized reporting "just the facts" bored her silly. Now that she has much more content to report to her muse, Nancy loves writing women's fiction and romance full-time. Critics have deemed her work "funny, smart and observant." She resides in Florida with her husband and daughter. You can reach her at www.nancyrobardsthompson.com and Facebook.com/nancyrobardsthompsonbooks.

This book is dedicated to Katherine Garbera
for helping me dream up the heroine of
The Cowboy's Runaway Bride
and for your unwavering friendship.
Kathy, you're the sister of my heart.

Chapter One

Lady Chelsea Ashford Alden cast a wary glance over her shoulder as she approached the front door of the gray stone cottage.

The place looked dark and formidable—cold and utterly unwelcoming—like it didn't want to be friends. It was so contrary to her university roommate Juliette Lowell's vibrant personality. Hard to believe Juliette lived here. However, in the dark, Chelsea could see the numbers on the house matched the address her friend had given her.

The fingernail of moon hanging high in the inky Texas sky wasn't her friend, either. It did nothing to light the porch. Then again, maybe the darkness was her best ally, cloaking her in shadows, hiding her from the monster that had sent her running to Juliette for refuge in the first place.

Life as the Earl of Downing's daughter didn't offer much latitude or forgiveness. In fact, sometimes it seemed as if people were standing back and waiting for her to fall. When she didn't, others were looking for opportunities to pull the rug out from under her or stick out a leg to trip her up.

Which was why she was in Texas.

She was tired of the limelight; tired of the pomp and pretense; tired of people using her; tired of watching her life play out on the covers of the British tabloids. Because God knew what the paparazzi couldn't confirm, they invented or they paid off acquaintances to create stories for them. She had experienced that compliments of a reporter named Bertie Veal, who had stalked her since university.

Most recently, he'd colluded with her ex to ruin her life. There was no worse betrayal than when someone you trusted in the most intimate way sold your most vulnerable moment to the press.

Chelsea tried to blink away the image, but it was burned into her brain. Intimate footage she didn't know existed until it had appeared on the tabloid's website.

She shuddered at the thought as she lifted the welcome mat in search of the key Juliette had left for her. The video had set off a humiliating chain reaction, the worst of which was her father's embarrassment and disappointment.

The look on his face had been devastating. It had

cut her to the quick when he and her mother had told
her she was on her own to solve the problem, that it
was best for all if she distanced herself from the family until she'd cleaned up her mess—as if by virtue
of simply leaving the country, London's upper crust
would forget she was their daughter.

At least they would pretend to forget. In the meantime, it was very clear that Chelsea was cordially invited to stay away until she'd gotten her life together.

The first step in Plan Damage Control was to make
freelance trash reporter Bertie Veal leave her alone.
The only way she would accomplish that was to disappear. Celebration, Texas, was the perfect place to
hide because it was the last place in the world anyone
would think to look for her.

No one would recognize her here. Most Americans seemed interested in the Buckingham Palace
royals. They didn't care about the antics of the two-
bit daughter of an obscure earl. American tabloids
were all about Charles and Camilla, Wills and Kate,
or movie stars spotted without makeup and rap sing-
ers caught cheating.

Chelsea switched on her phone's flashlight app
and shone it on the wooden floorboards, but found
nothing.

She tried the door, but it was locked. Juliette was
a wedding planner and she was in San Antonio on
business this weekend. She'd made it clear that Chelsea was welcome and apologized for not being there
when she arrived, but duty called.

After a wedding reception Jules had dreamed up

had been featured in Southern Living, her business had skyrocketed.

Chelsea was happy for her friend and glad that at least one of them had her life together. She assured Juliette she could manage, and they'd bid their temporary goodbyes with promises of a long catch-up as soon as Juliette got home.

The only logical hiding places for a key on the front porch were the doormat and a rocking chair. Again, she used the flashlight feature on her phone to search around the chair, but she came away empty-handed.

Perhaps Jules had left it on the back porch. They'd been in such a hurry when they'd talked that only now did it dawn on Chelsea that Jules hadn't mentioned a specific location for the key—only that she would leave it on the porch. Or maybe Chelsea had misunderstood. How hard could it be to find a hidden key?

The flash of headlights warned of an approaching car. Chelsea sank back into the shadows, deciding she was grateful for the cloak of darkness that concealed her. As the vehicle continued to move down the road she breathed a sigh of relief.

After the car was gone, she made her way to the back of the house away from the street to see if she could locate another hiding spot for the key.

When Chelsea and Juliette had roomed together at university, the two had weathered stronger forces than Bertie Veal. Well, nothing worse than discovering Hadden Hastings, her ex-boyfriend, had sold a video he'd secretly recorded of Chelsea and him having sex, but she and Jules had gotten into their share of trouble over the years. If they hadn't been knee-deep in it together, they'd gone to great lengths to cover for each other. That was what made them such good friends.

When Chelsea had phoned Juliette and told her she was in trouble and had given her the bare-bones rundown of Hadden's betrayal, she'd insisted Chelsea seek refuge with her in Celebration.

Chelsea and Juliette had both known Hadden Hastings at university. He'd been part of their group of friends. But Chelsea hadn't dated him until the year after they'd graduated.

When she ran into him after she got home from a year of doing relief aid work in Africa, she'd seen him with different eyes. He'd suddenly become datable. He'd been fun and funny and romantic and sympathetic to her post-university quandary—after all, he couldn't seem to find his place in the world, either.

He'd charmed her and she'd fallen for him.

He was the last person she'd ever thought would secretly record their lovemaking, much less sell the footage to Bertie Veal. The betrayal hurt as much as the humiliation of having a "sex tape" published for the entire world to view. The press ate it up because there was nothing quite as titillating as a noble scandal.

Chelsea lifted up the mat at the back door and ran her hand over the rough surface of the wooden floorboard.

Nothing. No key there, either.

Then she lifted up the various flowerpots and tipped the planters, all to no avail. As a last resort, she called Juliette, but the call went straight to voice mail.

"Hello, Jules. It's Chelsea. I'm so sorry to bother you because you're probably knee-deep in first dances and cake cuttings right now. But I made it to your house and I can't locate the key. Please give me a quick ring when you have a moment. It's probably in some painfully obvious place that I'm not seeing. You know me." She forced a laugh. "Anyhow, I hope the wedding is going well. I can't wait to see you. Toodles, love."

She disconnected the call and was just about ready to give up and return to the car when she noticed that a small window near the back door was open a few inches.

It wasn't optimal, but it was a way inside.

The window was small—tiny, in fact—and a bit high off the ground. And why had she chosen to wear a skirt today? Well, it didn't matter now. It wasn't as if anyone was lurking about, hoping to catch a glimpse of her knickers.

Chelsea stared up at the window and sighed.

It appeared to be her last recourse. She could either make it work or wait in the car until Juliette called her back. It was getting chilly out here. She'd much rather wait snug and safe inside.

She dragged over a patio chair made out of fat plastic pipe with a woven nylon seat base and positioned it under the window. Kicking off her wedge sandals, she tucked her phone and rental car key into one shoe and climbed up onto the chair. It wobbled a bit and she grabbed the window ledge to steady herself.

Chelsea was a solid five foot nine inches in bare feet. Hoisting herself up and inside that tiny window would be a challenge, but this was no time to fret. She couldn't overthink it. The sooner she got inside the house, the sooner she could relax.

She got to work on removing the screen. It took more effort than she thought it would. In the process, she broke her right index fingernail into the quick, which smarted like bloody hell. The pain had her performing a little jig, which caused the chair to rock unsteadily. But a moment later Chelsea persevered and popped the window screen out of its track. It clattered as she dropped it onto the porch floor.

Now it was time for the most challenging feat of the evening: stuffing herself through the small opening. The window looked into a small bathroom and was positioned just above the bathtub. A double swag shower curtain framed the tub. Beyond that she could make out a commode and a pedestal sink. The door to the room seemed to open into a hallway, but that was all she could see in the dim light.

With one deep breath, Chelsea used all the arm strength she could muster to pull herself up. As she labored, she managed to get a foothold on the house's cold, gray stones and used them to walk herself up the wall.

She just might pull this off.

With one last grunt and upward push, she managed to tip herself inside the window…sort of… During the effort, her foot caught on the chair—how the bloody hell had that happened? If she'd tried to do that on purpose she wouldn't have been able to. Nonetheless, the chair seemed to be attached to her foot. With a swift kick and a smart shake, she managed to free her lower limb. The chair crashed to the ground, echoing in the otherwise silent night, and leaving her precariously half in, half out of the window, faltering like a teeter-totter trying to find its balance.

With her arse hanging out in the most undignified manner, she was sure there was a life metaphor hidden somewhere in this situation. But this was no time to ponder it. She was going to fall one way or the other, and after all the work it had taken to get this far, she wasn't about to start over.

With one last forward thrust, Chelsea tumbled inside. As she twisted to break her fall, the bathroom light flicked on. Chelsea screamed as she registered the huge man hulking in the threshold.

Based on the racket he'd heard, Ethan Campbell thought he might have cornered a couple of raccoons that had fallen down the chimney or gotten into Juliette Lowell's house through an open window. The last thing he'd expected was to catch a tall, gorgeous blonde breaking and entering.

But there she was looking guilty as hell, standing in the bathtub, tugging up on the neckline of her blouse and smoothing her bright pink skirt into place. The open window was a yawning black hole behind her.

With her wide eyes and tousled long hair, the Beatles' song, "She Came in Through The Bathroom Window," suddenly took on a whole new meaning. Ethan tried to ignore how pretty she was and stepped forward to show the woman he meant business.

There had been some burglaries in Celebration over the past few weeks. Was this woman part of a ring?

"What the hell do you think you're doing?" he asked.

He didn't wait for her to answer and he didn't take his eyes off her as he reached into his jeans' pocket for his phone to call the sheriff. She was barefoot, he noticed. He also registered her long, lean, tanned legs and the barely there hint of cleavage that winked at him as she crossed her arms.

He forced his gaze back to her face. She stared at him, big-eyed and mute. She looked scared, like a cornered cub. He had a hard time believing Goldilocks was here to ransack the place. Nonetheless, she wasn't supposed to be here.

No one was.

So what was she doing?

When he'd noticed the strange car parked in the Juliette Lowell's driveway as he'd headed home from the stables, Ethan decided to investigate.

Juliette was in San Antonio facilitating one of those fancy weddings people paid her good money to plan. That was why Ethan had decided to stop and investigate.

His neighbor kept him apprised of her travel schedule and that's why he knew damn good and well *no one* was supposed to be in this house tonight.

"I'll ask you again," he said, waiting to hear what she said before he dialed the sheriff. "You want to tell me what you're doing in here, sis?"

The woman stared back at him silently. Those huge eyes of hers—were they blue or green?—still locked with his.

"No?" he asked. "Okay. Maybe you'd rather talk to the cops?"

That broke her silence. "No, don't call the police. Please."

Did she have an accent? He couldn't tell. Might just be nerves.

She held up her hands surrender-style.

"Well, then you'd better start talking—and fast. Are you alone?"

Aw, hell. He was such an idiot. She could have accomplices. They might already be in the house. She could've been the lookout. Albeit, a noisy one. But still…

Ethan glanced in the mirror, which provided a side view into the dim hallway, and listened hard, trying to detect sound or movement, anything that indicated they weren't alone.

He didn't hear a thing.

Yeah, wouldn't it be just like him to meet his maker after being distracted by a pretty face. It wouldn't be the first time. Well, figuratively, anyway.

As a safeguard, he placed the call to 911.

"No! Please don't. My name is Chelsea—Chelsea

Allen. I'm here to visit my friend, Juliette Lowell.
Please don't call the police. I can assure you that's
not necessary. Just call Juliette. She'll tell you I'm
welcome here. *Please*. Hang up. We don't need to
involve the officials."

This time there was no trace of an accent in her
voice. He must've imagined it before. Because now
her words were crisp and enunciated. And panicked.

And she was so pretty.

Oh, for the love of God almighty...

She did know Juliette's name. Which didn't automatically guarantee that she was a friend. She might
have known the house would be empty tonight and
the place would be a good target.

Juliette's business was just starting to take off.
She was even getting some press about it. Who knew
what kind of riffraff news of her success might at-
tract? Though Chelsea Allen didn't look like riffraff.

"Please hang up," she pleaded again.

Ethan shook his head and gestured to the window
behind her. "When you visit friends, do you always
enter through the bathroom?"

Her eyes flashed before she glanced over her
shoulder in the direction he pointed. "Of course not.
It's just that…"

A frustrated little growl gobbled up the rest of her
words. Ethan half expected her to stamp her foot or to
turn around and scale the wall in an attempt to leave
the way she came in.

But instead, she put her hands on her hips and apparently tried to turn the tables on him. "If Juliette is

not at home, what business do *you* have in her house? Who are *you*?"

He frowned at her tone. "I'm the one who's asking the questions here, and as soon as the sheriff arrives, he will take over for me."

"No! I'm sorry. Please hang up. I mean, you do realize that calling emergency services could keep them from responding to a true emergency, don't you? Just call Juliette from your cell. If you're in her house you should have her number. Right? She will tell you that we're friends and that I'm absolutely welcome here."

Ethan hesitated. She had a point. But before he could disconnect, the operator picked up.

"This is 911. What is your emergency?"

Chapter Two

"Hey, Joyce, it's Ethan Campbell," he said. "False alarm on that 911."

Chelsea finally drew in a breath after she heard him retract the police call. *Ethan Campbell.* So that was his name. Chelsea racked her brain trying to recall if she'd ever heard Juliette mention him. Campbell... Sounded familiar. But the way he was glaring at her as he talked to the sheriff's dispatcher addled her mind and made it difficult to remember her own name, much less her college friend's list of boyfriends past.

"Nope. Everything's under control, but hang tight. I'll call you back if the situation changes."

Pinned by his midnight blue gaze, she stood frozen, weighing her options. At least she had enough sense to realize most of the choices sponsored by the

fight-or-flight adrenaline rush weren't very practical…
or smart—like grabbing the phone out of the guy's
hand and tossing it into the toilet or scaling the wall
and going out the way she'd come in.

Both plans spelled disaster.

If she did the grab and flush, Ethan Campbell
would probably lock her in the bathroom and call
the sheriff from Juliette's landline. The last thing she
needed was for the police to show up. Because where
the police went, media usually followed.

Of course, if he locked her in the bath, she could
climb back out the window. But she wasn't a gym-
nast or a contortionist. So she wouldn't be very fast.
She wasn't even remotely athletic. It had taken forever and every ounce of strength she'd possessed to
hoist herself up and climb in the window. Her muscles
were still shaky after being taxed the first time. She'd
be deluding herself if she thought she was capable of
using that route for a speedy and successful getaway.

Bloody hell, if she did escape, where would she go?

A chase would ensue; the cops would be on her
heels.

Maybe she could simply push past Ethan and make
a run out the front door. That seemed like the least
shady option. But there was no getting around him. He
was a big guy. Being tackled and held by those rugby-
player arms and pinned by those shoulders might have
been quite nice under other circumstances. But right
now his considerable bulk filled the doorway, blocking the only other viable exit, eliminating that option.

"Yeah, I thought I'd caught the burglar at the Lowell place," he drawled into the phone.

Burglar? Did she really look like someone who sneaked into homes and robbed people?

"Turns out it's a woman claiming to be a friend of Juliette's. Sit tight. I'm going to call her to confirm… No. I don't need backup. I got this."

Finally, they were getting somewhere.

He seemed to be quite familiar with her friend. Against her better judgment, Chelsea wondered why Juliette *hadn't* talked about this Ethan Campbell. He was tall and rugged and handsome—if you liked big, brooding, broad-shouldered men with Texas drawls.

And who in her right mind wouldn't find a guy like him attractive?

He'd be even better if he wasn't holding her hostage.

She reminded herself of that, and the fact that he seemed to be pretty well connected to the local authorities, which could be a problem. A *big problem* if he pressed her for personal information. That would mean she'd need to leave again because she couldn't take the chance of word getting out and Bertie tracking her here. Celebration was too small of a town to hide from a bloodhound like him. She was running out of options of where to go. Unless she wanted to hole up someplace alone. If she blew it here, it meant she'd have to go home.

That wasn't an option. At least not right now.

"If her story doesn't check out, I'll call you back and have you send the sheriff out."

Ethan was nodding at something the dispatcher was saying on the other end of the line.

"Joyce…" More talking. More nodding. "No. Joyce…It's fine…"

"Yes, I'm sure…No, I don't see anyone else with her. She's alone." He turned his gaze back on Chelsea. "Are you alone?"

Chelsea nodded and instantly regretted it. Maybe she shouldn't have said that. But if she hadn't they surely would've dispatched the authorities.

"Her car's out in the driveway…No. I didn't get the license number. It was dark when I got here. I wanted to make sure the perimeter was secured first."

Was the guy a wannabe cop or something?

More listening. More nodding. Chelsea strained to see if she could hear what the person on the other end of the line was saying, but all she could discern was a low hum of an indistinct feminine voice.

Ethan backed into the hallway and flicked on the overhead light. Now Chelsea could see a collage of black-and-white photographs housed in a multipaned black frame hanging on the wall behind him. One of the pictures was from Juliette's days at St. Andrew's, and as if by some miracle, there was a shot of her and Juliette and a group of their schoolmates huddled together at a Sussex rugby match.

"Good idea," he snarled into the phone. He turned to Chelsea and held out his hand. "Give me your cell."

"Why do you want my cell phone?" she asked.

Still pressing his phone to one ear, Ethan gestured with his free hand. "Phone."

Chelsea pointed to the photo behind him. Ethan squinted at her and shook his head.

"Look at the photograph behind you," she said, nodding in that direction.

When Ethan didn't immediately turn around, Chelsea said, "There's a photograph of Juliette and me on the wall over your right shoulder. If you'll simply turn around, you'll see I'm telling the truth."

With one last wary glance at Chelsea, Ethan cast a quick look behind him. He did a double take. "Hold on a sec, Joyce. Actually, I'll call you back if I need you."

After he disconnected the call, he said, "If you know Juliette so well, why did you break in?"

"She was supposed to leave me a key, but I couldn't find it."

He squinted at her. "Where was she supposed to leave it?"

"Under the doormat or someplace. She wasn't specific, and, as I said, I couldn't find it. That's when I saw the open window—"

Ethan held up his hand, silencing her.

"Give me your cell phone."

"I don't have it on my person at the moment."

His mouth twisted in a dubious expression and he grunted. "On your *person*? I've been giving you the benefit of the doubt. If you don't want to cooperate, I can call Joyce back and we can sort out what's what down at the station."

He held out his hand again, this time moving his fingers in a give-it-to-me gesture.

"It's outside on the back porch in one of my sandals." Now he was starting to irritate her. "I'm certainly not hiding it." She ran her hands down the silhouette of her body to emphasize that she was wearing a T-shirt and a rather snug skirt that didn't leave room for secret pockets.

When she realized that Ethan Campbell's gaze was meandering the same path her own hands had traced, she regretted issuing the invitation.

She cleared her throat and crossed her arms over the front of her body. "I tried to call Juliette, but she didn't answer. I left a message and then I saw the open window. I took off my sandals and set down my phone and car key before I came in through the window. If you'll check outside, you'll find everything."

She shrugged a jerky little motion to indicate her annoyance.

"Wouldn't it be better to just call Juliette's number from your own phone, anyway? I'm surprised you're not afraid that I might call one of my henchmen to come and break me out of here."

His brow shot up and she realized she'd probably said the wrong thing.

"You have henchmen?"

"That was supposed to be a joke."

"How about some identification?" he said, obviously not amused.

Great. Just great. If he saw the name on her ID, the cat could very possibly be out of the bag. Especially if he called the police back and gave her name to the sheriff. If they ran her ID through one of those fancy contraptions that compiled reports on people's backgrounds, she might as well leave right now.

"It's in my purse, which is in the car. I'm happy to go get it."

"Nice try," he said. "If I march you outside to get it, there's a chance you'll run. If I leave you alone to go look for it myself, you'll leave."

He lifted his phone and started pressing numbers.

"No, don't. Please don't—"

"I'm calling Juliette."

She let out her breath on a sigh. "I thought you were calling 911 again."

He didn't respond. Instead, he pressed the phone to his ear. She must've answered on the first couple of rings.

"Juliette, Ethan Campbell—"

He listened for a moment.

"Sorry to bother you—"

He nodded, opened his mouth to say something and closed it again.

Juliette always had been a talker. It was amusing to watch this tall, gruff, take-charge cowboy be silenced by her. How long would it take before he could get a word in?

If anyone else had been there she'd have wagered with them.

Alas, she was alone and had to enjoy the private audience to this amusing show. When Juliette got back into town, Chelsea fully intended to hug her friend just for being her—and, well, okay, for making

Ethan Campbell stammer as he tried to get a voice-hold in the conversation.

"Juliette—" he said. "Juliette—*Juliette*. Juliette—"

He held the phone away from his ear for a moment and looked up at the ceiling. Chelsea could hear her friend babbling on even though she couldn't tell exactly what she was saying.

Finally, Chelsea did the only thing she could. "Juliette, it's Chelsea!" she called in the loudest voice she could muster. "It's Chelsea *Allen*. Please tell this man you know me and I'm welcome in your home."

Even though Chelsea hadn't been able to understand exactly what Juliette had been talking about a moment ago, she could hear the dramatic silence on the line now and knew Juliette had heard her. She could only pray that Chelsea remembered the *code*.

Chelsea Allen was the name she'd used back in their university days when she wanted to lay low. Rather than unloading her full name, Lady Chelsea Ashford Alden, which always made people change. They treated humble, unassuming Chelsea *Allen* like a regular person. Not like the sister of a famous fashion designer or someone whose brother was likely to be the next prime minister. *Chelsea Allen* was a nobody, and nobody wanted anything from her. Sometimes it was just so much easier to keep things simple. It had been several years since she and Juliette had been out together and she'd played the Chelsea Allen card, but surely Juliette would remember. Of course she would.

Frowning even more pronounced than when he'd

first cornered her, Ethan put the phone back to his ear. "Juliette, do you know a woman named Chelsea Allen?"

Juliette was still talking. Ethan's gaze flicked to Chelsea. As he listened his frown faded to a scowl.

"Yes. She's right here. Standing in your hall bathroom. Yep…Sure…Yeah. Right here in your bathtub, to be exact…No, she's not taking a bath…I caught her coming in through the shower window…It's a long story…No, she's fully clothed…Juliette, listen to me. All I need to know is whether or not she's a friend of yours."

Chelsea couldn't help it. She laughed out loud.

Buggers, she was still in the bathtub. She steadied herself with one hand on the wall and stepped out of the tub onto the black-and-white-tile floor.

A moment later Ethan held out the phone to Chelsea. "Juliette wants to talk to you."

She couldn't resist a smug smile as she took the phone from him.

"Jules? Hi!"

The sound of Juliette's warm laughter emanated across the line. "Chelsea, oh, no! Oh, my gosh. I'm so sorry. I was supposed to leave a key for you. I completely forgot to set it out before I left. Obviously, I forgot to close the bathroom window, too."

"Jules, it's okay. Will you tell Deputy Dawg to stand down, please?"

"You always did know how to make an entrance."

"I know, right? But for future reference, I'd rather use the front door than an open window. Scaling walls isn't my best sport. Please tell Ethan it's okay for me to be here. He's about ready to have me hauled off to jail."

With the phone pressed up to her ear, she brushed past him because she was starting to feel a bit claustrophobic in the bathroom. As she made her exit, her shoulder grazed Ethan's very solid chest. If she hadn't found the guy so annoying, she might've found the sheer masculine bulk of him quite sexy.

"Oh, Ethan's bark is definitely worse than his bite. He's a warm and cuddly teddy bear once you get to know him."

Warm and cuddly? More like ripped and solid as steel.

"And you're speaking from experience, I presume?"

Juliette snorted. "Um, *no.* I'll tell you all about him later. For now, give him the phone and I'll tell him you're welcome to be there. Make yourself at home. Help yourself to anything. There's tea in the cupboard by the stove and I just froze the rest of a homemade lasagna. I'll be home tomorrow afternoon. We certainly have a lot to talk about."

Chelsea glanced at Ethan, who was not even trying to pretend he wasn't listening. There was no way she could tell Juliette that escaping from the mess that had become her life was going to be a lot harder than she thought. She'd already been forced into hiding, and on day one of hiding in Celebration, Texas, she'd nearly had a run-in with the authorities.

There was a long pause on the other end of the line

and Chelsea could virtually hear Juliette's wheels turning with unasked questions.

"We certainly do have a lot to talk about. I'll tell you when you get home." She locked gazes with Ethan. "In the meantime, will you please tell the teddy bear I'm welcome to stay?"

Ethan snorted. "Teddy bear?" But she ignored him.

"Thanks, Jules. I appreciate this so much."

Chelsea Allen was hiding something. That much was certain. Ethan didn't know what, but Chelsea had seemed jumpier than a box of bullfrogs on a trampoline.

It went beyond being startled after unexpectedly confronting someone inside a house she'd assumed was empty. His gut was telling him that the woman was hiding something, and his gut was rarely wrong.

But after Chelsea had finished talking to Juliette, she'd handed the phone back to Ethan, and Jules had told him in no uncertain terms that Chelsea was not only welcome at her place, but if she wanted to come and go through the bathroom window, too, that was her prerogative. That was the thing about Juliette Lowell; she was sweet and naive and tended to only see the best in people. That was exactly why Ethan intended to keep an eye on this Chelsea Allen.

At least she was easy on the eyes. It wouldn't be too big of a hardship. But since Juliette had given her blessing for Chelsea to stay, he'd have to continue his neighborly duty from afar.

After he'd hung up the phone, he'd gotten in his

truck, called Joyce back and reported that everything had checked out with Juliette. Then he'd headed to Murphy's Pub. The place he'd been headed to before he'd been waylaid by the strange car in Juliette's driveway. Tonight the Dallas Cowboys were duking it out with the Miami Dolphins and all he wanted to do was belly up to the bar and watch the game.

As he pulled open the pub's front door, he was met by the sound of cheers and hollers. He glanced at the big-screen TV over the bar. The Cowboys had landed a first down, setting up a first and goal situation.

He muttered an oath under his breath because he'd missed the play.

He'd intended to get here in plenty of time to order his dinner—the cheeseburger platter with the works and a nonalcoholic beer—before kickoff, but thanks to Chelsea Allen he had missed nearly the entire first quarter.

Murphy's was crowded tonight, but there were still a few open spaces at the bar. A lot of people had turned out to see the game. On football nights, Murphy's ran specials on beer and their very own signature *Cowboy burger.* Ethan claimed the closest seat and settled in, raising a hand in a quick greeting to Jack Murphy, who was at the helm of the bar.

"Hey, bro," Jack said. "I was wondering where you were tonight. Be right with ya."

Murphy's Pub was one of Celebration's best-loved community gathering spots. It was a casual place and one of Ethan's favorite haunts. It was the kind of place where he could get out and be among people yet not really feel obligated to interact or explain why he was drinking sweet tea or nonalcoholic beer at a bar on a Saturday night rather than imbibing like the rest of the drunken fools.

The long teak bar ran the length of the wall to the left of the entrance. Murphy's bartenders prided themselves on their ability to mix any drink known to mankind, plus several originals that had been invented on the premises and named after local notables.

One quirk of the joint was they were proud of the fact that they only stocked a standard offering of American beers. None of those frou-frou microbrew abominations that seemed to be sprouting like mushrooms everywhere you looked these days. Ask Pop Murphy for something like that and he was likely to direct you to the local cantina Taco's or to a trendy start-up in Dallas.

But it didn't matter to Ethan since he had been sober for two years, three months and one week to the day. All he needed was his favorite brand of nonalcoholic beer, which the Murphys always kept in stock for him.

Even though he couldn't say staying sober today was any easier than it had been the first day he'd made the decision to go cold turkey and turn his life around, each day he stayed out of the bottle and in control of himself was its own victory. He wasn't about to break his winning streak now.

Some who knew of his struggles thought he was crazy to hang out at a place like Murphy's. They thought he was making it extra hard on himself by surrounding himself with the poison.

No. He had a handle on the drinking. Everything was under control. He didn't have to give up going out. He'd worked damn hard to get here and he had no intentions of sliding back into that dark hellhole he'd landed in after his divorce.

He was a recovered alcoholic. That didn't mean he had to be a shut-in, too.

One day at a time. The AA slogan had been his mantra when he was going through the hardest times. Now that he was stronger, now that he was sober, he liked to test himself by sitting at Murphy's bar, watching everyone else tip back a few too many. The smell of bourbon might tempt him, but it would never break him. Never.

Jack came back with an open bottle of fake brew and set it down on a napkin in front of him.

"Thanks, man," Ethan said and ordered his dinner.

Jack Murphy wrote it down and walked the ticket over to the kitchen window at the far end of the bar.

"Order," he called to the cook as he hung the green ticket on a clothespin strung at the ready in the order pass-through window between the bar and the kitchen.

Family owned and operated for more than a century, Murphy's was an institution around here. It was one of the oldest businesses in downtown Celebration, and had occupied the same spot since the Murphy brothers had opened their doors in the early 1900s. Not only had it survived prohibition, it had also expanded into abutting spaces over the years and had grown into the place it was today.

As Ethan nursed his drink, he squinted at the television, trying to catch up on what he'd missed of the game. It was still scoreless, but the Cowboys were making good use of their turn and were inching closer to a touchdown. At the very least they should get out of this with a field goal.

At least Chelsea Allen hadn't made him miss anything important. As he took a long draw from the amber bottle, he wondered what she was doing in that house all alone tonight. But before he could swallow, he reminded himself that it wasn't his business. Juliette had said she was welcome. Chelsea and whatever she was hiding wasn't his concern. If he knew what was good for him he'd put her out of his mind.

Juliette was due home tomorrow afternoon. Since Ethan was watching her dog, maybe he'd help her out and take Franklin home and make sure everything was still copacetic, that Chelsea Allen hadn't worn out her welcome.

It was the least a good neighbor could do.

When the TV network took a commercial break, Ethan relaxed. Inhaling the scent of booze, stale beer and fried food, he let his gaze sweep the joint to see who'd come out tonight. As he suspected, it was the regular crowd. Most of them had come to Murphy's to watch the game and grab some dinner like he had.

Some had no interest in sports and danced to the music that played from the jukebox in the adjoining room. Others were crowded around tables, laughing and talking. Another subset, like his friend Aiden Woods, had come out to shoot pool. Looked like Aiden was beating Miles Mercer. Aiden's wife, Bia, the editor-in-chief of the *Dallas Journal of Business and Development*, sat at a nearby table with Miles's wife, Sydney, sipping red wine and sharing animated conversation.

All the other pool tables, which took up a good portion of the front room, were occupied. They always seemed to be in demand. As usual, Murphy's was rocking with a good cross section of people from the Celebration community who kept the place buzzing with good energy.

"Hey, Campbell, I hear you caught the burglar." Zane Phillips slid onto the empty bar stool next to Ethan and ordered a shot of bourbon, neat.

Good news traveled fast around this town. Since Zane had heard, that meant Ethan was going to be the butt of a few good-natured jokes for a while, but he still wasn't sorry for making sure Chelsea was on the up and up.

"Yep." Ethan took another long pull from his drink. "And she was hot."

Zane's right brow shot up. "I guess being the self-appointed neighborhood watch captain has some perks, after all."

These days, everyone in Celebration was a little jumpier since the break-ins had started three months ago. Now neighbors were extra vigilant and took even more care to look out for each other. It was the decent thing to do, even if it meant calling in the occasional false alarm. Better safe than sorry.

"Just being neighborly," Ethan shot back. "I told Jules I'd keep an eye on her place while she's out of town. I saw a strange car in the driveway. I let myself in with the key she gave me and checked it out. No big deal."

"But she was hot, huh? Are you calling dibs?"

Ethan slanted a sideways glance at Zane. *Dibs?* What kind of lame-ass question was that? Besides, Zane had a girlfriend. Granted, the relationship was probably nearing its expiration date. Zane was a serial monogamist. He tended to date one woman at a time, but he never could make a permanent commitment.

When Jack set a platter heaped with a bacon-mushroom cheeseburger and onion rings down in front of Ethan, he trained his focus on his meal.

"So, who is this chick?" Zane asked as Ethan bit into his burger.

He took his time chewing and swallowing. "An old college pal of Juliette's, apparently." Ethan turned his attention to the game on the big screen. He'd come to Murphy's tonight to watch the game, not talk about Juliette's houseguest. "You want to meet her? Go knock on the door."

Zane Phillips was one of his best friends. They'd grown up together and Zane had even stood up for him as best man when he married Molly. He wasn't sure why the thought of the guy getting his grubby paws on Chelsea rubbed him the wrong way. He signaled Jack for another round and hoped Zane got the hint that he didn't feel like talking.

"All kidding aside, it's too bad you didn't catch the bastard," Zane said in a rare moment of sober good sense. "Whoever has been committing these break-ins is still out there. We have to make sure everyone is still on their guard."

Ethan nodded. The Cowboys scored and the place erupted in a cacophony of shouts and cheers.

"On another note, Rachel over at Bistro Saint-Germain said Lucy says she's finally going to open that party barn she's been talking about."

Lucy was his baby sister. Since she'd moved back home from California last year, she'd been threatening to turn the old barn down on the lower forty of their family's farm into an events venue.

Since she seemed to approach life in fits and starts, going gung ho until she lost interest on the project du jour, this idea had become known as the *party barn*.

"Yeah?" Ethan said, taking another bite. He'd stopped expending too much energy on his little sister's whims. It was hard to take her seriously after the fourth or fifth time that she'd jumped into something with both feet, only to move on to the next big thing.

"Sounds like she's serious about this," Zane said. "Maybe the twelfth time's a charm. I told her to invite me to the grand opening party."

Ethan harrumphed. "Don't hold your breath."

He wasn't worried that the party barn might actually become a reality. In all fairness, Lucy wanted to make the place a venue for weddings and other swanky events. She'd latched on to the idea after Juliette's wedding planning business had grown legs and had become a runaway success. Juliette had offhandedly mentioned that the closest wedding venue to Celebration was the Regency Cypress Plantation and Botanical Gardens, which was on the northern edge of Celebration. Lucy swore their grandparents' old barn was an untapped gold mine. Ethan didn't get it. The dilapidated pile of kindling needed to be burned down, not cobbled back together.

It wasn't that he didn't support Lucy. She and their brother, Jude, had inherited some money and equal interest in the family's 900-acre ranch. Since Jude was living the high life on the Professional Bull Riders' circuit, he and Lucy had left Ethan with the task of reviving Triple C's once floundering horse-breeding business. Ethan had worked hard to turn it around and breathe new life into it. Since the breeding arm of Triple C was all his doing, the siblings had mutually decided to divvy up the land, each claiming a specific 300-acre area. Ethan got the land with the stables and the home where they'd grown up. Lucy had chosen the plot with their grandparents' old house and the barn. Jude's was untouched acreage.

Lucy could do whatever she wanted with her piece of land. She was perfectly within her rights to turn it into an events venue. Hell, she could turn it into a zoo if she wanted. It was her call. However, over the past three years she'd had the attention span of a fruit fly. She'd already blown through every cent of the money she'd inherited after their parents died and she'd maxed out her credit cards and was left with the debt.

Ethan had helped her out financially until she could find a job with a steady paycheck that allowed her to start paying off her cards. As far as Ethan knew, she was still paying. Now that she was supporting herself, he wasn't going to enable another whim. When she'd asked Ethan to cosign for a loan so she could have some party barn start-up money, he'd declined.

If he was completely honest, his refusal wasn't just tough love. Ethan had often worried that his siblings might have the same alcoholic gene that had almost gotten the best of him. It ran in their family. In fact, it had cost their father his life. Their dad had been sauced the night of the car crash that had killed him. For a while it had been touch and go for their mother, who had landed in the ICU.

She'd lived, but she'd come out of the accident a paraplegic because of damage to one of the lower thoracic nerves. She passed away about a year later.

The disease hadn't hooked its claws into Jude, who seemed to have his act together—even if he never did come home. Ethan still worried about Lucy. She was only twenty-five. She had done some things in the past—like getting caught drunk skinny-dipping in the pond out back of old man Jenkins's hunting lodge—that made him question whether or not she was immune to alcohol's hereditary choke hold.

For some ridiculous reason completely out of left field, Ethan found himself wondering if Chelsea

Allen, the woman who'd already proven herself capable of breaking into houses, had ever been skinny-dipping.

As he chased away the inappropriate image with a sip of his beer, for a split second he craved a shot of something a hell of a lot stronger than nonalcoholic beer.

After Ethan's own hard-traversed path to sobriety, he worried that being in a party environment—even if it would be mostly wedding receptions—wouldn't be good for Lucy.

Sure, she was a grown woman, but she would always be his little sister. She and Jude were all the family he had left. His stance against the party barn stemmed from simply wanting to protect her. Jude may have been the prodigal brother, but Ethan was the protector. As any good big brother would, he wanted to hold back the tide and keep it from drowning her.

Even if the jury was still out on whether or not she was susceptible to the alcoholic gene, her previous, half-baked business ventures indicated she might not possess entrepreneurial instincts, either.

Obviously, she'd been talking about the party barn enough that word was starting to get around town. She hadn't mentioned any more about it to him. But really, was that so hard to believe? Sometimes he felt like he was the last to know anything. Such as how he'd had no idea that Juliette had such a beautiful friend. Whether or not that friend was hiding something or hiding *from* something, Ethan couldn't deny that she'd been front and center in his brain all night.

He hadn't had this kind of reaction to a pretty woman in a very long time.

He'd definitely stop by Juliette's tomorrow and see what Chelsea Allen was up to.

Chapter Three

The next morning when Chelsea's eyes fluttered open, it took her a moment to remember that she was safe in the sanctuary of Juliette's spare bedroom, where there was enough floral damask to rival Queen Mary's gardens at the Regent's Park. There were roses everywhere: on the duvet, the curtains, the wingback chair and tufted ottoman. It was so Juliette and it warmed Chelsea from the inside out.

She luxuriated in a long, slow, full-body stretch and then squinted at the clock on the nightstand to check the time. It was after nine o'clock. She should get up and get a wiggle on. Really, she should, she thought as she sank deeper into the warm bed.

Her body and mind had needed the rest. It dawned on her that this was the first time she'd slept through the night without waking since her life had blown up in the press last week, when she'd been humiliated and reduced to being the subject of lewd jokes and perverted voyeurism. Her ex-boyfriend had recorded them without her permission and released the footage, yet she was the villain. Her siblings couldn't look her in the eyes. Her parents didn't even want to see her face, much less help her solve the problem. They had made it perfectly clear that it was her problem. She needed to make it go away—or at least go away until it had passed.

Recently, it had been the last thing she'd thought about before she went to sleep and the first thing on her mind when she'd awoken. Until today.

This morning the first thought that had crossed her mind was flowers.

She felt safe here. Not that the press couldn't find her in Celebration, Texas. But with neighbors looking out for neighbors and scaring away those who didn't belong the way Ethan Campbell had last night, it would certainly make it more difficult for anyone to sneak up on her the way the reporters had in London.

Chelsea pressed the heels of her hands into her eyes, determined to exorcise the media demons. She drew in a measured deep breath, held it for a few beats and exhaled.

Visions of the reporters went away, but thoughts of Ethan Campbell remained.

In the light of day he didn't annoy her as much as he had last night. Of course, she was rested this morning and that made the whole world look better.

She took another healing breath and reminded herself everything would be okay.

Eventually.

She would put her life back together and maybe even look back at this time and laugh. Well, perhaps not laugh. That was pushing it, but she was resilient and she would be fine soon enough.

In the meantime, she had a lovely place to stay and the company of a good friend with whom she looked forward to catching up.

She'd have to figure out how to be helpful and not get under foot. She and Jules had roomed well together at university because they understood each other's quirks and idiosyncrasies. She knew Juliette well enough that she was confident she would be able to size up how her friend felt about Chelsea's invasion the moment she walked through the front door.

Chelsea would not outstay her welcome—though deep down she hoped Juliette would be just as happy to see her as Chelsea was to reconnect with her.

But she was getting ahead of herself. First, tea. Before that could happen, she must get up and put the kettle on. She swung her legs over the side of the bed, stood and pulled on her fuchsia yoga pants.

After Ethan had grudgingly growled off and left her alone last night, Chelsea had made a mad dash outside to get her handbag and suitcase out of the car. She'd managed to make it back inside without drawing any more attention to herself. Or, who knows, maybe Ethan had informed the town that Jules was cool with her being there. She hoped he hadn't told too many people. Juliette had lamented before that people in her hometown could be rather nosy. Some considered it close-knit and neighborly. But Jules had confessed that sometimes, despite good intentions, having the entire town in your business felt a little stifling. As Chelsea drew water and set the kettle on the stove, she hoped they wouldn't be in *her* business—or, more aptly, in Chelsea Allen's.

As she waited for the water to boil, she had a nose around Juliette's cottage. It was cozy and neat as a pin. A mix of old-world charm with modern accents, it was as posh and unique as Juliette herself.

The overstuffed sofa was piled with throw pillows in luscious jewel tones and rich floral patterns. The rough-hewn parquet floor was laid in a herringbone pattern that looked as if it had been lifted from a Belle Époque Paris apartment. The walls were painted a warm, welcoming shade of pale blue, which set off the white crown molding that hugged the tiptops of the home's tall walls. An antique Persian rug anchored the room and presented an interesting contrast to the modern wood-and-glass coffee table.

Chelsea had studied interior design at university and had even done a short stint at a high-end London firm. She loved what Juliette had done with the place. It was as spot-on as any project Chelsea might've planned.

She picked up a small obsidian elephant from an end table and traced a finger over its smooth, curved surface. She'd brought it back from Africa for Juliette.

A year out of university, she'd landed a great job

with a design firm, but then she'd learned about the international aid organization Voluntary Service Overseas and its world aid efforts.

She'd grown up so privileged it seemed the perfect way to give back. Everyone thought she was crazy when she made the decision to leave her design job, which her sister, Victoria, had helped her land, in favor of shipping off to Africa.

Despite the rolled eyes and reproach she'd received from her family and their accusations that she refused to grow up—and this sojourn was just an excuse to put off true responsibility—she maxed out her time in Africa helping to further the organization's poverty-ending efforts.

She'd been changed by her experience.

When the cost of a frivolous designer throw pillow could feed a starving family for a month, decorating the homes of the überwealthy seemed wrong on so many levels. After she aged out of VSO, Chelsea couldn't bring herself to go back into the design business. Instead, she took a job with the non-profit End Hunger London, which garnered more familial huffs and eye rolls because it wasn't one of their chosen charities. However, because of her family's connections, she was able to draw a respectable amount of recognition and support to the organization.

Even though she never sought personal attention, for a short while, the press deemed her an angel. Until they grew bored with that and they decided to turn her into the devil.

The minor tabloid attention had actually worked

in her favor for a while. After she'd helped get End Hunger London up and rolling, she was ready for a change. The prestigious London firm Hargraves Designs had courted her and hired her as a designer. It was the time for a change. She'd worked for the greater good—and would continue to volunteer and use her high-profile status to raise awareness. It just seemed like the right move. But everything fell apart after Hadden's revenge.

Hargraves wanted edgy, not skanky. They'd let her go, without even giving her a chance to defend herself.

Determined not to turn loose of her good mood, Chelsea returned the elephant to its place and pushed the memories from her mind. She spied several other things that Juliette had purchased when the two of them had traveled together during school—a hand-blown vase from Murano, a beautiful mirror made from vintage plates by Austrian designer Christine Hechinger. The memories made her smile.

But the thing Chelsea found the most endearing, and the most interesting by far, was the plethora of pictures her dear friend had scattered about the place in frames on the walls and on easels as centerpieces of shelf and tabletop arrangements.

Chelsea didn't have to look hard to find several pictures of herself with Juliette. But she couldn't locate a single photograph of Jules with Ethan Campbell. Not that she was looking—or at least she hadn't realized she was looking until it registered that she found his photographic absence strangely satisfying.

On the phone, Jules had denied anything but a platonic, neighborly friendship with Ethan, but they'd only spoken about him for a moment. Then again, Juliette certainly wouldn't have used that opportunity to regale Chelsea with details of a friends-with-benefits arrangement with her hunky neighbor. Not with Ethan standing right there.

Actually, it might've been better if she knew that Juliette *had* hooked up with Ethan, even casually—especially casually—because according to *the friendship code* that would make Ethan off-limits.

And how ridiculous was that thought? But wait... wasn't that guy, that professional bull rider that Juliette had a thing for, named Campbell, too? John... No... Was it Jude? Jude Campbell. Yes. That was it. She hadn't heard Jules mention him in ages. She made a mental note to ask about the connection when Juliette got home.

In the meantime, Chelsea didn't dwell on either of the Campbell men as she soaked in the rest of her best friend's home, focusing on what a treat it was to be there at last.

Though Juliette was born and bred in Celebration, the United Kingdom had always held a special place in her heart. Chelsea used to tease her about being an anglophile because she had loved everything British. Jules had, of course, returned to Celebration, and that was where she had started her business, but her friend had infused enough of England into her Texas home that she had taken the culture with her. The best of both worlds, Chelsea mused as she lifted a frame

containing a photo of a corgi puppy. Ahh, this must
be Franklin. Juliette had been so excited when she'd
texted with the news that she was adopting a puppy
from a litter of a corgi that belonged to a local friend.

She was eager to meet the little guy. Since Jules
was away, someone must've been watching him. Too
bad she couldn't go pick him up and have him here
when Jules got home. She'd do just that if she knew
where he was, but she didn't. And she didn't want to
call Juliette and risk interrupting her at work. But she
could text her, and Jules could answer at her conve-
nience. After a momentary hesitation about whether
or not it was smart to venture out, she made up her
mind that while she would mostly keep a low profile,
she had no intentions of sequestering herself while
she was here. Nothing said sketchy like a guest who
holed up in the house. Plus, she wanted to see where
her friend lived.

When they were at university together, Chelsea
had wanted to visit Juliette's hometown—she used
to joke that she wanted to meet a real cowboy—but
Juliette had always steered away from spending their
holidays here and they had opted for more exotic
locales such as Paris, Milan and Ibiza. After they
graduated, though they'd taken care to keep in touch,
they both had gotten so bogged down with life after
university—Chelsea going to Africa and Jules putting all her time and resources behind her wedding
planning business—that they hadn't seen each other
in person in three years. If there was one upside to

this scandal pushing her away from London, it was this chance to reunite with her best friend.

She sent the text and the kettle whistled. Chelsea returned to the kitchen, turning off the burner. She opted for the Taylors of Harrogate Yorkshire Gold from the selection of fine loose tea in Juliette's cabinet and spooned two teaspoons of the leaves into the mesh strainer, set it in the cup and poured steaming water over the top.

Her tea hadn't even had time to steep properly before Chelsea heard keys rattling in the front door.

What in the world?

She wasn't expecting Juliette until this afternoon—possibly even early evening. If Ethan was back, letting himself in without even the common courtesy of a knock, she would have several choice words for him. He might have a key, but that didn't mean he was free to use it and enter at whim while she was here alone.

She left her tea on the kitchen's marble-topped counter and walked into the living room, steeling herself to make it clear she wasn't pleased. She'd had it up to here with guys who thought they could push their way in and—

"Chelsea!" Juliette stepped into the living room, leaving the door wide open as she rushed toward her friend. "You're here! You're really here. I'm so happy to see you."

For the tiniest fraction of a second something that resembled disappointment zinged through Chelsea. But it wasn't disappointment. How could she be disappointed that Jules was here and she wasn't going to get the chance to tell off Ethan Campbell when the last thing she wanted was him barging in?

And she was elated to see Juliette, whom she was so busy enfolding in a warm hug that Ethan Campbell completely left her mind.

Well, maybe not completely.

"It's about time you got here," Chelsea said, holding Juliette at arm's length to look at her. "You're just as gorgeous as ever."

And she was. With her perpetually tanned olive skin, long, dark hair and sky blue eyes, she had always been an exotic beauty. Only now she seemed more…grounded. More sure of herself. And why not, with her business booming?

"I left early so I could get back as fast as I could. Now that you're here I may never let you leave. But what's going on? What the hell has Hadden Hastings done now? You know I never liked him."

Why wasn't she prepared for this? She knew she was going to have to tell Juliette the whole story. But she struggled to find the words.

"You must be exhausted," Chelsea said. "Why don't you kick off your shoes? I just boiled some water. While you're getting comfortable, I'll make you a cup of tea."

"That sounds heavenly." Juliette gave Chelsea another quick hug before she disappeared down the hall. "But I want to hear everything. Every last detail."

That was what she was afraid of.

When Juliette returned, she'd traded in her business suit for a soft-looking pink tracksuit.

"You were in San Antonio?" Chelsea asked, hoping to distract her by changing the subject.

Juliette nodded as she plated a couple of muffins and set them and the two mugs of tea on a wooden tray.

"It was a gorgeous wedding. The daughter of a big family that made a fortune in the spice trade."

"The spice trade? What is this, the fifteenth century?"

"Believe it or not, I think that's when they started the company." The two went into the living room and settled themselves on the couch. "But enough about them. What's going on?" Juliette sipped her tea. "Is your mother being impossible again?"

"I wish it were that simple." Chelsea ducked her head. "So I take it you haven't heard?"

"What's going on?" Concern overtook Juliette's face. "You said something about a video Hadden sent to the media. Is everything okay?"

As hot tears began to burn her eyes, Chelsea shook her head. She tried to console herself with the thought that if Juliette hadn't heard about the scandal, maybe it hadn't made its way across the pond.

Juliette reached out and put a hand on Chelsea's arm. "Honey, talk to me. Tell me what's wrong."

"Hadden's quite proud of himself, I'm sure."

Chelsea drew in a deep breath. She just needed to say it. It was like jumping off the high dive; if she thought about it too long she would paralyze herself.

"Before Hadden and I broke up, he filmed us having sex. Once word got out that Thomas might be a contender for prime minister, Hadden gave the tape to the media."

Juliette nearly snorted her tea and was overcome by a coughing fit. When she finally regained her composure, she said, "Are you kidding me?"

Chelsea shook her head. She couldn't force words around the lump of shame that always swelled in her throat when she tried to talk about this.

"That little turd. You could sue him. You could sue him and the media that released it. They didn't have your permission."

"No, they didn't have my permission. I would've never allowed it. I would've never allowed Hadden to record us if I had known. The problem is, I don't have solid proof that Hadden was the one who released the footage. Obviously, you and I both know it couldn't have been anybody but him. There was no one else in his flat while we were intimate—"

Her voice broke and she stared at her hands in her lap. She was so ashamed. Even telling her best friend in the world made her feel as vulnerable and dirty and humiliated as the moment she first found out.

"How dare he?" Juliette railed. "It's called slut-shaming, you know? God, I hate that term. It doesn't do the female gender any favors. Even though it's not intended to be derogatory toward women, it sounds like it is. It is a misnomer. It should be sex-shaming. Please know I am not by any means calling you a slut. You're not. You're the victim here. Don't you see that? This is the epitome of double standards."

"I appreciate your support. I feel pretty crummy

right now. I feel shameful and dirty, but I will never allow Hadden to force me to play the victim. You know me better than that. However, my family thinks *they* are the victims. They want me to disappear, just go away—" she made a shooing motion with her hand "—until this whole ugly mess blows over. I am officially a liability to Thomas's future. So I have been cordially invited to get lost. Thank you for taking me in. I couldn't think of anywhere else I wanted to go."

Juliette threw her arms around Chelsea and enveloped her in another of her famous bear hugs. "I am so glad you're here, honey. Though I wish it were under different circumstances. This isn't your fault, Chels. Hadden is a misogynistic pig. He's a creep. Why is he getting no flack and you're taking all the heat? Why are we not prosecuting him?"

"Because he blurred out his face in the footage. No one can prove it's him."

"And the fact that you dated him for over a year never entered into the tawdry equation?"

"Of course people have speculated, but there's no proof."

Her face burned and she buried it in her hands. Juliette reached out and rubbed her back.

"I am just incensed about this. I mean, I know you would never willingly open your bedroom door. It's such a violation of privacy. But here's one thing I don't get. Why is it still so shameful for a woman to embrace her sexuality, but a man gets points for dipping his wick?"

"That's the age-old dilemma," Chelsea mused.

"One would hope that by now we'd evolved beyond that pathetic double standard. But times like
this prove it's alive and well because everyone has
branded me a slut and seems to be taking great pleasure in shaming me."

"But you are not a slut! I know the tabloids went
to town on you a few years ago when you worked for
End Hunger. They tried to turn you into the poster
child for party girls. What was that creep's name who
kept hounding you?"

"Bertie Veal. He's still up to his antics. He's the
one who broke the news about the tape. I just hope
he doesn't get wind that I'm here. If he does, I'll have
to leave because I don't want him to start bothering
you. Let's hope he doesn't remember we were university roommates."

"Bertie doesn't remember me. I was never on his
radar. But he was pretty obsessed with you. Actually,
I think he had a crush on you, but he knew you were
out of his league. It's like the playground bully who
pulls a girl's ponytail when she won't pay attention
to him. Bertie needs to get a life."

"Sadly, selling stories to the paparazzi *is* his life.
After Hadden sold him the tape of us, Bertie has been
insufferable."

"But you really haven't done anything more than
the average twentysomething. Your father just happens to be the Earl of Downing and your brother
might be prime minister. That makes you a prime
target. An interesting target."

Juliette shrugged as if it was no big deal.

Chelsea knew Juliette meant well. But she wished she could tell her friend this wasn't making her feel any better. Similar arguments had been bandied about beyond the tabloids and in the conventional news media. All it managed to accomplish was to draw more attention to the fact that pictures and videos were at the fingertips of anyone who cared to call them up on the internet and watch the peep show. She'd come to Celebration to get away from this. Not to dwell on it.

"Yet, I'm sure Hadden is getting high fives and slaps on the back for being such a big man. Can't they find out the original IP address of the person who leaked it? I mean, your brother is a member of parliament. He knows the queen, for God's sake. Can't he get the Secret Intelligence Service on it? You do have an attorney at least, don't you?"

Chelsea buried her face in her hands for a moment before answering.

"Thomas helped me retain an attorney and he has an old school chum who is working on getting the video removed from the internet. My brother is doing what he can, but he's walking a fine line. The problem is, the video is like a virus. It's removed from one site and it pops up on three more."

"Oh, honey, I'm sorry."

Her father was more concerned that Hadden's vendetta might derail Thomas's shot at being prime minister should his party come to power than he was that his daughter's privacy and dignity had been violated. As far as her parents were concerned, this entire ordeal was her fault. If she'd been more rooted, more focused on something constructive rather than floating about trying to find herself, Hadden would've never had the opportunity; this disgrace would've never happened.

"The point of the scandal was to get back at me by bringing down Thomas and making him look bad during this time when every eye in the UK is on him. I just—" Chelsea felt tears brimming again, and she covered her face with her hands. "I can't, Jules. I just can't do this right now."

Juliette set down her tea, got to her feet in a flash and put her arms around Chelsea. "I'm so sorry. That was insensitive of me. I didn't mean to make you feel bad. This is not your fault. Your privacy was violated in the worst way possible. I can't stand the fact that that smug asshat Hadden Hastings is walking around with his head held high while people and the press are treating you like it's the puritanical seventeenth century and you should have a big red *A* pinned to the front of you."

Maybe it was because her emotions were running high, maybe it was because she was so tired of feeling so small and dirty, but something about the farfetched *Scarlet Letter* reference struck her as funny.

"If you're likening me to Hester Prynne, I'm not married, and thank God I didn't get pregnant with Hadden's child." But saying the facts out loud didn't sound as humorous as they'd sounded in her head. "Look, I appreciate you taking my side, but can we please change the subject to something more interesting?"

As Juliette nodded, she still looked as if she was spoiling for a fight with Hadden.

"I've been dying to know whether or not your neighbor Ethan Campbell is related to your old boyfriend, Jude Campbell. He is. Am I right?"

Juliette grimaced and Chelsea was surprised when her eyes darkened even more. "Yes. They're brothers. But I haven't seen Jude since I moved back to Celebration after college. He's been away living large on the Professional Bull Riding circuit. As far as I'm concerned, he can stay away."

"You're still nursing the Jude wound?"

Juliette chewed her bottom lip instead of answering.

"Well, Ethan seems pretty attentive," Chelsea said.

"Yeah, he's a great guy. He and his brother are as different as night and day."

"So, are you interested in Ethan? I mean, come on, Ethan is pretty darn hot, even if he is a little uptight. You could do a lot worse."

"Ethan is like a big brother. He's just a good guy who looks out for me."

"*Looks out* for you, huh? I think he has his eye on you."

Juliette flinched. "Ethan? No. Not a chance." Her mouth flattened into a distasteful straight line and she shook her head. She might have made the same face if Chelsea had asked her to eat the soggy loose leaves from the dregs at the bottom of the teapot. "He is not my type. There's definitely nothing happening in that arena."

And there it was, the companion to the strange satisfaction she'd felt earlier when she'd looked for Ethan's picture among Juliette's home gallery and didn't find it.

"I mean his brother Jude and I were pretty serious for a long time."

"Do you ever hear from him?"

"Nope, and I'd rather not talk about him." Her smile seemed a bit forced and her nod a little too resolute.

"All right, but you know I'm here if you ever do want to talk." Juliette nodded and Chelsea knew it was time to change the subject. "Thank you for letting me stay with you, Jules. I won't impose too long. If it gets to be too much having me under foot, I can find a place to stay in town."

Juliette put her hands on her hips. "You can stay with me as long as you like. I'm so happy you're here."

Chelsea grimaced. "You might not want to give me an open-ended invitation. Because I just might take you up on it."

"Maybe you should."

Sweet, generous Juliette. The thought about house-guests and fish came to mind, and even though she didn't want to argue it right now, she knew she *should* find alternate lodging as soon as she got her bearings.

"It's such a lovely day," Juliette said. "Let's take

our tea outside to the patio. I think we could both use some fresh air."

Chelsea followed her outside. The backyard looked transformed in the light of day. Her gaze skittered to the bathroom window she'd used to gain entrance last night and she found herself reliving the start she'd felt when she saw Ethan Campbell's muscled frame blocking the doorway. The chair she'd used to boost herself up was still turned over on its side, exactly where it had fallen the night before.

Chelsea walked over and picked it up, returning it to the patio table where she'd found it.

"Part of the crime scene from last night," she said sheepishly.

"I see," Juliette said. "I'm so sorry the key wasn't under the mat like I said it would be. We've had some break-ins around here. I'd taken it inside and I was in such a rush to get to this job, it completely slipped my mind to put it outside again like I promised."

The two of them settled themselves at the table and each reclaimed her mug of tea.

"It's not a problem." Chelsea smiled. "If there has been crime in the area, you shouldn't leave the key outside. Not even for one night. And you probably shouldn't leave the bathroom window open, for that matter."

They sipped in companionable silence for a few moments.

"So, is your gorgeous neighbor married?" Chelsea heard herself asking before she could think better of it.

"Why? Are *you* interested?"

"Absolutely not," she snapped. "I'm just curious."

Okay, well, under a different set of circumstances she might be. She tended to have a thing for tall, dark-haired guys with blue eyes and mile-wide shoulders. But now was not the time to indulge such fancies. "I'm here to disappear, not to land myself in deeper trouble. The even more pressing matter is to find myself a place to stay."

Though maybe a temporary fling with a handsome cowboy would be a good way to keep her mind off her troubles. She'd just have to be careful. Make sure it was on her terms.

"You're staying here," Juliette said. "End of discussion, okay?"

"You're too good to me," Chelsea said.

"It's the least I can do. How many times over the years did I stay with your family?"

Chelsea snorted. "Trust me. Your presence never inconvenienced them because they were never at home."

Chelsea's gaze scanned the backyard, which she realized was actually a beautiful, well-tended English garden in full bloom. Juliette always had loved her flowers. Especially English gardens.

"At least when you stayed with me at Longbridge Hall you never caused a commotion like I did last night," Chelsea said. "And you must've gotten up at the crack of dawn to make it back so early. See, I'm already being *that* guest."

"I was on the road by six, but you gave me an excuse to get out of there."

"Better you than me." Chelsea chuckled and raised her mug to her friend. "This is my first cup of tea."

Juliette laughed. "You've never been a morning person, have you?"

Chelsea gave a *you're-right*, one-shoulder shrug and sipped her tea.

"Look, I know my place isn't fancy, but—"

Chelsea held up a hand and stopped her. "Don't be ridiculous. Your home is lovely. I'd choose it any day over Longbridge Hall. But really, Jules, you don't need a long-term houseguest skulking about when you get home from a job."

"I'm not going to argue about this. You could never be a mere *houseguest*." Juliette reached out and put a hand on Chelsea's arm. "You're the sister I've always wanted."

"A sister who's toting a lot of baggage these days." Chelsea's cheeks warmed and she dropped her gaze to her teacup. Would this humiliation ever fade? This was Jules, after all.

The timing couldn't have been worse given Thomas's prime minister candidacy, but maybe this was the boot to the seat she'd needed to start getting her act together.

Chelsea heard the sound of a car door shutting and a dog barking.

"That sounds like Franklin," Juliette said, pushing away from the table and standing. "Ethan must've brought him home."

"Ethan?" Dear God in heaven, did all roads in

this town lead to Ethan Campbell? She ignored the thought that hoped so.

"Yes, he watches my dog when I go out of town."

"He seems to be a neighborly kind of guy, doesn't he?" Chelsea said, mostly to herself.

As they rounded the house, they saw Ethan standing on the front porch, knocking on the door.

"Hey, neighbor," Juliette said, casting a sidelong glance at Chelsea as she bent to love on her little dog. "We were just talking about you."

"You were?"

But Juliette was too busy cooing words of adoration and praise to her wiggling four-legged love to answer Ethan, whose gaze had locked with Chelsea's. He nodded his greeting and she felt her cheeks warm.

"Hello," she said, careful to keep her accent in check.

"Yes, I was just telling Chelsea that you're so good to look out for Franklin and me while I'm away. You didn't have to bring him home. I was coming over later, anyway."

"You were?" Ethan asked.

"Yes." She gave Franklin a hand signal and he followed her onto the porch. "This afternoon I'm looking at the barn with Lucy. Didn't she tell you?"

Who was Lucy? Ahh, his girlfriend, probably.

Made sense. Guys like Ethan Campbell usually had a girlfriend—or a wife.

A voice inside her reminded her that she knew nothing about Ethan Campbell beyond his being the eyes and ears of the neighborhood watch team.

And the fact that he was tall and muscled and good-looking as sin. But good-looking guys were the root of all the trouble she was in now.

Good-looking guys…guys who were tall and had broad shoulders were her Achilles' heel. She needed to stop being so shallow, stop allowing herself to be wooed by the promise of washboard abs. Because judging by the way his body went from broad shoulders to a strong, broad chest and veed perfectly into slim cowboy hips, she'd just bet there was a six-pack hiding out under that chambray work shirt.

She really should strive to be a better person and look beyond the physical…beyond the deliciousness of blue eyes and curly brown hair and focus on more important attributes—like the way Ethan's biceps had bunched and muscled as he held open the screen door and gestured for Chelsea to enter first.

All that and good manners, too.

"No, Lucy did not tell me you were coming over to look at the barn," he said, that familiar irritation he'd displayed last night coating his words today. "I hear she's starting up with that nonsense again. Juliette, don't encourage her."

He closed the screen door behind him, keeping his hand on it so that it didn't slam. Score another point for the cowboy with manners.

"Ethan Campbell, why wouldn't you want your sister to do something that made her happy?"

Sister?

Lucy was his *sister*?

Well, then. Score one—a big one—for Chelsea.

She bent down to stroke Franklin's velvety-soft ears and to hide her grin. "Nice, Franklin," she cooed. "It's good to meet you."

She focused on the dog's little corgi smile and the eraser-pink tongue that lolled to one side of his mouth, giving him an affable look. She'd always thought the corgi breed, with their happy personalities and short, stubby little legs, were the *court jesters* of all dogs. They made people happy just by being in the same room. That was why she was smiling, not because Lucy was Ethan's sister.

"I do want my sister to be happy," he said.

She wasn't smiling at the way his biceps were flexing again as he braced his hand against the doorjamb or at the way his eyes crinkled at the corners when he looked concerned.

"You know her track record when it comes to seeing things through to the end. She has a tendency to abandon projects when she loses interest. She doesn't need to waste any more money. She's still paying off debt from that fabric business she left school to start."

Juliette sighed. "I get that this is a big endeavor. It's huge. But now that my business is booming, I'm in a position to send a lot of my business her way."

Ethan must've noticed Chelsea's puzzled expression. "My sister wants to turn an old barn on the outer edge of our property into a party barn."

He gave his head a quick shake like it was the dumbest idea he'd ever heard.

"Not a *party barn*," Juliette corrected. "It's an events venue. There's nothing like it for miles around here. It's a completely untapped market and a great idea that she needs to take advantage of before someone else does. Barn weddings are all the rage right now."

Franklin walked over to his mistress, sat down and leaned against her leg as if showing his support.

"I seriously doubt many people would want to get married in a barn, out here in the middle of nowhere. The place is falling down. It's more of a shanty than a barn."

"That's why we need to renovate it," Juliette said.

"What's that going to cost?" Ethan crossed his arms in front of him. There were those biceps again, beckoning her from under his long-sleeve shirt.

Hello there, lovelies.

"Chelsea is a designer," Juliette said. "She might be able to give us an idea of the scope involved, and she and I can help Lucy bid out the work."

Chelsea blinked. "Oh. What?"

"The work on the barn. You have to see it, Chels. It has so much potential."

"I'm not licensed," she said. "Not here."

"Well, you have a design degree. You wouldn't be doing the work. Just rendering an opinion. Helping Ethan see the place's potential."

Ethan was frowning at her as if she couldn't convince him that the crown jewels had worth, but Juliette was nodding and looking so hopeful.

"Chelsea doesn't want to get involved." Ethan was talking to Juliette, but he was still looking at Chelsea.

"I don't mind giving it a look-see and offering my

opinion." Chelsea raised her chin, a defense under his scrutiny. "That's not exactly getting involved, is it now?"

"So y'all are going to gang up on me." Ethan laughed—a humorless sound—and shook his head. "I'll definitely be there for the walk-through, then. Because I'm not about to turn you all loose at Lucy's whim." He pinned his gaze on Chelsea. "Especially if *you're* going to be there. I knew you were trouble the minute I laid eyes on you."

She might have found his words offensive if not for the mischievous sparkle in his eyes that was more of a sexy challenge than an accusation. It made her breath catch before it sent her stomach into a rushing spiral.

Trouble? Oh, Cowboy, you have no idea.

Chapter Four

"Basically, you're working with a blank canvas," Chelsea said. Ethan watched her turn around and survey the interior of the old weathered barn. "Anything is possible."

Anything? If they asked him, he'd say it would be easier to burn the damn thing down and start from scratch.

With its dirt floor and wood rot that let daylight in through the cracks—*blank canvas* wasn't how he would've described the place, but they hadn't asked him. Chelsea was the expert.

The woman was full of surprises and apparently full of hope for this godforsaken place.

Or maybe she was just trying to be polite and not dash Lucy's dreams.

Pretty *and* polite.

That was a lethal combination.

Last night he hadn't thought *polite* was one of her attributes. But then again, last night he probably hadn't made the best first impression, either. He'd been gruff and she'd been feistier than an old barn cat that had been cornered by a skunk.

Polite hadn't exactly been on the table last night.

Today was a completely different story. She was freshly scrubbed and makeup-free. Her long, blond hair was pulled back in a ponytail, accentuating high cheekbones and a bottom lip that was slightly fuller than the top, giving her a look of near innocence. Near, but not quite.

She wore a simple blue T-shirt that brought out the color of her eyes and hugged her curves in all the right places. The woman standing in front of him this morning looked like a different person from the one he'd nearly had arrested last night.

Ethan had to make a concentrated effort not to stare at her. It helped when he reminded himself that Ms. Polite and Pretty was in cahoots with Juliette, and the two of them were filling Lucy's head with all kinds of dangerous ideas that would probably cost a fortune.

This initial consultation might be free, but he worried about the pretty picture Chelsea would paint as she convinced Lucy that she just couldn't live without all the bells and whistles a designer could provide at a steep markup. Wasn't that what designers did? Especially ones who entered a house through the bathroom window and managed to sweet-talk him out of turning her over to the sheriff.

"So you're saying we can do anything we want?" Lucy's eyes lit up.

"Whatever your budget will allow," Chelsea qualified.

Ethan braced himself. How much was that *budget* going to set his sister back? He had to be the voice of reason. "*Budget* is the key word, Lucy. Maybe you should finish paying off your debt and save some money before you jump into this."

His sister ignored him.

The only thing of value Lucy had left was this property. She didn't have any money. She'd spent the small amount of cash she'd inherited on her stint in graphic design school in New York and her subsequent move to California where she'd leaped right into a bad business deal. A friend she'd met in design school had talked her into moving out West where they'd endeavored to design their own line of fabrics. Ethan had warned her to do some due diligence before she rushed headlong into the partnership, but Lucy swore she knew what she was doing, that she had everything under control. Even though he'd seen the train wreck coming from a mile away, Ethan was fool enough to leave her to her own devices. Because, of course, Lucy was a grown woman. Even if she was his little sister, she was old enough to make her own decisions and suffer the consequences of her actions.

It was true. He knew it. But it didn't make it any

easier to watch his sister setting herself up to crash and burn again.

A party barn? Out here in the middle of nowhere?

People got married in churches or hotels or parks, not in gussied-up barns out in the middle of an overgrown field.

But what did he know? Juliette and Chelsea seemed to think it was the best idea since the invention of the telephone. And he did trust Juliette.

His sister had always been attached to this ramshackle pile of kindling that they called a barn. Always had been, ever since their grandparents had lived in the bungalow next door.

They'd been gone for nearly fifteen years and Lucy had moved into their house when she'd returned from California last fall.

While he knew the house and the land meant too much to her to sell, if she mortgaged the house to secure a loan she could inadvertently lose it all if she made another bad business decision. Lucy was headstrong and sometimes she latched onto ideas like this the way a pit bull grabbed hold of a soup bone. There was no reasoning with her, no loosening her grip on anything once it took root.

He had the sinking feeling thanks to the pretty picture Chelsea had just painted, he might be too late to talk some sense into her.

"Could we add on a second story, so while a wedding was going on down here, the caterer could be upstairs getting everything ready for the reception?" Lucy asked. "After the ceremony, the guests could walk right up to the reception. Ooh! Or you know what would be cool? What if we had two areas upstairs? One area where the guests could have hors d'oeuvres and cocktails, and another part we could keep separate where the dinner and dancing would take place once the bride and groom were done with photos. Could we do that?"

Cha-ching.

"Actually, that's a great idea," Juliette said. "In other barn venues we've had to hold the ceremony outside so the caterer could set up the reception inside the barn. If it rains, it creates big problems. So if a second story is feasible, it would solve a lot of problems. At least the bride would have peace of mind that the weather wouldn't wreck her day. Can we do it?"

All eyes turned to Chelsea. "As I said, it depends on your budget." She glanced at Ethan and seemed to weigh her words. Maybe she was taking what he'd said to heart. "But sure. The ceiling is high enough that it could work. Do you have a contractor?"

"Sounds expensive," Ethan preempted with his reality check before Lucy could get even more attached to the idea.

But he was too late. "I don't care if it's expensive," Lucy said. "Anything worth doing is worth doing right."

"Where are you going to get the money?" he asked.

His sister waved him off with a flick of her hand that suggested she didn't want to be burdened with the details.

"True, it's not going to be cheap, but it could be

done in stages," Chelsea offered. "Potentially, you
could fix up the interior with the plan of adding a
second floor or a loft later. At least that would allow
you to open for business and start bringing in some
income. If there's a wedding season, you could plan
the additions during the slower months or you could
work around them."

Ethan did an internal double take. That sounded
like a sensible plan. At least she wasn't trying to over-
sell Lucy. Maybe he'd judged her too harshly. He
glanced at his sister to gauge her reaction and noticed that Lucy was staring at Chelsea intently. "You
look so familiar," she finally said. "Have we met before today?"

"I don't think so." Chelsea shook her head. "Maybe
you've seen me in the photos at Juliette's house?"

"Maybe, but probably not," Lucy said, staring a
hole through the woman. "Chelsea Allen…? Who is
it that you remind me of? Even your name is familiar to me."

"I have pictures of her all over the house. That's
probably where you've seen her," Juliette said. "Where
were you planning on building a bride's room?"

It took Lucy a couple of beats to tear her gaze away
from Chelsea.

"You do know you'll need to plan space for a
bride's room," Juliette said.

"Sure. Yeah. I mean, no. I hadn't thought about
it being out here. For now, we could use my house.
Maybe we could build a bride's room into the plans."

"What's a bride's room?" Ethan asked. "Is that

something you can build in here, or are we talking about building another structure?"

"A bride's room is a place for the bride and her entourage to get ready before the wedding," Lucy said.

"Wouldn't she get ready at home?" The way all three women turned to look at him, he knew he'd just asked a dumb question. He didn't care. How was he supposed to know these things unless he asked?

"She might not want to put on her wedding dress before she arrives," Chelsea offered, but he must've looked confused because she continued. "Frankly, if I were getting married, I wouldn't put my gown on until just before the ceremony. It might get wrinkled or dirty. A bride's room would give her a place to dress and prepare for her wedding day. Plus, it's bad luck for the groom to see the bride before the ceremony on the day of the wedding. It would have to be out of the way so the groom doesn't see her before she walks down the aisle."

Chelsea started walking toward the north side of the barn and he followed, hearing Juliette say something to Lucy about Shay and Kyle Brighton's wedding on Saturday. The entire town had been invited, including Ethan. Even though weddings weren't his favorite thing to do on a Saturday night.

"So, you've never been married?" He had no earthly idea why he asked Chelsea that question.

"No, I haven't. Have you?"

He watched Lucy link her arm through Juliette's and steer her toward the opposite side of the barn.

They had their heads together, scheming, no doubt, as they exited the building.

"Divorced. When I got married the ceremony sure as hell wasn't in a barn."

"Barns are a newer trend in wedding venues." She stopped in a patch of sunlight that was streaming in through a shuttered window. Dust motes hung in the air, and Ethan was taken by how naturally pretty Chelsea looked in the soft afternoon light. The back-lighting made her look like an angel the way it played off her blond hair, illuminating it like a halo.

For a split second he had a crazy thought that maybe she'd been sent to save him. But as soon as the thought raced through his head he realized how pathetically asinine it was to think that and shoved it out of his brain harder than two drunks in a bar fight.

"Barns may not have been as fashionable when you tied the knot," she said. "How long ago was it?"

Even though he was the one who'd brought up marriage, he didn't want to talk about his own failed endeavor. It didn't hurt like it used to. The pain had faded once he'd gotten sober and realized that he and his ex made so much more sense as friends. It was as if sobriety had washed the letdown out of his system. In fact, now that they were divorced, he and Molly were on great terms.

"A long time ago," he finally said. "So, if wedding barns are a fad, does that mean next year something else will be all the rage and the barn will just be a barn again? Or in this case a wildly overimproved barn?"

"Not necessarily. Of course, I don't know this area, but I think a venue like this, done right, of course, will become pretty timeless. And Lucy can rent the facility for other uses besides weddings."

That was what he was afraid of. "We'll have to check into noise ordinances. Maybe that's the reason Celebration doesn't already have an outfit like this."

She shrugged. "Maybe so. It's a good idea to make sure Lucy checks into that before she spends any money."

"Or not," he said.

"Excuse me?"

"I'd rather she not do this venue thing."

Chelsea looked truly stunned. "I understand that Lucy is your sister, but she's an adult," Chelsea said. "Does she need your approval?"

"She can do whatever she wants. She doesn't need my approval."

"Not that it should matter, but Juliette believes in her. Why don't you?"

Ethan drew in a slow, measured breath. The phantom scent of hay and oats and horse hung in the air, even though it hadn't housed animals for the better part of fifteen years. "I do believe in Lucy." He stopped himself before he said too much, that he had his doubts about her ability to focus and follow through with a business like this. It was the truth, but he didn't need to share it with the world. "I have my reasons."

The words sounded a lot gruffer than he'd intended. He could tell by the way Chelsea's eyes flashed that he'd offended her.

"I'm sure you do and that's fine." She held up a hand. "It's none of my business, and I really don't want to get in the middle of it. If you'll excuse me, I'll go find Juliette and Lucy."

She turned to walk away and he should've let her go, but damned if he didn't hear himself trying to explain.

"Lucy hasn't had the best track record," he said.

Chelsea stopped and turned back toward him. Her face was neutral, but there was something in her eyes that encouraged him to keep talking.

"She's spent the past few years since our parents died searching for something that she hasn't found yet."

Chelsea's face softened. "I'm sorry for your loss."

"They've been gone for a few years now, but thank you."

The cicadas chose that moment to end the whining vibrato of their symphony. Quiet hung between Ethan and Chelsea like a sheer curtain.

"I don't want Lucy to get in over her head again," he said.

"She can't figure that out by herself?"

"She hasn't yet."

"So this isn't her first business venture, I take it?"

He shook his head.

"And let me guess, you're the big brother who steps in and always saves the day?"

"I wouldn't put it that way, but around here that's what big brothers do."

"Of course they do." The corners of her mouth turned up. He wondered how someone could look so sad when they were smiling. "I think it's universal. I have two brothers at home who always tried to fight my battles for my sister and me, too. But you know what? Sometimes a girl just has to take a chance. We don't always need to be saved. And the world doesn't end if we make a mistake now and then."

"Are you saying you've made mistakes along the way?" he asked.

"Of course I have. I'm human, Ethan."

Hearing her say his name triggered something inside him, a kind of strange tightening in his stomach. He ignored it.

"I would've taken you for someone who knows exactly what she wants and where she's going."

She shook her head. "Obviously, we don't know each other. I don't know you or your sister, but…" She hesitated a moment. "May I give you a piece of advice that will go a long way toward strengthening the brother-sister bond?"

He nodded.

"I know how it feels to come from a family that doesn't take you seriously," said Chelsea. "Lucy seems like a sweet, smart woman. Give her some credit. Don't do that to her."

"Do what to who?" Lucy asked. She and Juliette had returned.

"We were talking about planning and zoning and permits," Ethan said. "All the fun stuff."

Lucy frowned.

"We were wondering why there isn't already a venue like this in Celebration," Chelsea offered. "We were curious if maybe planning and zoning regulations were prohibitive."

"I've often wondered the same thing," Juliette said. "Why isn't there a venue here? The Regency Cypress Plantation and Botanical Gardens is just about the only game in town, unless you want to venture all the way over to Dallas. The Cypress is a good twenty miles away. Even if you're willing to drive that far, the place is booked out for nearly two and a half years. Good luck getting in in a reasonable time. Shay and Kyle booked their wedding about three years ago. Who wants to wait three years to get married?"

Juliette looked at Ethan. He shrugged.

"I have no idea," he said. "That's not my area of expertise."

"Of course, sometimes you get lucky and there's a cancellation," she continued. "Remember how fast Anna and Jake Lennox had to plan their wedding when that spot opened up all of a sudden?"

Ethan shook his head. He had no clue.

Juliette clucked. "Stop acting like you don't know what I'm talking about. You went to their wedding."

"Yeah. But how would I know about their time frame? I couldn't even tell you how long it took Molly to plan our wedding."

"Maybe that's why you're not married anymore," Lucy said.

"Ouch," he said. "Harsh, sis."

Lucy waved him off and turned to Chelsea, who was a much more accommodating sounding board than he was.

"The way I see it," Lucy said, "we will be providing a community service by opening this venue."

Juliette made noises that indicated she agreed. She turned to Chelsea.

"The Gardens are booked solid because they're the only game in town. It used to be a working sugar plantation back in the early nineteenth century. Since then, it's been refashioned into a much sought-after venue for parties and special occasions. Its history is what gives it the charm.

"When our friends Jake and Anna grabbed that unexpected cancellation, they had to put their wedding on the fast track and plan everything in three weeks. It was madness, but it was a beautiful wedding. If we do this place right, I believe we can give the Regency Cypress a run for their money."

She paused. "What do you want to call this place, Lucy?"

"I don't know. I'm still thinking about it."

"Keep thinking," Juliette said. "Because I believe our barn has so much charm that we will have a waiting list of people wanting to reserve dates, too. And, before I forget, since we will all be at Shay and Kyle's wedding on Saturday, you can see what kinds of services I provide and get an idea for some of the things we will need to think about for the renovation."

So they'd all be there? "Does that mean you're coming, too?" Ethan asked Chelsea.

She shook her head. "I wasn't invited. I don't know Shay and Kyle and I wouldn't want to crash the party."

"Nonsense," Juliette said. "I'm not going to leave you sitting at home by yourself. You can come along and help me. I can always use an extra set of hands."

"Sure, as long as I won't be in the way," Chelsea said. "I'd love to help."

First the impromptu consultation; now Jules was recruiting Chelsea to work as a wedding planning assistant. Ethan considered cracking a joke about Juliette paying her at least minimum wage, but that gave way to a warm satisfaction that she would be there. Suddenly, he wasn't dreading this wedding as much as he had been.

Chapter Five

Chelsea had been reluctant to venture too far out into public, but it dawned on her that now that Ethan and Lucy knew she was *visiting*, it would look weird if she spent the entire time holed up inside the house. Actually, it would look downright suspicious. Besides, she was happy she could help Jules.

On Saturday morning Chelsea went with Juliette to the Regency Cypress Plantation to help her set up for the wedding reception. Apparently, the bride had someone helping her at the church. This gave Juliette and Chelsea the entire day at the reception venue. Chelsea helped with everything from stringing tiny white twinkle lights and swagging yards of tulle across the ceiling and assisting the pastry chef with the wedding cake table, to rolling up her sleeves and helping Juliette create the head table for the bridal party. She moved heavy round tables and chairs into the perfect arrangement for the guests, and after that she laid the tables with linens and place settings and the sweetest floral centerpieces made of pink peonies and white hydrangeas and sprigs of green. Wait…was that mistletoe? It sure looked like it.

"Jules, is that mistletoe in the centerpieces?"

"It is. And I'm glad you mentioned it." Juliette picked up a large box that had been pushed back into a corner. "We need to hang these mistletoe bunches in places where people can stand under them and kiss."

"But it's not Christmastime," Chelsea said. "Why are you putting up mistletoe?"

Juliette smiled. "My mission is to make dreams come true. I give the bride and groom whatever they want. Mistletoe is kind of their thing because they met at a wedding that had a mistletoe theme and they decided they wanted it at their wedding, too. Even if it is May, their wish is my command."

It was cute for a couple to have their own special tradition like that. How nice it would be to share a romantic fancy like that with your soul mate, Chelsea mused as she hung the round bunches of greenery that were interspersed with baby's breath and tied with a pink ribbon to match the flowers in the centerpieces.

By the time they'd finished setting up, Chelsea had decided that working like this was the perfect cover. Who would think to look for a humiliated British heiress behind the scenes of a Texas wedding? Besides, Americans weren't that tuned in to the UK tabloids, and even if they were, the majority wouldn't give two thoughts about her sex tape, what with the Kardashians and other reality TV stars misbehaving on a daily basis. In fact, her misadventure might even seem a bit tame comparatively. Or at least a bit anticlimactic since she hadn't tried to capitalize on the scandal. She just wanted it to go away.

It seemed that everywhere in the world, famous people or wannabe celebs had adopted the stance that bad publicity was better than being overlooked. That wasn't Chelsea's philosophy, of course, and she couldn't quite wrap her mind around the trend of relishing public shame. She simply wanted to disappear until everything had blown over and John Q. Public had forgotten her. But keeping busy like this was one step better than disappearing because while she was working, she had actually forgotten about the problem that had brought her here in the first place.

"Okay, I think we're good to go," Juliette said, standing back and surveying the room.

The place really did look fit for a princess bride with the tulle, twinkle lights and flowers, and all that mistletoe just begging people to kiss.

"This was fun. If you need a hand on other jobs while I'm here, I'm happy to help."

"Thanks, love," Jules said. "I just might take you up on that. Now, let's go change out of our work clothes and into our party dresses. The fun is about to begin."

Juliette had lent Chelsea a dress and a pair of heels to change into. Since Chelsea had packed her bags on the fly before leaving London, she'd only brought along casual clothing. She certainly hadn't foreseen attending posh events while she was away. Especially not a wedding.

However, Juliette was right about needing to freshen up and change into appropriate attire after hefting tables and hauling ladders. Chelsea was already exhausted, and the real work—when the bridal party and guests arrived for the reception—hadn't even begun. The grunt work was only the preamble. Apparently, a wedding planner's job wasn't done until the bride and groom left for their happily-ever-after and the last guest cleared the building. Chelsea had always appreciated that Juliette was a hard worker, but until now she had no idea of the amount of exhausting work required to pull off Jules's job. From the outside looking in, her friend made it seem effortless.

They changed clothes in stalls in the ladies' loo and then touched up their makeup at the communal mirror.

"You really do earn your pay, Jules," Chelsea said. "I'm impressed."

"I love my career. It simply doesn't feel like work to me."

"Well, you're darn good at it."

"Thank you. When I see my brides and grooms looking so happy, it's worth every bit of effort."

"And, of course, they pay you handsomely."

"Yes, there is that." Juliette blotted her lips, smoothing her bright pink lipstick, which looked so smart with her olive complexion. "But that's the frosting on the cake. The real compensation is loving what I do."

"You're lucky to have found your calling," Chelsea said. "I'm beginning to think that finding the perfect career might rival finding the perfect man."

The thought had her mind skittering back to Ethan Campbell and talk of his marriage to the woman named Molly. Had Ethan been Molly's perfect man? If she married him, she must've thought so in the beginning. He seemed like a decent guy, even if he was a little overly protective. Why had Molly let him get away?

"Nothing is perfect," Jules said. "Well, except for the weddings I plan. Those have to be perfect. But you'll find yourself soon enough. It was a shame what happened with Hargraves Designs."

Chelsea died a little inside. Just when she'd gotten her mind off the damn tabloid story, there it was, jumping out at her like an ugly jack-in-the-box.

Initially, Hargraves had thought her name would lend cutting edge panache to the traditional studio. She was supposed to help them connect with the younger, hipper, moneyed generation. But her stock went down the tube once the video scandal had broken. They couldn't distance themselves fast enough. In the span of hours, she'd gone from being an asset to a crushing liability. They'd gotten rid of her faster than the queen's guard would dispose of a bat caught in the royal coiffeur.

Still, she was truly thrilled for Juliette. In fact, seeing her best friend's happiness, knowing that finding one's place in the world wasn't a myth, renewed her hope.

Maybe this sojourn to Celebration would help her sort things out. At least she'd have a chance to get her head on straight. It would be nice to have some quiet time, time to hear herself think. Maybe alternating the quiet with busy days like today would help her figure out her next step.

She finished touching up her eyeliner, ran a brush through her long, blond hair and pinched her cheeks to heighten the color. With that, she decided to call it good.

"What's next?" Chelsea asked Juliette, who was gathering up her makeup and stashing it in her tote bag.

"Would you mind putting our things in the car while I do one more walk-through before the bride and groom arrive? I want to make sure I didn't miss anything?" Juliette glanced at her watch. "Guests should already be gathering in the lobby for drinks and hors d'oeuvres. The new Mr. and Mrs. should be here in the next ten minutes or so."

"I'd be happy to," Chelsea said as she hoisted her own bag up onto her shoulder and took Juliette's from her outstretched hand.

A small crowd of wedding guests had already gathered in the lobby when Chelsea left the ballroom on her way toward the parking lot. Instantly, she picked out Ethan in the crowd. He was wearing a white dress shirt with a blue tie and was holding his suit jacket. Even from this distance she could see that the tie brought out the azure of his eyes. He was a good-looking man. No wonder her gaze had automatically landed on him.

Lucy was with him, standing by the bar. She was talking to a guy with dark, wavy hair. While Lucy seemed oblivious, hanging on to the guy's every word, Ethan saw Chelsea watching them. He smiled and began walking toward her.

"Let me help you with that," he said, opening the door with his right arm and taking the two totes and garment bags with his left. They didn't weigh a ton, but they had been cumbersome enough that they would've made it challenging to juggle her load and open the doors herself. Ethan scooped them away as if they were nothing.

"Thanks," she said. Her mind skittered back to the mistletoe in the ballroom and she wondered if Ethan would kiss anyone tonight. "I was taking those to the car. I can handle them if you need to get back inside. I'm the one who is working today. You're a guest."

"I wouldn't have offered to help if I thought I might miss out on something in there," he said.

Somehow she didn't believe that. In the short amount of time she'd know Ethan, she'd learned that even though he was gruff, he always seemed willing to lend a hand.

"Well, in that case, I'll lead the way," she said. "The car is just right over there. And thanks, Ethan."

Juliette's SUV chirped when Chelsea clicked the key fob.

"You're welcome," he said as she opened the hatch

and stepped back for him to deposit the bags. "You look real pretty today. Red is a good color on you. Looks nice."

She didn't know why, but she suddenly felt shy.

She finally mustered, "Thank you. You clean up pretty well yourself." It was true. The tie and pressed white shirt was a different look for him, but he wore it well.

He smiled at her again as he slammed the hatch, and the two of them walked side by side back to the building. She caught him slanting a glance at her and she racked her brain for something to say. Why was she so bad at this? She'd always been good at making small talk. Why did he make her nervous? She wasn't a schoolgirl.

"Has Lucy given any more thought to the suggestions I made last week for the barn design?"

"I don't know. She hasn't said anything. You might want to ask her tonight. But right now she's talking to Zane Phillips. I'm sure the barn is the furthest thing from her mind."

"Zane is the guy she's with inside?"

Ethan nodded.

"Are she and Zane dating?"

His laugh was sardonic as he opened the door. "No."

His answer was so resolute she was almost sorry she asked. *Almost*.

"Don't you like the guy?"

"Of course I do. He's like a brother to me—to both of us. Come over here and I'll introduce you to him."

Scanning the crowd, she hesitated. "Maybe later? I need to get back inside and see if Juliette needs my help with anything else."

"Save me a dance?"

Something in the way he was looking at her made her nerves bunch and swarm in her stomach. The feeling took her breath away, but she managed to say, "Sounds like a plan."

Chelsea felt his gaze on her as she made her way back to the ballroom and stepped into the sanctuary of the empty hall, shutting the door behind her.

"How does the crowd look?" Juliette asked as Chelsea handed her the keys. "Are guests starting to arrive?"

"Yes, there are a lot of people out there. Tell me about Zane Phillips."

"Zane Phillips?" Juliette did a double take. "Did you meet him?"

"No, not exactly. But based on what Ethan just said, I think Lucy might have a thing for him and I'm not entirely sure Ethan is okay with that. Is he really that controlling?"

"Who, Zane?" Juliette asked as she adjusted the flowers in one of the centerpieces.

"No, Ethan."

Juliette snorted. "No, Ethan is not controlling. Not when it comes to Lucy's thing for Zane. Ethan happens to have a lot of sense when it comes to that matter. Zane loves the ladies. I'm sure you will be no exception, but he is dating someone right now— supposedly. Listen, everyone in town knows that

Lucy has had a crush on Zane for as far back as—well, for as far back as I can remember, anyway. Zane loves to flirt. Ethan's just being the protective big brother."

"How can you believe that's not controlling? He doesn't want her to date Zane. He doesn't want her to open the barn venue. Even you want her to open the barn. Help me understand."

"Ethan is a good guy, Chels. He's just a little cautious. He's endured some hard knocks with his divorce and losing his parents, but he'll come around about the barn. I mean, it just makes sense. Look at this place." She made a sweeping gesture with her hands. "It's a gold mine. Lucy has a real opportunity by giving it some competition. Even so, Ethan just wants to make sure his little sister doesn't get hurt. He holds his family tight. You can't blame a guy for that."

Chelsea didn't mean to judge. Family was everything to her, too, despite how her parents had reacted to the Hadden debacle. She and Ethan had that in common. Except in her case, she was the little sister with the overly protective siblings; she was the one who didn't measure up.

Juliette's phone dinged with a text. "The bride and groom are here. We can open the doors to the ballroom. Shay and Kyle and the bridal party will make their grand entrance in about ten minutes. If you will help me get everyone in here, then you can go enjoy yourself."

"Enjoy myself? I'm not a guest. I'm the hired help. Remember?"

"You're a volunteer," Juliette said as they moved toward the doors. "It's understood that you will be paid for your efforts in wedding cake and dances with handsome cowboys."

"Well, if you put it that way, how can I refuse? Except, I don't know the bride and groom. Won't I be one step up from a wedding crasher? I could take a cab home."

"If you can get a cab to come all the way out here, you're certainly free to go, but I wouldn't count on it. Dorothy, you're not in London anymore. We're a community here and since you're my friend, you're automatically one of us. So join the party and enjoy yourself."

Chelsea must've still looked dubious because Juliette said, "Don't worry. I'll introduce you to Shay and Kyle after they get inside and get settled."

"Okay."

Really, what choice did she have? She did suppose wedding cake and handsome cowboys sounded like the ingredients that dreams were made of, especially if it meant dancing with Ethan Campbell. And possibly two-stepping underneath a ball of that mistletoe.

That could be fun. Her stomach did that strange bunch-and-dip thing it had been doing since she first saw him.

Yeah, *uh*, no. There would be no kissing anyone tonight, no matter how tempting the mistletoe or the cowboy.

Chelsea stuck close to Juliette, helping her direct

guests who had picked up their table numbers in the lobby as they waited to enter the ballroom.

Once again, she picked Ethan out of the sea of people and noted where he was sitting—table eight. Somehow he had made it past her, either getting direction from Jules or finding his own way. It wasn't that difficult. It wasn't as if he needed a map or a guide. In addition to Lucy and Zane, two more couples were seated at the table. She wondered if someone else would be joining them to fill that open seat. Zane's girlfriend, perhaps? Ethan wouldn't have asked her to save him a dance if he was with a date. But maybe Shay would try to play matchmaker and seat a single woman at the table?

Chelsea wished she would've thought to sneak a peek at the seating chart earlier. She'd had it right in her hands when she'd set up the seating assignment table in the lobby. Of course, she could go out and ask the table attendant, Susan, for the list. However, there was no time for that because Juliette was motioning her over to meet the bride and groom.

The next half hour flew by in a series of dances— bride and groom, mother and son, father and daughter— champagne toasts and the herding of more than two hundred and fifty people through the buffet line. It was exhausting, but finally Juliette shooed Chelsea away.

"You have been such a help, but your work here is done. Now, go get something to eat."

Chelsea's stomach growled at the suggestion. She'd been so busy working she hadn't realized until now that she was ravenous. "Would you like me to make you a plate, too?"

"No, but thanks. I need to coordinate the cake cutting time with the caterer. I'll grab something later. But you go. Relax. Enjoy yourself."

With that, Juliette was off on another mission, leaving Chelsea on her own.

It appeared that all of the guests had made it through the buffet line. Chelsea went through, fixing herself a small plate with prime rib, potatoes and salad. She glanced around the room. The empty place at Ethan's table was still unoccupied. She hesitated a moment, trying to decide if she should invite herself to join him—he had asked her to find him after she was finished working and suggested they dance. But with wayward thoughts of mistletoe and cowboy kisses still lingering, maybe it would be a better idea to disappear into a quiet corner in the lobby away from everyone. In the lobby she could sit down and take off the pinching heels. The shoes were gorgeous, but Juliette's feet were half a size smaller than hers and the loaners were killing her. Not to mention, she really did feel like a fish out of water in this big ballroom full of strangers who were well acquainted with each other.

So, this was what a party looked like when you didn't belong, she thought. Except for Jules, Lucy and Ethan, the rest of the people in the room didn't know her. Of course, she would've experienced the same sensation if she had crashed a wedding in London. But Chelsea was so used to being surrounded by friends that being on the outside looking in was a strange, lonely feeling. She reminded herself that solitude was exactly what she wanted. She hadn't come to Celebration to mix and mingle and make new friends. If she knew what was best for her she would retreat into the lobby, disappear into that enticing corner and mind her aching feet.

As she turned toward the door, she noticed that Ethan looked as alone as she felt. Lucy was talking to Zane; the other couples at the table seemed to be wrapped up in their own animated conversations. And there was Ethan, eating his dinner solo in the middle of these people who were his community, his friends.

And then he caught her staring. As their gazes crashed into each other, Chelsea's stomach rose and then dropped like a falling elevator. When he waved her over, it was too late to pretend like she hadn't seen him. Really, if she was honest with herself, she didn't want to pretend. So she took her aching feet and her racing heart over to table eight.

As Chelsea approached the table, Ethan stood and pulled out the empty chair next to him.

She really did look gorgeous in that red dress. He hadn't been able to take his eyes off her since he'd entered the ballroom.

"Please join us," he said when she got closer.

His invitation drew the others out of their private conversations. They looked over to see who he was talking to. When they saw Chelsea, the guys at the table fell all over themselves standing up. It was almost like something from an old-time cartoon.

"Thank you," she said. "I hope I'm not intruding."

"Of course not," Ethan said. "Everyone, this is Chelsea Allen. She's a friend of Juliette Lowell. She was helping her out setting up for the wedding tonight."

He went around the table making introductions.

Lucy beamed at Chelsea as she put a proprietary hand on Zane's arm. For the first time, Ethan didn't mind his sister's attempt to cozy up to Zane and claim her territory. Zane was a good enough friend to know better than to mess with his sister. Zane had known Lucy long enough to know she'd always had a thing for him, but with his reputation of playing fast and loose with hearts, Ethan had faith Zane wouldn't cross that line because he'd never break Lucy's heart.

Chelsea, on the other hand, was fair game. Since Ethan had *no game* and Zane was nothing *but* game and his girlfriend wasn't here tonight, Lucy's innocent attention might level the playing field. At least it might distract Zane enough to give Ethan a head start.

Huh. A head start for what? Maybe he was no better than Zane in that he wasn't looking for anything more serious than some good company tonight. Did it stand to reason that since Chelsea was Juliette's friend, maybe she should be off-limits, too?

"Chelsea, I'm so glad you're here," Lucy said. "I saw you earlier, but you were busy and I didn't want to interrupt. I have so much to talk to you about. Zane, Chelsea is the fabulous interior designer I was telling you about. The one who has been giving me such great advice about converting the barn."

Ethan didn't like the greedy way Zane was devouring Chelsea with his eyes.

"An ace interior designer and a wedding planner?" Zane asked, all swagger and confidence. "Sounds like you're multitalented."

"Actually, I'm not a wedding planner at all," she said as she unfurled her napkin and placed it in her lap. "I was simply an extra pair of hands helping out tonight. And I only offered some suggestions about the barn. It was nothing groundbreaking, but I was happy to help."

"According to Lucy you helped crystallize her vision. I think she wants to hire you."

"Oh, well, no." Chelsea's cheeks colored. "I'm only visiting for a while. I couldn't commit to seeing a job through to the end. But Lucy has a brilliant mind. I'm sure she will take the suggestions I've offered and make them completely her own."

"Where are you from?" Zane asked.

"England. Jules and I went to university together."

"If you're from England, why don't you have an accent?" Lucy asked.

"I was wondering the same thing," Ethan said. "Ninety-seven percent of the time you sound American, but sometimes the way you turn words and some of the words you use sound vaguely British."

Chelsea's nose wrinkled, drawing his attention to the spray of freckles that he was becoming quite fond of. She was the perfect blend of girl-next-door sweet and sexy self-confidence.

"Like what?"

"Like saying we went to *university* together," Lucy said. "Here, we go to *college*."

"Well, in the UK, we go to university." She smiled and gave a cute quick lift of her right shoulder, one of her mannerisms that was becoming familiar. "I guess I speak the way I do because I have a lot of American friends."

"Look at her," Lucy said to no one in particular as she nodded toward Chelsea. "Who does she look like? She looks like someone and it's been driving me crazy. Who is it?"

Lucy glanced at Ethan. He shook his head. Granted, Chelsea was a beautiful woman, but she didn't remind him of anyone. She had a look that seemed unique to her alone and it, along with her mannerism and Britishisms, was only one of the things he found so alluring about her.

Lucy sighed. "It will come to me—" The music changed into a lively country tune. "Oh! I love this song. Come dance with me, Zane."

After Lucy dragged Zane onto the dance floor, goading him into some sort of group line dance, the other two couples drifted back into their worlds, leaving him and Chelsea alone amidst the wedding's jubilant chaos.

The music was loud and Chelsea was still eating her dinner; the combination made it difficult to carry on a conversation. Finally, when she set down her silverware and pushed away her plate, Ethan was at a loss for conversation starters. He'd never been one for shooting the breeze and he didn't have the patience for small talk. But sitting there imitating an uncommunicative log didn't feel right, either. So he asked her the first thing that came to mind.

"Did you hear they caught the burglar?"

"Really? The one you mistook me for?" She cocked a brow and smiled at him.

"I suppose I deserve that, but in my defense, I was only looking out for Jules. It's not every night that I catch someone breaking and entering in through the bathroom window."

"That's the only reason I'm not holding it against you."

She was surprisingly easy to talk to, blending just enough sass and good humor that he discovered she didn't take herself too seriously. Something shifted in that moment and they fell into an easy rhythm. The song ended too soon and Lucy came back without Zane. She settled herself at the table and inserted herself into their conversation.

"So, I've been thinking about getting a tattoo," Lucy said, leaning in.

What the— "Why do you want a tattoo?" *And more important, why do you feel the need to discuss it right now?*

"Why not, Ethan?" Lucy rolled her eyes. "Why should I expect you to understand? You've never done anything spontaneous in your entire life."

He could be spontaneous. The only reason he

wasn't was because someone had to be responsible. Their brother, Jude, was making money riding bulls for a living, and Lucy had been in school and then in California and now she was back in Celebration making noise about this barn. That left Ethan to run the family's Triple C Ranch. It was hard work that required a strict routine, and routines didn't leave much room for spontaneity.

That was fine with him.

He wasn't going to defend his work ethic. Not that it would matter. Lucy was carrying on about the tattoo again.

"Yeah, I saw this one. It was a Sanskrit saying or something like that." She was studying her fingernails as she talked. "I have no idea what it said. It was on this very classy woman." Lucy looked up and leaned in even closer, as if what she was about to say was top secret. "Okay, confession time. Tabloids are my guilty pleasure. Especially the European ones. Don't judge. I have to look at those on the internet because I can't get them here. But anyway, this poor woman got caught in a majorly compromising position, if you know what I mean."

Ethan shifted impatiently. He had no idea what she meant and frankly he didn't care. He tried to catch Lucy's eye to send the nonverbal message to stop already, but Lucy wouldn't look at him. She was talking to Chelsea.

"Yeah, the story was something about her ex-boyfriend going rogue and publishing their sex tape.

Pretty humiliating, huh? But I digress. That's how I saw her tat."

Oh, hell. He loved his sister, but sometimes she had no shame. Why the hell was she talking about sex tapes and tattoos at a wedding and with someone she barely knew? Chelsea was obviously embarrassed by it because she had turned as pale as the white tablecloth and was sitting ramrod straight in her chair.

"Lucy, really?" Ethan said. "Stop." He turned to Chelsea. "I apologize on her behalf—"

"No, it's okay, Ethan." Chelsea cleared her throat. "So, Lucy, did you actually watch this tape?"

Lucy scrunched up her face as if she was truly disgusted by the suggestion—despite the fact that she was the one who brought up the subject.

"Oh! No way. I didn't want to watch it. Plus, I was afraid if I clicked on it I would get a virus on my computer or my phone. Is it possible to get a virus on your phone?"

"Yes," Chelsea insisted. "Be careful about that. Phone viruses will erase all your photos and contacts and steal all your passwords."

Hmm. He'd never heard of a phone virus, and he had a sneaking suspicion Chelsea was messing with Lucy, which would serve her right.

"Don't watch things like that, okay?" Chelsea said. "No good can come of it. If this so-called boyfriend released that tape without the woman's consent— that's just wrong. Sometimes guys do that to shame women. It's just wrong."

What kind of a jerk would do something like that?

"I did see the pictures, though." Lucy shrugged and she pursed her lips. "That's how I saw this *particular* tattoo. I mean, it was really different. It was *classy*."

"Lucy, just stop, okay?" Ethan said. He looked around, trying to locate Zane, hoping he would come back and distract Lucy. Right about now he would pay him to dance with his sister.

"A lot of people have Sanskrit tattoos," Chelsea said. "It's sort of a thing right now. Everybody's getting them."

"Everybody?" Lucy said. "Does that mean you have a Sanskrit tattoo?"

"Seriously, Lucy," he said. "Stop. End of this discussion. Chelsea, how about that dance you promised me?"

Lucy knew.

She *knew*.

Bloody hell. She'd figured it out and Chelsea was nearly paralyzed by the thought of what Lucy might do with that info.

Her heart thumped wildly and her legs felt like rubber as she followed Ethan out onto the dance floor away from Lucy. If Ethan hadn't asked her to dance, would Lucy have aired that bit of dirty laundry right there in front of everyone?

The grilling about her accent was bad enough. The fake American accent thing was only supposed to be used on rare occasion and when she was in a predicament. The Chelsea Allen persona was a means to an end, an alter ego to throw people—mostly drunk men—off the scent of Lady Chelsea Ashford Alden. If she had known she would be interacting with Juliette's friends—if Ethan hadn't surprised her and thrown her into survival mode—she would've thought better of using the fake accent. Now she was stuck, because she couldn't very well tell them she was just kidding. Life tended to get messy when things got real.

The only reason she hadn't excused herself from this conversation was because she thought playing it cool might throw Lucy off. Of course, she didn't have a way to get back to Juliette's until the wedding was over and it was too late to hide in the lobby corner, but that was beside the point. If she left the reception now, even to take a long walk around the grounds, she'd all but confirm Lucy's theory that she was, indeed, the hapless woman with the *classy* tattoo.

A spiral of Sanskrit words inked permanently on her derriere.

As if the situation couldn't get worse, the music shifted to a slow tune as they stepped onto the dance floor. Ethan didn't give her time to object. He simply pulled her into his arms and they proceeded to sway to the country ballad.

"I'm sorry about what happened back there at the table," he said. "I hope she didn't embarrass you."

He smelled good.

His cheek rested against her temple. The nearness of him, the feel of his solid arms around her, gave her the momentary delusion that she was safe. If she closed her eyes and blocked out everything but the feel of him and the smell of his citrusy aftershave, she could believe it. Well, if not for that compulsive voice in her head reminding her she was anything but safe, because wild card Lucy could expose her at whim.

In a sense she was safer on the dance floor...in Ethan's arms.

"Your sister does tend to fixate on things, doesn't she?"

"That's what I've been trying to tell you. She can be pretty intense."

"Do you have any other brothers and sisters?" Chelsea asked, eager to change the subject.

"A brother, Jude. He's a professional bull rider, off traveling the world."

"Two cowboys in one family?" she said. "You dance very well, considering."

"Considering what?"

"Considering I thought cowboys only two-stepped."

"Don't believe all the tall tales you hear," he said.

"Are you going to shatter my romantic notions?"

"You're a romantic, are you?" he asked.

He shifted his hand to the small of her back. She could feel the warmth of him and it unleashed a shiver of something that resembled desire.

"I suppose I was once. Not anymore."

"Why not? Did another cowboy ride off with your heart?"

No. Hadden Hastings was about as far from a cowboy as a man could be and— "I've told you something you didn't know about me. Now it's your turn to tell me something I don't know about you."

"Like what?"

She thought for a moment. As she did, her gaze drifted to the table. Lucy wasn't sitting there anymore and Chelsea couldn't decide if that was a good thing or not.

"Have you lived anywhere other than Celebration?" she finally asked.

"I moved to Chicago right after college."

"Chicago? That's a surprise."

"Why?"

"I guess I never pegged you for a big city kind of guy. What brought you to Chicago?"

She felt him stiffen a little and pull back ever so slightly. "My wife got a job. It was an offer we couldn't refuse."

His wife. Oh.

Inviting the specter of his wife was a sure way to kill any possible romantic notions. Maybe that wasn't such a bad thing. So she gave in to that part of her that was overrun with morbid curiosity and could not close the door on his past.

"Her name was Molly, right? You mentioned her that day at the barn."

"Yep."

"What was her job?"

He was quiet long enough for Chelsea to wonder if she was being too nosy.

"I'm sorry," she said. "We don't have to talk about it if it makes you uncomfortable."

"No, it's okay. She and I are still good friends. I don't mind talking about her. She is a pharmaceutical sales rep and she still lives in Chicago. We were high school sweethearts and we were probably too young to realize we had no business getting married since we didn't even know who we were or what we wanted out of life, but that didn't stop us. We got hitched right out of college. We had agreed that we would stay in Celebration and take over the Triple C, my family's ranch."

"Triple C?" she asked. "Does C stand for Campbell?"

"It does. My granddad was the one who founded the ranch. He named it after my dad and his brothers. I always wanted to come back here after college and work with the horses. But Molly wanted the big city."

"I love horses. It's been so long since I've been riding."

"We'll have to go sometime."

"Thank you. I would love that."

She stared up into his blue, blue eyes as they swayed together to the slow country love song. The singer was crooning something about his eyes being the only thing he didn't want to take off his lover. In a flash she imagined Ethan undressing her. The feel of Ethan's hand on the small of her back and the thought of him making love to her sent a ripple of longing shivering through her.

She needed to get the conversation back on platonic ground. The best way to do that was to talk about his ex-wife.

"I'm sorry, I interrupted you with questions about the ranch. So you wanted to stay in Celebration, but you ended up moving to Chicago?"

"Yes. Molly's dream job came along and we moved

to Chicago. We came back to Celebration and we got a divorce." He shrugged, as if shaking off the hurt. "That's when I learned you could love someone but never really know that person. I thought we wanted the same things. But we didn't. It sort of felt like bait and switch. But in the end I knew one of us was going to be miserable if we stayed together." He shrugged again. "We were just kids when we made those plans. People change. How can you know someone who doesn't even know what she wants?"

His words hit home. She didn't know what to say. So she waited for him to continue, but he didn't. So they danced, silently swaying to the love song.

Finally, he asked, "What about you? What's your story?"

On some level, she'd known a question like that was coming. That's how intimacy worked. When two people were getting to know each other and one confided something personal… She knew it was her turn to offer something…to meet him halfway by sharing something of herself. But what was she supposed to say about herself? No, it wasn't a good idea to encourage this…this…whatever it was that made her want to put her head on his shoulder and lose herself in him.

Her trepidation was validated when she spied the wedding photographer snapping pictures of people on the dance floor. Lucy had shattered her false sense of security when she'd recognized her; there was a chance others might be familiar with the scandal, too. That's why Chelsea didn't want her picture in Shay and Kyle's wedding album.

"My story is I would love another glass of wine," she said, turning her back to the camera. "Let's go get something to drink and I will tell you anything you want to know."

Within reason, she added silently.

With the photographer on the loose, Chelsea wanted to stay a safe distance away. She couldn't take any more chances.

Ethan handed her a glass of red wine and he sipped something clear and bubbly.

"Is that club soda?" She gestured to his glass.

"It is."

"Are you the designated driver?"

"Actually, I don't drink. Alcohol and I don't get along."

"If this bothers you—" she held up her glass "—I can have club soda, too. Or just water."

"The only thing that'll bother me is if you don't enjoy your wine."

"Are you sure?"

He nodded.

"Fair enough," she said, feeling a little awkward about touching her wineglass to his seltzer water, but knowing it would be worse if she didn't.

It took a strong man to admit that he and alcohol didn't get along. She found his honesty refreshing. Apparently, there was more to Ethan Campbell than first met the eye, complex layers that ran much deeper than she'd realized. She realized how little she knew about him and how much more she wanted to know. But for now, this was a good start.

She turned to him and said, "I promised you my story in exchange for wine. What do you want to know?"

He was just opening his mouth to speak when one of the bridesmaids materialized. "You do know you're standing under the mistletoe, right?" She pointed toward the ceiling. Ethan and Chelsea both looked up. Sure enough, they had planted themselves right under one of the green orbs.

Those who were around them started chanting, "Kiss! Kiss! Kiss! Kiss!"

Before she even knew what was happening, Ethan placed his hand on the back of her neck, leaned in and pressed his lips to hers.

It was a tender kiss. Whisper-soft, but lingering. He tasted of lemons from his club soda and something else that was uniquely him…and quite delicious. For a moment the entire world telescoped and disappeared until it was just the two of them, his lips on hers, his warm hand, which had somehow slipped beneath her hair to rest, skin on skin, on the back of her neck.

A bright flash of light shocked her senses and dropped her with a thud back in the here and now. When Chelsea pulled away from Ethan, she blinked at the sight of Lucy standing there with her cell phone aimed at them.

"Smile, you two," Lucy said. The flash blinded them as she snapped yet another shot.

Chapter Six

The kiss had rocked Chelsea's world, shaken her down to the core. Much more than she cared to admit. It was a kiss that she'd felt all the way to the center of her. But then she'd realized they had an audience and their kiss had been captured in a photograph. She'd murmured something about needing to catch up with Juliette and had beaten a hasty retreat. Ethan hadn't come after her, making it pretty clear that he, too, was fine putting some distance between them.

However, Lucy seemed eager to talk when she caught up with Chelsea.

"Come take a walk with me," Lucy said. "I think you need to get some air."

They'd gone outside and walked past the porte co-chere to a bench next to the fountain in the center of the driveway. They were far enough away from the valets and guests who were leaving early that they wouldn't be overheard. The sound of the water and the noise of purring car engines provided an extra sound screen to give them enough privacy to talk.

Lucy spoke first.

"Lady Chelsea Ashford Alden, I presume. Should I curtsy or something? Because you're royalty, aren't you?"

"Bloody hell," Chelsea muttered under her breath in full accent. A wave of nausea rippled through her. She had forgotten how awful it felt to face people who knew about her fall from grace, people who had seen the evidence. "No, I'm not royal."

"But you have a title."

"That's because my father is the Earl of Downing. Lucy, what are you going to do with those pictures?"

Lucy shot her a smug look.

"Erase them, please," Chelsea demanded.

"No, they're great," Lucy said as she scrolled through them on her phone. "Here, look."

She held out the cell so that Chelsea could see, but stopped short of handing her the phone.

Sure enough, there she and Ethan were, locking lips. She started to breathe a sigh of relief because in the shot, Ethan's face was blocking hers. He could've been kissing any blond woman in a red dress. But it was the second shot that sent the premature sense of relief sailing right out the proverbial window. In that picture, both she and Ethan were squinting right at the camera, looking like wildlife caught in headlights.

When you put the two photos side by side, there was no mistake who Ethan Campbell had been kissing in the first picture.

"What do you plan to do with the pictures, Lucy?"

"I haven't decided yet."

"Please don't put them on social media." She hated how desperate her voice sounded.

"Why not?" Lucy asked coyly.

"For obvious reasons. You know what I'm talking about." Oh, dear God, Lucy already knew about her predicament. Was she going to have to spell it out for her? She really had hoped that she would've exercised a little compassion. Actually, Chelsea still couldn't tell what her motivation was, if she was just getting a kick out of torturing her or if she really did have plans for the photos—like extortion.

Chelsea cleared her throat, trying to dislodge the lump of frustration and panic that was nearly choking her. "I came to Celebration to get away from the press. I wanted to get out of the public eye so I could get my life back together. When the *Tattler* released that video clip, it not only turned my life upside down, but it hurt my family, too. If you publish those pictures— even on social media—I'm afraid chaos will start up all over again. Will you please take pity on me and delete them?"

"But it's such a good picture of you and my brother. I haven't seen him look this happy in ages."

"He looks startled. He doesn't look happy. Neither of us looks happy in those pictures. Look, Lucy, what do you want from me?"

Lucy was looking down at her phone again. "It's simple, really. I want your design services."

"I'm already helping you. Are you blackmailing me?"

"Why?" She looked up at Chelsea with big, innocent eyes. "Would it work if I did?"

Now it was Chelsea's turn to stare at Lucy, and she was sure she was looking at her as if she had two heads, but Chelsea really was at a profound loss for words.

Lucy must've noticed how uncomfortable Chelsea felt because she immediately said, "I'll pay you, of course. It's not like I'm trying to blackmail design services out of you."

"But you are implying if I choose not to continue with your project then you'll plaster the photos of me kissing your brother all over the internet?"

"You don't have to put it that way."

"But that seems to be the only offer on the table."

"You don't have to make it sound so criminal. I've always believed that when you do something for a friend the friend should do something for you. I'll keep the photos and your identity safe, you help me get my barn in shape to open."

"I didn't realize we were friends."

"Of course we are. And we're going to be even better friends by the time this is over. Plus, there's a special built-in bonus just for you. You'll get to spend more time with my brother. I think you two make an adorable couple."

Couple? One kiss under the mistletoe at a spring

wedding did not make them a couple. She thought about asking Lucy what Ethan would think of her little game of extortion. She also thought about simply pulling the phone out of Lucy's hands and deleting the photos herself, but instead she opted for a more sensible right of refusal.

"I'm not licensed to work as an interior designer in the US."

"You don't have to be licensed. I'm not asking you to take down walls."

"But you were talking about adding that second story. I can't help you with that."

"Someone else can handle that part, Lady Chelsea."

"Please don't call me that."

"Why not? If I had a title, I'd insist people called me Lady Lucy. Not only do you have the title, you have the vision to get my barn into shape. You described exactly what I want. I'm not asking you to stay forever. That would be up to you and my brother. Still, can't you think of this as a win-win? I get my barn designed and you get to spend more time with my Ethan."

The crazy thing was Lucy's win-win didn't sound altogether bad. She had to admit that she was excited about the kiss—er—the *project*. Yes, the *project*. She'd never had a chance to see a design task through from start to finish. At least it would be a way that she could keep herself busy when she wasn't helping Juliette. And, in a sense, helping Lucy pull this old barn into shape so that she could open the

wedding venue in Celebration would also be helping out Juliette, because it would give her a venue
closer to home.

"We might be able to work out a deal, but I need
something from you, Lucy."

"Anything. Just name it."

"I need for you to give me your word that not only
will you not sell or post those photos anywhere, you
also have to promise me that you will keep my secret, too. Juliette knows, but I don't want anyone else
in Celebration to know the reason I'm here. Do we
have a deal?"

"I can't promise that nobody else in Celebration
reads the British tabloids, but you have my word that
I will not sell you out. I won't tell anyone else what I
know about you and I won't sell or post the pictures."

Lucy stuck out her hand. As the cool evening breeze
ruffled the nearby hedges, Chelsea regarded Lucy's
proffered hand for a moment. She wanted to believe
her. She seemed like she was pretty up front about
everything. Maybe Chelsea was naive, but she really
wanted to believe Lucy was a decent person.

To prove as much, she shook her hand.

"Actually, as a show of good faith and in the spirit
of working together, I'd like for you to delete the
photos right now."

A mischievous look colored Lucy's eyes. "I'll do
one better. I'll send them to you and erase them on
my phone. Because I'm willing to bet that not too long
from now you're going to want a picture of your first
kiss with my brother. What's your phone number?

I mean, I'm going to need your number anyway if we're going to be working together. Giving me your number will be your good faith gesture."

As Chelsea rattled off her digits, the whole bizarre situation struck her as funny. Nothing in her life had ever been conventional. Not even her first independent design job, where a photo of a first kiss served as the contract.

The photos came through on a ping, and Chelsea checked to make sure she'd received them both. When she looked up, she saw Lucy holding up her phone and, one by one, sending the pictures to the trash can icon.

"They're gone, okay? I mean, you can check my phone if you want."

Chelsea took Lucy's phone and scrolled through all the photo albums. There were several selfies of Lucy making silly faces, a couple of shots of the barn, photos of Lucy with some girlfriends and a few from tonight of her and Zane with their heads together.

They really would make a handsome couple. But the two of Chelsea and Ethan were gone. They weren't even in the recently deleted bin.

She handed the phone back to Lucy.

"Are we good then?"

Chelsea nodded.

Lucy drummed her manicured nails on her phone case. She looked as if she wanted to say something. But Chelsea remained quiet, letting her speak first.

"I don't want you to think that I really would

blackmail you. Obviously, you don't have to do this if you don't want to."

"I don't mind helping you, Lucy. You and I are sort of kindred spirits. I know you've been searching for your place. Juliette really thinks this wedding barn might be a good thing for you."

"I love the sentiment," Lucy said. "But how exactly does that make us kindred spirits?"

"Because I understand what it's like to be searching and how it feels when no one takes you seriously."

Chelsea told Lucy about her successful siblings and how her ex's releasing the tape had cast a shadow over her entire family. That was why she'd left London. The embarrassment that had made her sick to her stomach had nearly paralyzed her when she realized the way it affected her family.

"I'm sorry, but I just have to ask," Lucy said when she was finished doing as she promised. "Why did you let the creep film you if you didn't want it splashed all over the internet? Nowadays, you just can't be too careful or too trusting."

"I didn't know he was filming me," Chelsea said. "We'd been dating a while. I never dreamed he would do something like that. I trusted him. Am I foolish to trust you?"

"No! You *can* trust me," Lucy said.

"I hope so, because if you tell anyone who I really am, word is bound to get around. If the press shows up I'll have to leave Celebration. I won't be able to finish your barn."

"I understand."

"If the press does get wind—even if it's not your fault—you understand I'll have to leave. I decided to come to Celebration and stay with Juliette because I didn't want to hide out in my flat in London. Celebration is a much smaller town than London. If anyone gets wind of this, I'll have no choice but to leave."

"I already told you, your secret is safe with me. I promise I will not say a word to anyone. But you might want to think about confiding in Ethan. He's a good guy and he could be a great source of support."

That was exactly what she was worried about and that was exactly why she wouldn't be confiding in Ethan. She could get used to kisses like that, and that was the last thing she needed right now.

"There you are." The sound of Ethan's voice breaking through the night air as if they had conjured him startled her even more than seeing the camera flash go off. Concern commandeered his features as he looked back and forth between Lucy and her. "I've been looking all over for you two. Is everything okay?"

Chapter Seven

Ethan couldn't stop thinking about that kiss. It had been spontaneous and she'd kissed him back as if she'd liked it as much as he had. But then she'd gotten spooked when the damn camera flash went off. When he'd found her outside by the fountain with Lucy, she'd asked him to take her home because she wasn't feeling well.

The drive was mostly silent. He wasn't sure if he should apologize for kissing her. The only reason he didn't was if she truly was angry at him, would she have gotten in his truck for a half-hour ride back to Celebration?

As she stared out the passenger window, he'd pondered all these things as they drove through the inky night.

Where was she hiding that fancy tattoo? Based on

her reaction to Lucy, Ethan was sure Chelsea had one somewhere on that body.

When they'd reached Juliette's house, he'd walked her up to the door. His instincts had told him to give her space, not to kiss her, even though he ached to taste those lips again.

Instead, he joked, "Are you using the front door or the bathroom window tonight? I can give you a boost if it's the latter. I pride myself on being a gentleman like that."

"You're a funny guy, Ethan Campbell." She held up a key ring, letting it dangle between them. For a moment the way she looked at him made him think she just might lean in herself. Maybe even invite him inside. But then she closed that figurative door. "And you are most definitely a gentleman. Thank you for rescuing me. Good night."

It was fine. He could respect that. It was probably for the best. He wasn't looking for anything permanent. She was only visiting Celebration. Who knew how long she would be there?

He had no idea what was going on inside that pretty head of hers, but the kiss proved—at least to himself—he was not a stick-in-the-mud.

If he was honest with himself, tonight something had awakened inside him. He was feeling things he hadn't felt in a very long time. While he wasn't looking to fall in love, spending more time with Chelsea Allen just might be the cure for his *old man syndrome*, a condition that he was just realizing he'd been suffering. He and Molly had been divorced for five years now; he'd been sober for more than two years. Somehow in that time he had stopped living. Life— that was what he'd felt in Chelsea's kiss. She had such a zest for life—maybe some of that zest would rub off on him. Since she wouldn't be there long, maybe they could see each other. She just might be a good interim step in the right direction. Someone to prime the pump, get him back out there in the world again. But he knew he needed to take it slow.

The Triple C was a relative newcomer compared to other ranches in the area. Ethan's granddad had started the business back in the '40s. After his grand-dad had passed, Ethan's dad, Leroy, had inherited the ranch along with the responsibility to nurture and grow the ranch so that future generations of Camp-bells might continue the legacy. The only problem was that Leroy loved the bottle more than the busi-ness and his drinking began to get in the way. After a while, the only thing that kept the Triple C afloat were the good people that Leroy had working for him. Or so Ethan thought. But after the car accident, which killed Leroy and paralyzed his mother, Ethan realized the business was in worse shape than it ap-peared on the surface.

That was a period of time when his whole world seemed to be crashing down around him. The way he dealt with it was by following in his old man's foot-steps and numbing the pain. He'd nearly followed in his old man's footsteps by finishing off the job of destroying the Triple C Ranch. Thank God he'd woken up and chosen to get himself sober before he lost everything.

He hadn't always been unspontaneous. There was a time when he'd loved nothing more than to laugh and have a good time with friends over drinks. When his marriage started heading south, the drinks blotted out the pain and blurred the reality of just how unhappy he and Molly were together. That was a long time ago. He was a new man. Now the only way to stay on track was to stay on schedule. He got up at five thirty every morning, showered, dressed and brewed himself a big cup of joe. He was in his truck by six fifteen, ready to start his daily rounds of the ranch's 900 acres. The pastures and breeding barns were confined to the 300 acres he'd inherited, but he enjoyed touring the entire property for reasons both practical and spiritual.

He liked to drive around the Campbell land not only to experience the sheer beauty of it but also to remind him of how blessed he was to have inherited the operation and how close he came to losing it before he'd gotten sober. If ever he was tempted to take a drink when he was stressed or tired or lonely, all he had to do was jump in his truck and take in the visual reminder of his blessings. It was better than any twelve-step program—well, maybe not better, but it was a good kick in the ass when he needed to get back on track.

On regular days, when he toured the Triple C, he kept an eye out for things that might cause concern—

signs of predators, an anxious horse, a broken fence, a mare that might not be bonding with her foal. He reported the problems to his assistant manager, who made sure the issue was fixed.

After he finished his morning rounds, Ethan usually returned to his office, where he would spend a couple of hours answering emails, poring over results of races in which the ranch's progeny ran and reviewing the veterinarians' reports of which mares were in foal and which were heading out to the breeding shed that day.

That Monday Ethan finished his morning's work around nine o'clock. He went into the office kitchen, filled two metal to-go cups with coffee, grabbed a couple of muffins that his bookkeeper, Allison, had brought in that morning and drove over to the barn on Lucy's property.

Saturday night when he'd taken her home, Chelsea had mentioned that she was going to head over to the barn this morning to help get Lucy started.

Saturday night things between them felt tenuous—as if it might be the beginning of something good or if there was too much pressure it might all go up in smoke. If he came on too strong he might ruin everything.

So silence had reigned.

Today, however, was a new day. Even if he still felt her kiss on his lips and the mystery of her secret tattoo still haunted him, they needed to talk about the barn before this project got too far out of hand.

* * *

Chelsea jumped at the sound of the barn door opening behind her.

She whirled around to see Ethan sporting two cups of something and a small brown paper bag.

"Good morning," he said. "I thought I might find you here."

"I guess so." She gestured to the goods he was holding. "Either me or someone else. What do you have there?"

He held out one of the cups as he approached. "I come bearing gifts."

"Aw, you shouldn't have. But I'm glad you did. Thank you. I could use a break right now. I've been here since about seven o'clock."

"Alone?"

Chelsea nodded.

"Where is my sister? Why isn't she helping you?"

"She'll be in a little later."

Lucy had texted her last night with some good news. After she'd gone back into the reception, she'd run into Connor Bryce, who, according to Lucy, was an old family friend. She mentioned something about his being a wheelchair-bound veteran who had recently met and proposed to the love of his life. Saturday night at Shay and Kyle Brighton's wedding, Lucy had talked Connor and his fiancée into considering her barn for their ceremony and reception. She was having breakfast with them at eight o'clock this morning. Since everything was so new and up in the air, she had specifically asked Chelsea not to mention the meeting to anyone. Not Juliette and especially not Ethan. In fact, the only reason she told Chelsea was because they were supposed to meet at the barn this morning. Chelsea had cheered her on and assured her that she was fine getting started without her. After all, if you didn't have business, there was no use having a venue.

Of course, she didn't know Lucy very well, but aside from the pseudo-blackmail stunt, this go-getter attitude made her seem a lot more responsible and on the ball than people gave her credit for. Of course, the proof would be in the results, but they hadn't even finalized the concept, and Lucy was already out securing clients. Time would tell.

"This is exactly what I was afraid of. There's work to be done and Lucy is nowhere to be found."

Chelsea waved him off.

"Don't be so hard on her. Because really, it's fine. In fact, I was enjoying the peace and quiet."

"Until I barged in."

One side of his mouth quirked up. She was beginning to realize Ethan Campbell had a dry sense of humor that she didn't always get at first. But at least he *had* a sense of humor.

"I don't know yet," she said. "It depends on what's in the bag."

She pointed to the brown paper bag he was still clutching in his left hand.

Smiling, he said, "You don't miss anything, do you?"

She lifted her chin and shook her head.

He handed her the bag. "Actually, these muffins are something that shouldn't be missed. The Triple C's bookkeeper, Allison, makes them from scratch. She calls them chocolate pecan pie muffins."

Chelsea peered into the bag. "Oh, Lord, that sounds like an addiction waiting to happen." She claimed one and handed the bag back to Ethan.

"I think we need to sit down and give these our full reverence," she said. "Do you have time?"

"If I didn't, I'd make time."

Chelsea blinked; her heart stuttered but she refused to read anything into his words. Or into the fact that he had brought her coffee and a sinfully delicious breakfast treat.

"Let's sit over here." She gestured to an old army trunk that was one of the few things still inside the barn other than a ladder, some sawhorses and an old shovel.

The trunk wasn't very big, so their knees knocked when they sat down. Neither of them seemed in any hurry to give the other more personal space.

They sat there in companionable silence, enjoying the coffee. And he was right, the chocolate pecan pie muffin was to die for.

"This is so good. Why haven't you married her, Ethan? Anyone who makes muffins like this would surely make the perfect wife."

"Someone beat me to the punch. Otherwise, I just might. Though people might gossip about the age difference. She could be my grandmother."

"I suppose you wouldn't want to cause a stir."

"Speaking of potentially causing a stir, I'm concerned that Lucy isn't here helping you. This is sort of par for the course for her."

Chelsea turned to face him. Now the top of her calf was pressed against his upper thigh. Real or imagined, she could feel the heat of his body seeping into hers. "Will you do me a favor?"

"Anything."

"Have some faith in your sister. I think you will be pleasantly surprised. I hope you will. But you have to give her a chance to prove herself."

He regarded her for a moment and she could see the wheels turning in his head. She figured he was probably doing his best to choose his words wisely.

"You are my sister's biggest advocate. Do you always root for the underdog?"

"I suppose I could turn the tables and ask if you always expect the worst of people. But somehow I think you're just particularly hard on your sister. Ethan, Lucy will live down to your expectations and she would probably live up to them if you gave her some credit."

"I'm trying to be realistic."

"I understand. I was always the underdog of my family. I know how it feels when everyone expects the worst of you."

Ethan scowled as if he found that hard to believe.

"The other day you said your brothers don't take you seriously, but that's not the same thing as expecting the worst of you."

Chelsea shrugged. She felt as if she was dancing

along a dangerously fine line between explaining her reasoning and telling him too much.

"All I'm saying is I know how it feels to have a family who doesn't respect what you do."

"How can they not respect what you do? You have talent. I can see it, even in the few suggestions you've given Lucy."

He raised his brow and stared off into the distance somewhere as if he was processing everything. For a moment she worried that maybe she had overstepped. She half expected him to ask who she thought she was to come in and stir things up when her own life was such a mess. Then again, Ethan didn't know that about her and she needed to take care to keep it that way.

"If I am hard on her, it's only because I care. I don't want to see her get hurt. I don't like to see the people I care about get hurt."

He reached out and tucked a strand of hair that had escaped her ponytail behind her left ear. For a moment she thought he was going to lean in and kiss her again. Like he had Saturday night. Today it was just the two of them alone in the barn. No mistletoe. No people goading them. No cameras to capture the moment. Just the two of them doing this unsure pas de deux. She didn't know why they were both so nervous.

It was just a kiss. And what a kiss it had been.

When she had been alone with her thoughts yesterday and the memory of his lips was still fresh, all she could think about was how they'd lost themselves for a moment, how she'd lost herself and momentarily forgotten how Hadden had betrayed her.

Now they were talking around it—about everything but the kiss. It seemed like they were pretending it had never happened.

She reminded herself that she was in no position to get involved with anyone. Even so, if he leaned in right now and kissed her again, she'd let him.

Except Lucy chose that moment to push through the door.

"Chelsea? Oh, Ethan! Good! You're both here." Her exuberance shattered the spell between Chelsea and Ethan. They managed to find the personal space that just moments before had seemed nonexistent. "I have great news."

Chelsea could tell by the way Lucy was nearly brimming over that the meeting with the potential first client must have gone well.

"Let's hear it," Chelsea said. "Don't keep us waiting."

Lucy shot Chelsea a knowing look, but proceeded to deliver the news as if it was a surprise for both of them.

"Are you ready for this?" She didn't wait for them to answer. "Put away all your doubts, dear brother. I have secured my very first client for the *Campbell Wedding Barn*. Do you like the name? That's new, too. I had to name the place since this is really going to happen."

"Details, please," said Chelsea. She glanced at

Ethan, who was looking dubious, impervious to Lucy's effervescence.

"Ethan, Connor Bryce and his fiancée have agreed to be my very first clients and have their wedding and reception at the Campbell Wedding Barn. They are going to come out for a tour next week."

Ethan flinched. "Are you kidding? I mean congratulations on scoring your first gig, but aren't you afraid you might scare them off if you show them the place looking like this?"

Lucy shook her head. "I warned them that they would have to come with an open mind, that the place would be undergoing renovation soon. They promised to bring their imagination, and I promised to give them a discount."

Chelsea was holding her breath, waiting for Ethan's response. Lucy must've been doing the same because the place was unnervingly quiet.

"Did you discuss dates?" Ethan asked.

"We did. They want to get married next month."

"That's impossible," Ethan said. "How in the world are we going to get the barn in shape in a month? The plans that you have been discussing could take six months to complete. For that matter, you don't even have plans drawn up or permits drawn. I just don't see how we can do it."

Even though he was being pessimistic, the fact that he kept saying *we* was a good sign.

"I believe we can do this," Chelsea said. "I'm not licensed in Texas, but I can draft the plans and we can get an architect to pretty them up and sign off on them. It should be enough for permitting—at least according to what I read when I looked it up."

Again, Lucy and Chelsea were holding their breaths, waiting for Ethan's reaction. Of course, Lucy didn't need his approval, but Chelsea already understood that family unity was important to these two.

Ethan's face softened. He shrugged. "How soon do you think you can have the drafting done?"

"If Lucy and I can finalize the design, I can draft up the plans using a program I have on my laptop. I can finish it in a day or so."

"Of course, we will pay you," Ethan said.

"Since I'm not licensed, I don't know if that's even legal. Please consider my design services my business-warming gift to you."

Looking a little skeptical yet resigned, Ethan said, "Looks like we have our work cut out for us. Let me know when the plans are ready and I will help get them to the right people down at City Hall so we can expedite the permitting process. Right now I have to get back to work.

"I'll talk to you later," Ethan said to Chelsea. Then he turned to Lucy, "I'm proud of you, sis."

After Ethan had shut the doors, Lucy squealed, grabbed Chelsea's hands and began jumping up and down.

"This is really real." She stopped jumping. "Or if it's a dream, don't wake me up because I don't want to know."

Chelsea smiled at her. "It's as real as you want to

make it, Lucy. The power is in your hands and you're off to a great start."

Lucy looked around the place dreamily. "When I walked in, you and Ethan looked like you were getting cozy." She smiled. "I told you this would be a win-win."

"I have no idea what you're talking about." Chelsea tried not to smile, but she was having a hard time. "Even so. We'll make this happen."

"Are you talking about the barn," Lucy asked, "or your romance with Ethan?"

Chapter Eight

Chelsea was a woman of her word, Ethan thought as he held open the door of City Hall and they stepped out into the sunny spring morning. She and Lucy had finalized a simple design that required minimal construction and could be completed within a few weeks if they all pulled together and worked hard.

Chelsea had drafted the plans in record time. Lucy had prevailed upon an architect friend to look over the drawings. After the guy had signed off and rubber-stamped it, Ethan and Chelsea handed the blueprints off to the permitting department. Lucy had offered to come, but Ethan had given her a pass for selfish reasons. He wanted to be alone with Chelsea.

The clerk had promised it wouldn't take very long to get an answer—a day or two at the most. First of the week at the very latest, since the planning and zoning committee was meeting on Thursday.

They'd done all the paperwork. Now they waited.

"That seemed easy," Chelsea said. Her perfume, something light and floral, teased his senses as she walked next to him down the sidewalk in downtown Celebration.

"I'd hold off on making that comment until after we get the permits," Ethan said.

Chelsea wrinkled her nose, and the way she looked made his heart compress and then beat a little faster. "Do you foresee there being a problem?"

"No. I hope not. You just never know with bureaucracies. Especially since this is a two-part process. Not only are we asking them to approve the building plan that you so graciously helped Lucy bring to life, but we're also asking for a zoning variance for the property. As it stands the barn is zoned for private use, but the more I looked into it I don't think we should have a problem because the Triple C is zoned commercial. Even though we generally don't have parties in the breeding barns—or at least not the kind of parties we're talking about—I'm hoping the area of the ranch that is zoned commercial will set a precedent."

"Let's hope for the best. You seem pretty connected with all those bureaucrats. If it's based on popularity, you shouldn't have a problem."

Ethan didn't know why but he found it satisfying that she saw him in a favorable light. Maybe it was because they'd gotten off to such a rocky start when they first met. She was too polite to say it, but it was obvious she thought he was a hard-ass. Of course, he thought she was breaking into Juliette's house, but looking back on the situation, even he thought he needed to lighten up a little bit.

That was just one of the ways Chelsea Allen seemed to be good for him. She was helping him realize he needed to get out of his own way, out of his head—that he needed to live a little. Hell, she was making him want to do a lot of things he thought he'd never want to do again.

City Hall was located on the south side of Celebration Central Park. Across the lush expanse of green grass, he saw that a group of food trucks had gathered in the public parking lot.

"Are you hungry?" he asked.

"I'm always hungry," she said.

"Those food trucks over there are new to the area, but they have been getting rave reviews. I've always wanted to try them. Are you game?"

"I didn't bring my purse," she said. "Maybe another time?"

"Carpe diem," he said. "My treat."

Who said he wasn't spontaneous? He wasn't even irritated with Lucy anymore for calling him that. Sometimes the best cure was for someone to hold up a mirror so a person could see himself more clearly.

After his divorce he had allowed inertia to set in. He would own that. But things were changing now. Life was opening up.

He smiled at Chelsea. For the first time in a long

time he wanted to step out of the box he'd been living in for the past five years.

They walked over to the food trucks, arms bumping, hands brushing occasionally. They laughed and talked about everything and nothing in particular as they sat on a park bench eating pulled pork and cinnamon doughnuts. It was nice just to be.

"Do your parents live in London?" he asked.

She dabbed at the corners of her mouth with a napkin. "Just outside the city in a place called Longbridge. But they travel a lot."

"You have what—three siblings, if I remember correctly?"

"Two brothers and a sister. All of them older."

"What do they do?"

She frowned for a moment. "Um… My sister works in fashion. One brother is a doctor—he's quite brilliant. The other is a…bureaucrat."

"So you're the one who should know how to work the system and all its red tape," he said. "Since you have a bureaucrat in the family."

"I don't know about that. British and US zoning isn't exactly apples to apples."

"True. Are your parents retired? You mentioned that they travel a lot."

She laughed. "Why are you grilling me?"

"I'm not. I just want to know you better. I want to unravel all the mysteries of Chelsea Allen."

"I don't quite know what to say."

"I do. Chelsea Allen, you are an enigma."

"Why do you say that?"

"Because it seems like there is a whole lot about you I still don't know."

Ethan shrugged and she smiled. Once again the image of an angel came to mind. But he knew angels didn't kiss like that and they didn't have curves that tempted him to touch her in a way that was anything but innocent.

No, Chelsea Allen was no guardian angel, but that didn't stop him from wanting to believe that she might be the one who could save him from himself. She might be the one who could pull him out of this rut he'd dug for himself over the past five years and start living again.

"You know what I want to do?" she said.

"What do you want to do?"

"I want to go swing on that swing set over there. I haven't done that since I was a kid."

"Let's do it."

They got up and started making their way across the green, manicured lawn toward the empty playground.

She turned to him as they were walking. "I told you about me. Now it's your turn. Tell me about you."

"What do you want to know?"

"Everything."

Their gazes snared for an electric moment and the corner of his mouth quirked up, revealing a dimple in his left cheek. It was a little mesmerizing. She realized even if she didn't do much while she was staying

in Celebration, Texas, she could pass the time looking
at his dimple and be a very happy woman.

It's the little things in life.

"I've been divorced for five years. I was a mess for
about three years after we split up, but I'm sober now."

They sat on adjacent swings but angled themselves
toward each other.

"When did you become friends?" Chelsea asked.
"Saturday at the wedding, you mentioned that you
and Molly are good friends now."

"Actually, we are so much better as friends than
lovers and especially better at friendship than being
married. We just didn't want the same things in life,
but we didn't realize it until after we'd tied the knot.
Things between us didn't smooth out until after I
sobered up."

She didn't quite know what to say. He was very
forthright about his struggle, but she wanted him to
take the lead in pressing further. So she walked the
swing back and pushed off, pumping her legs to start
the swinging momentum. It would give him an easy
out if he wanted to move away from the subject.

She was surprised and glad when he continued.

"My drinking started getting out of hand when
we moved to Chicago. We both traveled a lot for our
jobs."

"You mentioned that she was in pharmaceutical
sales, but what did you do?"

"I worked for an agricultural company in feed
sales. Not very exciting, but I had a huge northwest-
ern territory. Like I said, it involved a lot of traveling."

He got up and stood behind her, grabbing her around the waist. It was nice to feel his hands on her and she was a little disappointed when he gave her a gentle push. She stopped pumping her legs. She didn't want to go too high because she wanted to hear every word that he was confiding.

"When I was on the road I would have a couple or three beers every night—sometimes four or five. When I was home and Molly was away, I would meet up with friends every night for drinks. When she was home and we were together we would drink. There was a lot of booze involved. I was holding a lot of anger and resentment inside and that's how I numbed it. I hated living in Chicago, but I did it for her because it made her happy."

They continued that touch-push rhythm as they talked. Each time his hands were on her back, a shiver of awareness shimmied through her.

She didn't want it to stop there. She wanted to kiss him again to see if it really was as good as it had been at the wedding. Would she see sparks again?

"I don't see you as a big city kind of guy."

"I'm not, and moving away from Celebration wasn't the life plan that Molly and I originally made when we got engaged. We'd been sweethearts since high school and we'd always talked about a future together. We'd planned on going to college together. Then we were supposed to come back to Celebration and I was going to work with my dad and eventually take over the ranch after he retired. She went to business school and was supposed to keep the books and manage the business end. We'd talked about raising our kids here and living happily-ever-after. I'll bet that sounds pretty boring to someone who grew up in a place like London."

She adjusted her grip on the swing's chain, tipping her head back to look at him as she swung out. "No, not really. It's nice here. I can breathe and hear myself think."

"Yeah, but it'll get old after a while. Trust me."

"Are you over this place?" she asked.

"Me? No. I'm so deeply rooted here I can't see myself living anywhere else. Wouldn't mind traveling now and again, but this is home. Molly thought she wanted it, too. She thought that marriage and kids and family would be enough. But how could she know what she wanted when she didn't even know herself?"

"People change, I guess," Chelsea said, slowing down to a stop. "Do you think you'll ever get married again?"

"Marriage is hard. It's not the fairy tale people make it out to be. We're all human. We screw up. We make mistakes and sometimes we end up wanting different things than we thought we wanted. That's growing as a person. I get that. If you don't grow you're stagnant and that comes with its own set of tests. The challenge is when you're married and you change in opposite directions. One day you wake up and realize you love someone, but never really knew that person."

"Did you just wake up one day and decide you didn't want to live in Chicago anymore?"

"The path wasn't that direct. We'd been in Chicago a couple of years when my folks were in an accident that killed my dad and left my mom in a wheelchair. Lucy was only fourteen. Molly and I left our jobs and came home to take care of everyone and the ranch. Molly was really good to Lucy and Mom, but I knew that wasn't where she wanted to be. Then Mom died less than a year later."

Chelsea dragged her feet, stopped the swing and turned to him.

"I'm so sorry."

He gave a one-shoulder shrug. She understood, because what was there to say?

"Did Molly go back to Chicago?"

He nodded. "We'd only planned on staying until we could get Mom to the point where she was taking care of herself. She still had use of her arms and she could get around in a wheelchair. Molly kept saying that we needed to give her as much independence as possible. She was right. No grown woman wants to be treated like an invalid. But Lucy was so young and Mom never fully recovered."

With the palm of his hand, he thumped his chest in the area of his heart. "She was never the same after Dad was gone. Lucy swears she died of a broken heart."

"It sounds like it."

"After she was gone, I couldn't leave Lucy—she'd just turned fifteen. She'd just started high school and both of her parents were gone. Jude took off to ride bulls. Frankly, I wanted to stay and run the ranch. It was selfish, but it was the truth. It was the only piece of normal I could grab. I wanted to make sure my little sister was okay and I needed to make sense of things. They offered Molly her old job back in Chicago. The short version is we tried living apart for about a year and a half before we knew it wouldn't work and then we decided to split. There's a three-year period tacked on the end that's a little fuzzy and involves me nearly losing the ranch—you wouldn't have liked me then. That's why I got sober and haven't had a drink for the past two years and that brings us to now."

Tears welled in Chelsea's eyes. She was speechless.

Ethan Campbell was a good man. He was strong and solid and kind. Sure, he was a little short on patience, but he battled his demons like a gladiator. He was the kind of guy who sacrificed and didn't go all bitter martyr on everyone. He looked out for his family and neighbors and the community. He was even friends with his ex.

Here he was sharing his deep-hearted truth, but she'd only glossed over the surface of her life, which seemed so shallow by comparison. What was she supposed to tell him? *I've dated a lot of men. The one I got serious about proved I'm a poor judge of character. When my parents discovered our sex tape was all over the internet, they told me they didn't want to see my face again until I'd cleaned up the dirty mess. And, oh, yeah, Chelsea Allen isn't even my real name.*

That was rich. It was her life in a nutshell.

Would Ethan be as magnanimous toward her if

she dug deeper and told him the whole sordid truth of what brought her here? Judging by what she knew of him, he might be.

Still, right now things were so good and he looked at her like she was some kind of goddess. She couldn't bear the thought of him looking at her any other way—like she was tainted and dirty and done.

She would be leaving Celebration as soon as she'd put her life back together. In the meantime, Ethan Campbell made her want to be a better person. Was it so bad that she wanted to try to live up to that standard? Was it so wrong to want a fresh start without the permanent stain of her past fouling the future?

"I guess fate has a funny way of stepping in." She stood up and turned to face him. "Do you believe in fate, Ethan?"

"I don't know. Maybe."

The next thing she knew, Ethan's arms were around her waist, pulling her close. His lips were skimming her cheek. His eyes were an unfathomably dark shade of blue, like blue suede or a dusky sky, and they were full of desire.

Her heart hammered against her breastbone.

She wasn't sure who moved first, but it didn't matter. The world went away as his lips met hers and her hands fisted into his shirt collar, pulling him closer.

This time it was different than when they'd come together under the mistletoe. It felt all at once brand-new and like coming home. He tasted like hope and heartbreak, but it was over before it had a chance to blossom into more.

So how was it that in the span of maybe ten heart-beats a lifetime of possibilities flashed through her mind in living color so vivid they imprinted there?

This could be good.

How could this be so good and the timing so bad? Of course, she could make the bad go away. All she needed to do was tell him the truth about who she was and why she was here. But if she told him the truth, he might just get up and walk away.

Better now than later, she told herself. But somehow the pep talk didn't ring true.

He'd rested his forehead against hers. A shadow swept across his features but it didn't hide his desire. She breathed in his smell that was becoming so familiar—soap and leather, the citrusy scent of his aftershave—all male and intoxicating and so very arousing. Desire, heady and irresistible, engulfed her. She tried to ignore the contrast of clean male juxtaposed with the texture of his work-worn hands as he caressed the back of her neck. It was heavenly.

His mouth tempted her again and she leaned in for another taste, a taste that awakened a voracious hunger inside her. As long as they were kissing, they didn't have to talk, and if they didn't talk, she didn't have to tell him the truth.

At least not yet.

His lips parted and he deepened the kiss. Chelsea wanted to consume him. She wanted their bodies to succumb to this intense heat and meld into one.

But all too soon they returned to earth, landing with a thud. She tried to assess how he was feeling. She bit her bottom lip, gaping at him. His blue eyes seemed to be amazed and even darker—almost pitch—with wanting. Or maybe she only imagined his desire because she wanted him to feel the same things she was feeling, to have been as affected by the kiss as profoundly as she had been.

Since Hadden betrayed her, she thought no one would ever be able to break through the wall that she'd built around her heart. A wall designed to keep people out so they never got the chance to betray her the way he had.

"Should I apologize for that?" he murmured, his hand still in her hair, their foreheads still touching, her lips still tingling and craving more.

"No," she said.

"Good. Because I'm not sorry."

"Then definitely don't apologize. Because I'm not mad about it at all."

She bit her bottom lip. "Well, actually, I was quite mad about that kiss. But not in an angry way. More like a crazy about it kind of mad. So don't hesitate to do it again."

Chelsea climbed up the ladder to sweep the cobwebs off the barn's rafters. She'd attached an old towel that Juliette had bequeathed to the cause to a long-handled paint roller and voilà! Instant cobswabber.

The height of the ladder coupled with the extension of the wooden handle gave her extraordinary reach, all the way up to where the high walls connected with the roof.

The barn hadn't been occupied in ages. From the looks of it, it was entirely possible that these nether regions had never been cleared of cobwebs—even when the place had been in use. But the wood had to be cleaned before they could paint.

The guy they'd hired to help clean up had needed to leave before he finished the job so he could make it to his son's lacrosse game. He'd offered to stay, but Chelsea had sent him on with good wishes to his son for a winning game.

Chelsea didn't mind. Since they were paying him hourly, she would save Lucy a bit of money by finishing up the chores herself. Juliette was out of town on a job for the weekend. Chelsea had run home, fixed a quick bite to eat and let out Franklin before returning to the job site. A designer's duties usually didn't entail custodial services, but she didn't mind. It was nice to keep busy.

Juliette's house was lovely and warm and comfortable, but Chelsea had felt restless and cooped up. Better to expend her anxious energy on something productive rather than drive herself and the dog crazy by pacing about the place. This point was driven home when Franklin had tried to herd her toward the couch when she was pacing. If she was irritating the corgi, she knew she needed to get out and do something productive. So she'd come back to the barn. Plus, there was a better chance that she might run into Ethan at the barn than sitting on the couch watching the telly with the dog.

She hadn't seen him since yesterday when he'd brought her back to Juliette's after the park. It was clear that they were both a little confused about what to do next.

He'd excused himself, saying he needed to get back to the ranch to do his rounds. She'd welcomed the distance because she needed to put things into perspective.

She could still feel the power of his kiss on her lips. The lingering effects shot an arrow straight down to her lady parts, and they were begging her to get to know Ethan Campbell much better.

After she had a chance to step back and give her ovaries a chance to calm down, common sense stepped in and reminded her that it wasn't a smart time to lose her wits over a handsome cowboy.

But her ovaries begged to differ. To hell with what she *should* and *shouldn't* do. She was attracted to him. He was attracted to her. They were consenting adults. What was wrong with having a little fling while she was here? She'd said she wouldn't allow Hadden to cast her in the role of victim. What better way to break out of that corral than to ride that cowboy until all her troubles fell away?

And where would you like him to send the souvenir recording?

Bloody hell! Decent people didn't do things like that.

Ethan was friends with his ex-wife. He hadn't

sought revenge. He wasn't inclined to slut-shame her because she hurt his feelings.

She remembered a saying in a needlepoint picture hanging up in Juliette's house: *I'm a grown-ass lady and I do what I want.*

So there. She would do what she wanted.

For now she took a moment to survey the structure from her high perch. Already, they had a long, hard row to hoe if they were going to get the place ready for Connor Bryce's party. Actually, she was going to suggest that they have a grand opening party before Connor and his fiancée's wedding reception so that they could work out any kinks.

She hoped the subcontractors would be conscientious about showing up on the promised dates and times. Ethan had said they would and that their work was of exceptionally good quality. Probably one of the perks of living in a small town like Celebration, Texas, and knowing the people you hired. If they didn't deliver what they promised when they promised, the person who'd hired them knew where they lived.

They'd know soon enough, once the plans were approved and the real work started.

She couldn't imagine such service in London. Even though this was her first job as head designer—er, okay, so she was the *only* designer on this project and she was donating her services—the process seemed a far cry from the horror stories she'd heard at Hargraves.

Of course, as a newbie, she'd never been allowed

to roll up her sleeves and run with a project. Her days were filled with important tasks such as sorting fabric samples and culling through product lists, identifying and deleting discontinued items and searching for suitable replacements.

In the short time she was with the firm, Geoffrey Hargraves had allowed her to choose three light fixtures for a movie star's London flat. The client got to pick her favorite. Chelsea had never learned which one the client chose—nor had she known the identity of said movie star because of the firm's steadfast rule that a client's privacy was to be protected above all else. She knew better than to ask and Geoffrey certainly didn't volunteer the information. So that was the extent of the creative input she'd been allowed to give during her few weeks at the firm. Then the scandal had broken and she'd gotten the boot before she had a chance to prove herself.

There was something strangely fulfilling about conceiving an idea in her imagination and knowing she could watch it take shape right before her eyes.

She hoped Lucy would find a similar feeling of accomplishment once her business began gaining momentum.

Lost in thought, Chelsea swiped the long-handled dust mop as far as she could reach across the slanted ceiling. How ironic it was that she'd been searching for herself in London's hubbub and it had never seemed to fit. *She* had never felt like she fit, despite the fact that London, with all its posh parties, was home and its fancy people were her people. But they weren't really. It had always felt so superficial, but she hadn't realized the shallowness had been the root of her discontent. She hadn't known it until she'd gotten away from it and had been forced to face herself in the quiet.

Who knew she'd be more content alone on a Friday night cleaning a barn than clubbing in Ibiza? Even more of a shock was who knew she'd connect with herself in a place like Celebration, Texas?

London had been the puzzle piece that looked as if it *should* fit, but didn't quite match up. No one would've ever known it really didn't belong until the rest of the pieces were set in place and the picture was off and a piece was missing elsewhere. Celebration seemed a good fit for the puzzle that was her life. At least for the time being she could catch her breath and get in touch with her heart. And maybe get to know Ethan Campbell a little better.

The squeak of the barn door opening startled her out of her reverie. She flinched and lost her grip on the wooden pole and it fell from her hand, landing with a clattering thud at Ethan's feet.

Chelsea's heart thudded and the butterflies that had been her constant companion since she'd arrived swooped in formation.

"Good grief, Ethan! Don't sneak up on me like that."

Bloody hell, and she'd let the accent slip.

He held up his hands surrender-style, but her accent didn't seem to have registered with him. "Don't fall off the ladder. I didn't intend to sneak. I had no idea you were in here. What are you doing here this late?"

Her heart was still thudding and she placed a hand on her chest as if that would help it settle down.

"I'm working," she said. "Kenny French needed to leave for his son's sporting event. He wasn't finished with the cobweb dusting and I thought I would wrap it up for him. It will save Lucy some money. For that matter, why are you here?"

Thank God you're here.

"I'm sorry I scared you. I was driving home and I saw the light on and came in to turn it off."

She laughed and loosened her death grip on the side of the ladder. "Please don't leave me alone in the dark."

Her lips tingled as she thought of yesterday's kiss, the feel of his lips on hers, his strong, capable hands on her body and how she'd hated it when he'd said good-night. What would it be like to be alone in the dark with Ethan? Her heart rate kicked up again and a slow burn of approval started deep in her belly. What would he do if she climbed down from the ladder and proceeded to jump his bones?

"I wouldn't dream of it," he said.

"I beg your pardon?"

"I wouldn't leave you in the dark. Not alone, anyway."

Ethan bent down and picked up her dust mop. From her perch on the ladder, she could see that grit and dust from the floor now stuck to the cobwebs.

If she kept using it, she would scatter dirt and dust all over and make the mess worse.

"You're going to need a clean towel," Ethan said.

She frowned and started down the ladder. "Or I could simply rinse off that one."

"There's no water out here. They won't have it turned on until next week after we get the permits."

"Does Lucy have a spigot outside her house?" Chelsea asked.

"Speaking of, where is my sister and why isn't she out here helping you? Again."

With both feet now planted firmly on the ground Chelsea stepped away from the ladder.

"She had another business meeting tonight. I don't mind working by myself. The quiet is kind of nice."

Ethan studied her in that unapologetic way of his. The man was such a study of contradictions. On one hand he was gruff and a little rough around the edges, but on the other, he was so comfortable in his own skin, so completely unselfconscious. A refreshing change from the guys she was used to. Ethan Campbell, all long, tall, six-foot-something of him, was a take-me-as-I-am-or-leave-me-the-hell-alone kind of guy. Chelsea had to smile to herself because she was ever so tempted to take him exactly as he was right here, right now.

"You don't strike me as the type who thrives in solitude," he said.

How on earth had he come to that conclusion? "Why would you think that?"

The dimple in his left cheek winked at her again. He was flirting with her. Her heart soared.

"I can usually get a pretty good read on people."

"Is that so?" she said, trying to play it cool.

He nodded.

Swallowing the urge to come clean and confess everything to him, she put her hands on her hips and tilted her head to one side. "Tell me, what else do you think you know about me?"

She'd learned a long time ago not to give anything away. If he'd learned something, say, about the video, let him broach the subject first. If he knew anything. And she was betting that he didn't. Praying that he didn't.

God, please don't let him know.

He studied her for a moment and her heart thudded with each passing second.

"I think you're one hell of a hard worker and I think you look like you could use a break. Want to come to my place and have something to drink?"

She started to protest, but he stopped her.

"Come on. It's Friday night and the two of us are standing here in an old barn. We can do better than this."

She always had been a sucker for dimples. His dimples in particular.

"Well, since you put it that way. How can I refuse?"

After she stepped outside, he clicked off the light and shut the door. The night air was springtime cool, and she caught a whiff of something heady and wonderful perfuming the air.

"What is that lovely scent?" she asked, lifting her face into the evening breeze.

"That's jasmine. It grows hardy out here. That's it over there, climbing the fence."

"Mmm. I could bathe in it. It's intoxicating."

He followed her to the passenger side of his truck, opened the door for her and held her elbow, helping her into the Ford's cabin. When she turned to thank him she saw him draw in a deep breath.

"Funny how you can get so used to something you don't even notice it anymore," he said. "It is nice."

They made small talk as they followed a dirt road that was bordered by white post and rail horse fencing on either side. The path cut through a large stretch of grassy land. It led to a ranch-style house that sat a good distance off the highway.

The amber porch light welcomed them and illuminated two rocking chairs and several barrel planters brimming over with an assortment of colorful flowers.

"Is this your house?" she asked as she climbed the steps.

He nodded.

She couldn't recall the mental picture that had come to mind when she'd pictured Ethan at home, but it hadn't been quite like this.

"It's nice," she said as she stood on the porch, squinting out through the veil of inky evening, trying to get the lay of the land. There was a lot of it, for as far as she could see.

Some kind of night creature chirped in the distance. "Does all this property belong to you?"

"Lucy, our brother Jude and I each own a third." He turned the knob on the unlocked door. They stepped inside. "We decided it would be easier to split it into three equal parcels. Lucy owns the area surrounding the barn. This part is mine. Jude owns the property over on the west side. We each inherited about three hundred acres."

"That's a lot to take care of." She glanced around as she followed him into the living room. The eighties-era decor was rustic, but the house seemed neat and tidy. Chelsea imagined that it probably looked exactly as it had when Ethan was growing up. Since his parents were gone he probably found some comfort in that.

"It keeps me busy," Ethan said. "I have my routine. As long as I stick to it, upkeep's not a problem. I like keeping busy."

"You and I have that in common," she said. "We both like to keep busy."

He cocked a brow, as if he might have read something into her words. But then he nodded and gestured to the couch. "Make yourself comfortable. Would you like something to drink?"

"A glass of wine?" Her hand flew to her mouth. The words had no sooner escaped her lips when she realized what she said and that he probably didn't keep alcohol in the house.

She waved her hand as if to erase her mistake. "Actually, water is fine. I'm sorry, Ethan. I didn't mean to be insensitive."

He shook his head. "You don't need to apologize. I wish I could offer you wine, but I don't have any. We could go to Murphy's Pub if you want. They have a good wine list."

"I don't need wine. I'm sorry. I shouldn't have—"

"You don't have to tiptoe around the subject when you're with me. You're not the one who has a problem with alcohol. You can have wine when you're with me and you don't have to apologize for it."

She thought about the people she used to go out and about with in London. The parties, the mornings when she would sleep until noon because she was nursing a headache from overindulging the night before. She'd never thought she'd abused alcohol. Not even after Hadden recorded their intimacy unbeknownst to her. Maybe if she had been more cognizant it wouldn't have happened.

It certainly wouldn't hurt her to abstain for a while.

"How about some coffee?" she asked.

"Coming right up."

She followed him into the kitchen, which also looked like it had been frozen in all of its eighties grandeur, with its ivory-painted cabinets, sky blue tile backsplash, butcher-block countertops and light blue-and-yellow linoleum floor.

Just like the living room, it was neat and clean. Everything seemed to be freshly scrubbed and in its place. An honest kitchen for an honest man. Just like Ethan, it was unapologetically bona fide. No arrogance. No pretense. No airs. It was what it was and there was beauty in that.

As she watched him spoon coffee into a filter, the old familiar tangle of anger at Hadden and self-loathing for landing herself in this degrading situation knotted in her stomach. She felt like such a fraud standing in Ethan's house, pretending to be someone she wasn't, someone virtuous and honorable. The person he deserved didn't hide her name or her reason for being here. She certainly didn't fake an American accent for fear that she would be found out for who she really was.

Again, the sudden need to confess everything to him swept through her with gale-force intensity.

What would he think of her if he knew her real story?

What would this man, who took pride in carrying on his family's legacy and fiercely protected his little sister, think of her if he knew the truth?

What would he think of her if he saw the recording?

The humiliation of disgrace bloomed on her cheeks as he turned around to say something to her.

"Are you okay?" he asked.

No.

"I'm fine." She mustered her best lying smile. "Why would you think I wasn't?"

He watched her for a minute.

Maybe she wasn't as good at deception as she thought.

"You looked upset. Are you— Is this okay? If you're uncomfortable—"

The coffeemaker started hissing and chugging.

"I'm not uncomfortable," she said, hanging tight to her enunciated American accent. She just couldn't seem to let go of it. "I promise."

Her last words were softer. Because she really was okay being here with him. No, more than okay. She wanted to be here. That part wasn't a lie. She just wished it all could be aboveboard.

She wanted to kiss Ethan again. In full self-disclosure, she wanted to do more than kiss him. She hadn't felt that way about a man in a long time. Ethan Campbell was built from different stock than Hadden Hastings.

But she was getting ahead of herself. Right now they were having coffee. It was a chance to get to know a man who seemed to be interested in her for herself. Not because of her brother's political connections or because her sister could score front-row seats at any number of fashion week shows.

His lopsided grin brought his dimple out to play. "Good, because I'm glad you're here."

Chelsea experienced a moment of clarity. This was how it should be between a man and a woman. Organic attraction. Nothing premeditated or conditional. With Ethan, she could glimpse the potential to becoming the person she always wanted to be. This person she was pretending to be now.

This was nice…and intimate.

"So, I never asked. How long are you staying? It seems a shame that Juliette has to be away so much of the time you're here."

"It's sort of open-ended right now."

He looked a little surprised. "Are you on vacation or between jobs?"

"It's a long story," she said.

"I have all night," he returned.

That deep Texas drawl wound its way down her spine like a velvet caress and sent a shiver that reached all the way to her core. That was a loaded statement, and there was that inflection in his voice that she could take all sorts of different ways.

"What a coincidence. So do I."

Chapter Nine

Ethan couldn't deny the spark of longing that surged through him. He wanted her. He hadn't wanted a woman like this for a very long time.

There had been other women since Molly. Most of them had been one-nighters, especially before he'd gotten a handle on the drinking. But since he'd been sober, the idea of sex for sex's sake didn't appeal to him as much. Sure, he still had needs, but sex to numb, sex to forget himself for a while, just didn't seem worth the hustle anymore. Living in a small town like Celebration, it wasn't really feasible to sleep with your neighbor or the bartender at Bistro Saint-Germain and expect to remain platonically friendly. Word got around. Women started comparing notes.

Things felt different with Chelsea. It wasn't just

because she was leaving soon. At first he thought it might be convenient, but she was Juliette's best friend. Juliette had always been like family, even though she wasn't seeing his brother, Jude, anymore. By virtue of friendship, it took Chelsea out of the one-nighter category.

So, where did that leave them?

Chelsea was the first woman in a very long time who had thawed his frozen heart and warmed him to the idea of something more than casual sex, something more than friendship.

They had taken their coffee into the living room and were sitting comfortably close on the couch. They'd talked about the barn; they'd talked about horses and going riding sometime this week; they'd even talked about the weather. It wasn't that they'd run out of things to say as much as it was that with each exhausted topic, the urge to kiss her, to touch her, to pick her up and take her to his bed, edged out his ability to keep up a conversation.

But he didn't want her to feel like he'd brought her here with ulterior motives.

His eyes fell to the creamy expanse of her neck, which looked enticing and smooth beneath the V of her T-shirt. He forced his gaze back up to meet hers.

Finally, she reached out and took his cup and set it on the coffee table. "Would you stop being such a gentleman and kiss me?"

That was all it took.

She melted into him. He bent his head, and as if she sensed the subtle movement, she tilted her head up and met his lips. The feel of her in his arms—the way she fit so perfectly—reminded him of when he'd kissed her at the park. They hadn't spoken of that kiss. He thought he'd be just fine with that, but the minute he'd walked in and saw her on that ladder tonight, he knew he wanted to kiss her again. No, not just kiss her, he wanted to make love to her. Judging from the way she was holding on to him, she didn't seem to mind venturing out of the friend zone, either.

Her body, so close and supple, made him yearn to explore her swells and valleys. His hands got a head start on doing just that. He kissed her gently at first then more insistently as he pulled her flush against him.

"You are so beautiful," he said, trailing a finger down her jawline. Then his lips followed the path his finger had traced.

She sighed. It was almost inaudible, but he felt it when he found her lips again. He tightened the embrace in response; his hands swept down her back, over the slight rectangle of bare skin where her cotton shirt met the waistband of her low-slung jeans.

As they deepened the kiss, his tongue swirling around hers, her response was so invitingly erotic that he didn't even realize the rasping moan echoing in his head had escaped from his own throat.

He pulled back, trying to read her, needing to make sure she wanted this as much as he did. If she didn't, he would honor that, but they needed to stop now. He needed to take her back to Juliette's and they needed to say good-night.

"Are you okay with this?" he asked.

"I'm more than okay." She looped her arms around his neck and brushed a feather-light kiss on his lips. "Ethan, I have a feeling we're both going to be even better very soon."

When she covered his mouth with hers, it was all he needed to extinguish any doubts that she wanted him as badly as he wanted her. He longed to show her exactly how hot he burned for her.

He took possession of her body, craving the feel of her hands in his hair; the searing heat of her touch on his shoulders, trailing down his back; the white-hot ecstasy of skin on bare skin as she slid her hands underneath his shirt. They held each other so close he could barely breathe. But her kiss was the only air he needed. She breathed life into him, imbued him with something he hadn't felt in a very long time. Something he'd been missing. He was finding it in a woman who was getting under his skin as deftly as she crawled in through bathroom windows. Breaking and entering.

Breaking down his barriers and entering his heart.

Even if it would be temporary.

Right now he had to have her. He couldn't get enough of her. Just like earlier when he'd had a hard time finding the words to explain what he wanted, how he felt. She'd met him halfway, bridged that gap. Now all he could do was show her how he felt.

With Chelsea in his arms, the heaviness he had been carrying around was lifted off his shoulders and out of his heart. He held her close, afraid that if he turned her loose, she might slip away. He kissed her more urgently this time, taking possession of her mouth, craving the shared heat.

Her skin was smooth and her body was firm with a sexy, feminine strength that had him summoning every ounce of self-control to keep from taking her right then and there.

"Let's go into the bedroom," she murmured, as if reading his mind.

He kissed her deeply as he backed her down the hall—tongues thrusting, hands fighting with buttons, teeth nipping gently at tender skin.

Their ravenous slow two-step finally landed them in his bedroom.

Need guided his hands as he explored the swell of her breasts and skimmed her belly until he found the tail of her T-shirt and slid his hand underneath. When his hands found her breasts again, she drew in a ragged breath. As he moved his thumb over her nipple, hard as a rock even through her lacy bra, a low moan escaped her lips and he nearly came undone.

She was spellbound by his touch. He pulled her shirt over her head, and got rid of her bra, jeans and panties.

"Where is it?" he murmured, brow arched in a way that was so sexy it nearly made her come undone.

"Where is what?" she answered in her most playful voice.

"That tattoo." He ran his hands down the side of her and slid them underneath her so that he cupped her bottom with his hands, pulling her close. She could feel his arousal.

She smiled up at him. "What makes you think I have a tattoo?"

"I gathered as much from that conversation about tattoos we had at the wedding. You made a pretty good argument that even classy women have them, and you're probably the classiest woman I've ever met. Ever since then, I've been trying to imagine where a classy woman hides her wild tattoo?"

Chelsea's breath hitched in her throat. Oh, no. He knew. If they were going to make love, if this was really going to happen she should tell him everything right now, before they went any further.

"On her wild side, of course." Chelsea wriggled out of his embrace and turned around to show him the spiral of Sanskrit words tattooed on the right side of her derriere. "It means, *live with no regrets—contentedness is the only path to happiness*."

A low, sexy growl that sounded like approval escaped his throat. He moistened his lips with his tongue and kissed her again. Even though this relationship, this fling—whatever it was they were doing—was temporary, she should tell him the truth. She wanted to trust him. She did. She had to or she wouldn't be able to give herself to him. She couldn't lie here with him, vulnerable, exposed, allowing him to break through her personal barricades, inviting him to partake of her body, if there wasn't mutual trust.

"Ethan, I need to explain something—"

"*Shhhh*. Not right now." He kissed her on the forehead and eased her onto the bed. "Wait right here. I'll be right back."

She watched him undress in a small shaft of moonlight that filtered in through a slim gap in the drawn drapes. The faint light illuminated the room just enough so that she could see his muscled body, the long-limbed ease of his gait as he rounded the bed, the plane of his taut stomach, the bunch of his biceps as he bent to pull something—a condom, she guessed—from the nightstand drawer. He lowered himself down onto the bed next to her, stretched out beside her and rose up on his right elbow so that he was looking at her.

"Are you okay?" He ran the pad of his thumb over her bottom lip. "Is this okay?"

She nodded.

Say something.

"We don't have to do this if you're uncomfortable."

"No, I'm fine."

She needed to tell him the truth, but she couldn't focus on words with Ethan's hand tracing circles on her bare stomach. She shivered, unsure if the frisson was induced by guilt or her overwhelming desire for him.

Or maybe both.

Definitely both.

As she watched him slide the condom down his considerable length, all she could think about was what that big, strong body of his would do to hers, the pleasurable heights to which he could take her. The delicious thought pushed the explanation that she'd been piecing together—the words she should be saying right now—out of her head. The clarification of who she really was—why she was in Celebration, why she'd given him a fake name—faded farther and farther into the back of her mind until all she was aware of was the hunger in his eyes and the way moonlight played off his dark brown hair. She ran her fingers through locks that curled defiantly at the nape of his neck, working her way around to push wayward strands off his forehead.

Her confession had to come right now...

But right now he was addling her with gentle caresses and soft kisses that paid homage to her body's most sensitive places—the tender and oft forgotten spot at the base of her ears, the dip where her neck gave way to her collarbone, the ticklish zone under her arm, revealed when he laced his fingers in hers and pinned her arms over her head. He trailed sweet kisses down her body until he reached the private place hidden between her thighs and his tongue found its way to her center.

He held her under his spell, captivated by pure bliss until she cried out in pleasure that was so powerful it pulsed off her in waves.

Ethan's gaze locked on hers as he settled himself between her legs and thrust gently to fill her. She gasped and raised her hips to meet him and take him all the way in. She reveled in the sensation, in the wonder of this man inside her.

They both held still for a moment as if they were afraid to break the fragile spell of their joining. She looked into his eyes—eyes that were the deepest shade of blue she'd ever seen, like India ink or a midnight sky—and she smoothed her hands down his back to cup his bum, holding him there.

"You feel even better than I imagined," he whispered before he lowered his mouth to hers for another kiss.

She pulled him closer, sinking in and savoring the deliciousness of him.

Finally, when he pulled back to look at her and she smiled up at him in a lusty daze, he began to move inside her, slower than she wanted, each movement purposeful and deliberate, promising to drive her mad.

As he thrust again, she rose up to meet him and he slipped his hands beneath her bottom and shifted her so that he could go deeper. Her body ignited with a glorious passion so intense that it flared from the inside out and only got better when he began pumping his hips a little faster.

Chelsea wrapped her legs around his hips as the golden warmth gathered in her belly and blossomed outward. Each stroke, deeper and deeper, brought her closer to release. Her body shook from need as she reveled in the sensation of his every move. Ethan steadily increased his rhythm, and his breathing was heavy and raspy against her ear.

When the pleasure wave crested, a moan escaped her lips. His mouth found hers again. Her release was suspended for a moment that seemed to stretch into eternity before finally spilling over. Ethan's kiss caught her cry of pleasure and it seemed to fuel his own.

"Chelsea," he groaned as he made his final powerful thrust.

Ethan's eyes closed and his body tensed as the orgasm shook him. Chelsea slid her hands up along the rigid muscles of his biceps and shoulders until her fingers curled into his hair. He hovered above her for a moment, breathing hard. He looked sexy as hell and quite satisfied. She tried to pull him down on top of her, but not before he kissed her again as if drawing a sustaining life's breath from the final moments of their coupling.

Finally, he collapsed next to her, turning her body so that she spooned against him. He pulled her in close with a possessive arm so that her body was flush against his.

Feeling warm and protected and utterly spent, she curled into him, basking in the heat that radiated off his skin.

Their lovemaking had zapped her energy; yet the physical closeness, the way he continued to hold her, filled her heart. Even as her body gave in to the satisfied weariness, every muscle in her body relaxed. If she could only quiet the voices in her head that nagged, *You should've told him. You need to tell him.*

She would.

Soon.

Just not right now.

Chapter Ten

It was nice making coffee for two and bringing a cup to Chelsea in bed. Even so, Ethan hated to wake her up. Instead, he wanted to crawl back under the covers next to her and make love to her for the rest of the day, shutting out the world so it was just the two of them.

However, Ethan had awakened to a text from Tyler Jennings, the vet who looked after the Triple C's horses, saying that Calendula, a mare they were looking to breed with a stallion on Kingston Farms, was ready to go. Since they were inseminating the old-fashioned way, they'd been on standby for signs that the time was right to deliver Calendula to her stud, and the time had come.

Crawling back into bed with Chelsea sounded a hell of a lot better than delivering a horse.

His body responded, seconding the motion, but good sense reminded him he had a short window to load up Calendula and drive her over to the Kingston ranch in Burleson, about an hour southwest of Celebration. No matter how much every primal cell in him protested, Ethan knew he couldn't put off the transport or they'd have to wait another month for Calendula to complete yet another cycle.

Chelsea looked beautiful lying there with her blond hair spread all over his pillow. He set the hot coffee on the nightstand and sat down next to her on the side of the bed. As he brushed a wisp of hair off her forehead, her eyes fluttered open. She blinked a couple of times as if trying to orient herself. Then a slow smile spread over her face.

"Good morning," she said, stretching luxuriously, reminding him of a sleek, golden cat. Her voice was husky with sleep.

"Morning." He knew he was grinning like a damn fool, but he couldn't help himself.

"Is that coffee I smell?"

"I brought you a cup. Black. Just how you like it." Even though he'd just learned how she took her coffee last night, it felt intimate. Like he knew her. It seemed like he did. She felt comfortable and familiar in the best way. A way that made him hungry to learn more. He handed her the mug and she scooted up to a sitting position, modestly covering her bareness with the sheet as she accepted the cup.

"Thank you," she rasped. "Wow. Coffee in bed. I could get used to this."

So could he. He would bring her coffee every morning if it meant he could wake up next to her.

"Sorry to get you up so early," he said. "Turns out, I have to deliver a horse this morning. I didn't know about it until after the vet had done his rounds."

"Is everything okay? I hope it's not an emergency."

"Nope. Just nature calling. She's ready to be bred."

"You don't do the breeding here?" she asked.

"Sometimes," he said. "This is a special arrangement and it's easier to transport a mare than it is to wrangle and move a ton of bucking stallion. We've been on standby for days and the vet just gave me the green light that she's ready to go."

"Oh, I'm sorry. I don't want to make you late. I can leave." She held out the cup, trying to give it back to him, but he waved her off.

"No, take your time. Drink your coffee. I have some things I need to do before I leave." He stood. Before he turned to go, he added, "In fact, why don't you come with me?"

He hadn't planned on asking, but he heard the words slip past his lips before he could overthink it.

"To deliver the horse?"

He shrugged. "Yeah, it's over in Burleson. A couple hours away. It might be nice for you to see some of the countryside. We can drop off the horse and grab lunch on the way back. I can have you back here by early afternoon."

She made a noise as if the suggestion surprised her. "You know how I love horses."

Yes, he did know, and it added to what was already turning into a good situation.

"Well, then, that settles it. You have to come."

"But I'm not exactly dressed for the occasion." She glanced down and then a wicked smile tugged at the corners of her lips. "I'm not exactly dressed, period."

"And you look amazing, exactly the way you are." He leaned down and captured her mouth with his. Her lips were warm from the coffee and tasted like heaven.

She pulled back, nipping gently at his bottom lip. "I'd better pass and let you take care of business. And I need to—" He kissed her again, showing he didn't intend to take no for an answer. But she persisted, "I need to take care of business, too, over at the barn. Time is ticking if we're going to have that place in shape for the grand opening party."

"I think I know of a party that would be much more fun…" He kissed her long and slow. "And some business we could take care of together." He took the cup from her hands and stretched out next to her, finding her lips again. She responded by deepening the kiss, and for a few moments they lost themselves in each other. Until she shattered magic with one single word.

"Franklin."

"No. Um…I'm Ethan."

She laughed. "I could not be more aware of who *you* are, but I need to get back to Juliette's so I can feed the dog and let him out to take care of his own business. Poor dog is probably about ready to burst, if he hasn't already. I took him out about nine o'clock last night before I went to work at the barn. Juliette is counting on me and I'm sure he's wondering where I am."

Ethan propped himself up on his right elbow and marveled at her beauty—fresh-faced and perfect in all of her imperfections—and there weren't many. With his free hand he ran a finger down to the sexy place where her cleavage peeked out from the edge of the sheet, enticing him to unwrap her and explore the rest of her all over again. In the early morning light, he was sure she would be even better than last night. She was a natural beauty—wide-set, crystal-clear blue eyes, high cheekbones, Cupid's bow mouth, small, upturned nose made even more alluring by that spray of freckles and the way it wrinkled when she smiled. He wanted to photograph her with his mind, exactly the way she looked right now.

"That's an easy fix," he said. "I can drive you back to Juliette's and tend to the dog while you shower and get dressed. I would recommend jeans. Although, as I said, I'm particularly partial to what you're wearing now. In case you needed fashion advice."

She laughed as she swatted him away. "I can see I shouldn't take fashion advice from you. You'll get me arrested for indecent exposure. So you need to let me get out of bed. Otherwise, I might just keep you here all day."

"I didn't realize that was an option," Ethan said, tracing her jawline with the pad of his finger. "Because it is very tempting."

"No. It's not an option." She turned her head and captured his finger with her lips, giving it a playful suck. He could tell by her smile that she was fully aware that her actions were contradicting her words. "But I'll go with you and I know of a very exclusive party happening when we get back. And you're invited. So the sooner we deliver that horse…"

She pursed her lips and cocked her right brow. She looked so damn sexy it was all he could do to keep from taking her again. But from somewhere in the back of his mind the voice of reason prevailed. He inhaled a deep breath, which was supposed to help him put himself back together, but it smelled of her, of them.

The only safe bet was to remove himself from temptation and start getting the trailer hitched to the back of his truck—a most unsexy option, but nonetheless, the only option. But not before he claimed one last, long, sensual kiss.

With their lips still touching and her hands fisted into the front of his shirt, she whispered. "I can't recall ever looking so forward to a party in my entire life."

Calendula was a fine, muscular red bay Thoroughbred with black points. Chelsea stroked the mare's nose, admiring her beautiful chocolate eyes, graceful neck, and gorgeous long legs. She'd opted to stay outside with the horse as Ethan wrapped up business in the office. Being out here in the fresh air and open country, dressed casually, reminded her of how much she used to love to ride and how much she was longing to get into the saddle again.

When Ethan brought her home, Chelsea had texted Juliette and asked to borrow a cap and a casual T-shirt. Generous Juliette had given her the go-ahead to help herself to anything she needed. So Chelsea had donned the hat, threading her ponytail through the open space in the back and pulling it down onto her forehead, pairing it with sunglasses, dungarees and Tim McGraw concert T-shirt. She'd reproached herself after kissing Ethan so openly out in public the other day. While she'd gained a false sense of security in Celebration, even though it was highly unlikely that anyone would recognize her—especially dressed like this—she needed to be careful.

Still, she didn't need to make herself crazy, which is why she'd decided to spend the day out with Ethan. Lucy recognizing her had been a fluke. How many other people from the Texas hill country would recognize her in this context? She'd probably have a better chance winning the lottery than being spotted in the crowd. She wanted this time with Ethan. She wanted to be a normal person who was out with the guy she liked, doing the normal things normal couples did. No pressures to look or act a certain way and certainly not being singled out as tramp, a slut, a whore—as the woman whose most intimate moments had been broadcast for the world to see. She shook the thought from her head, determined not to let it cloud her mood.

"Can we go riding tomorrow?" she asked Ethan

after they were on the road again. "I should be at a pretty good spot to take a break by then—even after playing hooky today. It's been so long and I really miss it. There aren't many opportunities to ride in the city and it's been ages—years, in fact—since I've had time to get out to the country."

He slanted her a glance. "Sure. We can go anytime you want. Just name it. Did you have your own horse when you were growing up?"

"I did. His name was Bromley. I loved that horse like family."

"What happened to Bromley?"

"He got old and I got busy. I haven't been riding since he died."

In the distance she spied a colorful collection of neon and steel. It looked like a festival of some sort.

"What's going on up there?" she asked, happy for a valid reason to steer the subject away from Bromley and possible segues to Longbridge.

"That's the Celebration Spring Fair. It just started a couple of days ago."

"Let's stop. Can we?"

"Yes. Let's take a day off and go to the fair. Even if it's just for a few hours."

"I thought you had a tight schedule you needed to stick to?"

"I do, but that's what assistant managers are for. Let me make a call and we can make a day of it."

She felt as giddy as a child at the thought. "I've never been to a fair like this."

He laughed. "This is the best days of my youth in

one tacky, neon-lit diorama. I grew up going but it's been a few years since I last went. When I was a kid I used to raise livestock to show through 4-H."

"I wish I could've seen you as a little boy. I'll bet you were adorable."

He parked the truck and made his calls and the next thing she knew, they were in the thick of things.

The air buzzed with the faint sound of music from a country concert happening on the other side of the fairgrounds. Chelsea didn't recognize the tune because it was muffled by the sounds of the generators that powered the rides and the screams and laughs of the revelers who seemed to be having the time of their lives. The sum total created such a festive atmosphere Chelsea couldn't help but smile.

The air was heavy with the smell of livestock, diesel fuel and a mélange of food aromas wafting from the various vendors on the crowded midway.

Chelsea had never seen anything like the food offered for sale: spaghetti and meatballs on a stick, pizza cones, deep-fried Twinkies and candy bars, frozen, chocolate-covered Key lime pie. There was even a stall featuring chicken-fried bacon.

"Do you want to grab some lunch?" he asked.

"Here?" she said.

"Of course. Who doesn't love fair food?"

"I don't know. I've never had fair food, but I think I've gained five pounds simply smelling it. I don't suppose they'd have a salad stand, would they?" She was joking about the salad, of course, but not about never having tried fair food. And part of her—the part that was tired of trying to conform to the standards her family and the media had set for her, the part of her that had been trying to please everyone but herself—wanted to take a bite of every single unhealthy, nutrient-void junk food delicacy. Maybe even two bites. Especially the more traditional carnival fare that Ethan was pointing out now—the funnel cakes and French fries and corn dogs and gossamer-pink cotton candy. Especially the cotton candy.

"You've never had fair food?"

She shook her head. "I told you, I've never been to one of these things."

"That explains why you don't know that vegetables—unless they're fried or buttered corn on the cob—are against the law at a county fair. I think it's a capital offense."

He narrowed his eyes. "I can't believe you've never been to the fair."

She shrugged and shook her head again. "In the UK we have livestock shows, but I've never had the opportunity to attend."

"Never had the opportunity, huh?" His mouth quirked up on one side. "In other words, this really isn't your gig?"

"Hey, I was the one who suggested we stop. Don't try to make me out to be some sort of snob."

"You? A snob? Heavens, no. And since you're in such an adventurous mood, I'll get a wide sampling." He gestured toward the food stalls. "That way you can have the authentic Texas county fair experience."

True to his word, he purchased a lot of food. It

bordered on being obscene. But it was glorious. They found a picnic table in the shade and took their time eating. There was so much food and it was all so delicious that she thought he was going to have to carry her out of there, but after they'd finished, Ethan grabbed her hand and pulled her to her feet.

"Let's go walk it off," he said. "I've introduced you to my favorite foods, now I want you to meet my favorite rides." He laced his fingers through hers as they walked the midway.

He held her hand so unselfconsciously that she couldn't give in to her own uncertainty—the thought of being openly affectionate in public…again…with this man…in this new…this…romance? Affair? Whatever it was that they were doing… It made her insides zing in a little cha-cha. She closed her fingers around his rather than pulling away. Since she was throwing caution to the wind, she decided she wouldn't even stop him if he tried to kiss her. In fact, she kind of wanted him to kiss her, right here, right now. Because the only thing that seemed more delicious than all the food at the fair was Ethan's lips.

Really, what was the worst thing that could happen if they kissed right here out in the open? They might draw attention to themselves and someone might recognize her. In that cap and behind those glasses?

Fat chance.

People might look at them in a get-a-room way, but out here no one cared if they kissed. Out here they were nobodies. She was a nobody. Anonymous.

Un-newsworthy. And she couldn't remember the last time she'd felt so free.

In that instant she realized she had a choice: she could either hide away and let Hadden win or she could take back her life. Have fun for the first time in a long time with a man who made her think and feel things she hadn't felt in a long time.

She chose to ignore the little voice that nudged her—if she wanted this to work with Ethan, she knew she had to tell him the truth.

But not right now.

Right now the sun was shining and the gentle breeze was blowing and the warmth of Ethan's hand in hers made the late-spring morning almost perfect. She hadn't been this happy in ages. There was a chance that he might pull away, might be angry with her for not telling him the truth before now—or he might not want to associate with a woman with a past. He might not want any part of...*this*...of them...after she told him the real reason she'd come to Celebration.

So, right now all she wanted was this day. She knew she was being selfish, but she was going to enjoy herself being a woman who was falling for a man.

Tonight.

She would tell him tonight. In the meantime she held Ethan's hand as they walked down the midway. She hugged him when he won her a bear by throwing a ball and knocking over a triangle of bottles. They rode the rides, shared some cotton candy and she didn't balk when he stopped at a booth that was selling kisses for two dollars each to raise money for disabled veterans. Ethan slapped down a ten-dollar bill.

Only, Ethan didn't collect five kisses from the cute redhead who was working the booth. He turned and gathered Chelsea in his arms, tipped her backward and planted a toe-curling kiss on her mouth right there in front of God and everyone who cared to watch.

When they finally came up for air, he said, "That should count as five kisses, shouldn't it? I wouldn't want to waste your time with piddlin' pecks on the lips."

Then, without another word, he swept her off to the Ferris wheel. He put his arm around her, and they sat in silence, the big bear he'd won for her at their feet as the ride carried them up, up, up above Buxton County. He pointed out Celebration to the north and Burleson, where they'd just delivered the horse, behind them.

People would eventually get bored with the video. Their interest would shift when something fresh and more exciting came along. Even though it made Chelsea feel like a freak in a circus sideshow, she clung to the reality that Hadden and Ethan were apples and oranges.

Ethan, who had seemed so gruff and private, a solitary island of a man. Yet he actually wanted to spend time with her.

He was taking time out of his busy day to be with her.

Where Hadden, who loved to be in the public eye, had only been around when there was something in it for him—a chance to further his connections or feed his political ambitions. He'd never come around to take her to the fair or kissed her high atop the Ferris wheel.

When Ethan captured her mouth with his, thoughts of Hadden scattered. After several heated minutes when they finally came up for air, she realized their car was stopped at the very top.

The spring breeze was a little cool up there. It brought with it the faint sounds of the fair below. The people and the other rides on the midway looked magical and tiny from this vantage point. She felt a million miles away from everyone who could hurt her, everyone she could disappoint.

"You're quiet," Ethan said. "Everything okay?"

"I was just thinking I'm glad I'm not afraid of heights. It's nice up here."

"Yeah, I can't think of anyplace I'd rather be right now. I'm starting to remember what it's like to live again, to have feelings for someone again. Until now, it's like I've existed in a fog."

He kissed her again.

When the Ferris wheel jerked into motion, he leaned in so that his forehead was resting on hers. All she knew was she wished they could stay like this forever. Because up here in the clouds, only the best things seemed possible. This thing between them seemed real. It seemed like it could actually work.

Chapter Eleven

Chelsea and Ethan stayed at the fair until early evening. After a quick check-in at Juliette's house to take care of Franklin, they'd grabbed a nice dinner at a steak house in downtown Celebration and spent the night at Juliette's because Chelsea felt guilty about leaving Franklin alone all day. He was sure to miss his mom since she wouldn't be home for another two days. But not *that* guilty. It had been a wonderful day. One of those gift days that was so unexpected and so perfect, it couldn't have gone better if she'd planned every detail. That was the thing, days like this weren't planned. They were lovely presents in beautiful wrapping—like a day at the fair and spending the night in Ethan's arms.

The next morning, Chelsea dressed in blue jeans

and a simple blue cotton blouse. She and Ethan had plans to go riding this afternoon, but first she needed to get some work done over at the barn. Lucy was meeting her there at nine o'clock and they needed to get a lot accomplished today to make sure everything was ready for the party. Chelsea planned to go in early to get a jump on things since Lucy had held down the fort yesterday while she was at the fair with Ethan, insisting that Chelsea take the day off.

After she applied a quick coat of mascara and dabbed on some lip gloss, Chelsea dried her hair in the hall bathroom. She couldn't stop thinking about how natural it was becoming to wake up next to Ethan every morning. Okay, so it had only happened twice, but that was the point. It felt as if they'd been together a lot longer. They were so comfortable together—not in a boring, too familiar way. It just felt right—seeing his face first thing when she opened her eyes; him in the kitchen making coffee for them; her getting ready for the day; them sitting down to breakfast together.

She turned off the blowdryer and set it down, staring at herself as realization engulfed her. This *thing* that was happening between them really could work.

More than that, she *wanted* it to work. She'd never met anyone who made her feel so safe, so whole, so adored. Yesterday he'd told her he had feelings for her, that everything had changed the moment he'd caught her coming in through that bathroom window.

She turned and looked at the window over the tub. It looked like any other unobtrusive bathroom window, yet the butterflies swarmed as she remembered that night. Who knew that an act of desperation—one that had nearly brought the police—would change her life?

Acknowledging the possibility for them made it suddenly hard to breathe. She braced her palms on the counter and inhaled sharply, half checking to see if the madness of this feeling would pass, but it clung to her like a second skin. This was night and day from how it had been with Hadden. She'd broken up with Hadden because she couldn't see a future with him. She could never love him like *this*. This is how it was supposed to be.

Here she was falling in love with Ethan Campbell. It was the last thing she'd wanted, the last thing she'd intended to do, when she left London to come to Celebration, but here she was with her heart in her hands, fully prepared to offer it to him.

What was more was she was pretty sure not only would he take it, but that he would handle it with the same mix of kid gloves and fierce protectiveness that he handled everything else that meant so much to him.

She went back into the bedroom, brushed her hair and pulled it back into a ponytail. She sat on the edge of the bed and tugged on her red Doc Marten's boots. They weren't exactly work boots—and they certainly weren't cowboy boots—but they were the best bet for the job. She remembered what he'd told her about his ex-wife, Molly, about how the breakup of his marriage had taught him that you could love someone but never really know that person. The bad experience had made him cautious and in the course of being careful he'd stopped living. He'd told her yesterday it was as if he had been existing in a fog, and then he'd opened up and confessed that since he'd met her, he was starting to remember what it was like to feel again, to live again.

She took her time lacing up the boots because she knew when she went into the kitchen, she had to tell Ethan the rest of her story. No more stalling. No more excuses.

If they could just get past this, the truth would set them free. But *being honest* was key.

She had to check herself for a moment to examine why she wasn't giving Ethan enough credit to see this as not a big deal. It was her own trust issues rearing their ugly heads. Even if she hadn't loved Hadden enough to see a future with him, she'd trusted him and he'd betrayed her. Now she was going to have to reopen that wound, and all the humiliation that went along with it, and confess that not only had she been pretending to be someone else from the moment she'd come in through that window, but that the reason she was running was because she'd embarrassed herself and her family.

But if Ethan was falling for her, if he was willing to trust her with his heart—to trust again for the first time since his marriage—she owed him the truth.

Her stomach knotted at the thought. But she couldn't put this off any longer. She checked her reflection in the full-length mirror one last time, squared her shoulders and started toward the kitchen, saying a silent prayer that he wouldn't walk out on her once he met the real Chelsea.

Ethan's kitchen repertoire wasn't vast. In fact, it was pretty lean. But he certainly wasn't starving. Bacon and fried eggs was his go-to breakfast. He grilled a mean steak; he could scare up a pot of chili that had garnered an honorable mention at the annual Celebration Chili Cook-off, and he was working on a top secret barbecue sauce recipe for the local pit master competition later this summer. But banana pancakes were his breakfast specialty—the secret weapon he pulled out when he was trying to make a good impression…or when he was falling in love. Actually, the only other woman he'd made them for was Molly, and she wasn't even a big fan of pancakes. But when he'd seen the ripe banana in Juliette's kitchen, he'd been inspired to make them for Chelsea.

He was just setting the plate with the pancakes in the oven to keep them warm until Chelsea finished getting ready when his phone rang.

The phone's display showed the name Ben Harper, his stable hand.

"Morning, Ben. Whatcha need?"

"Hey, Ethan, sorry to bother you so early, but Lulabelle has gone into labor. Tyler is with her now. Thought you'd want to know in case you wanted to come on out before your rounds."

Lulabelle was another one of the Triple C's high-bred ventures. They bred her with a stallion that had fathered a Thoroughbred that had won the Triple

Crown a few years back. Ethan knew she was close to foaling. But did it have to be now?

He must be pretty far gone on Chelsea if he was grousing about this important business venture. He had to check his attitude. Chelsea could enjoy the banana pancakes without him. It just meant he'd have to make it up to her.

As if on cue, she entered the kitchen, clutching the coffee mug he'd brought her first thing and looking so damn good it set him back on his heels. There had been a time after he and Molly had divorced, when the pain was still fresh, that he thought he might never be able to feel this way again.

Sure, he needed time to heal, but maybe the reason it had taken so long was because he was waiting for Chelsea. Of course, he hadn't known it at the time—who could know something like that except in hindsight? But damn, this was good and she was worth the wait.

"Good morning, beautiful," he said.

"Good morning." Traces of her British accent were stronger than usual. She probably wasn't fully awake yet, but he liked the sexy rasp of her voice.

She walked over to the coffeepot and poured herself another cup. With her back still turned, she said, "Ethan, I'm sorry to do this so early, but we need to talk."

We need to talk.

The four words no man who was falling in love ever wanted to hear. Suddenly, he was glad to have a legitimate reason to put off this *talk*.

"Are you okay?" he asked.

She turned around and her face was so clouded with emotion that she didn't even have to answer. Whatever she was about to lay on him wasn't good. Hell, he should've known better than to get carried away.

"I hate to do this," he said. "But my stable hand just called and I have a horse in labor. I have to get out there now. Can we talk tonight?"

She nodded. Maybe he was imagining it, but he could've sworn she looked a little relieved. Maybe he was searching for any glimmer of hope. Maybe he was deluding himself.

"If this is moving too fast for you, we can slow it down to a comfortable pace." He grabbed a pot holder and took the plate with the pancakes out of the oven, removed the foil and set them on the table. "Eat breakfast and let's not rush to any rash conclusions. Let's talk about it later, okay?"

Chelsea tried. She really did. She'd gone out there and told him that they needed to talk but he had that emergency and just like that, fate had granted her a few more hours.

As she worked in the barn she tried to figure out if this was a blessing or a torment. Choosing to look at the positive, she racked her brain for something— anything that would allow her to make the most of the reprieve.

But how?

What could she do to turn this around?

She took out her frustrations sanding a rough board that might be a source of splinters if a guest leaned up against it.

Of course, it wasn't a given that Ethan would run. He might take it all in stride… He might even think it was sexy… Um, no. She wouldn't want a man who thought like that.

But he probably would take his cue from her delivery. If she presented it as if the hangman was coming, he would of course see it as gloom and doom.

Oh, bloody hell. If only it were that easy. Ethan had a mind of his own and it was highly unlikely that she would be able to lead him to the emotional conclusion she wanted him to have. He would think what he thought. She needed to prepare for the worst, but hope for the best.

The tape did not represent who she was and if he was scared off that easily, he wasn't the man for her. She had enough negativity in her life; she didn't need someone who couldn't stand by her when the chips were down.

Too bad her heart didn't see it that way.

"Hey, girl!" Lucy's bubbly voice filled the air. "You're here early."

Chelsea forced a smile. "I have a lot to do to make up for my absence yesterday."

Lucy waved her away. "Are you kidding? You deserved a break, as hard as you've been working. Did you have fun? You and my brother certainly have been spending a lot of time together. I haven't seen much of him, and when I have seen him he has been like a changed man. I don't know what you're doing to him, but keep on doing it. Um… That sounded vaguely dirty. So consider it rhetorical."

Chelsea couldn't help but laugh. While she had no desire to discuss Ethan's and her sex life with Lucy—or with anyone for that matter—Lucy might be able to help her with something else.

Chelsea set down the piece of sandpaper. "I've been meaning to say, I appreciate how you've kept my secret, Lucy."

Lucy's right eyebrow shot up. "Certain people may find me lacking in certain areas, but one thing no one can accuse me of is betraying a friend when I have given my word about something."

A friend.

Lucy really did consider her a friend and it touched Chelsea to the very core of her being. She had a lot of acquaintances, a lot of hangers-on—people who wanted something from her, or more aptly her brother, Thomas, who could do political favors, or her sister, who could serve as a stepping stone into the fashion industry. Chelsea, of course, could provide an introduction to both of them. She was a quick study. It only took being used a couple of times before the wall went up and the lock on the gate to her intimate circle stayed securely in place.

Lucy wanted nothing from her. Well, okay, Lucy wanted something from her. But at least she was up front about it. And Chelsea found that to be a breath of fresh air. This was a way she could contribute—a way that she could prove she was good at something.

Actually, Chelsea felt as if she was the one benefiting the most because she had finally found her place.

"You are a good friend, Lucy. I need to ask your opinion on something. I need your advice."

Lucy straightened her shoulders and leaned in toward her. "Of course. Is everything okay?"

Chelsea felt her eyes brimming and Lucy put her hand on Chelsea's arm. "Oh, my gosh. What's wrong? Let's go sit down."

They made their way over to the army trunk where Chelsea had sat with Ethan the day he'd brought her muffins. In many ways it was the day when everything had begun. Or at least one of the days. According to Ethan, everything had snapped into place for him the moment he saw her crawling in the window. Ha! What a sight that must've been.

"Okay, spill it," said Lucy. "What's wrong?"

"I have to tell your brother the truth."

Lucy's expression transformed from concern to puzzled to realization. She nodded. "I see. So I guess this means things between the two of you are pretty serious?"

Chelsea shrugged. "Maybe. Yes? I think so. Lucy, he told me he hasn't been this happy since things were good with Molly."

She stopped at that because it didn't feel right sharing any more intimacies. She had never been one to kiss and tell, and she knew how it felt to be betrayed by someone who did.

Lucy didn't push her any further. She simply nod-

ded as if she understood perfectly. And she probably did.

"I started to tell him this morning, but he got called
away on an emergency with one of the horses. I did
say I needed to talk to him. We are getting together
tonight." She knew she was rambling, but she needed
to get it all out.

"He doesn't even know my real name. He doesn't
know why I'm really here in Celebration. And most
of all he doesn't know about the video."

She felt her face flame. "What's he going to think
of me when he finds out?"

Lucy drew in a deep breath and looked as if she
was weighing her words. "If this relationship is turning into something serious he needs to know the
truth—"

Chelsea's phone chimed, signaling a text. Lucy's
gaze fluttered down to Chelsea's phone. "Well, speak
of the devil. That texter is my brother." A sly smile
spread across her pretty face. "Go on, pick it up. I
know you want to."

If it had been anyone else—or any other time in
her life she would've ignored the text in favor of the
conversation because it was just rude to let electron-
ics dominate. But this was Ethan.

Bloody hell, she was in a bad way over him.

She purposely took her time picking up the phone
and opening the text message so that she didn't appear as desperate as she felt.

What she saw nearly made her drop her phone.
Ethan's text read:

Look at us. We made the paper. We're famous.

There was a picture of Ethan and her in a lip-lock in front of the kissing booth at the Celebration Spring Fair.

Apparently, the photo had gone out over the news-wire and the *Dallas Morning News* had run it on the front page of the entertainment section, promoting the fair as weekend fun.

If tabloid reporters were paying attention to the newswire or even if they had secured sources to be on the lookout, now they could track her to Celebration. The only thing she could do was leave before they got here and turned Ethan's life upside down.

Chapter Twelve

The call came through minutes after she'd picked up Ethan's text. She'd barely had a chance to show Lucy the picture he'd sent when her phone rang. The sound startled her. At first she hoped against hope that it wasn't Ethan calling to get her reaction. But a minute later talking to Ethan seemed like a dream as she stared at the new message notification on her phone. She didn't recognize the number, but it was an international calling code and she knew who it was even before she picked up the message.

"Are you okay?" Lucy asked. "You look like you've seen a ghost."

"In a way I have. Actually, more of a monster than a ghost."

"Who is it?" Lucy demanded, taking Chelsea's

phone out of her hand and looking at the screen to see for herself. "Are you going to listen?"

Reflexively, Chelsea gave a quick shake of the head, as if Lucy had suggested she jump into a viper pit. Essentially, picking up the message, hearing that creepy voice, amounted to the same thing.

Still, there was a slim chance that she was wrong—maybe it was a family member calling from a different number; she hadn't talked to them since she'd landed Stateside. Now she'd given the press something else to write about. Even if she wasn't well-known in the States, a well-crafted story about a British noble hiding from scandal in the US might generate some interest. Especially if the creep used the angle that she was the sister of the likely new prime minister.

She could sit there and speculate all day. The only way she would know what she was dealing with was to listen to the message. She took a deep breath and pressed the playback icon and put it on speaker so Lucy could hear.

"Lady Chelsea, you looked smashing in today's paper." The cockney accent made her cringe. *"However, I am deeply troubled that if you were game to grant a photo that you didn't come to me. As you know, I do feel a bit proprietary when it comes to breaking news about you. Never fear, my darling, I'm getting a good sense of where you're hiding. Why don't you give your good pal Bertie a ring? You know I'll find you in a matter of days if you don't. Looking forward to seeing you. Toodles."*

"What the hell was that?" Lucy's eyes were so wide Chelsea was sure her friend would have nightmares.

"That monster is the reason I have to leave Celebration as soon as possible. This creep has been badgering me since university. I even changed my phone number before I left for the States, but he managed to get it. Now I'm afraid he will come here. I have no choice, Lucy. I have to leave."

"You always have a choice," Lucy said. "You don't have to run away from this son of a bitch. You need to tell Ethan and he will help you, Chelsea."

She shook her head again. "No. I can't. If I do, I'm afraid Ethan will go after him."

"Right," Lucy said. "That's the point."

"Wrong. The point is if Ethan goes after him—even if he enlists the help of the authorities—it will draw even more attention to the original story about the tape. I can't let that happen. I can't embarrass Ethan that way."

"Instead, you're going to break his heart?" Lucy said. "That's not much better, Chelsea."

"I've already made up my mind. I can't stay here and wait for Bertie Veal to find me and wreak havoc on the people who have so generously taken me in."

"You could get a restraining order," Lucy bargained. "Or what if you just sat down and reasoned with him? Isn't it worth a try, rather than running... again? You can't keep running, Chelsea."

She didn't want to keep running. She'd rather stay

right here with Ethan, maybe set up a design studio and make a life for herself—with him.

She thought about Lucy's suggestion of trying to bargain with him, but two seconds later she realized it was a bad idea.

"There is no bargaining with the devil, Lucy. You don't know who you're dealing with here. The guy is a parasite, a bully, a thug. He ticks just about every box that describes a sociopathic personality. He will stop at nothing to get a story that he can sell to the tabloids. He doesn't care if he destroys lives. That's how he makes his money. If he thinks you're trying to protect me, he will go after you. Think about what that could do to your new business, to Juliette's. He could ruin everything you've worked so hard for. Bertie Veal is the devil incarnate. My only choice is to leave before he tracks me to Celebration. I'm so sorry I can't stay for the grand opening party, but you're almost finished. You're almost there. You've got this. I know you're going to be a big success."

"I don't want you to go."

"I don't want to go, but I can't stay."

Lucy looked crestfallen and they sat and stared at each other for a moment that seemed like an impasse—two headstrong women who were used to getting what they wanted even when no one else could see the possibilities. Only this time what they wanted was beyond their reach—at least for now.

Finally, Lucy broke the silence. "Please promise you won't leave before you talk to Ethan."

Chelsea's stomach bunched and knotted. "Of course." She did owe him that much.

"How can you leave before the party?" Ethan said. "You promised Lucy you'd help her get to that point."

After Chelsea had left Lucy, she'd texted Ethan and asked him to come to Juliette's house after he'd finished with work. She had decided it was best to meet on neutral territory rather than asking him to meet her at his house or at the barn. While she waited for him, she booked herself on the first flight out of Dallas, packed and tidied up so that the place would be shipshape for Juliette. She'd called her friend to tell her about the turn of events and that Lucy had agreed to care for Franklin until Juliette returned. In similar fashion to Lucy, Juliette had tried to reason with her to stay—she suggested she tell Ethan and see if he could help get this guy off her back.

"You know, Chels, as long as you keep running, this guy will keep stalking you. You need to do something about it. If your folks won't help you, I can put you in touch with people who can."

"And it will get ugly before it gets better. I just can't put my family—and you and Ethan and Lucy—through any more crap."

"You know I love your family, but I'm disappointed in them for throwing you to the wolves."

"They might argue that I led the wolves to the door. Look, you know I love you. You're my best friend. Actually, you're family. I appreciate all that you've done—how you've let me disrupt your life hiding out here—but I have to handle this my way. It's time for me to go."

A knock sounded at the front door and Chelsea's heart leaped into her throat before it plummeted. "Ethan's here. I'm telling him everything. I need to go."

"Chels, call me later?"

"I will." With that, she disconnected the call and steeled herself to do the right thing.

Within the short span of five minutes, Chelsea saw Ethan's mood go from hopeful to flummoxed to prickly.

"I told Lucy from the start I might not be able to stay," Chelsea said when she tried to explain why she had to leave. "She knows it's time for me to go and she understands. I wish you would."

"I wish I understood, too. I thought things were good between us, Chelsea. Can you help me understand what went wrong? Can we at least talk about it?"

The look on his face was breaking her heart. He obviously thought she was rejecting him. She wasn't. If he only knew. She stared at her hands as if they might show her an answer. Or at least give her some direction about what to do next.

But of course, he didn't know the full story.

"Ethan, this morning when I said I needed to talk to you, it wasn't about me leaving. Actually, I didn't know I was leaving until later. Until after you sent me the photo from the paper."

"Now I really don't understand. What was so

reprehensible about that picture that it's driving you away?"

"There is nothing reprehensible about the picture. Ethan, I—"

She clamped her mouth shut. In the midst of this craziness, she'd almost told him she loved him. She did love him, but it didn't matter and it would only make things harder if she confessed her feelings.

So she did the only other thing possible. She told him the truth. "I haven't been completely honest with you, Ethan."

He was frowning at her, as if her revelation hadn't surprised him one bit. Had he known all along that she was hiding something? Of course he hadn't known. Still, he sat there, arms crossed, looking annoyed and defensive in his staunch silence.

The phrase *he who speaks first, loses* came to mind, but Chelsea knew there was no getting around it. She had to be the one to break the silence.

"Let me start from the beginning. The night I met you, I wasn't planning on running into anyone. I certainly wasn't planning on seeing you again or falling for you. My name isn't Chelsea Allen. It's Chelsea Ashford Alden. Chelsea Allen was a name that I used to use sometimes when Juliette and I would go out and I was trying to fly under the radar."

His brows drew together. "Fly under the radar? What does that mean? I understand that sometimes women don't want to be bothered, is that what you mean?"

"No, I mean fly under the radar, as in not being recognized."

"Why? Are you someone famous who I'm not familiar with?"

She shrugged. "Sort of. My father is the fifth Earl of Downing. My brother is Thomas Ashford Alden. Does that ring a bell?"

He did not look impressed, which was fine. She didn't expect him to be up on British politics.

"It's quite likely that my brother will be the next prime minister of Great Britain—"

"And you couldn't trust me with that?" He shook his head and got up and paced the length of the room. She wanted to give him time to let this sink in before she told him the real reason she was running.

"If your father is an earl, does that make you royalty or something?"

"Yes. Sort of. I'm at the very end of the line for the throne, but that doesn't mean anything."

"Well, yeah, it really does. It's who you are. Why didn't you tell me? I get using the fake name when we first met, but Chelsea, we've seen *a lot* more of each other since then. You could've told me. You could've trusted me."

The bottom dropped out of her stomach. This was it. This was the moment she'd been dreading. But she had to tell him. There was no holding back.

"Ethan, please sit down. There's more. There's a reason I lied to you."

She told him everything—about Bertie Veal, about the secret recording, about Hadden selling it to the tabloids after she broke up with him, about her parents' mandate, about running from the reporter who seemed hell-bent on ruining her life.

"He's bound to find me and I have to leave before he tracks me here—to you and Lucy and Juliette. You don't need that in your life. You don't need to be linked romantically to someone who is known around town as *that woman—the one in that video—wink, wink, nudge, nudge.*"

She paused and it was the stupidest thing—her heart thudded against her breastbone and she was hoping he would gather her in his arms and tell her everything would be all right, that he would love her and protect her and make sure that Bertie Veal never hurt her again. But he just sat there looking through her with a vaguely horrified expression on his face.

It was the look she'd feared since the moment she realized that she could love this man. But he had fallen for Chelsea Allen, a woman who didn't even exist.

Chelsea had been gone four days and Ethan had felt every ticking second like a dagger to the heart. Leave it to him to fall in love with a woman he couldn't have. That was why he hadn't gone after her, hadn't begged her to stay. This had nothing to do with inferiority complexes or male pride; he simply knew when he was facing an impossible battle. It wasn't that he was being a defeatist, he was being a realist.

It was clear from the moment Chelsea told him she was leaving that she couldn't wait to get out of this town. If Molly, who had been born and raised here, had been loath to stay, why would someone like Lady Chelsea Ashford Alden—someone of noble birth, who had gone to the same college as the Duke of Cambridge, the guy who would likely sit on the throne of England. Hell, the fact that Chelsea could even say she was in line for the throne was daunting. He refused to kid himself that someone like that would want to give up the jet set for life on a horse ranch that was rooted just as deeply in him as London was in her.

He wasn't even angry that she'd lied about her name and had evaded the truth about her background. Okay, he was at first, but not now. The reason he was letting her go without a fight was because it was simply good horse sense.

He was still a little too raw to contemplate the prospect of being *just friends*. After she'd told him about the video that creep had sold to the tabloids, Ethan had given in to curiosity and spent the better part of an afternoon online, searching the web for stories about Lady Chelsea Ashford Alden. He could not find the infamous video and he wouldn't have watched it if he had. He could only hope that somehow her well-connected family had been successful in helping her wipe the video off the internet.

One thing he did find online was a story about Chelsea and him that was written by Chelsea's stalker, titled, *Could This Be Love for Lady Chelsea or Just Another Spring Fling?* The con artist had ripped off the photo of Ethan kissing Chelsea at the fair, the one that had originally appeared in the *Dallas Morning News*.

Pain and a sense of loss as raw and real as the day that Chelsea had told him she was leaving stung every nerve ending in him, tempting him to sign off and leave well enough alone. But he couldn't. He wasn't sure if he was punishing himself or soothing himself by reading story after story about this woman he thought he knew.

Though the web seemed to be cleansed of the video, plenty of sensational and obviously fabricated stories remained. He came away from the search with the sound conclusion that the Chelsea Ashford Alden he saw on the web, the one depicted in all those trumped-up tabloid stories was not the same woman he'd fallen in love with. That was not Chelsea. The person in the tabloids was an exaggerated figment of a desperate reporter's imagination.

Chelsea wasn't any different than any other woman who had done her share of having a good time, raising a little innocent hell. At least she'd steered clear of substance abuse and she didn't let alcohol rule her days and nights. He'd witnessed that firsthand. No, the Chelsea Ashford Alden he'd met was kind and generous and decent. She was also beautiful and charismatic and the daughter of a well-connected, high-profile family. That made her the perfect target for a sleazebag like Bertie Veal.

It also didn't change the fact that she was in England and he was in Texas. Lady Chelsea Ashford Alden would never be content in a small town like

Celebration. So Ethan threw himself into his work at the Triple C and pretended that he didn't have a huge gaping hole in his chest where his heart used to live.

Chapter Thirteen

On the day of the grand opening party, which was a trial run before hosting Connor Bryce's wedding reception, Ethan dressed in khaki slacks and a plaid button-down that he had taken the time to press so that he'd look presentable for Lucy's big night.

He had to give credit where credit was due. She had stuck to her guns and brought this dream to fruition. He was proud of his little sister. That was why he was determined to make this night about her, not about the person who was conspicuously absent tonight. He missed Chelsea. The ache lingered like arthritis in his soul. But as with all adversity he'd ever faced in his life, he learned to live with the pain, to push through it and carry on.

Tonight would be no different. He would go to the

party, help Lucy however he could—though Juliette, party planner extraordinaire, seemed to have everything under control. He would be there as a source of support and do his best not to think of Chelsea.

She'd been gone two weeks now. Every single day of that time he'd had to consciously restrain himself from calling her. His heart longed to see her one more time, but his head reminded him it was hopeless. He wasn't looking for a long-distance relationship. He certainly wasn't about to pin his hopes on her having a big change of heart and trading in the glitz and glam of London for him at the Triple C Ranch.

That was just how it was. The truth hurt, but as with everything else he would survive. Or so he told himself. It had become his mantra. If he repeated it enough, someday he might believe it.

The party started at seven. He wasn't much for shindigs like this. So when he'd called Lucy and asked her if she wanted him to come early and she had assured him she and Juliette had everything under control, he decided to do his evening rounds of the ranch, checking to make sure everything was buttoned up for the night.

The sun was hanging low in the western sky, bathing everything in soft tones of gold and orange, red and blue, showing off as it bid the world good-night and prepared to tuck itself away. Another day done. Since she had been gone he'd started feeling a little sadder at this time of night. During the day, when the sun was hotter than the hinges of hell, it burned right through him, numbing the pain. The vast blackness of the night threw a cloak over his emotions. Thank God he hadn't reached for the bottle. He'd been tempted because it was the one sure way to anesthetize the pain. In fact, a couple of times he'd had to call his sponsor and have him talk the bottle out of his hand. He wasn't going to let losing her break him.

The urge for a drink was always the worst at twilight. He remembered his mom calling this time of night the *blue hour* and now he understood why.

Tonight, as with every night for the past two weeks, as he drove by the pastures and the stables he saw reminders of Chelsea everywhere he looked. In the shadows of the oak trees, in the distance by the post and rail fence, in the rolling hills that graced his land. Her specter lived there.

How long was it going to take to exorcise her?

This morose thought was particularly irritating because she wasn't dead. He couldn't even pretend like she was dead to him. He couldn't hate her. He couldn't call her names or scoff at her way of life because he still loved her. The only thing she was guilty of was coming from a different world—and for that matter, he was just as damn guilty as she was. Actually, he shouldered more of the guilt for not trying to meet her halfway. For letting her go without trying to salvage something of them or letting her know he was willing to be her friend. They could do that long distance, couldn't they? Couldn't they be friends?

No. He didn't want to be her friend.

But for the first time since she'd left, he realized that he wasn't good with completely cutting her out of his life. He had no idea how she felt because they hadn't talked. No one had made the first move to reach out to the other. Suddenly, it seemed ludicrous not to man up.

Glancing at the dashboard clock that glowed neon-green, he noted the hour and his brain calculated the time difference between Celebration and London: six hours. If it was seven thirty here, that meant it was one thirty in the morning there. It was late. But it was a Saturday night. He wondered what she was doing. Was she home asleep? Or was she out with friends… or out on a date? Even though he had no right, the thought kicked him in the gut.

He pulled the truck over and took out his phone. He brought up the last text they had exchanged, the one where she had asked him to meet her at Juliette's house the night everything went down. For about the millionth time, he racked his brain, trying to think of something he could've done differently that might've changed the way things turned out.

Of course he came up with nothing. Except the nagging reminder that he could've asked her to stay. But he couldn't ask her to trade in the big city for small-town life. And he was back at square one.

This train of thought had become part of his nightly routine and was as intrinsic to him as doing rounds of the property.

What a terrible way to end things. He'd been so caught off guard by her revelation. He'd honestly thought she had called him there to say she needed space, that things were moving too fast for her. He'd been idiot enough to believe all he had to do to make things right was give her a little room and she would realize how right they were together. Hell, he didn't need to be joined at the hip with the woman he loved, but he sure as hell needed the two of them to want the same things. Been there done that with someone who wasn't on the same page. It never ended well.

The reality check still wasn't resonating. It was bouncing around his brain like a ping-pong ball, but the message of good sense wasn't reaching his heart.

He scrolled up past the text that had decided their fate and read happier messages.

Chelsea: What do you want to do for dinner tonight?

Ethan: I'd like to have you in my bed.

Ethan: Want to go riding this afternoon?

Chelsea: Are you talking horses or...? :)

The playfulness made him smile through the ache. If someone didn't know better they might think the relationship was solely based on sex—and God, the sex had been off the charts. It had rocked his world. But there had been so much more.

If he texted her now, she'd get his message first thing in the morning… That banked on her being home sleeping. If he texted her, she could reply whenever she was ready.

He scrolled past the record of them, back to the blank screen and typed:

Hi, doing my rounds of the ranch. Realized that we never got to go riding. The next time you visit Jules, let's make that happen.

He started to delete the message. In fact, he did erase the part that said *let's make that happen*, but after staring at it for a while, trying to figure out what to write instead, something that didn't sound bitter or pathetic or too presumptuous— For God's sake was he actually sitting here second-guessing himself over a text message?

It was a text to a friend. Nothing more. So he retyped it and pushed Send before he could talk himself out of it. The overwhelming urge to wash away the sickening insecurity with a tall, cold draft nearly overwhelmed him. He gripped the steering wheel with both hands until the wave passed.

He was better than that. He'd worked too damn hard to get where he was, to stay sober this long and rebuild his life, to fall off the wagon tonight. He needed to go put in an appearance at Lucy's party and then he would get the hell out of there.

As he reached for the gear shift, his phone signaled an incoming text.

His gut tightened as he picked up the phone and saw Chelsea's response.

Hello, stranger. Good to hear from you. You must be a mind reader. I was thinking about you and Lucy.

Tonight is the big grand opening trial run, isn't it? How is it going?

I'm on my way to the party now. I know it's late there. I hope the text didn't wake you.

You didn't wake me. I'm at a party myself. My love to you and Lucy. I'm there in spirit.

Since she was out on the town, he debated whether or not to respond—it didn't escape him that she hadn't picked up on the bit about going riding. But both of them knew that was just an icebreaker. He wasn't going to hold his breath, waiting for her to come back to Celebration. Maybe if they corresponded as friends, someday he would make the trip to visit her in London. It was already feeling complicated. That was why he decided a quick *gotta go* reply would be the best way to keep it casual.

Thx. I'll share your message with Lucy when I get there. Talk to you soon.

He tossed his phone onto the passenger seat and drove to the barn. The parking lot was already crowded with cars and trucks. It looked like the entire town of Celebration had turned out to support Lucy's new endeavor.

He managed to maneuver his truck into a space on the unpaved area behind the building and made a mental note to mention to Lucy that she should consider adding more paved parking. As he rounded the barn heading toward the front door, he could hear the sound of a band playing a Luke Bryan tune mixed with the convivial sound of happy people at a party. Good for Lucy. He hadn't realized it before, but this really was her wheelhouse. If anyone knew how to have fun, it was his sister. And he truly meant that in the most supportive way. He checked himself before he opened the door, which was festooned with twinkling white lights and a wreath made of wheat stalks and checked ribbon.

Just because he wasn't in the mood for a party didn't mean he would bring the shade to his sister's big night. As his hand rested on the door handle, he wondered if he should've brought her flowers to celebrate the occasion. He even considered leaving to get some, but he knew it was as much a stall tactic as it was a congratulatory gesture for her. The best gift he could give her was his presence and a good attitude.

And the sooner he did this, the sooner he could leave.

He pulled open the door and stepped inside and through the throngs of people, the first person he saw was Chelsea.

When Chelsea caught sight of Ethan, her knees almost buckled. She had been nervous about making the trip, but she had wanted to be there for Lucy. The two of them had kept in touch since she'd left Celebration. She'd been giving Lucy final design advice. The Campbell Wedding Barn still had a long way to go before the place would be finished, but it was presentable enough to serve as a rustic venue. They'd work out the kinks in this trial run grand opening party so that they'd be as prepared as possible to give Connor Bryce and his bride the wedding reception of their dreams. But that was Juliette's and Lucy's territory. She would make sure the place looked as fabulous as possible.

Lucy had all but begged her to come back for the party. The tipping point happened when she'd learned that her brother's old university pal, who was now a high-powered barrister, was able to help cleanse the internet of the offending video and teach Bertie Veal and Hadden Hastings a lesson. Not only did Thomas's mate scare the bejabbers out of both men by threatening an invasion of privacy lawsuit—referencing the civil suit against Gawker Media was enough to keep Hadden in check—but Thomas's chum had also implied that if Mr. Veal persisted in stalking Chelsea, he just might find it difficult to gain reentry to the United Kingdom if he left again. It seemed old Bertie had some past indiscretions that had as of yet remained unflagged, but that could easily be changed with a couple of phone calls.

Thomas's friend assured Bertie and Hadden they were welcome to challenge him, but they would certainly end up wishing they'd left well enough alone. It was their choice: mess with Chelsea and suffer consequences, or refrain from harassing the Ashford Alden family and have a happy life. The choice was entirely theirs.

The gauntlet was leveled a couple of weeks ago, and neither Bertie nor Hadden had so much as glanced in Chelsea's direction.

It was almost like starting over. She'd realized that the place she wanted to make her fresh start was Celebration, Texas.

Of course, she had no guarantee that Ethan would welcome her with open arms. The text he'd sent had been the first communication they'd exchanged since the horrible night when everything crashed and burned.

Just because his text had been warm, it didn't mean he wanted anything beyond friendship—not after her confession that she had lied to him.

As she watched him walk toward her, the butterflies that he always seemed to induce had come to life again, proving that she still had it bad for him. No, not just bad—oh, who was she kidding? She was in love with the guy and in this moment, she wanted nothing more than to win him back. She had no idea how he felt about her, but she was going to exhaust every avenue before she gave up on Ethan Campbell.

As he closed the distance between them, she was so giddy-nervous she thought she might jump out of her skin. She clutched her cranberry and soda so tightly she had to make a conscious effort to loosen her grip so that the glass didn't burst in her hand. She raised the other hand in a shy greeting as he approached.

She couldn't read his expression. His eyes were intense but his face was otherwise neutral. She couldn't figure out if it was a shocked-but-happy-to-see-her neutral or if he was coming over to ask her to leave.

She found her words in the nick of time. "Great party, huh?"

"You're here. You came back."

"I wouldn't have missed this for the world."

He opened his mouth to say something but shut it again, his brow furrowing as if he was trying to process everything. Finally, he said, "It seemed so final when you left."

She swallowed the lump in her throat. "That was before I knew that Celebration was a safe place—*my* safe place."

The side of his mouth quirked up into that half smile that she missed as much as a drowning woman missed air. She hadn't realized how much she missed it—how desperately she'd missed him—until now. She'd been pining for him, but the magnitude of it hadn't hit until this very moment.

The pull of attraction was strong, but attraction alone wasn't what Chelsea needed. She needed to know that Ethan could forgive her. That maybe, just maybe, he could love her for who she was, despite her stupid mistakes and everything that made her who she was. Because she loved him.

"You never answered my question about going riding."

"I figured we have plenty of time for that since I'm moving back."

She hoped he'd meant it. That it wasn't just a rhetorical conversation starter.

"Did you really mean it, Ethan?" Crap. She hadn't meant to say that out loud. But she did and there was no taking it back now. "Because I hope you did. I mean, I hope you meant you want to go riding with me. Because after I left I was afraid that you never wanted to speak to me again, much less see me again. I never meant to lie to you. I don't make a habit of lying to people I care about. But I realize you might feel like you don't even know me. I wouldn't blame you if you never wanted to see me again."

"You're wrong about that—on both accounts. I know who you are now and I understand why you did what you thought you had to do. I couldn't care less about the video. I didn't watch it."

"It's gone now," she said. "Thomas worked his magic and took care of it and Bertie Veal. He won't be bothering me—us—anymore. That's the thing about big brothers—"

"I love you, Chelsea. Why would I never want to see you again?"

His words—those three words—made the room expand and contract and then tilt on its axis. When she finally regained her equilibrium, she said, "Well, that's good to know because I love you, too, and I was really hoping that we could talk about what we were going to do about this love predicament we seem to have found ourselves in. If we're in love, it seems a little counterproductive to not talk and not see each other. In fact, I'll confess that I don't think I've ever been as miserable as I've been these last weeks that

I was in London. I had so many things I wanted to talk to you about and—"

The next thing she knew her world actually was tipping on its axis because Ethan had gathered her in his arms and had smothered her rambling words as he covered her mouth with his.

"That's what we're going to do about it," he said after he righted her and set her back on her feet.

Her head was spinning, but she had enough presence of mind to say, "So, you don't think it's a bad idea for me to move to Celebration and open a design business?"

Ethan pulled her close and whispered in her ear. "That's the best idea I've heard in ages. The only thing that would make me happier is if you'll marry me. I nearly let you get away once, but I won't let that happen again."

Her entire body zinged with elation. "Ethan Campbell, are you proposing to me?"

"I don't have a ring, because I hadn't exactly planned this." He fell to one knee. "Chelsea Ashford Alden, will you make me the happiest man alive and agree to be my wife?"

Before she could answer, she realized the music had stopped playing and every eye in the house was watching them.

"Yes!"

The room erupted into a rousing round of applause and the band began the strains of a romantic country love song that Chelsea recognized but couldn't recall the name of.

"This is for the happy couple," the singer said and everyone cleared a path so that Chelsea and Ethan could have the dance floor.

As they swayed to the song, she gazed into his eyes. "Let the records show that not only was that the most romantic proposal ever," she said, "but probably one of the most spontaneous, too. No one will ever call you unspontaneous again."

"I don't care what anybody calls me as long as they call me your husband."

* * * * *

Look out for Nancy Robards Thompson's contribution to THE FORTUNES OF TEXAS: THE SECRET FORTUNES *continuity, available May 2017, only from Mills & Boon Cherish.*

MILLS & BOON®

Cherish™

EXPERIENCE THE ULTIMATE RUSH OF FALLING IN LOVE

MILLS & BOON®

EXCLUSIVE EXTRACT

Sheikh Ibrahim al-Ansari must find a bride,
and quickly… Thankfully he has the perfect
convenient princess in mind—his new assistant,
Ruby Dance!

Read on for a sneak preview of
THE SHEIKH'S CONVENIENT PRINCESS
by Liz Fielding

'Can I ask if you are in any kind of relationship?' he persisted.

'Relationship?'

'You are on your own—you have no ties?'

He was beginning to spook her and must have realised it because he said, 'I have a proposition for you, Ruby, but if you have personal commitments…' He shook his head as if he wasn't sure what he was doing.

'If you're going to offer me a package too good to refuse after a couple of hours I should warn you that it took Jude Radcliffe the best part of a year to get to that point and I still turned him down.'

'I don't have the luxury of time,' he said, 'and the position I'm offering is made for a temp.'

'I'm listening.'

'Since you have done your research, you know that I was disinherited five years ago.'

She nodded. She thought it rather harsh for a one-off

incident but the media loved the fall of a hero and had gone into a bit of a feeding frenzy.

'This morning I received a summons from my father to present myself at his birthday majlis.'

'You can go home?'

'If only it were that simple. A situation exists which means that I can only return to Umm al Basr if I'm accompanied by a wife.'

She ignored the slight sinking feeling in her stomach. Obviously a multimillionaire who looked like the statue of a Greek god—albeit one who'd suffered a bit of wear and tear—would have someone ready and willing to step up to the plate.

'That's rather short notice. Obviously, I'll do whatever I can to arrange things, but I don't know a lot about the law in—'

'The marriage can take place tomorrow. My question is, under the terms of your open-ended brief encompassing "whatever is necessary", are you prepared to take on the role?'

Don't miss
THE SHEIKH'S CONVENIENT PRINCESS
By Liz Fielding

Available February 2017
www.millsandboon.co.uk

Give a 12 month subscription to a friend today!

Call Customer Services
0844 844 1358*

or visit
millsandboon.co.uk/subscriptions